MIRROR AND BONE

BY

ANDREW SHIELDS

BLADES
IN THE
DARK

MIRROR AND BONE

First Printing: 2019

ISBN: 978-1-7327586-4-3 (paperback)

Cover art by John Harper

https://shieldsuppublishing.wordpress.com/

For the last several years, I have seen a variety of Andrew's work on *Blades in the Dark*. I have read his excerpts in the Blades book, talked with him over G+ posts, and used his Heist Deck. To me, one thing is very clear: Andrew's mind lives in Doskvol. In cold, cramped, soggy streets where you're just as likely to die of infection as you are assassination.

Over and over as I read the book, I had to put it down to jot down some notes. Ideas I'd work into a session of Blades, or prompts to start off a score. The world not only feels alive in *Mirror and Bone*, but you can almost make out the moving pieces beneath the story. If you're a fan of of *Blades in the Dark*, this book feels like exactly what you'd expect of a heist gone sideways.

Mirror and Bone does a wonderful job of showing scoundrels both plying their trade and suffering the consequences of their actions. Even as they are planning a job, they have to watch their backs, as their target is doing all he can to hunt them down. They suffer loss, they change, and several times they have to decide if they are really doing the right thing. This look into their private lives raised the stakes of their choices, and kept me wondering how they were going to get through alive—I already knew they weren't making it out unscathed.

In a delightful nod to Herbert Asbury's *Gangs of New York,* Andrew weaves together the stories of how the underworld and the world of politics are all connected. How nobles and people in power both use and depend on criminals to carry out their dirty work, and how bold scoundrels—often those equipped with blackmail received from doing said dirty work—can move pieces around at the highest levels. Reading about the Silkworms and the River Stallions, I'm reminded of the stories of Tammany Hall and the Five Points Gang, the Whyos, and the Gophers, all tangled up in each other's business, legitimate and otherwise.

Blood curses. Dissertations on vampirism. Exploration of the ghost field. Demons. Andrew's story truly takes place in a haunted Doskvol. The nuances of the Forgotten Gods and their followings, the functions of spirit wells, and the tools Whispers use to ply their trade are all central components of *Mirror and Bone.*

As a person often frustrated by the presence of magic in any setting, specifically because it typically lacks internal consistency and only functions as needed to move the story along, reading *Mirror and Bone* reminded me of interlocking puzzle pieces. They may be individually indecipherable, but collectively they paint a wonderful version of Andrew's take on a haunted city.

Sean Nittner,
Cutter at large
2019

CHAPTER ONE

The end of the world is no excuse for increased social mobility. It is easier for a ghost to press against the natural order of things and re-enter the world of the living than it is for a poor man to acquire respectable status in Doskvol. It is more natural for a demon to form a cult to worship it than it is for a person of merit to earn recognition as new aristocracy. I suspect that is because when the supernatural flooded into the world, Doskvol's elites were presented with a new reality and had to adjust. They feel no such helplessness in the face of lowborn trying to make inroads into their ranks.

— From "Historical Ruminations of the Fall and Subsequent Taxation," by Aletha Sventon

ROWAN HOUSE, SIX TOWERS.
18ᵀᴴ ELISAR, 848. HOUR OF SONG, 2 HOURS PAST DUSK.

The lightning tower projected a field that hissed and crackled as it vaporized the snow swirling across it. Wind sluiced through, flexing the field and distorting its stark blue light over the straight avenue that led to the enormous mansion, the center of all the activity in the area. Normally the streets of Six Towers were almost solemn, the wide lanes hardly trafficked. Tonight, this street rang with the clatter of carriages, bleats of surly draft goats bawling at each other, laughter of the wealthy, and strains of music welcoming the invited to come in out of the cold. Braziers flanked the avenue, with servants struggling under the weight of coal buckets, moving up and down the street as they kept the flames bright for the guests.

Inside one of the lacquered and gilt carriages, a woman sighed with exasperation. "This is a terrible idea," she said.

"It's not that expensive, though, if you consider the stolen carriage and the fact we pay our fake servants with shares of loot rather than daily rates," the man opposite her shrugged. "Come on, Red, I bet some part of you misses these fancy parties." His smile was wide and inviting, but she resisted his charms with practiced skill.

"Our criminal discount does not validate our goal here," she said through her teeth.

"Well thanks for playing along even if you don't approve," he replied, cocking his head at a speculative angle. "You're the only one in the crew besides myself that I can trust to behave at a proper social event."

"Keep up the flattery, Saint. It suits you," she replied. She leaned back. "For what it's worth," she added, "you look ravishing tonight." Her smile widened, black lipstick parting to reveal pale, even teeth.

"Oh, this old thing?" he replied airily with a gesture. "I find that green and white really offset my eyes and my elegant paleness," he grinned. "Plus, it's got shiny boots and a proper cut around the joints, designed for ease of swordplay." He paused. "Or running," he shrugged, sharing an inside joke.

"Plus I'm half your age, you lecher, so we'll fit right in with the other couples there," she said as she took a moment to survey the street.

"How old do you think I am?" he protested.

"You're not pushing forty?" she replied, eyes still drifting on the street.

He paused. "You're older than twenty," he said, eyes tracing the smooth curve of her jawline, throat, shoulder. "We're no more than fifteen years apart."

For the first time, she smiled. "Look at you. All flustered." She shook her head. "Vanity."

"What, about my age, or my lecherousness?" he demanded, almost playful.

"Either," she shrugged. "There are products on the market to suppress signs of both."

"Hilarious," he replied, rolling his eyes. "Do you mind if we review our objectives here again?"

"Actually yes, I do, it's insultingly vague," she frowned. "You think Lord Rowan is up to no good and you want us to network and find people in the know who might gossip about it, now or later. Or, if we're stunningly lucky, find out what his sinister plot involves." She paused. "And no stealing," she added.

"No stealing, right, I tried to really hammer that point home in the briefing," he agreed. "So glad it stuck."

"With me, sure," she said dismissively. "But I pay attention. I'm reasonably clever. The Hammer is fine, he doesn't suffer from sticky fingers. But Gapjaw?" She shook her head. "I wouldn't leave him alone."

"No, we won't, the Hammer will be with him the whole time." Saint pulled out a compact and snapped it open, checking his eyeliner and blush. "I'm not sure which of us is wearing more makeup," he murmured.

"I can tell you who needs more," she replied, arching an eyebrow.

"You do shoot to kill, don't you," he muttered, smudging at his jawline, then abruptly snapping the compact shut and putting it back in his coat. "Close enough."

The string quartet was getting louder, and finally the goat strolled up to the position in line where the nobles could join the party. The Hammer jumped off the footboard at the back of the carriage, opening the door with a flourish. Saint held Red's hand, transferring her stability to the Hammer, who eased her down to the red carpet. Saint followed, offered Red the crook of his elbow, and strode confidently up the carpet, aiming smiles at the guards, staff, and hangers-on crowding the site.

While many of the broad granite steps sweeping up to once-grand buildings in the Six Towers neighborhood were broken and dangerous, these stairs had been re-leveled and fixed by master masons. Brass rods held the carpet down. Ahead, the columned face of the ancient house had been scrubbed and repaired. Massive red and white banners flanked the entry way, showcasing the family crest. Matching planters overflowed with radiant plants in the center, gently glowing and encouraging the greenery around them to flourish and expand.

At the top of the stairs they approached a man in a flawless black suit who extended his gloved hand to them. Saint smiled in return, giving him two invite cards.

"Welcome Lady Elania Sudureun and Lord Michaels Torrent," the steward announced in a penetrating voice. He put the invitations on a table behind where he stood, and a servant slipped them into a box. "You may enter," the steward said, officious.

Red and Saint swept by, strolling through the massive bronze and iron doorway, following the red carpet into the manor itself.

A balcony surrounded the foyer along the walls, with doors leading into the shadowed secrets of the vast mansion estate. Two staircases descended from the balcony, merged, and formed one broad avenue to the main floor. A wide curving corridor connected the entry to the ballroom on one side, and the parlor and dining hall on the other. Elaborate signs were painted on chalkboard, indicating that the main events were in the ballroom and parlor.

"You take the séance," Saint said with a nod to the elaborate painting of a crystal ball consulted by a long-nailed hand. "I'll take the dancing."

"Without a partner?" Red asked, eyebrows up.

"You'd slow me down," he shrugged. "I'll cut in where it's most strategic."

"Or fun," she frowned.

"Or fun," he agreed. "Remember, we're leaving the stolen carriage here, so when you're ready to go just, you know, slip out," he grinned.

"I think I can remember that," she said, only a hint of acid in her voice as she took in the beautiful gowns and elegant suits that now moved around her. Something in her eyes was lost, as though she was surrounded by ghosts.

"You okay?" Saint said, trying to catch her eye.

"Don't you worry about me," Red replied, and she turned her back on him, headed for the dining hall.

The steady influx of aristocrats and notables continued unchecked, but the massive foyer did not get crowded.

*

As the valets took the goat and carriage, Gapjaw climbed down from the buckboard and joined the Hammer. "There are some really fancy goats here," Gapjaw observed, scratching at his broad girth as he looked around the wide lane back to the stable.

On a normal day it would seem empty, but tonight there was a mass of goats, carriages, and servants choking up the approach. Some of the goats had the traditional cornrow weave of hair, serving as both decoration and armor. Others had been dyed and fancifully groomed to subtly alter their shapes. Some had been subjected to hair treatments to make the coarse goat hair smooth and flowing so it looked like a wig, dyed and styled. The fancier goats had horn decorations, like fake jewels glued to the curves, or toppers put on the end, or horns cut off and capped.

The pair headed up the stairs to the back entry, where two guards in yellow and white stopped them. "Servants down the stairs," one said gruffly with the air of a man who has said the same thing over and over until it lost all meaning.

Gapjaw and the Hammer exchanged a glance, then headed down the stairs to the low-beamed basement where a bar had been set up on one end, and trestle tables filled much of the space in the "L" shaped room. The basement resembled a vast common room in a tavern. A fireplace roared with burning bundles of compressed algae, releasing heat, light, and a comforting sour stink.

After they each got a sizable cup of fungal brew, the two men shouldered through the crowd surrounding the bar and followed the aisle down the trestles, making their way around the corner and back to find another staircase headed up. This entry had a pair of square-jawed men in yellow and white.

"Hello there, I need to pop upstairs and give my master his reading glasses," the Hammer said, his blunt features sincere as he held glasses up pinched between his fingers. "Otherwise imagine his embarrassment," he said seriously.

"Won't be able to read," Gapjaw explained, nodding solemnly.

"You can't go upstairs. Your master is on his own," the guard said.

"But there's a really short list of things my master can do on his own," Hammer squinted. "You know how they get. And who will get in trouble."

The guard frowned. "I don't care if he hangs you by your thumbs and hooks a hagfish to your scrotum," he clarified.

"That's very vivid," Gapjaw said to the Hammer.

"I can feel the kind of a tugging sensation, yeah?" the Hammer agreed with a gesture at his nethers. "I don't like this man's misuse of the gift of poetry."

"Any other time we'd have to do something about that," Gapjaw nodded.

"Not tonight, though, best behavior," the Hammer admonished.

"Best behavior," Gapjaw agreed. "So, we were thinking about joining up with your outfit. We really, really like your uniforms," he said with a nod to the yellow and white coats and breeches under the crossed baldrics, a pistol on one side and a cutlass on the other.

"Fancy hats," the Hammer clarified.

"What's the name of this outfit then?" Gapjaw asked.

The exasperated guard traded a look with his partner, then straightened. "We are members of the North Hook House Guard," he said. "I wouldn't bother applying if I were you." He glanced over the two servants with a disapproving eye.

"What?" the Hammer said, taken aback. "I'll have you know I served the Emperor in the Unity War. I'm a veteran, and I have more experience around tactics, scouting, artillery—the things I've done for the Immortal Emperor are things no man should have to do," he said, eyes wide, slightly hoarse.

"Let me tell you what you *didn't* do for the Immortal Emperor," the young guard replied, steel in his voice. "You didn't take care of yourself, so now you're mired in lard. You let your training go, you'd have to practically start over. And you have no idea how modern technology works; to make it in the North Hook House Guard you have to know the fundamentals of the security systems, and be prepared to install, repair, monitor, use, calibrate, and uninstall them as needed. Not much call for *artillery,*" he said, warming to the subject as he glanced over at Gapjaw. "How about you, old man? You serve the Immortal Emperor too? Get some medals for getting your damn fool limbs shot off?"

"Wow, this fella must not know many veterans," Gapjaw said, serious, putting his hand on the Hammer's forearm. "I'm surprised you've not run into more people who taught you not to speak that way about those who served."

"What's your name, son," the Hammer said, oddly composed.

"Captain Myles Strank," the North Hook guard replied. "If you want to try and go somewhere with this, I welcome you to waste your time further."

"I think we're done here," Gapjaw said, keeping a sideways eye on the Hammer. "Thank you for your time." He put his arm around the Hammer's shoulders, and leaned on him, steering him to pivot and leave the stairs.

"That kid is a jackass," he said long before they were out of earshot. "Sorry you had to see that."

"It's fine," the Hammer replied under his breath. "For the first time, I'm glad Saint involved us in this party." He stopped, turning, evaluating Strank with a critical eye. Strank met his gaze fearlessly. "Did you know," the Hammer murmured to Gapjaw, "before I was a soldier, I was a teacher?"

"I didn't know that," Gapjaw said.

"It's true," the Hammer nodded. "And I still have this love, you know? At a deep level. Of imparting knowledge. Of seeing understanding dawning in the eyes of someone learning something new."

"Just not today," Gapjaw invited the Hammer to repeat.

"Not today," the Hammer agreed, eyes glittering.

Strank slowly smiled, then looked away from the Hammer, indulging in some small talk with his partner. When he looked again, the two men were gone.

*

Saint drifted along the thready current of guests, exchanging pleasantries, complimenting those who looked like they needed it. He ended in the drafty cavern of the ballroom, three stories high, with two levels of balconies. The vast chandelier had platforms, and musicians had climbed down a ladder flanking the chains holding it up, so music drifted down from the crystal and the lights above. Another ensemble was set up on the stage at the end of the ballroom, ready to provide dancing music when the time for ambient music ended.

The side curve of the ballroom was set up for catering, and Saint gravitated towards it. His eyes were busy tracing faces, outfits, military honors, and social clusters. He found himself at the elbow of a young woman in a trailing glory of pink, maroon, and white, a mix of satin and crushed velvet. He smiled at her, pivoting to give her his full attention.

"Why, Doctor Tyrconnell, what a pleasure to see you here!" he said with a broad smile.

"Oh, hello!" she said, trying to recover from her surprise. "You recognize me in this! That's impressive," she clarified. "Where did we meet again?"

"The symposium on pre-Fall architecture," Saint lied smoothly. It seemed inappropriate to mention that he knew she frequented a brothel in the Ease. "What do you think of this Rowan upgrade?" he asked, gesturing around.

"Pretty neat," she shrugged with half a grin. "I'm always happy when these old buildings get fixed up instead of being left to rot." She shook her head. "I guess six months ago his aunts still had the place, and were living in here like hoarders." She took in the ballroom. "It's been a busy six months."

"But there's no way he could have fixed up the whole estate in that time," Saint said.

"Oh no, that will take a decade or more. Just the areas that are open right now. Maybe the kitchen, maybe a bedroom or two. All that's—astronomically expensive," she said. "But still, don't cross the velvet rope." She smiled, gracious.

"Where do you think he gets the money?" Saint wondered aloud, shaking his head.

"Old money coffers, of course, but Rowan wouldn't risk depleting that. Probably his security company," Tyrconnell shrugged. "He purchased an interest in one of the bigger security companies and they've been offering high tech security to noble houses." She looked around. "I don't see much installed here yet."

"High tech security, eh," Saint said, looking slightly confused as a sinking feeling dragged at his stomach.

"Localized electroplasmic barriers, integrated power systems, that sort of thing," Tyrconnell said as she closed in on the catering table. "I haven't gotten a look at the systems yet because it's all still very 'invitation only.' So I imagine the money's good, hence," and she gestured around meaningfully. Then she turned to the nibble tray, selecting choice bits of sweet pastry and savory fish using a pair of toothpicks.

Saint offered her a cheery enough 'Good luck!' and drifted with the crowd once again. Just in time for the welcome speech.

Servants used mallets on chimes that hung from straps, brandishing the chime with one hand and ringing it with the other. The same tone rippled through the room, almost surreal as the resonance of one overlapped another, and another. The room quieted.

A man wearing a fancy mantle of red and white mounted the podium at the side of the stage at the end of the ballroom, and everyone gravitated towards it. He planted his hands on the side of the podium, impressive in the cut of his clothes and in his bearing.

"Greetings, and thank you for coming tonight," said the host. "I am Lord Cleith Armeide Rowan IV. I know some of you have come tonight for a sneak peek at what the North Hook House Guard will be able to offer later this year, and I look forward to showing that to you—but only the few," he said with a winning smile. "The rest of you will have to wait until the technology is perfected and standardized for mass production. In the meantime, drink, dance, and intrigue to your hearts content," he said with a grand gesture. "Thank you for coming to bear witness that the Rowan family remains central to securing the beating heart of Doskvol." He stepped down off the podium amid gratifying applause.

"Good thing Lord Torrent has an invitation," Saint muttered to himself. Then, he started working his way through the crowd towards the private display lineup.

He reached the line, where the steward smiled at him and extended his hand. Saint offered his card, glancing around like he was waiting for confirmation of a sure thing. The steward waved him through, and he found himself in an antechamber with several doors and a dozen expensively dressed aristocrats biding their time. A servant passed with a tray loaded with wine goblets, and Saint plucked one with practiced ease. He did not try to make small talk; this was the wrong venue to draw attention to himself.

"Lord Torrent," said a man at his elbow.

Saint turned to see a man in an Inspector uniform, dark with hints of color. "Yes?" he said, as though there was no danger his disguise could be penetrated.

"It is your turn to be checked for weapons or recording devices," the Inspector said. "This way." He led Saint to an alcove in the back, and Saint stepped in—

—blow landed in his kidney, driving him forward to where a couple of the house guard snatched his elbows and hauled him around, flinging him down to the ground. He crashed down unable to pull in a breath for a moment, and a man loomed over him.

"Saint Suran, leader of the River Stallions," said the man. "You are wanted for questioning adjacent to a number of incidents, and I've got a number of exceptions prepared to bind you by law to stand trial. Many as I need, really," he shrugged.

"Didn't even bother with a disguise," the Inspector mused, staring at Saint. "Brash."

"Who the hell are you?" Saint demanded, breathless, looking at the shadowy figure next to the Inspector.

"There will be plenty of time for that," the man sneered, then the head bag dropped over Saint's vision and tightened around his neck.

*

As Red entered the study, the otherworldly tone was already set. Wood paneling and heavy drapes soaked up the reverberation of the electrophone and harpsichord duet, so the sound seemed to hang independently of its context, twining through the air and tugging the guests together like a tightening stitch. Incense curled up into the lamp light, coiling and twisting as people moved into the otherwise breathless room.

The room was deceptively stifling, considering its size. A six-sided table was under a shaded bulb, the electroplasmic light unflinching. There were seats at the table, and also in a ring around the table for spectators. In the corner, the electrophone warbled and wailed like an underwater stringed instrument, its ethereal tones stalked and pinned in place by the brittle tinny chords of the harpsichord.

Red aimed for the center of the crowd, trying not to stand out. She had picked up a handful of salacious gossip that could likely turn out to be actionable, but she had not sensed a way in to Rowan's inner circle.

The doors to the study creaked towards each other, then closed with a decisive click of the latch. There were about twenty people in the room, looking around, suddenly attentive as the lights dimmed for just a moment.

The people quieted as awareness rippled through the crowd, and they turned to see the Iruvian mystic standing by the table, a boy at her elbow dressed in a turban and silks.

"Behold," the boy said confidently, his voice projecting, "you now stand in the presence of Madame Starshine Selkovinaed, Mystic of the Seventh Tower." She graciously seated herself at the table. Her face was lined and loose with age, her hair under a turban, her face flanked by earrings and necklaces. Her costume managed to be elaborate without being cartoonish, and she had an air of dignity and bearing that gave her stature as she sat at the table.

Madame Starshine spread twenty cards, then she swiftly dealt five of them to the remaining spots at the table, still face down. The boy rounded the table, flipping the cards. "Please join Madame Starshine for the séance. Lady Vestine Arran. Lord Timoth Welker. Captain Vond Comber. Lady Elania Sudureun. Sergeant Mara Haig."

Red blinked twice as it sunk in that her alias had been called to the table, then she surrendered to grim resignation and put on her most gracious smile, rounding the table to where her card was flipped. She demurely glanced around at those standing in the immediate area, and of course a gentleman stepped forward to pull out her chair. Cool, she surveyed the variety of ages and attitudes that joined her at the table.

In a city ringed with lightning towers to keep out the ragged storms of ghosts, a séance was something of a luxury for those isolated from danger. Captain Comber and Sergeant Haig in particular seemed unimpressed with the proceedings, where Lady Arran and Lord Welker looked excited. Red tried to keep her hand from shaking as she felt her nerve thin out. Adrenaline seeped into her blood stream.

Madame Starshine had a reputation as a powerful medium, able to summon and control ghosts. That could happen here, and the possibility chilled Red to the bone. She dared not draw attention by trying to back out, so she leveled an uncompromising gaze at the mystic, as regal as she could be.

"Tonight, we will reach out to Shaw Rowan, an occultist who died three centuries ago, and ask him for his blessing for the present." Madame Starshine's movements were birdlike, her eyes bright, and she finally addressed those at the table personally as though no one else was in the room. "He was wise and powerful, and his blessing on the house would be a strong omen of good times to come. Thank you for being a part of this auspicious effort," she added with an acknowledging nod. "Now still your thoughts," she said as the boy lit the candle in the center of the table. "Take each other's hands, a united circle of warm and living blood to contain our call until it is strong enough to reach our special guest." She smiled as the guests complied, shifting her shoulders in a wiggle that betrayed her sense of satisfaction. "This is good," she purred. "I can feel our united presence behind the Mirror. Some of you are quite strong there. Bright, and hot," she whispered. "Let us begin."

She composed herself for a long moment, then murmured in ancient Hadrathi, "Gaze we now upon the flame." The boy repeated the phrase in Akorosian, a hushed whisper. Those at the table obediently stared at the candle flame.

"Now the flicker is felt," she soothed, an ancient phrase. For as the candle flickers, it flickers in the mirror—the slimmest fraction of a second later. Madame Starshine attuned to the Mirror, and her attention thinned it somehow, so those at the table felt the rest of the world fall ever so slightly out of synch. The steady flame of their life energy moved an imperceptible nudge closer to the Back of the Mirror.

Red let out an involuntary moan as the itch began; the damnable itch in her blood, under her skin. Her eyes widened with alarm, and she glanced over at Madame Starshine, who met her gaze with a look of surprise.

"The flame, child," Madame Starshine admonished, and Red felt heat building in her, preparing to sweat in the cool room. But she was in the grip of things, now, her hands held by others, and with a peculiar helplessness she once again directed her attention to the steady flame.

"Now thin the obfuscations that surround us, that truth may stand before fire as in olden times," Madame Starshine whispered, the fluid words spattering and hissing like water dropping into a hot pan. "I call to you now, on the site of your death. Shaw Rowan, let me be your vessel, that you may speak through time and the Mirror." The young man in the background threw a handful of dust into a brazier. It hissed, sending a curling column of smoke out that filled the room with a pungent haze.

Suddenly the silence ran deep, leaving a ringing sound in the ears of the witnesses, and the temperature fell noticeably.

"Come to me, Shaw Sebastian Alaric Rowan," Madame Starshine whispered, still in Hadrathi. "You may speak through me, O Lost One."

Red let out a thin whine as her ribs burned in her torso, her hands shaking as she gripped the suddenly sweaty palms of those flanking her. She squeezed her eyes shut, baring her teeth, and for a moment there was an unbearable sensation. Then she felt that plunge into a desperately needed cold submersion, and her eyes opened again, ringed with pale blue fire.

"I think I like this one better," Red breathed, a plume of cold breath falling from her mouth.

Madame Starshine stared at the ghost, shocked. "You mustn't harm her," she said in Hadrathi.

Red's face creased with puzzlement. "Nor she harm me," he breathed. "What—what have you done to this body?" Anger flashed across his features. "Are you trying to mark me?" the ghost demanded, twisting Red's voice to project deep menace.

"What—" Madame Starshine began, then the ghost of Shaw Rowan hissed, draining the room of twenty degrees of heat, and Red's body glowed, the light twisting out of a bright core and filling out glyphs.

Red's skin burned with writing, forbidden and terrible writing, with a glyph on her forehead and a row down her chest and back, smaller glyphs at each joint, limned out in the hellish and awful light of the darkest occult cursing. With the sizzling heat of meat cooking, the glyphs shone, and her clothing caught fire where the biggest ones blazed under her skin.

"Damn you!" Shaw roared, leaping up out of the chair in Red's body, breaking the circle. "I'll not carry this curse!" Shaw slammed the door between the front and the back of the Mirror, and the shockwave blew all the séance participants away from the table, tumbling on the floor, the electroplasmic light shattering as the candles were snuffed out.

Hysterically babbling and sobbing, Red scrambled through the dark room, eyes useless, her dress flickering with fire as glyphs still pulsed and burned her skin with every beat of her heart. Others exclaimed in dismay, clawing at each other to get out of her way as she stumbled unevenly towards where she remembered the door being.

Battering through the barrier seemed strange and simple, all in the physical world, and as the house guards perked up and realized something might be wrong, she tore her shoes off and sprinted across the foyer with the staccato slapping of bare soles on stone. Shoving past those who tried to stop her, she poured on fresh speed and vanished, out the main doors and into the snowy night.

Back in the study, the guests managed to re-light some of the lamps as the house guard barged in and immediately started helping people up and back to their chairs. Only Madame Starshine stood motionless, but profoundly moved.

"What—what was *that*?" Lord Welker demanded, absently rubbing at the hand that touched the cursed woman.

"I've never *heard* of curse-work at that level," the mystic murmured in response. "This is an ill omen indeed for Lord Rowan," she added. She looked Lord Welker in the eye. "That curse has touched the energy of his line." Her eyebrows raised. "He will need to find that girl," she breathed.

CHAPTER TWO

It was spring of 826, and this skinny kid with a flashy smile was making waves. A sadistic Bluecoat, Constable Gorloc, was cracking down on the neighborhood, especially the fancy ladies. One of them had a son who didn't take kindly to it, not at all. So he started playing the angles. One of Gorloc's men got taken down for gambling, another was caught with the wrong woman, another crossed the wrong crook and got knifed. This kid was stealing money and giving it to people Gorloc was squeezing. People started joking about his good deeds and his good looks, saying he was the Summer Saint there for a while; risks he was taking, people figured he'd be dead by fall. Doskvol doesn't really have much of a summer, you know? Well, he lived, just to spite the Bluecoats, and he kept the name; swapped it around to "Saint Suran" named for the hottest month. The name stuck at the afterparty of Gorloc's execution.

— From Orta Urra's half-sober bar tale, Ulsivet 18, 844

ROWAN HOUSE, SIX TOWERS.
18ᵀᴴ ELISAR. HOUR OF SILVER, 3 HOURS PAST DUSK.

"Your idea to check on the goats is unpleasant," the Hammer half-shouted over the din of goats who were none too happy about their close quarters in the rear stable.

Gapjaw didn't bother responding, his forehead drawn as he spotted the two guards outside the entrance, and the crew of six servants hauling feed for goats. They jammed in past the goats to get into the stable and glance around. Gapjaw chose his moment and headed up the ladder to the balcony. The Hammer was at his heels.

"This really isn't better," the Hammer growled, looking around the loft at the packed algae bales that collapsed with decay into shapeless wads. "I don't think anyone's been up here in years."

"Yap yap yap," Gapjaw said absently, eyes roving the space. "Like a little dog." He pulled a globe from his pocket and shook it, and it glowed to life with enough faint luminescence to see. He followed the dank and narrow aisle between bales. At the back of the loft there was a barred door. He shifted the bar and gave the door a push, and it drifted open over the back of the barn. The rear wall of the property was visible from here, as well as a path leading up to the house. If there were patrols around the barn, none were visible for the moment.

"Don't get cocky," the Hammer said, gruff. Gapjaw glanced around, then lowered a rope ladder, swinging around and scrambling down it. The Hammer followed.

Leaving the door open and the ladder down the wall, the two rogues headed up the path towards the back of the house, careful to keep screens of brush and trees between them and those managing the flow of servants, carriages, and goats. A few minutes later they stood at the back of a house that bore no resemblance to the noble Rowan House; it was a huge and ancient pile, wrecked where it stood, dragged by entropy into an inevitable dissolution.

Better still, no guards back here.

The Hammer gave Gapjaw a leg up, then Gapjaw helped haul him up. They made it up to the patio, then climbed the broken canopy. Facing the second floor exterior, they examined a couple windows.

One of the windows had been stuffed with the nests of venomous crows, to the point where the stone holding the ornate metal bars had corroded. On three, both men yanked at the cover, and it gave with a screech. Pushing it further out of position, they swiped the nests out of the way, quietly broke the window, and levered themselves inside one by one.

The walls were drifted to shoulder height with old books, piles of clothes, shapeless bags, and a generally potent mixture of trash and treasure. The air was thick with dust and decay, to the point where the two intruders pulled masks over their features not just to hide their identity, but to breathe.

They reached a back dining room, where the sprawling mass of hoarded junk and materials was like a crescendo frozen in time, starting around the door and building up to bury the far side of the room utterly. The table jutted out of the mass, and two rickety chairs served a pair of bare patches on the otherwise fully loaded table. A familiar, if twisted, stench emanated from the pile; at least one corpse was in there somewhere. Treading carefully, the intruders rounded the table and headed deeper into the house.

They paused under a skylight, looking up. Radiant plants shone down through the clear skylight like the dappling of stained glass. The skylight was ringed by planters on the roof. Radiant plants glowed and pulsed with their own peculiar rhythms, releasing deep shades of red and blue, brilliant hues of yellow and green.

The Hammer pulled out his paper and smoothed it open on the end table in the room. "So here's the shrunk-down floor plans," he muttered. "Saint thought we should head for the overlook, here. And I think we're in the Contemplatorium, here, because of that skylight." "As long as we don't actually have to contemplate something, I'm good," Gapjaw shrugged.

Following the meager light from the glassy orb, they passed through the clogged passages of the house, once breaking down a door because it was mounded on both sides by intractable garbage. They took more care to be quiet as they approached the Mirror Chamber from the back side, and heard the laughter and the murmur of speculation from a nearby crowd.

They carefully picked their way through what had once been a game room, the felt-topped tables vanished under mounds of refuse, the trophies on the wall swallowed up or jostled out of place by the tide of worthless material, once precious and stockpiled but now beyond all use. Cloth, furniture, and books dissolved together, the paper like mortar between the gravel and stones. On the other end, a balcony; Gapjaw and the Hammer took pains to tread quietly.

The Mirror Chamber was originally for study of dance or combat, with mirrors on all the six walls. It was also a smaller hall for entertaining more intimately than the grand ballroom. The game room's balcony overlooked the charming space that was about a hundred feet across, windowless, with a two story domed ceiling.

The center of the room was dominated by a massive throne. Cables snaked out of the throne to a number of stubby towers that jutted up like crooked ribs. There were posts and boxes here and there, a couple walls, a collection of peculiar equipment, and a countertop loaded with controls. Six house guards stood around the assemblage, and a slim man fussed over the console. His suit was stitched with Hadrathi sigils in vertical rows, and he had several amulets and charms visible as functional decoration.

An unobtrusive door to the side opened, and a black-clad servant rushed in. "Is it ready?" he hissed. "Lord Rowan is about to open the door!"

"Yes, ready," snapped the man in the suit. "Let them in." He closed his eyes, and when he opened them his slicked-back arrogance was softened somewhat by breezy charm.

"And this," they could hear from the back of the ballroom, "is the future of security in Doskvol. Follow me!" With that, the door to the ballroom drifted open, and Lord Rowan pivoted and strode into the Mirror Chamber, still borne up by the applause and music behind him. The elites poured in at his heels.

"Now that I have you all to myself," Lord Rowan said with a conspiratorial air, "I have something new to show you. It's rare enough in these days that anything can be called genuinely new, but these refinements are a massive leap beyond what is available now." The doors to the ballroom swung shut, and locked with an authoritative clack.

At that moment, a figure clad in black dropped from the ceiling to land behind Gapjaw and the Hammer; both pivoted, reaching for weapons as the man in black pulled his mask off.

"It's me," he hissed.

"Piccolo, blood and bones, I damn near killed you," Gapjaw hissed, his face purpling a little with stress.

"Don't flatter yourself, old man," the young man in black said, dismissive. "Where's Saint? He's supposed to be with them," he whispered, pointing down at the frilly mob.

The Hammer squinted down at the group. "I don't see him," he observed.

"I know that," Piccolo muttered through his teeth. "Do you know where he is?"

"Haven't seen him," Gapjaw murmured.

"Well, you two take notes on the grand unveiling, I'll go find him," Piccolo whispered in exasperation. He pulled the black mask back on, and melted into the shadows.

"Those were just the first tentative steps into what is possible as a new age dawns over our city," Lord Rowan continued. "Tonight you witness the close of one chapter, and the opening of another." His smile widened. "After this, nothing will be the same." He turned to the dapper man in the sigil suit. "Leslin?"

"Good evening, ladies and gentlemen," Leslin smiled. "As you know, every one of us has a certain sensitivity to the Ghost Field. We have the ability to alter our perceptions to understand and interact with different levels of what is real. Hard work and sacrifice have pulled this area of study out of the clutches of superstition, and into the reach of responsible adults, and what you are about to witness tonight is a new pinnacle of refinement and application for energies as old as the end of the world."

He rounded the console, glancing over its controls, largely a showman's act to heighten the tension. "I myself am an adept," he said. "I have an affinity for understanding and manipulating the rituals and energies of the Ghost Field. I am not a Whisper," he admitted, "but those are extremely expensive and demanding specialists to keep on staff. Adepts like myself are far more plentiful, and less prone to excesses of ego. We're worth the investment, because we are the key to the system."

Leslin extended his forearms, wrist up, and those assembled could see the flat metal disks implanted in his wrists. "These contacts are key to the system. Observe." He turned his back on them and mounted the stairs to the chair throne. Seating himself, he made a production of wiggling his fingers, then lowering his forearms onto the angled arms of the throne, so the metal in his wrists made contact with the disks on the throne. The servant standing to the side put a cabled helm on his head, so only his mouth and chin were visible.

"I am one with the machine," Leslin murmured, using the resonaters built into most of the peripheral devices to fill the room with his quiet statement. The aristocrats jumped, then applauded politely, some with a degree of enthusiasm.

Lord Rowan seamlessly took over, striding to the console before the applause died down. "We've tried security systems based on electroplasmic advances, have we not?" he said. "They turn out to be vulnerable. The fuel moves through cables that can be cut. The projectors can be sabotaged. It can be expensive to train staff properly, and when they make mistakes it can be catastrophic. Adapting a security system when lifestyle changes happen can be costly and poorly thought through, leaving gaps that allow very real dangers to enter our lives."

He glanced over the assembled gear. "We've studied the best efforts and used their most brilliant ideas as a launching point for an entirely new concept in security defenses. How many of you have experimented with cameras? Oh, several of you. So you know they're expensive, unreliable, and difficult to place and monitor in sufficient numbers. With this system, there are acid etchings that can be done to the back of mirrors, provided they are pure silver. Then the mirrors that you already have, that are already strategically placed, become conduits for a vigilant adept to watch your property and possessions."

Lord Rowan reviewed the crowd. "You there, young lady. Yes. Here is a slate and some chalk. Stand behind that wall, and write a number to show the mirror."

Blushing furiously, the young woman took the slate and chalk around the corner, out of sight.

"That's naughty," observed Leslin. "You were supposed to draw a number, not an apple."

She let out a cry of surprise, and ran around the corner, brandishing her slate with an apple drawn on it.

"And you, you've got critical business with me," Lord Rowan said as he smiled at a dapper older gentleman. "I don't want to hear it, so I'm going into my study." He approached the door that was built into one of the display walls, and paused to push a silver button on the wall. "I do not wish to be disturbed," he said. He winked at the aristocrat, then stepped inside and closed the door. The aristocrat strode forward and took the handle, then staggered back with a cry as a shock jounced between the knob and his hand.

"The amount of power can be adjusted,"Leslin explained, "up to lethal. But you have control, and you can also arrange for guards to be summoned to remove the intruder." He paused. "One way or another, no one makes it through that door." That smile again.

"How is it powered?" demanded a pale aristocrat, caught up in the moment.

"Condensation," Leslin said. "Sure, the startup of the system runs on electroplasm. Once the collectors are running, they draw in the loose energy of the Ghost Field and condense it down. If there is ever too little ambient energy, which we hope is a natural consequence over time, then you power it as you do with current systems. But consider the benefits. For one, the system is much cheaper to run, and on a size-able estate, it has plenty of plasm to condense. For another, the drastic reduction of plasm weakens ghosts who make it to the system, and if a ghost tries to interfere with the system, the very plasm that gives it form and power gets drained into the defenses. Finally, this drying up of ambient plasm means that any Whisper or adept that does try to conduct rituals or manipulate the Ghost Field is sorely disadvantaged." Leslin shook his helmed head. "Energetic dangers of the superstitious past become nothing more than fuel for a modern defense," he said.

Of course the aristocrats applauded that vigorously.

"But—but surely," one spectator cried, "one adept cannot be at all times on duty!"

The door opened, and Lord Rowan rejoined them. "Of course not. For a modest system, we include three adepts. Each time the system scales up, three more. Therefore, you always have one on duty, one sleeping, and one with time to pursue studies and the business of liv-ing. And in case of leave, or illness, or calamity, or heightened mea-sures, you've got a depth of adepts prepared on your system. Should you need more, each system we produce will have its own unique code that will be etched in the invisible side of the wrist lock."

"Can a proper Whisper take it over?" asked an uneasy man.

"That's the whole point of the glyph lock," Lord Rowan explained. "Unless the Whisper channels all energy through that symbol, which is not something they are trained to do, nothing you see here responds to them." He paused. "In fact, if a Whisper were to try and take over the system by brute force in the Ghost Field, the collectors would tear that energy right out of the aggressor." He looked several of the audience in the eye, one at a time. "This is not a toy, or a novelty. This is serious security for those who will no longer tolerate the swaggering criminal element in this city. I said it is time for a new chapter, and I meant it. Criminals capable of working around this level of security are few and far between. The tide of sloppy braggarts that we cope with now?" He slowly shook his head. "They are about to become extinct. And you can help be part of that."

"Where do we sign up?" asked an elderly woman.

"What I need from you now is a different kind of support," Lord Rowan said, clasping his hands behind his back. "I am one of the six members of the City Council, and because this is experimental technology, so far I have been denied permission to implement a security system for anything more than experimental and demonstration purposes." He paused. "You can see the future, right?" he asked in a quieter voice, drawing his audience in closer. "You can see a future where the unwieldly lightning wall projectors are unnecessary because these more efficient systems ring the city, and as we need more space..." he shook his head, eyes serious. "We *take* it," he murmured, leaning forward.

He let the moment stand, then he continued.

"If you support me here, now, at the beginning, when I need it," he said, "then you're first in line to get these systems when they get online." He shrugged the rest away. "If you place a financial sponsorship now, then that investment will be considered and factored into the cost of your system or systems when we are ready to start producing and installing in earnest."

He glanced over at his seneschal, then nodded curtly to himself. "That's it, my friends, that's the secret project I brought you here to see. Do talk things over with Darrington when you've reached a conclusion for us to document. Pledge support financially, and politically, and we'll remake this city." His smile was almost predatory.

"I think this registers as a disaster," Gapjaw muttered to the Hammer.

"Catastrophe," the Hammer agreed under his breath.

"I kind of want to smash it," Gapjaw added.

"How does that help anything?" the Hammer asked, brow furrowed. "Except to bring a world of heat down on us, attention we surely do not need."

Gapjaw looked down at the Mirror Room, trying not to feel petulant. A new thought bloomed in his mind. "We could *steal* it," he said slowly.

"It's too big," the Hammer retorted.

"Just the helmet. The box," Gapjaw shrugged.

"Saint said no stealing," the Hammer reminded him. "He was very specific."

"He didn't know about this," Gapjaw replied.

The two scoundrels contemplated the room, motionless among the clutter filling the balcony. Below, the mirrors reflected the throne and its attachments from various angles.

*

Saint bashed his shins on the squat steps jutting from the back of the wagon, and rough hands shoved him up through the doorway into the stinking box. It smelled of all the worst flavors that pour off the human body in distress. As the armored door slammed shut and the guards fumbled with the lock, the bag was tugged off Saint's head. He found himself face to face with a hulking Bluecoat. In an armored wagon meant to transfer maybe four to a side, the two of them considered each other for a moment.

"I'll confess I thought they'd keep me here for a while at least," Saint said with a shrug. "I guess we're off to the magistrate?"

The wagon lurched as the driver flicked the whip at the two goats pulling it, and its armored weight was reluctantly dragged into motion. The leather springs creaked as the box rocked along the back road. Saint squinted, looking out through the mesh. "It would be faster if we took Flockwood—"

The Bluecoat didn't even have to lean forward to fire his fist into the side of Saint's head, bouncing it off the hard wall of the wagon. Saint recoiled, jaw loose for the moment, struggling with the sharp pain jabbing through his skull. Shaking his head slightly, he re-oriented on the Bluecoat.

"No talking? Is that the—" Saint tried to dodge, but this time the Bluecoat grabbed the chain connecting his wrists, and yanked him forward into the punch that sent him whacking back into the wagon wall. Saint resisted choking on his blood, instead spitting a mouthful to the side.

"You're going straight to Iron Hook," the Bluecoat said with a measure of satisfaction. "It will take us about an hour to get there."

Saint watched him warily, and did not mention that was kind of a slow rate for a direct trip. His assailant smiled genuinely.

"Better," he said. "Mainly what I want out of you are screams, maybe some begging, some gurgling," he shrugged.

"What's this about?" Saint asked warily.

"It's about how you are going to catch a beating," the Bluecoat said reflectively, "then you're gonna get locked up and you're never gonna be a free again as a living person."

"No trial?" Saint said.

"Already fixed," the Bluecoat replied. "You really don't recognize me?"

"I really don't," Saint shrugged. He spat another mouthful of blood off to the side; more was leaking in.

The Bluecoat removed his helmet, and his dirty blonde tresses tumbled down. "I'm Clef," he said. "My brother was Ingvald. You knifed him in the back, and his boss? Hutton? That traitor, he just *watched.*"

Clef's face darkened with savage bloodlust, his breath uneven. "He *watched.* Now you and Hutton are *buddies,* and the Grinders are *pets* here in the city, and the new Skovlanders coming in gotta live by their rules." He shook his head. "That makes me *so mad.*"

Saint launched at him, trying to catch the fake Bluecoat's neck in a choke-hold. Clef was too fast for him, slapping his arm to the side, whipping a head butt into his face that broke his nose; Saint crashed back into the wall of the wagon, and this time Clef leaned back enough to heft up a leg and pound a kick into his chest, knocking his air out as black shapes popped and drifted in his vision.

"I hear you're clever," Clef said, still breathing hard more from rage than exertion. "You make friends. But you won't really be able to do that if you can't stand up." The huge man slid off the bench, dragging Saint's leg up and putting it on the opposite bench, and before Saint could squirm free Cleff slammed his elbow down on Saint's knee, snapping it into a recurve bend.

Saint let out his first scream.

Clef started laughing.

*

"I think that's the lowest the security is going to get," Gapjaw whispered to the Hammer. There were two guards, and the thin adept in a suit. The adept was making adjustments to a control panel, a distant look in his eyes.

"Those guards are probably two of their best," the Hammer observed.

"I sure hope so," Gapjaw growled, and the Hammer could not help but smile.

"I don't know. About trying to get at that thing," the Hammer nodded towards the throne.

Almost soundless, Piccolo dropped behind them. "It's been three hours," he breathed. "I can't find Saint or Red." He paused. "Why are you still here?"

"I'm thinking about stealing the helmet and box," Gapjaw said, nodding at the security setup.

"Didn't Saint say not to steal anything?" Piccolo replied in a whisper, a puzzled look on his face.

"But he didn't know about *this*!" Gapjaw hissed, gesturing at the security setup. An idea occurred to him, lighting up his face. "One for, one against, Piccolo can be the tiebreaker!" he growled.

"No, veto," the Hammer said, shaking his head. "We know how Piccolo will vote."

"Guys, it's time to go home," Piccolo muttered, almost stern. "So what we're going to do is to obey Saint and not steal anything—BUT," he added, holding up a finger to forestall Gapjaw's protest, "we're gonna kidnap the skinny guy."

"Okay good," Gapjaw agreed immediately, a wide smile revealing every one of his missing teeth.

The Hammer paused, pinching the headache away from the bridge of his nose, then he sighed. "Let's do it. What's the plan."

"My extraction is ready to go from the lower art gallery," Piccolo muttered. "Follow my lead."

Off they went, down to the end of the chamber. Gapjaw and the Hammer waited on the balcony, and Piccolo slid down a hastily secured rope, crouching twenty feet from the back of the display but now visible in all the mirrors, adrenaline threading its way through him.

Then he was off, sprinting with impossible strides, building up speed so before he was even spotted he leaped up and shotgun kicked the adept, slamming him off the console to tumble awkwardly down.

The two guards pivoted to see what caused the bang, but Piccolo had already dragged the stunned adept over his shoulders, and was racing back towards the lowered rope.

One guard whipped his pistol out, lining it up, and two reports from the balcony sent plumes of smoke over the Mirror Chamber as they also sent bullets into the guard; he flew back to smash an ancient mirror, tumbling down in a glitter of shards; they heard the slow toll of a bell behind the Veil, a marker of death in the city.

The other guard reoriented his shot, firing at Gapjaw, but his shot was low and burst another antique mirror. Piccolo raced over the shards and snatched the rope; he climbed as Gapjaw dragged the rope up, and the Hammer fired his second round, banging into the house guard's shoulder and pivoting him around.

The door to the ballroom crashed open and guards poured into the Mirror Chamber as Gapjaw ran through the shadows above, followed by Piccolo carrying Leslin. The Hammer retreated too, pulling up the rope so no one could climb after them. A few shots were fired, but with no clear targets; the culprits had a serious head start.

As they reached the side gallery, Leslin started to struggle, so Piccolo slid him down to the floor and the Hammer punched him in the forehead, knocking him out cold. The Hammer picked him up as Piccolo led the way down and around, to a window with a black "X" painted on the outside. He kicked the glass, blowing it out, and they saw a panoramic view of the river. Below, a steam launch moored, waiting. Piccolo tossed the rope down, and between the gear and the team effort, minutes later everyone was in the launch.

"Smooth?" asked the boat pilot.

"Safety, if it was smooth you'd be seeing my happy face," Piccolo frowned. "We lost Saint, and I'm not sure where Red is. And apparently there's a scary new security system. But we got us an expert," he grinned, squatting down in the unsteady boat and slapping Leslin's face.

Safety stared at them. "I thought the idea was *not* to anger Lord Rowan, one of the six City Council members, and draw his attention to our little operation specifically!"

The others blinked at him.

"I just heard 'don't steal anything,'" Gapjaw said, defensive.

Safety shook his head. "I guess we'll see how it turns out," he sighed.

The launch battered against the chop of a larger ship's passage, and vanished into the river's boat traffic.

CHAPTER THREE

Don't dig at it, there's nothing but madness and death down that path. But if you were going to poke around, I'd start at Claymark Bellfoundry. Of course you never heard of them, they went out of business over five hundred years ago. But once upon a time, they were the supplier of damn near every bell in Doskvol.

Then in the bitter cold of deepest winter, the Spirit Wardens showed up, shut them down, and relocated the bellfoundry into the Bellweather Crematorium. That's right, the bellfoundry and the crematorium in close quarters, 'neath the enchanted bells that ring on both sides of the Mirror every time someone in the city dies. Why did they do it? Was there a competition issue? Or was there a problem with the bells? Why did the bells start marking the deaths in the city anyway?

Those aren't the right questions. I've seen those bells. Carillon upon carillon, from giant bells the size of a coach to wee handbells in rows. I can say this, for certain; Bellweather has more bells in those towers than will fit in those towers. Now. Leave it alone.

— From Dava Mark's personal correspondence, Elisar 9, 812

BARKUL MARKET, SILKSHORE.
18TH ELISAR. HOUR OF FLAME, 5 HOURS PAST DUSK.

Draft goats pulled the wagon down the uneven street, guided by two burly Bluecoats seated on the buckboard. The wagon was flanked by six Bluecoats marching in a row on each side, armed and armored for battle. Their gear included metal breastplates, greaves on their forearms and shins, knee and elbow protection, rifles, and pistols. The set of their jaws, the tightness of their shoulders, and the energy of their movements spoke for them. They knew one way or another someone was about to die.

They rounded the corner to see an almost deserted street, the bustle of the Barkul Market drained to whispers and rubbish in a fitful breeze.

At the far end of the market, a rough barricade was built out of carts, doors ripped from their hinges, barrels, and smashed furniture. Several tousled heads were visible peering over the barricade, watchful.

A robed figure strode out of the shadows to the middle of the street, between the Bluecoats and the makeshift barrier. She turned, pushing her hood back to reveal solemn features tattooed with strange occult symbols. Squaring off with the Bluecoats, she stood unmoving.

"Out of the way!" hollered one of the men on the wagon. "We have City Watch business!"

"You are here for the leader of the riot," she agreed, her voice cutting through the background noise, easy to hear. "I'm not here to stop you—but I would ask you to wait."

"Wait?" growled the Bluecoat leader. "For what?"

"Give him a chance to surrender," she said. "Please."

One of the Bluecoats on the buckboard leaned over to the other. "She's with the River Stallions. They've got Niece, that Skov girl."

"Blood and bones," the captain muttered. He eyed the mysterious woman in the cloak. "What do we do?"

The other Bluecoat crossed his arms over his chest. "We give 'em a few minutes," he said under his breath. The restless Bluecoats held position.

Just for a few minutes.

*

"Line 'em up over there," barked the hoarse Skov, his beard bristling and his tunic spattered with blood. He sheathed his knife, cocking his head as he looked down at his handiwork; the Bluecoat sergeant was not recognizable, his face a mass of meat, his uniform black with blood. "Looks like we got a scarecrow to get their attention," the Skov growled.

"Captain!" one of the other Skov warriors said, "we've got their women and children against the barricade."

"Good," the captain nodded. "And the backside?"

"Locals clearing out," reported a Skov perched on a roof, looking down at the rest of the crew. "No sign of the law yet from the back."

"But there's a wagon out front," said the woman that walked out of the half-barricaded alley. She held her hands out to the sides, empty, but she wore the sword and dagger of a Skov warrior unapologetically. "Captain Rikard, you're making a knot in the fabric of my city."

"Combing out the likes of me is hardly womens' work," he sneered in return. "Who the hell are you?"

"Locals call me Niece," she replied. "I'm part of the group that figures out how new Skovlanders are going to fit in around here." She looked at the four dead Bluecoats sprawled on the street. "So far you're not impressing anybody," she shrugged.

"They started it," Rikard said, "and once they put a hand on my crew, they owed me a price." He looked her in the eye, wound tight with all the danger of a cornered bear. "It's a price I was happy to collect."

"Very fierce," she agreed, stopping a dozen feet short of the captain. "You've got fifteen crew, plus yourself. Fine warriors, all," she nodded, looking around at where about half of them were visible. "I'll give you a generous four to one kill ratio today, even on unfamiliar ground against the home team, who have metal armor and guns." She looked the captain in the eye. "This is where your ship's travels end. The masthead gets cut off, shields stripped from the sides, and she becomes a barge for the local canals, in service to the city, never again to cross the Void Sea. But you can console yourself," she said, "by thinking about the Bluecoats you killed. When you lost everything else." She looked him in the eye. "A stranger's grief is seldom satisfying for long."

"You figure me for surviving this?" he said, eyebrows raised. "Maybe so, once I've gotten my point across. That the Serpentine and her crew are not to be toyed with or bullied by the likes of this scum," he said, and he spat at a senseless Bluecoat corpse.

"When you melt back into the shadows, that's where we are," Niece said quietly. "If you come in to our city and make a lot of noise then try to disappear, you'll find the places that might shelter you will close their doors if you bring this much heat for no reason."

"No reason?" he protested.

"I don't want to hear it," she said. "I'm sure they were rude to you. Maybe even violent. But you killed some of them, and they're no more forgiving about that than you are. So if you want the rest of your crew to escape, you've got to pay a price." She looked down at the knifed Bluecoat. "Not so severe a price as this, and there will be pain." She met his eyes. "But you will likely live."

For a long moment he stared at her, eyes crazy wild with adrenaline, droplets of blood in his eyebrows and beard.

"Right," Niece said. "Who is Captain Rickard's second?"

"Hey," called out a square shouldered woman with an axe, standing in the nearby shadows.

"Your name?" Niece asked.

"Her name is Danika," Rickard growled, "and you're not talking past me or I'll slit you wide open."

"Danika can retreat with the crew while you are surrendering, and the Serpentine has time to resupply and shove off," Niece said, looking Rickard in the eye.

"Or they could mount a rescue," Rickard growled.

"Soldiers!" yelled the lookout by the barricade. "Over a dozen! Metal armor and rifles!"

Rage leaped up in Rikard's eyes as he glared at Niece. She crossed her arms over her chest and returned his gaze unflinching.

"You trying to distract me?" he demanded.

"No," she said simply. "Bluecoat snipers will be climbing up in buildings around this location. You may not get a fight at all, unless you pull back to somewhere with worse sight-lines."

"Rickard," Danika said urgently, "this is stupid, and we're losing time."

"They shoot you, no deal for anybody else," Niece said coolly, looking Rickard in the eye. "And if you are dead set on starting a war, the Bluecoats will spread the pain to the Skovs who are already here." Her smile tightened to a line. "Makes it hard to count on your kin to back you up when it's their heads on the block if you go down swinging."

Rickard stared at Danika. "What do you think?" he demanded.

"Hey, you say we start killing fools, we do it," she replied. "None of us signed on with a plan to get old."

"Captain!" said one of the broad Skov warriors, stepping forward. "I'll do it. I'll pretend to be you, go to jail. You keep sailing." His forehead was drawn together with concentration and fervor.

Rickard stared at him. "Konrad, I could not ask that of you. It will be bad," he said.

"You don't have to ask," Konrad replied, sincere. "I want to serve." He turned to Niece. "Would you vouch for me? Say I'm the captain?"

She looked over at Rickard. "I will, yes," she said.

Rickard thought for one more second, then nodded. "Do it," he growled.

"The fastest way out," Niece said, "is through that public house, down the hall to the left of the bar, to the basement, out to the canal. Bluecoats may not have that buttoned down yet." She paused. "Get your supplies, and get gone."

She turned to Konrad. "Put your hands on the top of your head," she said. She took two strides over to the barricade and hopped up, peering over. "Inkletta!" she shouted. "The captain surrendered!"

On the other side of the barricade, the lone robed woman standing in the street turned and looked at the Bluecoats. "He's all yours," she said. "Please don't let this get out of hand."

"What about the rest of his crew?" one of the Bluecoats demanded.

"Captain's coming out now!" Niece yelled.

"We'll sweep 'em up," the head Bluecoat growled without much conviction. "First things first." He drew his pistol, and gestured for the six Bluecoats to the left to go intercept the big man clambering over the barricade, his hands in the air.

Meanwhile Niece worked her way down the line of the barricade, tugging women and children loose of where they had been hastily lashed to the overturned wagon, barrels, and other debris. "Get out of here," she whispered, and as each was freed they either ran ahead to free others along the line, or darted along a side street to disappear into the city before the Bluecoats got closer.

Inkletta pulled back to the side, no longer between the Bluecoats and the Skovs. She watched, wary, as the big Skov approached the six Bluecoats. Two of the Bluecoats knelt, putting their rifles down on the street, unhooking manacles from their belts. They approached the big Skov, who stared at them, unflinching.

An ear-splitting scream tore out of the night sky, and a single flap of leathern wings bore an unexpected complication into the street. Everyone flinched a glance upward as the giant bat's erratic flight swayed down to home in on Inkletta. Before she had quite realized what happened, the bat opened his wingspan to almost seven feet, applying the airbrakes and crashing into her, wrapping his wings around her as she was blown off her feet to land square on her back covered in bat.

Winded and desperate, she managed to free a hand and grab the bat's face, sliding towards his eyes; one squinted shut as she touched it, the other was a metal ball, and it was hot to the touch—

—*cursework*—

Gasping with the flash of pain and vileness that blew through her, Inkletta wrestled with the frantic bat as he started mewling and clutching at her with his knobbly wing fingers, clambering at her with his feet as though trying to climb her.

Meanwhile Konrad made the most of the distraction, taking a big step forward and snatching both Bluecoats by the fabrics over their chests, hurling each one back at the other gunmen, confusing the situation momentarily. A gun discharged, and another, but neither hit the giant Skov at point-blank range.

The startled and distracted Bluecoats turned from the bat and fired a volley of shots at the big man as he leaped towards a nearby alley; one shot hit him for sure, but he made it to cover, smearing blood along a wall as he scrambled away as best he could.

The six Bluecoats that had tried to take him into custody managed to get to their feet and give chase, but the Bluecoat on the wagon gestured for the others to hang back. "It could be an ambush," he said. "Great spot for one, running through the alleys after a prisoner who was shot trying to escape." He paused reflectively looking over at where Niece was helping tug at the bat, who still scrabbled all over Inkletta.

Inkletta murmured some soothing words in Hadrathi to the bat, and her pupils flexed as she sensed at his life force. Feeling his fever, his terror and pain, his confusion, she blended her own thoughts and feelings in; the hot liquid panic that filled the bat spilled into her and cooled, and the bat stopped clawing at her.

"What the hell is going on?" Niece demanded through her teeth.

"Something terrible has happened to Red Silver," Inkletta replied, shifting the weight of the bat. "I don't know if her idea moved through Nails, or if he came to find me on his own, or both." With Niece helping, she got clear of the bat, and he resumed languishing, clawing at the metal ball in his eye socket.

Two Bluecoats loomed in the background. "I don't know what you're trying to pull," the first one growled, "but that distraction was a little too well timed."

"You were going in there," Inkletta said. "It would have been a bloodbath."

"So you figured you'd help your new Skov recruits escape?" the Bluecoat demanded.

"They're leaving town," Niece said. "Gave up their captain and headed for their ship."

The Bluecoat stared at her for a moment, then looked over his shoulder. "Round it up!" he shouted. "To the docks!" He ran over and mounted the buckboard as the wagon rattled back the way it came, the remaining Bluecoats jogging to keep up.

"Maybe I shouldn't have said that," Niece sighed, rubbing her face.

"We have bigger problems," Inkletta murmured. Nails had calmed down significantly, and she was scratching under his jaw, along the side of his face, rubbing his soft and alert ears. She let her eyes drift closed, and she felt the giant bat's heartbeat, three times faster than her own; she lined up her consciousness with it, and seeped into the bat's active fluttering mind.

"Something went wrong in Six Towers," Inkletta murmured through nerveless lips. "Sssh, ssh," she soothed Nails as the bat violently spasmed. "Can't go at it directly... fire.... Burning... she goes for water... can't do the water..." Inkletta looked up at Niece. "We need to get to Six Towers, now."

MISTSHORE PARK, SIX TOWERS.
19ᵀᴴ ELISAR. HOUR OF SMOKE, 11 HOURS PAST DUSK.

Niece stood in the back of the small boat, anchored with a wide stance, flexing the pole back and forth to keep the boat moving. Nails clutched at the prow like a horrifically adorable figurehead, and Inkletta sat right behind him, eyes half closed, sensing his connection to Red Silver.

"We've got the Mistshore Park up ahead," Niece murmured. "Are we getting close?"

"Close in on the park," Inkletta said.

The boat sloshed along against the waves from the river current, and they approached the shoreline, where thousands of tons of crushed rock created something like a beach centuries ago. The hull of the boat scraped along the gravel, and Inkletta leaped out to splash into the water, dragging at the boat, pulling it up out of the river's easy reach.

"I smell something burning," Niece said with a frown.

"There." Inkletta closed in on a longboat that had been tipped up-side-down. They saw wisps of smoke draining up out of the craft, thin in the pre-dawn light. A very dim glow was visible, as they focused on the overturned boat. They approached with caution, but Nails swept his wingspan a couple times, then dropped to the gravel in front of the boat, ears laid back, and crawled in.

"Think she has a fire in there or something?" Niece asked, wary.

"I don't know what I'm going to find in there," Inkletta said through her teeth, eyes fixed on the overturned boat, "but what I felt from Nails? Brutal cursework. Like, human sacrifice, dawn of necromancy, old school darkness." She set her jaw. "Don't freak out."

"See, that? That's sort of encouragement to freak out," Niece muttered under her breath. Then she squared off with the boat. "I'll go look."

"No no, better not," Inkletta retorted, taking hold of her elbow. "Just... I just needed a minute." She took a deep breath, then let it out. She approached the boat, dropped to all fours, lowered herself to lay prone, peered under the boat, and pulled herself forward with her elbows.

Red was splayed against the wood, cloth and flesh slightly hissing as the glyphs burned into her forehead and down her chi meridians pulsed with her heartbeat. That was the only light, and it was partially covered by the miserable bulk of Nails, drawn to his mistress and her suffering but repelled by the agony and revulsion of the cursework that bound her.

"Red?" Inkletta said, hesitant. "It's me, Inkletta."

"Oh, thank the Keeper of the Flame," Red gulped. "Nails, you're a very good boy. And—oh gods," Red quavered, on the edge of falling apart.

"I want to tip this boat over, and get you out of there," Inkletta said soothingly. "Niece is here with us, we want to take you home."

"No!" Red said sharply. "Not home! I'm—my blood is screaming," she managed. "I can hear it scream. I feel like everyone can hear—my blood—screaming."

Inkletta thought fast. "Right, the Mistress of Tides has a safe place where we can go. Okay? We'll go see the Mistress of Tides."

"Okay," Red whispered. "Okay good."

Niece was already by the boat, so when Inkletta stood, together they flipped it over easily enough. Niece only stared for a moment, then she pulled Red up, supporting her by ducking under her arm, hauling her over to the boat. A short struggle later they got the boat back out into the current, Red bundled up in two heavy cloaks in the bottom of the boat, Inkletta at the prow as Niece once again sculled at the stern.

"You're thinking it, I may as well say it," Niece said. "If Red showed up here, then something went wrong at the party. Sanction and the boys are probably looking for her as we speak."

"Let's get to the Mistress of Tides, then you can track down the boys, and I'll look after Red," Inkletta said. "This is... disturbing. Whatever hit her, it's not something she could have picked up tonight." She shook her head. "This kind of cursework... it takes time. You can't.... you can't dig this deep into someone's life force, into their blood, and..." She shook the feeling off. "There's a bigger picture here. It's not one we're going to like."

ZEPHYR STREET, MASTER MARKET, MAURO OVERVIEW, SILKSHORE. 19TH ELISAR. THIRD HOUR PAST DAWN.

The constellation of clouds assured only the faintest sepia light brushed the exposed surfaces of the market. Instead, it bustled with its own glowing fragments. Light shone from luminous jars and mirrored flames, radiant plants and hand-held plasmic torches. Niece guided the boat into a narrow canal alleyway that dead-ended by steps leading to a basement back door to the Overview. Niece held the boat steady while Inkletta hauled Red off the boat and up the stairs, then she backed out to go about other business.

Inkletta used her key to let herself in, and she swung the massive reinforced door shut behind her with a clang. Together, Red and Inkletta shuffled across the open space of the training chamber, removing a bar from another heavy door, descending down some stairs, entering a spherical chamber.

The walls had bands of sigils carved in and sanctified with rituals. As soon as they entered, three of the twelve bands glowed in response to their presence. Inkletta hauled at the door, pulling it closed, and she sat on a bench carved in a circle near the bottom of the sphere.

"You see the glyphs," she said, gesturing at the walls as she caught her breath.

"That keeps the noise in?" Red asked in a small voice.

"Yes, keeps the noise in," Inkletta agreed. "Seems you've regained some of your composure."

"A little," Red agreed, twisting her hands. "It's—humiliating. Being so—the way you found me."

"You were not overreacting," Inkletta retorted. "Now. Can you tell me how you got those marks?"

"Yes and no," Red mumbled, eyes down.

"Red," Inkletta said, firm, so Red's eyes flicked up to meet her own. "This is not the time to be cagey. You have to tell me everything so I can help you."

"I was pulled into the séance," Red said, brow furrowed. "Madame Starshine summoned the ghost of this occultist in the Rowan family, Shaw Rowan."

"I heard of him," Inkletta nodded. "Gifted, powerful, poor sense of judgement."

"Anyway," Red continued, "The ghost showed, but didn't settle in Madame Starshine. He picked me."

"Why did he do that?" Inkletta asked quietly, studying Red.

Red paused for a long moment. "I could just say I don't know," she began, "but that wouldn't be totally true. I—even before this, I get, I don't know, itchy sometimes. My skin doesn't fit right, my bones won't knit with each other. Some years back I got to—to self-medicating by riding."

"Ghost riding," Inkletta clarified. "Letting a ghost in to live out some impulse. You're talking voluntary possession for kicks."

"Yes," Red said, looking Inkletta in the eye. She gave Inkletta every chance to respond, then she looked back at her hands. "Sometimes it got rough. Almost killed me a few times. But—it was nothing like this. Like what Shaw did once he got in there."

Silence stretched between them and grew heavy.

"I have to ask," Inkletta said quietly.

"What did Shaw do?" Red echoed sardonically. She drew a deep shuddering breath, and let it go. "Those other ghosts must have gotten inside the curse too, and just not felt it. Not seen it. They didn't know what the curse was, but Shaw did. So he burst out before it would flow up or down history, get into his bloodline's fate."

"So—so the ghost didn't curse you," Inkletta clarified.

"No," Red mumbled, looking down at her hands. "But he turned it up. Lit the beacon."

"Red... what beacon?"

Red was quiet for a long moment. "I never told you my real name," she said quietly. "My real name is Gavrita Elena Soskitu Selraetas." She looked Inkletta in the eye. "I am the last of my line."

"Selraetas..." Inkletta murmured, her memory working. Her eyes widened.

"An insane Whisper by the name of Razor Wind made it his life's mission to wipe out my family line, when he was a young man," Red nodded. "You've heard the story. He went through the bother of genea-logical research so anyone who touched my grandfather Beren's blood was a target, and he murdered them all pretty horribly. Torture, muti-lation, and yes—cursework." She paused. "My parents managed to put me in what they hoped were safe hands when I was only three years old. The story I heard later was that Razor Wind destroyed my parents slowly, with ritual magic, branding their blood so that their issue or progenitors would light up the dark sky with a signal that was sure to draw Razor Wind to them to finish off the line. It was a masterstroke to try and mop up half-children, bastards, hidden heirs, and the like."

"No wonder it took you a year to warm up to me," Inkletta said softly.

"Whispers scare the hell out of me," Red muttered through clenched teeth. "Darnok the Miraculous was an adept who took me in, and when I was six and the runes started glowing through my skin, he..." She stopped, rubbing at her eyes.

The women sat in the quiet dimness together for a while.

"Darnok found a ritual and he committed suicide, using his life energy to cover my own," Red whispered, barely forming her breath into words. "I was... I was six."

"That's a heavy gift for a child to bear," Inkletta agreed.

"Even as a child my pretty face got me into a family, and my danger sense got me out, so I bounced around a little until I found—look, that doesn't matter. The main thing is that the enchantment Darnok bought for me was probably already wearing thin, and when Shaw revealed the cursework, it's out, and Razor Wind is on his way to finish me off."

"We are not going to let that happen," Inkletta retorted, stern. "You may have had a family of aristocrats, and they may have had the money to hire muscle and expertise to defend themselves, but what you have now is better." She paused. "You've got a handful of scoundrels who routinely invite personal danger for profit, and work together as a team to take on anything." She paused, ducking a glance at Red's face. "Does that help?"

"I mean, yeah, a little," Red admitted. "If you were smart you'd drop me and walk away. This is not—"

"Oh, Red, you know there's little danger of us doing the smart thing," Inkletta said with a warm smile, brushing Red's hair back from her face.

"I guess there's that," Red agreed, and a tentative smile almost broke through.

Inkletta smiled back, but the expression didn't begin to match the pit of fear in her gut.

Niece strode down the cobbled street, glancing over her shoulder, approaching the massive bridge across the river. Her walk slowed as she saw the beggar tucked back off the walking path, his cup out front next to a glow jar he probably painted himself.

"Hey there, stranger," Niece said. "What do you think of the local birds?"

"Noisy songs," the beggar replied, his smile thin. "Spare a coin?"

Niece looked him over, then looked down the street, and across the way, and behind herself, and her jaw set. "Great," she murmured.

The beggar leaned forward, rocking to his feet with alarming speed, lunging at her. She was ready, slapping his knife to the side and scoring a cut along his ribs as he twisted away from her thrust. He pivoted, slashing at her with his long and filthy nails, and she caught his wrist on her forearm, jabbing a cut at his armpit. He gasped, taking a couple big steps away then pivoting back towards her.

"You must be Rowan's people," she said, frowning.

His response was to raise his fist to his mouth, but even as he blew a handful of glittering powder at her she had her cloak up to deflect it; she leaped at him, and her blade punched through the cloak and into the beggar assassin's torso.

She retracted the knife and cloak with a long, low step back, and the assassin beggar dropped to his knees, then leaned forward and planted a hand on the paving, his other hand on the knife wound that slopped out blood to spatter on the ground.

"This—changes nothing," the assassin gasped.

"Your week's plans shifted, I'll wager," Niece retorted. "As have mine."

The beggar assassin fell on his side, pulling himself together. Niece squeezed the blood off her dagger blade and sheathed it, immediately regretting the fresh blood on her cloak. She looked at the dying assassin, and listened for a sound that carried on some medium beyond the mid-day breeze.

The assassin beggar's eyes went glassy. Far, far away, a Bellweather Seminary bell tolled a single simple peal.

Feeling eyes upon her, Niece retraced her steps, and did her best to vanish into the dim bustle of daytime traffic.

ZEPHYR STREET, MASTER MARKET, MAURO OVERVIEW, SILKSHORE. 19TH ELISAR. FOURTH HOUR PAST DAWN.

Inkletta quietly swung the door to the chamber closed, then turned to leave. She was startled to come face to face with the elaborate veils of the Mistress of Tides.

"My lady," she said, instinctively.

"You cannot leave," the Mistress of Tides said. "I have received word from Safety. Your crew's evening activities have provoked Lord Rowan to declare war on the River Stallions." She paused. "He is on the City Council," she clarified. "He has… resources."

"It's not safe for you to shelter us," Inkletta said breathlessly.

The Mistress of Tides waved that off. "I have acolytes doing meditation exercises in these chambers, and for the next while, those acolytes are you." She shrugged. "No one need know you are here. I can get word to Safety that you're out of danger."

"We have to suss out a way to hit back, if we give him time to hunt us we're finished," Inkletta said grimly.

"You know that I, and the Silkworms, and the Fairpole Council will help you," the Mistress of Tides replied. "Resist panic."

Inkletta hesitated. "Also, Red is cursed. That chamber dampens the signal, but… Razor Wind will be hunting her. Here, in Silkshore, possibly before the week is out."

Inscrutable behind her veil, the Mistress of Tides thought that over. "Sounds like we have much to do," she murmured, "to prepare for battle."

"Yes," Inkletta agreed, with the barest of smiles. "We do."

CHAPTER FOUR

In the summer of 823, Warlord Roytaa had claimed about a third of the Ease as his kingdom of decadence. He used nepotism and murder to replace most of the Bluecoats in the area with relatives, and he was creating quite a cesspit. He was into the occult, and conducted frequent rituals of protection and such, and a soothsayer once told him that he would be slain by Gapjaw, a crocologian that drifted through the canals at the top of the food chain. So when this punk kid managed to surprise him in his quarters and knife him to death, Roytaa wanted to know how it was possible. The kid just grinned and said "I must be Gapjaw." Sure, the kid was a smartass, but the more superstitious types noted the crocologian was never seen again. They wondered if this kid had somehow faced that monster in the darkness and taken its essence, just to kill the Warlord. Whether you believe the story or not, the name stuck.

— From "Occult Vignettes of the Dusk," by Sord Vortison

HIGH SIX RADIANT GARDEN, SILKSHORE.
19TH ELISAR. FIFTH HOUR PAST DAWN.

A distinguished man leaned into the curve of the shaped bench, one arm draped along its back, his free hand holding a modest book. He read by the light glowing from the depths of the massive oak behind him and spreading overhead, pale wood glowing in streaks through cracks in the bark, leaves breathing illumination from their delicate veinwork. The view laid out before him was spectacular; the overlook was higher than the Ease, offering a clear view of the neighborhood's silks and colors, like stained glass glowing up into the dimness of the broken sky.

He looked up as a man in black robes strolled along the path towards his secluded reading spot. The man was flanked by well-dressed pale assistants, possibly bodyguards. The man on the bench snapped his book shut and tucked it in his coat, and he rose to his feet.

"Greetings," he said. "I don't believe we've met." His smile could pass as sincere.

"Oh, I've taken pains to avoid your notice, Sir Belderan," the other man said with an equally artificial smile. He removed his hat and bowed low. "Cecil Soapstone, Solicitor," he said. Straightening, he replaced the hat on his head. "I'm here to prevent our inevitable disagreement."

"You work for Councilman Rowan," Belderan murmured.

"It is a lucrative retainer for a valued client, who is a real pillar of the city," Soapstone agreed. "I help him with his problems."

"I have taken care not to be one of his problems," Belderan said.

"It's the company we keep," Soapstone said apologetically. "Our connections; we pull on them, but do they not also pull on us?" He shook his head. "I cannot have you coming to the aid of the River Stallions. In fact, I believe you may be the key to a rapid resolution of the disagreement they are having with Lord Rowan." He paused. "A face-to-face conversation should clear it up nicely," he added, a quietness and finality in his tone.

"I see," Belderan said, expressionless. "What if I told you I have no connection to the River Stallions?"

"I would acknowledge the half-truth of the statement," Soapstone said thoughtfully, "then point out you also have an alias. You are also Trellis, leader of the Silkworms, that does in fact have association with that mob."

"You are a very well informed solicitor," Belderan observed.

"I work for a man who dislikes surprise," Soapstone shrugged. "As enjoyable as this conversation is, I believe we've reached the end of contextualizing what comes next." He paused. "I hope what comes next is peaceful and compliant."

"Do you think that's likely?" Trellis asked quietly.

"I hoped that by isolating you here, in your place of contemplation, where your security is lightest, we might avoid tiresome antics," Soapstone confessed.

"Reasonable," Trellis agreed. "A tactic that I myself would use, were I to come to you with the goal of removing your piece from the board. Peacefully," he clarified.

"So we understand each other, there's no going to the bathroom, no tying your shoe, no last smoke, no checking your messages, no vigorous scratching of an itch, nothing to eat or drink; you will refrain until you are in our coach, then you may indulge whatever idiosyncrasies you need to address." He stepped back, gesturing down the path. "Let's go."

Trellis regarded him for a long moment. "What if I compel you to carry me?" he asked.

"None of that," Soapstone shrugged. "You won't walk, then I kill you here, and leave your corpse among your life's work," he said with a gesture around the radiant garden. "I have two reasons to bother taking you alive. For one, you owe the River Stallions little and could greatly speed their capture. Secondly," he added slowly, "I admire your work. Your operations could be the subject of a year's study if there was a masterclass in what we do."

"Well then," Trellis said with the barest of smiles. "Let's go."

ATTIC, CRAMDEN'S PUBLIC HOUSE, SILKSHORE. 19ᵗʰ ELISAR. FIFTH HOUR PAST DAWN.

"Do you figure the light has shifted too far," the young man mused, gazing out the circular window of the attic loft.

"Tired of posing?" the artist asked, sardonic. He shrugged. "The light's fine, maybe another half hour." He resumed his work. "Got somewhere to be, Mister Kreeger?"

"Perpetually," Kreeger replied, his eyes distant. The artist paused, then redoubled work on the face, striving to capture something rarely on display.

Loud knocking rattled the door and shattered the mood. "Just a second," the artist muttered, dumping the brush and crossing to the door. He opened it a narrow gap, and it was shoved open enough to send him stumbling back.

Three burly Bluecoats pushed into the narrow loft, filling it. Behind them, an Inspector's black uniform was filled out by a somewhat haughty man.

"Kreeger? Allow me to introduce myself. I am Inspector Gant, and I've inherited some old cases that I think you might be able to help me with."

"Odd that you should feel the need to barge in to my sitting, for old cases," Kreeger said mildly. "Impatient, or have you got something urgent?"

"Still too soon to say," the Inspector sneered. "Care to join me at the station?"

"If it can wait, we still have half an hour of good light," Kreeger said, nodding at the window.

"Blood and bone," muttered one of the Bluecoats and the Inspector's sneer soured.

"You'll come with me now, and you'll be grateful I'm asking nicely," he snapped.

Kreeger's hesitation was fractional. "I'll get my coat," he said, shrugging off his dandy waistcoat and hanging it on a peg, pulling on his more functional oilskin greatcoat. "Which station shall we head towards?" he asked, feigning brightness.

"Just come on," the Inspector growled. They pushed out, and the artist closed the door behind them, heart still pounding from the potential danger.

They bustled down the stairs, through the smoke and noise of the public house, then out to the darkened street lit from a hundred directions by small efforts to push light against the city's shadow. Light paled the sky over the river, but on the other side of the tall buildings the light was lost; it did not approach the ground.

The cobbled street was on a hill. Confident cabbies and hurried merchants alike pushed their massive goats to drag carriages and wagons at potentially unsafe speeds up and down the thoroughfare.

"Mind telling me what this is about, seeing as how I'm cooperating?" Kreeger asked mildly.

"I'll be the judge of whether or not you are cooperating," Gant snarled. "You have a reputation for mischief, you do." He shook his head. "One day you're working for the Ministry, the next you're a gentleman of leisure. How do you afford that?"

"I work for my uncle, Lord Belderan," Kreeger replied. "The High Six is a boon for our family finances. And my needs are simple." He tried on a winning smile.

"Like having your portrait painted?" Gant sneered.

As they hustled down the sidewalk towards the parked carriage, Kreeger's alert glance picked up on a woman jumping up on some crates, pushing her hood back. He immediately recognized Niece.

And the worry on her face. And the hand signal to "get out of there."

"It's nice to know there's something to remember me by," he said as casually as he could. "Accidents happen."

He lunged forward, snatching Gant's harness, and slung him to the side. Gant staggered off the sidewalk, then tripped over his feet and fell—under the oncoming hooves of draft goats and a loaded wagon. His body was crushed as the wagon jounced and the goats screamed, almost obscuring the distant tolling in another world as Gant's broken body died.

One Bluecoat had the presence of mind to snatch Kreeger's shoulder, and Kreeger pivoted to pull the Bluecoat's pistol and fire it into his torso point-blank. The big man staggered back, and as Kreeger oriented on the next Bluecoat, a backhand knocked the smoking gun from his hand as another hand cannon was drawn and aimed at him. Kreeger hurled his whole mass into snatching the gun arm and shoving it aside; the gun discharged directly into the third Bluecoat, knocking him off his feet. Kreeger slung an elbow strike into the Bluecoat, to no effect, and he was hurled to the ground. The massive breech loading pistols had two shots each, and the Bluecoat cocked the hammer on the second shot as he lined up on Kreeger.

A glittering knife whirled across the street and slammed into the Bluecoat's shoulder, and his shot went wide, snapping into a cobblestone and ricocheting away. Kreeger drove a two-heeled kick into the front of the Bluecoat's knee, and he was rewarded by a meaty snap and strangled cry of pain. Rolling over, he took off, slipping into the crowd as the three Bluecoats struggled to recover from the rapid assault.

By the time they could look for him, Kreeger was gone.

ZEPHYR STREET, MASTER MARKET, MAURO OVERVIEW, SILKSHORE. 19ᵀᴴ ELISAR. FIFTH HOUR PAST DAWN.

A haze of incense hung in the narrow stone gallery, and the robed and veiled figure seated on the throne at one end was motionless. The faint strains of a harp drifted through the room, wandering and lost, a thin line between the distant street noise and the silence of shadowed stone. The occasional rustle of cloth and whisper of sandal on paving underscored the quiet rather than disrupting it.

A woman in a long robe rushed up to the figure on the throne. "Mistress of Tides," she murmured, "Spirit Wardens are approaching, fast."

The Mistress of Tides rose to her feet. "Go down to the underchamber and lock the door to the lower galleries, make sure the false wall is in place." She turned to another of her acolytes. "Everyone, here, in the gallery behind the pillars, armed. At once. We will likely shed blood."

Her attention turned to the entry chamber, where one of her acolytes tried to scurry in to announce the visitors, but he was shoved into a wall gracelessly by a mailed fist as four Spirit Wardens strode in, unapologetic. They wore expressionless bronze masks etched with protections, as well as unusually heavy armor; chainmail and breastplates. The leader had a full face mask, marking his status as a full-fledged Spirit Warden, Master of the Order. The others were initiates; well trained and prepared, but lacking the secret knowledge and elite training of their masters.

"Mistress of Tides," the leader said, his voice sharp. "I am here to bring you in for questioning related to some open cases."

"I do not choose to cooperate," she said coolly from behind the veil.

"Then I will press charges," the Spirit Warden said, not skipping a beat. "Mistress of Tides, you are accused of necromancy, plasmic sabotage, interference with the dead—"

"I sound dangerous," she said, her voice cutting through the litany and stopping it in its tracks.

"One way or another you come with me. Alive? Dead? That's up to you," the Spirit Warden snapped.

"Bold words for a man with only three friends," she observed.

"Highly trained—" he began, but her hand emerged from its long loose sleeve with a massive pistol; she lined up and fired, and the shot crushed the knee of one of the initiates; his leg flew out from under him as though it had been kicked by a draft goat, and he slammed face-down on the paving with a clang.

That was the signal, and an acolyte standing behind a column threw purple sand in the brazier; the room seemed to flex as the ritual activated, and all the charms, protections, spells, and runes safeguarding the Spirit Wardens burst with staccato flashes and snaps, staggering them as their equipment crackled and singed.

A dozen robed figures swarmed out from behind the columns as the Spirit Wardens oriented on the Mistress of Tides. The acolytes did not have pistols. They had slender spears and knives. They closed three strides to the Spirit Wardens as the armored men were drawing their pistols, and the trained acolytes aimed for gaps between plates, catching the Spirit Wardens off balance and driving them back to back in the center of the narrow gallery. Their pale steel weapons flicked and jabbed, and there was no hesitation as they cut at flesh to release its life force; they did not flinch from the spray of arterial blood they slashed loose.

In moments the intruders were cut down, except for the Spirit Warden, who had a slit across his inner elbow so he dropped his gun, and a cut in his ribs so his breathing whined with blood, and a savage stab wound that almost severed his Achilles tendon so he was on one knee. He struggled to move, then froze, as the Mistress of Tides stood before him.

"I don't care who sent you," she murmured, invisible behind her veils. "I don't care if there are more Spirit Wardens on the way. This is the heart of Gondolier territory, near the center of the Fairpole Council's power base, and if you declare war on me I will cease to allow you to harvest spirits from the dead of Silkshore. Instead I will gather them so that they may be used to make war upon you until your people *beg* me to forgive them." She paused. "Bring me in for questioning? I will not go with you. In your armor. So smug."

The Spirit Warden's voice shook. "By now—your *friends*—are in enemy hands," he wavered. "The boat people cannot stand—against the Council—the *City* Council," he panted. "You are making—"

With a clack, she jammed the pistol against the mask's eye-hole, and she pulled the trigger, blasting the Spirit Warden's head into pieces.

The Mistress of Tides looked at her attentive acolytes. "We knew something like this might happen, and you know what to do," she said.

Her will was made reality.

FOGGERT'S SUMP, SILKSHORE.
19TH ELISAR. TENTH HOUR PAST DAWN.

"Well, this is all your fault, so I don't see why you get to complain," Safety growled. He flexed his jaw against the stench, and leaned back against the slimy pylon.

"I have the River Stallion's best interests at heart in everything I do," Gapjaw grumbled, adjusting the luminescent jar. It sloshed a bit, sending weak ripples of light across the dank and gummy planks of the hideout. "How could we leave empty-handed?"

"I'm not having this conversation again," the Hammer said.

"I miss our hideout under the bridge," Gapjaw said with a squint. "It was just getting to the point where we have so much cool stuff there we can entertain and impress the other scoundrels." He heaved a deep sigh.

"I hate to think of Rowan's people all over it," the Hammer agreed. "Even worse, I'm worried about our people. Nobody knows where

Saint is, Red and Inkletta are holed up with the Mistress of Tides, and Niece is in the wind."

"Pretty awful," Gapjaw agreed. "All the pretty people are somewhere else, I get *you* to look at." He glanced over at Safety. "Are you sure we aren't overreacting by going to our most horrible and secret safe house where no one would ever go to look for us?"

"We are not overreacting," Safety said, jaw clenched.

"You're sure you can trust the message from the Mistress of Tides that she's got Red and Inkletta?" the Hammer pressed.

"I'm sure," Safety replied. "She left a message in the blind drop on Wolfagen Street, and that's the last time I get to walk down that street with my face visible until we get this resolved." He paused. "Rowan declared war on the River Stallions, just like I figured he would." He shook his head.

A voice drifted down from a shaft that led to the stinking lair. "I bought expensive sheets, you assholes," the voice echoed. Moments later, Piccolo was among them. "I bought silk wall decorations. Real furniture. And what do you guys do? You wreck everything," he said, harsh. "I owe money to three guys and suddenly they're everywhere I go, looking for me. So I have to go where no one would ever go on purpose or accidentally," he growled, eyes watering as he crossed his arms and stared around the filthy hole. "Because of the stench," he explained unnecessarily.

"You are the one that grabbed the guy," Gapjaw said, sour.

"I will kill you," Piccolo clarified. "In case you were wondering."

"Did you get the prisoner stowed where he'll never be found and we don't have to babysit him?" Safety asked.

"As per the plan for situations like this, I took care of it," Piccolo shrugged. "But I can't be seen out there right now. I can't go drinking, or walking down the street, or checking in with my fences—nothing." He scowled at the River Stallions.

"Look, we appreciate you coming along on the Rowan job," the Hammer said. "We were down Niece and Inkletta because of an unexpccted Skov raid that we just couldn't ignore. But now you're in it with us."

"Not just me," Piccolo clarified. "I'm with the Silkworms, and they're getting hit right now from all sides because they know you. Anybody else you put in danger by befriending." He shook his head. "At least we may be provoking Rowan to overextend," he said.

Gapjaw, the Hammer, and Safety looked at him.

"Right?" he prompted.

"Better get some sleep," Safety said, almost numb. "The ugliness is just getting started."

DANNERY RUN, SILKSHORE.
19TH ELISAR. FIFTH HOUR PAST DAWN.

The carriage door opened, and Trellis was the first inside, closely followed by Soapstone. Trellis sat with his back to the front of the carriage, facing Soapstone and his two assistants. The door snapped shut, and reins hit the flanks of the goats outside, tugging the coach into motion.

"Glyphwork," Soapstone explained, gesturing at the spidery symbols in the paneling. "Bulletproof reinforcement. Custom restraints and drugs if need be." He shrugged. "Let's agree to make this trip comfortable," he said, the glint in his eye suggesting he was fine either way.

"You said I could smoke once we got to the carriage," Trellis said. "It would settle my nerves."

"With these locks in place, you're stuck with us until we reach our destination," Soapstone said, considering. "Sure what's the harm?"

"You've searched me, after all, and taken my knife," Trellis agreed. "I suspect if you follow my work you know I have no interest in suicide."

"And if you hurt us," Soapstone agreed, "you'll provoke a disproportionate response." He paused. "I will deliver you to Lord Rowan today."

"Sure," Trellis shrugged, his nimble fingers pulling out his tobacco bag, clay pipe, and electroplasmic sparker. He readied the pipe and lit it, then leaned back, pulling in the smoke, filling himself with it. "That's good," he murmured, smoke jetting from his nostrils as though he was a dragon. He smiled, putting the kit away, loosely holding the pipe with practiced ease. Trellis refocused on Soapstone. "So how is Rowan these days?"

"Busy with the City Council, and his new company, and his many projects," Soapstone replied. "If you give us what he wants to know, you may have a future in his organization." His smile broadened. "Considering his projects, and what the future will hold, that's no small opportunity."

"I am not one to let an opportunity pass me by," Trellis shrugged. He blew smoke out at his captors, and smiled. "What can you tell me about your employer's new projects?"

Soapstone's smile was spare. "Not much. Not until after you've talked with Lord Rowan."

Trellis chugged out smoke along with a merry laugh. "Oh, that's precious," he said. "Rowan knows his plan, but he doesn't have your grasp of the big picture. If we're talking a future, I need you in the conversation." He shook his head, and took another drag on the pipe. "Aristocrats," he murmured.

"Aren't you an aristocrat?" Soapstone pointed out, arching his eyebrow. "Old money, no less."

"Certainly of a class traditionally too proud to countenance low-born like you, who make it on their merit—much to my personal consternation," Trellis agreed. "But people like Lord Rowan... they are entitled to everything. They feel they bear the heavy responsibility of shaping the world."

One of the assistants coughed, then subsided, sullen. The bullet proof windows would not lower. Pipe smoke curled and twisted in the air.

"What kind of weed is that?" Soapstone asked, trying to keep the distaste from his voice.

"Oh, you know I study radiants, we get into all sorts of odd botany," Trellis said as he looked down into his bowl. "This particular ghostroot blend was given to me by a Whisper as a birthday present. You can see ghosts in the smoke," he said with wide eyes and a gesture.

"Mistress of Tides?" Soapstone clarified, arching an eyebrow.

"Now you're just showing off," Trellis replied with a grin. "The other neat thing about it—this smoke can trap ghosts." He nodded, and Soapstone realized his danger too late. Trellis's eyes glazed as he attuned to the smoke, and he snapped the clay pipe in half. The smoke flexed. The three men jolted, eyes wide, and found they could not move. "Even ghosts still wearing their meat," Trellis murmured, looking Soapstone in the eye.

Trellis reached into his pocket and pulled out his journal, then stripped the end pages off the back and peeled two adhesive sheets from the interior, slapping them on the door latch and rubbing them into place; the glyph from the paper was visible on the door latch plate. Leaning forward, Trellis pulled Soapstone's knife from his belt, and pricked his thumb. Trellis jammed the knife into the back wall of the bulletproof coach, looking Soapstone in the eye, then he snatched the spiritbane charm from Soapstone's lapel.

"This could have protected you, had you activated it," he murmured. "I'll just hang on to it. If I need to be in touch, I'll send it back, and you'll know it's me." His grin was hard. "Thanks for taking me alive. Consider this a return of the favor."

Trellis pressed his bloody thumb against the glyph, the glyph flexed and writhed, and the door lock blew.

Hearing the disturbance, the driver slowed the cab, leaning over to look back at the door. The door banged open, and Trellis took a long step out of the cab, barreling into the people on the curb, who broke his momentum somewhat. Shoving his way rudely he was into the crowd and through it, even as the cab jolted to a halt and the driver stood, drawing his pistol; too much haze, too dim, and Trellis was gone.

Motion was already returning to those in the coach. Enough for Soapstone to contract his face to a grimace, and his hand to a fist.

Niece trod the back alley between the canvas shop exits and wind-breaks, her boots squishing in the offal and dankness of the slum market. She pushed a lashed sheet aside, and stepped into a back room shared by several shops. She sat down in one of two rickety chairs and let out a couple ear-splitting whistles. They vanished into the noise of the market.

She only had to wait a couple minutes. The door creaked open, and a tough old woman shouldered her way in.

"Rhya, thank the gods you're here," Niece said as she rose to her feet and embraced her aunt.

"I couldn't stop them," Rhya whispered in her ear, then gave her a squeeze. The old woman eased down into a chair. "So what is going on that you come see your aunt then?" she asked, and when she smiled, her rueful expression was wound around apple-red cheek knobs and an expanse of wrinkles. Her eyes were still sharp, and now, sorrowful.

"It's been a week for killing my way out of things," Niece replied, tense, in Skovlan.

"Week's not over yet," Rhya shrugged. "Don't you worry about me—"

The room seemed to fly apart as a handful of Bluecoats attacked, coming through the canvas and knocking down the stemcore prefab walls. The plan was obviously to overwhelm her in close quarters so she did not have a chance to fight back, but the closeness impeded their ability to coordinate, and they lumbered into the wrecked room with grasping hands and manacles.

Niece left her sword in its sheath, yanking a boot knife out and whipping a parry across a Bluecoat's forearm that left a nasty gash.

Another Bluecoat lunged at her, wrapping her up in a garlicky bear hug, and as she flexed against it the raw muscle of the man clamped hard and triggered something like panic, the enemy of any warrior. He flexed and shook her, and the knife twirled down out of nerveless fingers.

With a battlecry, Rhya slashed the man's ear off with her cleaver, burying the blade in his shoulder so deep it clicked on his collarbone. The Bluecoat spasmed, shocked, and Niece managed to pry herself loose in time to see the third Bluecoat jam Rhya down on the table, brandishing manacles.

Rhya's eyes reached out to Niece and caught her. There was a kindness there, and a fire, and permission.

Run.

Just run.

Niece could barely see as she ducked a wide-armed sweep and shoulder-checked the back of a stall, knocking the makeshift wall into the kitchen area and springing through to bash out the front, racing down the market's muddy alley, Bluecoats on her tail.

She knew this market. Under the bridge, then sliding to a halt under the Ministry's offal cart by the canal. No one would look into the cart too closely, or under it for that matter.

Boots pounded past, and the search widened. The criminal element shifted in response. The Bluecoats knew that any sort of stall-to-stall search now would be for show.

They did it anyway.

Niece was long gone.

INTERROGATION QUARTERS, IRONHOOK, DUNSLOUGH. 19TH ELISAR. NINTH HOUR PAST DAWN.

The ever-present screams did not fade, but Saint was somewhat numb to them as he lay on the paving stone, his neck shackle permitting him only the most shallow breaths, his many injuries throbbing but allowing molten flashes or cracks of darkness to flutter through him if he moved. The cell door rattled with a key, and opened. A bland man in a dark suit entered.

"You may not remember me, we met at the party," he said politely.

"You punched me," Saint clarified.

"A good shot," the man in the suit nodded. "I'm Cecil Soapstone, solicitor."

"You know, I might need a lawyer," Saint slurred. "I need—to—"

Soapstone nodded to his Bluecoat escort, who crossed to Saint and stepped on his disfigured knee. Saint let out a scream, and Soapstone almost smiled.

"Enough with the bravado," Soapstone said quietly. "We came at your team from every direction. And the Silkworms. Swept them all up." He crossed his arms over his chest. "Your use to us from now on is going to be scheduling appointments with your enemies in exchange for favors; you'll be useful for a while yet." At last, the smile arrived.

Unable to see much past the swelling of his eyes, Saint spat at the floor. "You didn't get Trellis," he slurred.

"Oh, you're so sure?" Soapstone sneered. "What if I told you we got him first?"

Saint pointed his ruin of a face at Soapstone, then managed a chuckle. "Oh. Oh, son. You missed," he managed to choke out.

Soapstone's expression darkened. The Bluecoat glanced over at him, feeling slightly nervous as a power dynamic he could only vaguely sense began to shift.

"You're going to die in here," Soapstone said, his voice cold.

"You better kill me now, while you can," Saint over-enunciated with his sloppy battered mouth. "Difference—between him an' you?" Saint's bounce of a chuckle grated bone on bone in his broken ribs. "He's too small ta hit. But not you." Saint peered at Soapstone through the one eye that wasn't swollen shut. "Trellis? Won't miss."

Soapstone glared at him for a long moment, then turned and left the cell, the Bluecoat locking it behind them.

Saint started laughing.

It was worth the pain.

CHAPTER FIVE

At the root of the crisis, you need three things from your leaders; applying consistent vision, demonstrating speedy reaction, and owning hard choices. That's how the aristocrats held on to power back when the world ended; they served the people with their leadership abilities.

Now they offer none of these essentials. The city wallows, rudderless in the murk, bled dry by those in power. Should a proper crisis rise, the city will crack along its fault lines, and the tectonic masses left will reveal local leaders.

The current flood of Skovlanders into the city is building the tension and may well lead to the flash-point that shatters the city's unity. An ironic outcome of the Unity War meant to weld Skovlan and Akoros together may yet be the fraying and dissolution of Doskvol.

— From "War of Politics, Politics of War," by Chen Roslith

CENTRAL LANDING, THE EASE, SILKSHORE.
20ᵀᴴ ELISAR. FIFTH HOUR PAST DAWN.

The air was saturated with the smells of frying food, canal boats, urban waterways, and unwashed bodies. Candles flickered on the tables, each one ringed in a decorative paper shade, muting and texturing the glow that suffused the low-beamed expanse. Two of its walls were open, facing the intersection of canals right outside.

An old man sat on a bench at one of the tables, his back to the wall that was painted with symbols that provided both decoration and perhaps protection from ghosts. His shapeless hat had a brim, and it was pulled low; a bushy beard further obscured his features, and he wore a heavy coat. He was halfway attentive to his work of penning notes on small papers, his attention otherwise drawn to his surroundings. Lord Belderan, the criminal mastermind known as Trellis, scratched briefly at his false beard as he turned his attention back to his notes.

His ears perked up, and he shifted position. Sounds of the tramp of purposeful marching resounded in the bustling space. There were dozens of other patrons in the Central Landing, working on boats or sitting at the built-in cafes, and alertness swept through them as well. Bluecoats clattered down the stairs in numbers, at all three obvious entries to the Central Landing complex. Behind them, officers of the Ministry.

Brows drawn together, Trellis thought fast as he hid further behind his cup of tea, draining it as he watched over the rim. The Ministry of Preservation with a small army of Bluecoats was guaranteed bad news.

A dozen, two, over three dozen Bluecoats. At least eight Ministry officials. Then Soapstone strode in their wake, flanked by bodyguards.

The Canal Coordination Office was at the end of the Central Landing, a famous and public nerve center for the Fairpole Gondolier Council's rule over the boating communities serving the canals of Silkshore. The Bluecoats unerringly closed in on it, and Soapstone went inside with a handful of others.

Trellis eyed the exits, and thought about slipping away, but a strong curiosity burned in him as he looked at the determined, sweating Bluecoats. Something was about to go down. He evaluated the density of the crowd; it was thick enough to hide him. More curious people were coming down the stairs and swarming into the Central Landing in the wake of the Bluecoats. He crossed his arms and leaned back, inscrutable. He did not have long to wait.

The door opened, and a slim man walked out and stepped up to the natural podium that was subtly worked into the half-balcony around the office. He looked out over the assembled crowd, and cleared his throat; he was pale and sweaty.

"As you know I am Trajan, and I speak for the Fairpole Council in business matters," he said, his voice lacking its customary confidence. "Please keep calm and hear out our friends from the Ministry. This is Officer Delreen, with the Lending Commission." He stepped to the side, trying to suppress the nervous glance over at Soapstone, who appeared unreadable.

Delreen stepped into the pulpit, frowning over the crowd. He had close-cropped hair, bulldog jowls, and a hundred pounds more fat than he needed. "Financial practices of the Ministry have been reevaluated, and the Silkshore customs and rates are going through a re-issuance." He paused. "About eighty five percent of the small boats operating in the Ease are leveraged in debt to the Ministry," he said, "primarily due to favorable lending laws that allow their owners to use the boats as collateral for loans to cover any sort of short-term need." Delreen steeled himself. "All debtors have three days to pay their debts in full, or their boats will be repossessed by the Ministry."

A moment of silence was all it took for that news to sink in, and the crowd reacted explosively, surging forward, shouts of anger from all sides. The Bluecoats braced in a defensive line and jammed the crowd back. It took all their strength not to be shoved into the canal.

Frowning, Trellis knew there was more to this, but it was time to go. He managed to slip through the crowd and head up the stairs, popping his collar against the wind and passing the knot of Bluecoats keeping an eye on the surface exit.

THE ADMINISTRATIVE PLAZA, SILKSHORE.
20ᵀᴴ ELISAR. SIXTH HOUR PAST DAWN.

The thin, hunched girl trudged along the cobbled sidewalk, her eyes flicking around, wary. She wore the dark and sensible frock of a clerk, one of many working in the Ministry offices fronting the plaza. She flinched as a man fell in step beside her.

"Easy, Jan," said Kreeger, offering her a brilliant smile. "Just going for a walk. No need to get excited."

"Someone will recognize you!" she hissed.

"You didn't," he pointed out, "and this makes me invisible," he added with a gesture at his groundskeeper uniform, somewhat stained. He had a litter bag slung over one shoulder, and a stick with a nail for picking up trash. "Unless you talk to me, so maybe have a seat." He smiled, and walked behind the bench, stabbing at papers and discarded food wrappers.

She sat down, color flushing her narrow features. "This is so dangerous," she managed. "There was an announcement this morning that you murdered an inspector and attacked Bluecoats, and if we hear from you there's a reward for information."

"That's good news," Kreeger said mildly. "Soon as we're done here, you run to the nearest Bluecoat office and collect that reward."

"What?" she hissed. "What do you want me to say?"

"I held you at knife point and demanded to know what was on the agenda for the cabinet meeting today," he replied. "I was dressed like a groundskeeper and smelled like rust and water." He paused, and stabbed at a crumpled paper. "What was on the cabinet meeting agenda today?" he asked.

"Bad news for you I'm afraid," she winced. "Lord Barteus introduced a report from an independent investigator concluding that the High Six was mismanaged and has become toxic. If the cabinet adopts the report, then the city will contract a reclamation service to pull anything of value from the site, then it will be demolished and sanitized."

Kreeger waited. "I feel like there's more," he muttered.

"I got a look at some of the upcoming agenda items, and one of them is looking for a new spot to build a Spirit Warden compound in Silkshore, to have a more direct and persuasive presence with the gondoliers," she said rapidly, looking around in a fog of anxiety. "Sir Dramach is bringing it forward, and he's a good friend of Lord Barteus."

"And Barteus is a good friend of Lord Rowan, I'm sure," Kreeger sighed. "Normally this would rest between sessions and be decided next cycle."

"You've got days, tops," Jan blurted. "That's all I know. Please don't come to me again."

"Run along," Kreeger said with half a smile. "Enjoy the reward money." He strolled through an "Employee Only" gate with his bag of trash, and the clerk got up and walked as fast as she could back towards the looming front of the ancient headquarters, looking for a Bluecoat.

The houseboat drifted on the lake in the cavern under Grotto Hill, almost motionless. On the upper deck, the Mistress of Tides sat by the cart full of scrolls, one unfurled across her lap for study, half a dozen acolytes attending her. They heard the approach of boots long before their visitor was visible, but still the Mistress of Tides did not look up.

"We must have words," the tall man said in sonorous tones. He wore the regal drape of the Council Whisper, and he was flanked by bodyguards.

The Mistress of Tides regarded him through her veils. "Very well," she said quietly.

"First of all, you should respect my station and show deference when I approach, as you are taking advantage of our safe house and sheltering within the power of the Fairpole Council," he frowned, his face hidden behind a spirit mask made of steel and porcelain.

"Thank you for your advice," she replied.

He paused for a moment, then continued. "One of your acolytes informed me about what you said to the Spirit Warden," he said. "How you feel you have the authority to send us all to war on a whim." He straightened. "You do *not* have the power to act unilaterally on behalf of the Council! Even as the Council Whisper I cannot do such a thing! If I hear that you have offered to decide issues on behalf of the Council again, I'll have you stripped of rank and exiled."

She regarded him, allowing silence to gather.

"Anything else?" she murmured.

The Whisper bristled. "No one can compel you to take any of this seriously, of course," he spat. "However, I do have the discretion to decide whether or not you shelter here. I cannot turn you in to the authorities," he strained, "but I don't have to harbor you. Pack your things and leave Grotto Hill. Be gone within the hour."

"You may have cause to regret that," she observed, her gaze level, felt if not seen behind the veils.

"You have your orders," he sneered, then he pivoted, striding away, his bodyguards in tow.

"Mistress?" one of the acolytes said, concerned.

"It is fine," she said with a dismissive gesture. "There are always places to hide in the Dusk. Gather our belongings and prepare to move."

SOUTH STAINS NEAR GRINDER HALL, SILKSHORE. 20TH ELISAR. HOUR OF SONG, 2 HOURS PAST DUSK.

Niece sat with her back to the weathered boards, one foot dangling over the dizzying chasm that ended in the canal sixty feet below. She tore a lump of coarse bread off the loaf and bit into it, vaguely surprised by the chewy mushroom bits. She frowned at the bread, then shrugged; next time she would be more attentive before shoplifting.

She looked down the way to where the canal met the river, and across from that, the upside-down ship hull that formed the Grinder base. It brought her some sense of peace to be near her kin, even if she dared not approach them. The Grinders squatted on the river shore behind a palisade torn from nearby buildings, and it was a major touchpoint for local Skovlander immigrants.

Now that night was firmly established, she imagined her uncle was on his throne, with his pet wolves, and now that the night was cooling off they'd be stoking the fire and sharing out food, and storytelling would start soon. She felt a stab of homesickness at the thought that tonight there would likely be singing, to remember the homeland in this strange place.

A low throbbing sound caught her attention, and she sat up straight, looking around. She could feel the powerful pulse of the engine, through the water and the land, up through the rickety building where she hid. One of the Doskvol warships that were normally at the docks had come down the river, and now was pivoting across the current, pointing upstream and holding position.

The ship had two decks, and it bristled with cannon. The back had a massive engine with screws under the surface. It was over half the size of the massive Leviathan hunting ships, and its sole purpose was war. Floodlights snapped on from its decks, playing across the hull of the Grinder base.

"No," Niece whispered through nerveless lips.

It wasn't the cannons that fired, but the mortars. The ammunition that crashed down on the Grinder hall was incendiary, and when it shattered the whole structure was bathed in hellishly pale fire that clung and flickered with unnatural intensity. Several more mortar shots blanketed the entire area inside the palisade with liquid fire. Fire that would suck the air out of anything under it, flash frying meat, suffocating victims with a lack of air before smoke inhalation could become an issue. The bowl of flame was unsurvivable.

There was no screaming because for those caught in that fire, there was no air to scream.

Just like that, the warship surrendered its fight against the current, slowly pivoting on the river, headed back to its dock. Niece could not see it go, through the tears that blurred the whole world as she felt the Mirror reverberate with an intolerable clangor of death tolls.

FOGGERT'S SUMP, SILKSHORE.
21ST ELISAR. SECOND HOUR PAST DAWN.

Gapjaw and the Hammer started as the ladder rattled, then Piccolo stepped into view of the dim lantern, and they relaxed.

Piccolo crossed the slick floor and lowered himself to sit next to the lantern. He held a number of ink-smeared papers in his fist. His face was unusually somber.

"Wake up," the Hammer muttered, kicking Safety's boot. The scoundrel started and blinked, then sat up and rubbed his face.

"You're back," Safety said to Piccolo.

"I have news," Piccolo replied. "The Grinders were firebombed by a warship last night. I have no idea if there were any survivors."

"By the navy?" the Hammer demanded, incredulous.

"By the goddamn navy," Piccolo agreed. "Also, all the boats in Silk-shore's canal trade that have debts with the Ministry, and that's most of them, have to pay off those debts by the twenty third or they lose their boats."

"What the hell?" Gapjaw demanded. "That—that will cripple trade in Silkshore! The financial losses alone are—are—that's a lot of math," he protested.

"There are some caveats," Piccolo continued. "If you have action-able intelligence on the whereabouts of members of the Silkworms or River Stallions, then you get an extension on your loan. If you capture one dead, your loan is forgiven. If you capture one alive, your loan and five other loans are forgiven."

"That still doesn't solve their problem," Gapjaw said, shaking his head. "What will they do for boats?"

"Lord Rowan is starting a new portage company," Piccolo said. "It's on this full page ad in every paper I lifted this morning. Rowan Ship-ping will hire those with experience with boats on the canals, at a basic salary." He paused. "I overheard a conversation that Rowan plans to buy the boats from the Ministry, at a fraction of the foreclosure rate, and use them for his company."

"That son of a bitch," Gapjaw breathed.

"Did he just buy the Fairpole Council?" the Hammer asked quietly.

"Can he just do that?" Gapjaw asked.

"He's got a kind of wealth and pull you've never seen," Safety re-plied. "He can do that, and worse."

"So if the Fairpole Council doesn't have our back, and the Grinders are down... are the Silkworms defeated? I mean the smart ones," the Hammer clarified.

"No word," Piccolo shrugged, "and I got these papers because there's supposed to be secret codes printed in them. I looked, and nei-ther Trellis nor Sanction nor the Mistress of Tides is reaching out." He sighed. "However, Kreeger, which is Sanction's former name, is wanted for murder and assault. He killed an inspector and shot up some Bluecoats."

"That's fantastic," the Hammer said, grim.

"No news from Red Silver or Inkletta or Niece," Piccolo continued. "In this case I don't know if that's good or bad, but I don't want to try to find them if they don't want to be found, and if they've got any brains at all, they don't want to be found."

"So what's our next move then?" Safety demanded. "Squat in this hole for a week and hope we don't start growing fungus?"

"In a week, it's a sure thing," the Hammer muttered.

"That's not me," Piccolo said, shaking his head firmly. "That's not *us*, or we wouldn't be in this situation. We take action! We may not think it through all the way," he confessed, "but it's bold, and it's daring, and we get results. And in the end, things work out pretty well for the survivors." He sensed his inspirational speech wasn't going well, so he waved that away.

"The problem here," he continued, "is that Lord Rowan doesn't have anything better to do than hunt down scoundrels. We need to give him something else to look at. Somewhere else to apply his pull and his bottomless war chest."

"Nobles generally look stronger than they are," the Hammer said.

"I put a lot of thought into this since I saw the morning news," Piccolo said. "Nobles care about two things; money and blood relations. He's outside the lines here, going after *groups* of people because of what *we* did, and that makes me angry." His mouth closed to a thin line, and his eyes glittered in the dimness. "I think it's time we start killing this asshole's family."

The Hammer blinked. "How does that help us?"

"He assumes he's driven us so far underground we can't strike back. I want him on the defensive too. Defense takes a *lot* of energy," Piccolo shrugged. "Protecting your holdings takes a lot of guards and equipment, both of which are expensive, both of which have weak points. He wanted to hurt us." Piccolo paused. "He did. He plans to keep on doing it. So... I want to hurt him back. Things he can't fix. Things money can't buy. I want to inflict wounds that political power and wealth cannot restore."

"You'd rather be angry than scared," the Hammer said, regarding him calmly.

"Yes. That," Piccolo said, pointing at the Hammer. "I am done being scared and I'm ready to be angry instead." He nodded. "Yes."

"It's not like we can protect the things we care about," Gapjaw muttered darkly.

"This could escalate things," Safety mused.

"Escalate?" Piccolo echoed, eyebrows raised. "He firebombed the Grinders and torched Silkshore's economy. We can't escalate past that."

"I'm in," Gapjaw said. "Lord Rowan is getting away with this, and I can't stand that. If I can hurt him, I will."

"Aristocrats," Safety said, and he shook his head. "What the hell. I'm in. I don't know if this is the best plan, but... I'd rather die fighting than from a fungal infection."

Piccolo turned to the Hammer, who sighed.

"Not me," the Hammer said. "I'll wait here. I need to hear from Saint, or Trellis, or one of our Whispers. I'll back a plan that's got some finesse." He paused. "The front line of war is chaos, and it's horrible. But it's behind the front lines that you learn that revenge is hollow, and just causing pain for its own sake..." He was quiet for a long moment. "I've learned my lesson. And if you need to learn it yourselves, I guess now's the time." He looked up at them, and his eyes were steady.

"No hard feelings," Piccolo said.

"No hard feelings," the Hammer agreed.

Piccolo looked at the other two. "Let's get the hell out of here."

They were gone, and quiet descended. The Hammer drew his long knife, and slowly sharpened it, hearing the echo of the slithering rasp carried by rotten brick and stagnant water. He settled in for a long day of pushing memories back into the past where they belonged.

CANTER'S LOWLAND, SILKSHORE.
21ST ELISAR. SEVENTH HOUR PAST DAWN.

"I know why nobody comes here," Gapjaw groused, "even in winter." The biting cold failed to suppress the foul stench of urban runoff into the bowl of land that only flowed into the canal when it flooded.

"The snow complicates things," Safety muttered, glaring out of the lean-to at the flurries that danced along the street, dusting the ruts in the alleyway.

"Don't worry about the snow," Piccolo replied, grim. "Just watch the far end of the Briar public house there. If Sanction saw my message in the paper he'll follow the street along then go down through that back gate. Take the stairs to the lowland, and we'll go meet him there."

"This plan seems sketchy," Gapjaw observed, scratching at his stubbled jowl.

"It's an emergency back-up meeting plan," Piccolo replied, testy. "Of course it's sketchy." He looked back over at the road across the way. "I paid an urchin to take a message to the printer this morning, for the evening edition, and the correction was made," he said, brandishing the paper. "I paid to have a comma turned into a period on the masthead."

The other two looked at him silently.

"It's how the professionals do it," Piccolo frowned at them. "Nuance, man. Nuance."

"I'll be damned," Safety murmured. He watched a figure with a lantern follow the road, and fumble with the back gate for a moment before heading down the stairs.

The three scoundrels bundled up, obscuring their features and shapes in heavy coats and scarves, then they crossed the street in the swirl of snow, heading down the stairs to the frozen-over slough behind the public house. The wreckage of broken furniture stuck up through the ice, and was littered along the back slope, and the smell was filth locked in coldness, like marrow in a bone.

Three figures squared off against one at a distance of twenty feet.

Piccolo pulled off his head gear, and smiled as Sanction pulled his scarf away.

"You got my message I see," Piccolo said quietly as they all walked towards each other, closing the distance.

"I haven't heard from the others yet," Sanction replied, "and I'm glad to see at least some of you ducked the sweep." He looked over his shoulder, then back at Piccolo. "So what the hell happened?"

"We were at Rowan's party, and we saw this amazing new security equipment he designed, so we kidnapped his lead adept developer," Piccolo said. "Stashed him in the unfindable place we used to talk about."

Sanction stared at him for a long moment. "There's a lot of blood on your hands for that," he said.

"Yeah, who knew Lord Rowan would go berserk and start tearing up the city?" Piccolo muttered. "Anyway what's done is done and that's in the past now, and we need a way forward. Get this Rowan guy off our backs. Got a plan?"

"In progress," Sanction replied with a slight frown.

"No problem, I've got one to keep us busy in the meantime," Piccolo continued, almost seamlessly. "Distract Lord Rowan from hunting us. Start killing off his family members. So he has to refocus on defense. Break his concentration," Piccolo shrugged. "I mean, what's he going to do? Come after us and everything we ever built, everything we love? Pfft. Already in progress. So, let's make it expensive."

Sanction looked thoughtful for a long moment.

"Your plan is terrible," he said. "But... it has appeal."

"What about your husband, Rutherford?" Safety asked. "Is he out of danger?"

"Why, yes, thank you for asking," Sanction replied. "He's traveling right now, in Iruvia. I sent him a wire. It's the best I can do." He shook his head. "That man can take care of himself," he said with a distant look in his eye.

"Then we're free to act," Piccolo said energetically. "Where do we start?"

Sanction suppressed a chuckle. "Your brilliant plan, and you don't know who is related to Lord Rowan. Or how to find out."

"We all have a place on this team," Piccolo said. "Mine is to provoke action and to carry out plans. You work on coming up with the angles."

Sanction paused again, looking troubled. "I don't know how," he murmured, "but I think I was followed." He shook his head. "We're being watched. I'd swear to it."

"Fugitive life is difficult," Safety agreed, checking his pistol. "You see things, hear things that aren't there. Except when they are." His eyes were hard.

"I say we run the way we came," Gapjaw said, "and flag down a cab."

"Then we get you checked out," Safety said to Sanction, "and make sure you're not sporting a tracer of some kind, for either side of the Mirror."

Sanction nodded. "Go."

The four rogues turned and ran, clattering along the cracking ice. They scrambled up the hill, and were almost run over as they spilled across the roadway to stop traffic by getting the in the way of a cab; the cabbie halted reluctantly. The others clambered in as Safety vaulted up to the buckboard, handing over a payment that inspired the cabbie to lash the already-grouchy goat to pour on fresh speed.

The noise of their jostling and jolting career through the streets was too much to allow conversation in the back, and Safety grimly held on to the buckboard up above.

Then they turned down an alley where the cobbles dipped down to a sheet of ice, and up out the other side. The goat stopped, and the rogues dropped out of the cab and continued on, sliding over the sheet of ice with practiced ease and climbing up into the hazy alleyway market. The goat backed up with aggressive daintiness, pushing the creaking coach, then reoriented on the road and strolled on.

"I know a place," Gapjaw said. "Quit serving me years ago over a difference of opinion, and he's expensive, but it's the real deal." He led the way down the alley as the rogues pulled their hoods, hats, and scarves over their features as best they could. The swirling snow meant everyone was trying to stay warm, so they did not stand out in the privacy-valuing crowd here.

After a couple blocks, Gapjaw stopped. "We're one alley over," he said, and he mounted the stairs to a corridor where a building had been half hollowed out to make a throughway, with a small café built into the other half of the building's main floor. They stepped away from the crowd, heading for the café and the alley on the other side.

Gapjaw grunted and staggered forward as an arrow slapped into his back, its energy driving him to fall on all fours. It took half a second for the feathered shaft in his back to register for the others, and they scattered to the walls of the narrow space, guns out, scanning the back trail.

"Blood and bone!" Gapjaw whispered, and he drunkenly scrabbled towards cover. "Hell of a thing!"

"Piccolo, you're no good to us here!" Sanction hissed. "Circle round! Or better yet, just—get out of here. Find Trellis."

"Yeah," Piccolo agreed, and he rushed at the far wall, jumping up and kicking off it, snatching an outcropping from a window box over the alley and pulling himself up as an arrow whizzed past his ankle. Sanction leaned out of his alcove, guessing at a window big enough for an archer to be inside, and firing off a round to smash the glass. Meanwhile bits of trim and fungal rot rained down as Piccolo climbed up the building fast, getting distance.

"I don't like our odds without Piccolo," Safety said across the alleyway to Sanction.

"He's no good here, pinned down," Sanction shrugged. "I think our best bet is to make the sniper come to us. Hand to hand range. You up for it?"

"Me? Sure," Safety shrugged. "Gapjaw?"

"Think it hit a lung maybe," Gapjaw wheezed. "Better not—take it out—until someone can help."

"Through and through?" Safety asked.

"Barbed. Stuck," Gapjaw managed.

"Great," Safety said. "Look, no offense, Sanction, but of the two of us I'm the fighting man. You drag Gapjaw, I'll do what I can to protect us all."

"Great," Sanction muttered. Then he rushed forward, dipping to drag Gapjaw's arm over his shoulder on the uninjured side, and hauled the gasping, swearing man forward as Safety followed backwards, eyes everywhere, pistol at the ready for a sign of the sniper.

Sanction staggered at the back counter of the café, and the clerk jumped out of the way as Sanction flipped the bar entry open and shoved Gapjaw through, towards the stairs down to the cellar. Gapjaw groaned and cried out as they jounced down the narrow stairs, and Safety took cover at the edge of the café, watching the alley.

Some instinct warned Safety the assassin was already underground, so he turned and vaulted the counter, clattering down the stairs after the others.

They were in a cellar, with a boarded up door and a pool and a locked grating in the wall.

"Everything is interconnected down here, I'll bet," Safety growled. "The killer could come from any side."

"We're probably all running blind down here," Sanction grunted as he tugged at the grating latch. "Nobody gets to scout these tunnels free and easy."

Safety stepped forward and crushed the latch easily with his metal hand. "I hope you're right," he said. "Our best bet right now is to keep moving." He wrenched the grating open.

An arrow pounded into Sanction's torso, hurling him back off his feet to slam into a cellar wall. The assassin lunged, pivoting, driving a fistful of arrow into Safety's throat; Safety put up his hand and the arrow clacked into it, and the rogue's other fist crashed into the assassin's jaw, knocking him off balance to the side.

Gapjaw, on his knees, was suddenly confronted with the staggering assassin. He shot him in the face, hurling the killer back to rebound from the wall. With the tip of his tongue sticking out, Gapjaw squinted, and fired the other round at close range right into the killer's head. A soggy whacking sound accompanied the breaching of the killer's skull, spraying a delta fan of brains and viscera on the floor and wall.

Gapjaw sank back, coughing bubbles and runnels of blood. "Yep—" he managed. "Lung."

Sanction awkwardly rose to his feet. "I knew we're wanted," he panted, "and get to wear heavy cloaks, so—" He knocked on the plated armor he wore under his greatcoat. "Help me." He managed to work at the straps, and Safety came to his aid, unclipping the armor and pulling the plastron off.

The plate stopped some of the arrow's force, so there was only a triangular stab wound two inches deep and half that in width.

"Some stitches," Safety said grimly. "You'll be fine."

Together they hefted Gapjaw and headed up the stairs. They did not approach the assassin's body to look for gear or clues. Assassins in that class tended to make it unwise to try and investigate them upon death.

Enough that a single bell chimed behind the Mirror.

Let the Spirt Wardens clean it up.

CHAPTER SIX

Oh, it was the Ebon Wings, in the Runwater Flats, in the east wilderness of Crow's Foot before the fires cleared 'em out. They were these tough leg-breakers, a gang working for the Crows, but they were all into that freaky Forgotten Gods worship and they were drinking from some spirit well down in the filth.

They fought ghosts, and ghosts rode them, and they threw ghosts like weapons; it was a crazy pack, generally hopped up on drugs and plasmics, and the Crows used them for terror tactics. The boss was Bloodletta, this crimson-haired fury. Back in the day, the word was she could "scream ghosts," whatever that means.

Her kid grew up practically living in the spirit well, and her nannies were freaky cultists. Before she could talk she was drawing Hadrathi symbols on people with charcoal, and she was tattooing everybody who would hold still by the time she was ten. By the time puberty hit she was a force of nature on both sides of the Mirror. So Bloodletta's kid was called Inkletta, a joke that stuck. Far as I know she's the last of the Ebon Wings, and that's just because she got out before they crossed the Ferals and perished.

> — *From Growler's entry in "Crow's Foot Ephemerals,*
> *a Collection of Oral Histories," by Crayla Hurantis*

MARKER THIRTY SIX, GHOST MARKET, SILKSHORE.
21ST ELISAR. EIGHTH HOUR PAST DAWN.

"You sure you know where we're going?" Sanction demanded, sweat rolling down his face. The snow had thickened, fat flakes dawdling down towards the floor of the alleyway, the buildings hunching and stoic as mats of snow formed on their ledges and windowsills.

"Unfortunately," Gapjaw grunted, a whine in his breath. "Follow—follow the stonecutter sideyard," he managed, nodding instead of pointing. Safety hefted the big man, refreshing his grip, and doggedly continued on.

"I am completely not in the mood for this," Safety said between his teeth as they staggered and stumbled through the fence and saw the massive three story frame that simulated one of the walls of burial niches in a typical cemetery, showcasing the different doors and carvings the stonecutter could provide. They pushed on past memorial ledge perches, stone skull boxes, and sentimental stone and glass hand boxes where the finger bones of loved ones could be wired into a forever-outstretched gesture for remembrance.

A low tool shed at the back had a grave marker leaned by the door with "Thirty Six" carved into it. They paused to catch their breath, trembling with exhaustion and pain.

"This is it. He's in here," Gapjaw said.

"The shed?" Safety retorted.

"Just go in there you ninny!" Gapjaw gasped, patience depleted.

Sanction worked the latch and opened the shed, and was surprised to see that the only thing in the shed besides a line of tools down one wall was a staircase leading down. It was flanked by stone statues, palms forward in a warning gesture.

"I don't like that," Safety panted, hauling Gapjaw in.

"What's to like," Gapjaw grumbled. "Down we go."

Sanction headed down the stairs first, one hand resting on the butt of his pistol. Gapjaw and Safety struggled down behind him. They reached the bottom of the stairs and followed a short hallway to a massive iron door in a stone frame. The only light was a single buzzing plasmic bulb set in the wall. Sanction rapped on the door with his knuckles, experimentally.

A view slot snapped open, and some smoke wisped out; Sanction could make out a pair of eyes, but little else.

"Password?" the voice demanded, thin and reedy.

"We can pay," Gapjaw wheezed.

The figure hesitated, then shrugged. "Close enough." The view slot snapped shut, and a process of opening locks and removing bars unfolded on the other side of the door. It eventually swung open, freeing a horrible chemical stink that mixed with decay in a sinus-searing fume. "Come in," said the doorman, a man so pale he was almost translucent, dressed indifferently in a house robe and sandals. His red-rimmed eyes and his jug-handle ears drew the eye until he smiled, the nasty expression surprising Sanction so he involuntarily dropped his hand to the knife pommel. Their guide pivoted and headed in.

They shouldered through the narrow hall behind the door, and followed the skinny man deeper in. Turning the corner, they found themselves in a parlor of sorts, with several people standing around motionless. The room was long, low, almost a wide hallway. The other end was taken up with a massive workshop that expanded out into wings with even more equipment.

"Wait, is this a wax museum?" Safety said, brows contracting as he took a closer look at one of the half a dozen motionless people standing around the parlor.

"No," Gapjaw said, his voice flat.

"I'll get Workshop!" the guide volunteered with another ghastly grin, and he loped off into the interior of the underground complex.

"Bleeding out in the alley does begin to regain some appeal," Sanction muttered, his expression somewhere between a wince and a squint as he reluctantly examined the smooth skin of a haughty woman dressed in fashions that peaked twenty years ago.

"We need to go somewhere that no one expects us to go," Gapjaw said, dogged. "That's here."

"You are not wrong," Safety muttered. Motion caught his eye, and he watched the slim man who emerged from a door and strolled towards them.

"Well well," the man said. "Look what the fugitives dragged in." A smirk crooked his face. "Keepsake, you just let these people in?"

"They can pay!"

"They *said* they can pay," the man corrected him.

"I am Sanction, and we need help; some physiking, and also a scan to see if we've picked up any tracers making noise behind the Mirror."

The newcomer slouched, his prominent and bony shoulders hunched, his white cornsilk hair limp and pulled out of the way. One of his eyes was stitched shut, but otherwise, aside from an instinctively detected asymmetry to his features, posture, and clothes, he seemed almost normal.

"I am Workshop, the Leech of the Ghost Market," the thin man said. "This is my assistant Keepsake. Is he not something?" he said with a fond smile.

"Just what I was thinking," Sanction said under his breath.

"He's got my son's face," Workshop said lovingly, stroking Keepsake's cheek while the young man grinned. "Most of his brain is Lafferty, a street urchin who learned his letters at my knee. Lafferty's brainstem gave out on me, though, the whole reptile timekeeper just wouldn't work. So I glued it to one donated by Sarala, the beautiful lawyer who got me acquitted in court." He smiled at Keepsake fondly. "Everything Keepsake is comes from someone I want to remember," he explained. Workshop glanced at his visitors, who were now more pale and nauseous than they had been a minute ago. "This one is built of the people I like," he explained, his tone more professional. "Cross me, and you go into the Hall of Cautionary Tales."

"Figuratively?" Safety squinted.

"No," Gapjaw wheezed as Workshop just gazed at him.

"I have sapphires," Sanction said, blunt. He pulled a box out of his lapel pocket and snapped it open, revealing four glittering blue stones.

"Those are very nice," Workshop said, eyebrows raised. "Let's get you fixed up!"

"Maybe deal with the tracer first?" Sanction suggested. "At least look for one?"

"It's your blood," Workshop shrugged. "Sure, if you're the suspect, follow me and we'll get you sniffed over." He looked at the others. "You might want to wait for me rather than have Keepsake stitch you up;

he has terrible big loopy stitches, pulls wounds together crooked. No pride in his work," he said, shaking his head. Then he took Sanction by elbow and led him off.

"Have a seat. Want a snack?" Keepsake offered.

"I really don't," Safety replied, his features tinged almost green as he looked at a taxidermed man standing against the wall, politely holding a tray.

Meanwhile Workshop led Sanction to a table. "Strip, and lay down." He busied himself with trays of tools on the countertop.

Sanction hesitated for only a moment, then stripped, wincing with every movement. His torso puncture started leaking more blood as he bent and strained to tug off his clothes. Then he was on the table. Workshop shoved down on a massive lever, and a sleeve popped up around the table and clicked into place, turning it into a tub. Workshop spun a wheel, and water started burbling up into the table/tank.

"C-cold," Sanction muttered, shifting and wincing.

"Don't be a baby," Workshop responded dispassionately without turning. "You up against adepts or Whispers, or what do you think put a tracer on you?"

"We pissed off Lord Rowan, and he has resources to hire assassins capable of guaranteeing their work," Sanction said, grim, squinting as the cold water flowed around his naked rump and back, rilling along his ribs.

"Bra-*vo*," Workshop said, eyebrows raised. "Should I expect a super assassin to come down into my shop and kill us all?"

Sanction squinted at Workshop. "You think this is funny?" he asked.

"A bit," Workshop shrugged. "Most of the people who come here to kill me are slack faced knuckle draggers, it would add spice to have a next-level deviant sociopath come for me. I've got some defenses that I've never gotten to deploy," he mused.

"Sorry to disappoint, but we shot him in the face and left his corpse in the basement of Lilora's Brew Pad, a couple blocks away."

Workshop leaned his elbows on the filling tank, looking down at Sanction. "You didn't touch the body or anything, did you?" he said, almost concerned.

"No, I know bett—better," Sanction managed, his lips turning blue, his jaw shuddering a bit with the cold.

"Leave it to the experts," Workshop said with a nod. He pulled on a massive glove. "I may just have to go take a look, with the proper precautions, once I'm done with you lot."

"Maybe give it some more time," Sanction said, and he let out a breath and sucked in another. "I don't want any lines between you and us."

"Harsh but fair," Workshop shrugged. "Fugitives are terrible at networking." He grinned, and the expression was not comforting. Then he twirled the wheel, cutting off the water flow. There was enough in the tank for Sanction to submerge. Workshop loomed over him once more, holding tongs with his glove, and in the tongs he gripped a gleaming golden orb the size of a fingertip.

"Huh," Sanction said, looking at it, steeling himself.

"Don't you want to know what this is?" Workshop prompted, grinning.

"Of course I do," Sanction lied.

"This is a distillation of alcahest," Workshop said. "My special modification is that I move it a quarter step out of phase. If I were to drop actual alcahest into this tank, then it would break you, the water, everything down to essential elements. Messy. But this is tuned to only target composites that are polluted with demon blood. Almost every tracer is plasmic, and most involve demon blood because it's the noisiest small substance to make a detectable ruckus on the Back of the Mirror."

"Now what?" Sanction asked.

"I drop it in, and it dissolves anything that isn't all-natural life force, or totally inert." Workshop paused. "So, if you've worshipped a demon, or allowed one to violate you, or anything I should know," he said with casual gestures.

"Drop it in," Sanction demanded. Workshop grinned, and let the sphere fall. The water warmed in no time to a pleasant steaming broth, and it glowed golden; Sanction felt a strange peacefulness, as though he was on a warm and stable lifeboat in the storm-tossed darkness of the Void Sea.

"Not bad," he murmured with a smile. "Not bad."

BREYAN STREET NORTH, SIX TOWERS.
22ND ELISAR. HOUR OF SONG, 2 HOURS PAST DUSK.

Fog trailed to wisps as proper night settled. The Vigilance public house was bustling with prosperous and happy patrons. Inside, the rooms were filled with light, drink, song, and off-duty guardsmen. Outside, the snow had stopped accumulating, but could not melt, so it blew around restlessly stalking the streets and alleys like spirits searching for an escape.

Those who did not work the next day were filtering in to the establishment, and finally those who did work the next day began to filter out. In groups of two or three they huddled into their bright yellow and white garb, and headed for lodgings. They easily ignored the beggars huddled in the alleys and along the streets, maybe half a dozen in easy view of the front door.

One pair of guards was headed down the streets under the crackle and hum of the electroplasmic lamps. The snowflakes glittered, caught in the light, and the shadows were long and solid. As the guards walked past a light post, one of the two guardsmen noticed his shadow cast before him, and that of his friend, but also a third shadow—someone right behind them. He frowned, and turned.

A meaty yet metallic whack rang out from the five-pound sledge that slammed across his temple.

The other guard let out a yell of surprise, stepping into a pivot, reaching for his gun, but the man following him was too quick. He sprang forward, snatching the guard's wrist and directing the gun barrel away; the guard strained to aim it back at him, and the attacker let the gun come back his way, flexing to force the barrel past him and down at the paving; he shoulder-checked the guard, sending him stumbling back.

The guard raised the pistol only to have it knocked from his hand with a sweep of the hammer, and the attacker's other hand lashed out to smack him in the bridge of the nose; as the guard staggered, blood filling his eyes and nose, he realized his attacker had brass knuckles.

The guard groped for his sword, but his attacker had the upper hand now. A hobnailed boot whacked down on the guard's foot as the attacker's elbow bashed him in the chest. The guard couldn't stumble back with his foot pinned, so he crashed down on his back, his head rebounding from the cobbles.

The guard was dazed for a moment, then he let out a cry as the attacker grabbed a fistful of his hair and dragged him into an alley beside a stone stable. Instinctively, the guard's hands sought the attacker's grip, trying to free himself, to no avail.

With a final ripping sound, the attacker slung the guard ahead of him in the alley, and discarded a handful of hair. The guard's scalp was freely bleeding, but he regained presence of mind to fumble for his sword. His attacker kicked him solidly in the face, and the guard flopped over on his back, half-conscious.

"Sword on the left side," observed the attacker in a rough voice. The guard blinked, trying to focus, and he realized what was going on just as his attacker whipped the five pound sledge down on the guard's right hand. Bones splintered, and the guard released an unearthly scream. He rolled over, pulling his maimed hand in close, struggling to rise to his knees as unconsciousness swarmed up behind his eyes, looming over him.

He vaguely made out the shape of his attacker dragging his friend into the alley and closing the wrought iron gate, then kneeling by the unconscious man and slugging the man's head with the hammer; that blow was certainly fatal. Nodding at the ruptured skull, the attacker rose, and returned to his other victim.

"Who—who are you?" the maimed guard demanded.

"You can call me the Hammer," his attacker replied. "And you're Captain Myles Strank," he continued, a sardonic mockery in his tone.

"What do you want?" the captain shouted.

"Well, two things," the Hammer said, reflexively twirling the sledge in his massive grip. "I got one. I wanted to wipe that smug smile off your face. You were rude to me once," he explained.

"Wh—what?" the captain said, struggling with how to respond to that.

"Doesn't matter," the Hammer shrugged. "My advice is to keep a respectful tone when you talk about veterans, going forward," he confided.

"Rowan's party?" Strank protested. "You attacked me for *that*?"

"That's one thing, there were two," the Hammer said mildly.

"This better be good, because you've assaulted a captain of the North Hook Hou—"

The spiteful threat was interrupted by a solid kick to the gut that doubled the captain over; he toppled in the slush of the half-frozen murk of the alleyway.

"You're very scary," the Hammer said. "Now, you said you were a captain, so I figure you know more than the average grunt. I lost someone at the Rowan party, he was ambushed somewhere and whisked away off-site. Hush hush, probably more house guard than Bluecoat if I had to guess." He paused. "I need to know who was involved with that, and where the target went."

"I'm not—"

The Hammer let out a noise somewhere between a grunt and a roar, and took a couple big steps around to flank the captain as he struggled to rise. He slung a kick into the captain's ribs that threw the man across the alley to smack into the stone wall, followed up with a step and a stomp that drove the captain's shoulderblade forward into the wall, so his shoulder gave with a crunch. Snatching the captain's hair, the Hammer yanked him back to flop down on his back, unable to breathe, and he dropped to one knee as he whipped the hammer down on the broken shoulder.

The captain was helpless with pain as the Hammer snatched his right wrist and straightened out his arm, between the broken hand and the shattered shoulder. One, two, three strikes reduced the hand to pulp. Breathing heavily, the Hammer rose again to his feet, staring down at the captain.

"I don't care," he said. "We can do this so you end up in a wheelchair fed by orderlies." He shrugged. "Or I walk away and leave you here." Again the hammer twirled in his grip. "You threaten me again and it's your right ankle. Tough to use a crutch on the side with the amputated arm." He was expressionless.

The captain's left hand closed on the sword grip, and the captain trembled with pain as he looked at the Hammer, torn between the risk of trying to draw the sword and the risk of not trying to draw the sword.

"I'll leave it in your other shoulder," the Hammer said, serious.

The captain's hand fell from the sword, instead bracing him to try and sit up. "Okay," he said. "Okay. I was part of the basement detail, we don't know each other's assignments."

"But," the Hammer said as his grip tightened on the hammer.

"But, but, but," the captain said, wincing as blood trickled down the side of his face, "there were some Bluecoats there. Rowan's solicitor, Soapstone, he had something going on there, something on the side. He had Inspectors there too. They were looking to sort out some criminal, he used the wrong forger to get an invite to the party. The forger squealed, Soapstone knew this guy was coming, and was going to teach him a lesson for being so brazen." He shook his head. "That's all I know."

"You have no idea where the Bluecoats took him," the Hammer said, his voice flat and unconvinced.

The captain paused for a moment, then shook his head. "Special arrangements. I overheard one of the Bluecoats saying they were going to take the long way round to Dunvil Bridge."

"And that's straight to Ironhook," the Hammer nodded. "Damn."

The captain paused, daring to look the Hammer in the eye. "That's all I know," he said, his voice trembling with agony.

"I believe you," the Hammer nodded. "Now. Do you pose a threat to me? Going forward? Like, 'this isn't over,' or 'you won't get away with this,' or 'you better kill me now, or I'll get everyone you know'?" He paused. "Anything like that you want to say? Feeling any of those sentiments?"

The captain locked his jaw and did his best to speak evenly. "I hope we never see each other again," he managed.

The Hammer nodded, then turned away and disappeared into the night. The captain watched him go, then passed out, motionless under the slow twirling descent of snowfall.

MARKER THIRTY SIX, GHOST MARKET, SILKSHORE. 22ND ELISAR. HOUR OF ASH, 9 HOURS PAST DUSK.

"What time do you figure it is?" Safety asked mildly, his arms spread along the rim of the hot tub as most of him was submerged in the dark waters.

"Won't be dawn for hours," Gapjaw mused, looking at Safety's metal arm. He eyed the connecting point, where the meat of Safety's torso and the knob of his shoulder joint were clamped in the metal of his prosthetic. "Never saw your whole arm before."

"Likely never will again," Safety shrugged, the motion distracting as it pulled muscle and metal together. "How are you doing?"

Gapjaw squinted up at the mosaic dome over the poorly lit hot tub room. "Workshop is a creep," he said, "but he knows his stuff. I'll be fine." His eyes drifted shut. "Or, maybe more accurately, that stuff he gave me to drink makes me feel like everything will just... work out." His grin was slightly silly.

Sanction padded into the dim room wearing only a robe, a towel over his arm. He looked down into the dark water of the tub skeptically.

"There's room for like six people here," Safety said mildly. "You can come in."

"It's great, there's these little fishies, they nibble," Gapjaw slurred through his grin.

Sanction hesitated a moment more, then put his towel down, shed his robe, and stepped down into the tub.

"I thought it would be warmer," he said through his teeth. The others chuckled, and he found his way to the seat underwater, relaxing back. "Workshop said this was part of the 'curing process.' I didn't ask if that meant, like, meat, or healing."

"He had me drink three different concoctions," Safety replied. "I hope we trust him, because pfft," he gestured. "Buncha guys broke in here now, I'd just let 'em take me." He splashed water at Gapjaw. "That guy's worthless."

"Yer mom," Gapjaw managed, and he snuggled back into the wall, looking up at the dome, and he sighed deeply.

"So..." Sanction sighed. "I was thinking we should figure out Piccolo." He gestured vaguely. "We sort of lost him."

"Oh yeah," Safety agreed.

"And maybe... maybe we should plan for... discuss my plan." Sanction blinked a couple times, then rubbed his eyes. "I have some next steps."

Gapjaw started snoring.

"Tomorrow maybe?" Safety slurred, arching an eyebrow, comfortable in his grin.

"Yeah, okay," Sanction said, leaning back. "Or, later today."

Safety was going to say something sharp about Sanction needing more drugs to relax and let it go for five minutes, but he couldn't quite find his way to the words, so he just made a rude noise and sagged back, letting the last of the tension drain out.

Sanction felt alone for a moment, but that did not distress him. He blinked and refocused as Workshop strolled into the room, noiseless, and stood opposite him.

"There you are," Sanction slurred.

"Why am I here?" Workshop asked.

"Because it bothers you that I trust you not to turn us in for fabulous rewards," Sanction replied, smiling. "You need a reason."

"Yes," Workshop agreed. "You are taking a tremendous risk, and I want all the cards on the table. Contingencies catalogued. Threats ranked." He paused. "You understand."

"Completely," Sanction nodded. He raised his hand out of the water, putting up a finger. "One, you got paid." He shrugged. "It's nice. Two," he raised another finger, "you get bored, and it's fun when things get stirred up." He raised another finger. "Three, untouchable people make you itchy and we're bothering untouchable people." He shrugged. "If you wanted to piss off the rich and famous, it would cost money to put an operation together like that. And some personal risk. So that's what's balanced against turning us in for a reward." He shrugged again. "You get some money; eh, you can get money. Maybe you get a pat on the head, maybe you get arrested, those are both—both." He sighed, gesturing. "Annoying." Sanction smiled. "But you let us go. Well. If this goes right, it helps your rep as a rebel. Makes friends in Silkshore. Irritates nobles. That's your list. The stuff you really want. The other side, pfft," he gestured dismissively. "Money." He shrugged.

Sanction looked at Workshop, who stood unmoving. "Well?"

Workshop did not respond. A minute or two later, Sanction was asleep.

ZEPHYR STREET, MASTER MARKET, MAURO OVERVIEW, SILKSHORE. 22ND ELISAR. SECOND HOUR PAST DAWN.

Six taps in a pattern. Red dragged herself up to her feet and crossed the chamber, opening the barred door. Inkletta ducked in, snow falling from her hood as she pushed it back. She put a basket down, and shrugged her cloak off.

"All quiet while I was gone?" she asked.

"All quiet," Red said, her voice hoarse. Red resumed her seat on the cushion in the center of the chamber, the curse runes glittering in time to her heartbeat.

"At least we have that going for us," Inkletta sighed, pulling food out of the basket. Dry fish, hardtack, a wheel of goatcheese dipped in wax. She hefted the jug she brought in, smiling. "I happen to know someone likes rum," she said.

"I don't know if I can eat," Red murmured, "but I'll take the rum." She paused, then nodded at the wall. "The next one is going," she said.

Several of the lines of defensive runes had crumbled already, and one of them looked as though it had been painted on with charcoal instead of etched into the stone. It was already ashing apart before their eyes. "This chamber won't be safe much longer," Red sighed.

"That curse is something else," Inkletta observed, muted.

"Every day that passes, I can feel him getting closer," Red replied. She rolled off the cushion and lay on her back, limp, staring up at the ceiling. "I think he can affect me through this curse. Even if I figure out where he is first, my only hope on my own is to shoot him at long range."

"Normally we could be marshalling our defenses, bringing in allies, preparing the ground, baiting the waters, setting up our ambushes," Inkletta said. "This timing with Lord Rowan is inconvenient."

"What *can* we do?" Red asked, still watching the ceiling.

"Part of that depends on the nature of the curse," Inkletta replied. "From what I have managed to find out, the structures and interlinked nature of the curse is the kind of thing that was explored by demonologists and necromancers in Alduara, specifically a cabal of scholars known as the Seventeen. They developed a kind of grammar and punctuation for each energy container, to make trains like the glyph tracks on your chi meridians."

"It's about the interconnection of everything, and abusing it," Red murmured, eyes half closed. "It's about following bloodlines wherever they lead. It's about every drop of my blood carrying the information about the whole, so that if information changes in one drop of blood my coursing circulatory system is altered." She paused. "It's about how the wind carries the sea foam to the clouds to fall as rain, refilling the ocean." Her eyes drifted closed. "It's about destiny and fate. Life and death and life. And death."

"What's useful here is that the Seventeen stole the language of demons to make their glyphs, to make sturdy enough containers to stay connected to the cosmic winds and geomantic tugs that keep everything in constant motion," Inkletta pressed on, hiding her concern. "Those glyphs in your blood anchor the webwork of alarms, and I think the key is that they are powered by demonic energy."

"How does that help us?" Red asked.

"I think we can mask the signal with a spirit well," Inkletta replied, eyes bright.

Red sat up. "A spirit well? Are you kidding?"

"Not even a little," Inkletta replied. "I got a good look at the gondolier map of known spirit wells in Silkshore, and some beyond their territory. They have a pretty good sense of where the rips are within city limits. Most of them."

"I thought spirit wells attracted spirits, and caused mutations, and corrupted reality itself with leaking energy from behind the Mirror," Red said.

"All true," Inkletta nodded, "but they are also a pure kind of energy, and they are associated with demonic essence. I think the key is that the spirit wells are another world's intrusion into this one, just as a demon is, so the energies feel somewhat similar."

"So, we buy time? Hide better?" Red demanded.

"Maybe," Inkletta agreed, "but maybe if we saturate you with energy from the spirit well, I can pry it loose at the roots. Or at least reduce its strength."

Red stared at her. "That sounds—dangerous," she said.

"Oh, yes," Inkletta agreed. "For you, for me, for the whole city."

A moment of quiet drifted past as they considered that.

"Well, why the hell not?" Red demanded, a new energy in her conviction.

"That's the spirit," Inkletta grinned. "You rest, and eat something, and enjoy the rum. I'll see if I can get word to the Mistress of Tides."

"She would improve our chances," Red conceded.

"Yeah," Inkletta said with half a grin. "A bit." She rose, pulling her cloak back on, and a few moments later Red was once again alone.

Red stared at the glyphs pulsing on her arm, glittering along to her heartbeat, then she shook her head and turned to the basket.

"Gotta keep my strength up," she murmured, and she picked up the bread.

CHAPTER SEVEN

You think this is the only place with weather? We're a coastal city, of course we get hammered with great storms and the like. Do you never look up to see the great gusts of energy boiling away as sheaves of ghosts are hurled through the defenses of the lightning towers? If you listen, they wail as the energy tears them apart. It was a wind that blew them into the city, but not a wind on this side of the Mirror.

I didn't realize there was weather on both sides of the Mirror until I was on the Fifth Star, one of the Strangford Leviathan hunter ships, before I captained the Shiv. A blind old man we called Seeker knew more about the hunt than anyone alive, and he growled to me that weather is the same on both sides of the Mirror; if there is low pressure, then the high pressure will flow into it. That's wind. Everything's built on that. Like gravity, everything drawn to the low point. That's why the climax of a hunt was so often a storm.

Now when I sense a shift in the weather on the backside of the Mirror, I wonder who is making a low point, and what they're doing with that energy. Changed how I saw Whispers and their rituals, that's certain. As the weather is fickle, I realized that what they do leads to consequences we'll never understand.

— From Captain Nyala's personal correspondence to his son Jack

FOG CREST ROOFTOPS, SILKSHORE.
22ND ELISAR. NINTH HOUR PAST DAWN.

Safety cautiously placed one foot in front of the other as he hunched over, slowly climbing the roof. The angle was not so steep he had to lay down, but it was plenty slick. The broad rooftop was coated with a patina of oil, and he knew if he fell it would be difficult to stop sliding. The massive industrial tower next to the building obscured the roof and surroundings in a drifting cinder-etched smoke.

At the peak of the roof, not fifteen feet away, he saw the pilings surrounding a crooked water tower that once supplied the factory next door, or possibly the run-down tenement below his feet. He approached the tower, enticed by the glow of a candle; the interior had been empty a long time, and someone might be sheltering in the tower now. He quietly approached the tower, and leaned close, trying to see inside.

"Easy," growled a voice behind him. Safety froze, then slowly raised his hands.

"Piccolo?" Safety said, not turning.

"Is that you, Safety?" Piccolo asked, a squint audible in his voice. He suppressed a cough.

Safety slowly turned. "You used to tell stories about learning stealth and roof races and such in the cinder cloud over the stacks." He paused. "It's close to the Ghost Market, so I figured it was worth looking for you here."

"You jerks dropped out of sight," Piccolo's silhouette shrugged. "You've been gone like a full day."

"And now we're looking for you," Safety said. "Want to come to the new hideout? We can keep this one as a backup."

Piccolo emerged from the rolling smoke, entered the water tower, and snuffed the candle. He stepped out a moment later with a bag. "Let's go."

"Why don't you lead," Safety suggested with a wry smile that was lost in the darkness of the cloud.

A nightmarish slippery climb in the dark carried them down to the street, where they blended in. Many cowled and cloaked figures scurried towards home as the afternoon wore on under a sky filled with the nuance and color of a fresh and bloody bruise.

"Catch me up," Piccolo muttered to Safety.

"We surprised and killed the assassin then limped to Gapjaw's Leech buddy, Workshop. We spent the night there, Sanction found us a new hideout this morning, and I've been out looking for you." He nodded. "All caught up."

Piccolo coughed, then cleared his throat. "Well that's something," he muttered. "At least you got the assassin."

Safety squeezed past a cart and headed down a pitch-black alley, shaking a glass globe to offer just enough light to maneuver. Faceless brick rose on both sides of the alley, barely five feet apart. They reached a walled-off entry to a courtyard, and Safety knelt opposite the sealed gateway to tug at a metal plate.

"They sealed the coal chute here when the building switched to plasmic systems," Safety muttered, "and this part of the cellar was walled off." He wrenched the metal plate aside and slid his legs in, squirming to drop out of sight. Piccolo was right behind him, pulling the plate closed. They were now in the candle-lit and dusty corner of a cellar with no other exits.

"Glad to see you," Gapjaw said, serious. "We were worried."

"And we'll need you for this next part," Sanction added, snapping his book shut and tucking it into his coat. "The plan is audacious, destructive, chaotic, and provocative."

"That's my thing," Piccolo said with half a smile.

Safety winced. "I kind of feel like we can do that on our own. Weren't you supposed to come up with a more subtle sort of plan?"

"My plan gets us what we need to carry out Piccolo's plan," Sanction said with a nod. "The target is here." He picked up a walking stick and gestured at a building marked on the crude street plan he had drawn on one wall. "This is an archive for the Ministry of Taxation's Silkshore satellite office."

"Sorry, I fell asleep for a second there," Gapjaw said, deadpan. "Make this interesting."

"The problem is getting information," Sanction explained. "We can't consult our normal experts, we can't conduct research, we can't involve our allies in finding out facts for us. So what we need is a succinct source where all the information we need has been collected and put within reach." He paused. "Part of the tax code that favors the members of the Council and accrues to them the benefits to which they are entitled requires them to submit genealogical research supporting their claims as to who belongs in their bloodlines."

"So for tax purposes, Rowan had to submit scholarly research on all his family," Safety said, realization dawning for the first time. "All of them!"

"Filed and indexed," Sanction nodded. "Available for city officials above a certain level to reference. Kept in the archives, out of reach of those not trusted by the Ministry to act on its behalf. If that archive substation catches fire," he said, "then it could be an accident. And if there's enough chaos, it will take time to determine what's missing." He shrugged. "By the time Rowan is notified that we have his family tree, he'll already know from us."

"I can get some accelerant," Gapjaw said. "Even as a fugitive. I know where to collect some—drippings," he shrugged.

"We will need some acid, an enhanced bar-cutting garrote, and some sacks of rats," Sanction said.

"You get the rats," Piccolo said with a blur of speed, pivoting to point at Safety before he could react. "I'll get the acid and garrote." He grinned widely. "I love your plans, Sanction."

"I guess I'll get the rats," Safety said through his teeth. "What's that about?"

"We need a narrative for how the fire happened. One that doesn't require scoundrels' involvement." Sanction cocked an eyebrow. "Rats in the walls. Plasmic systems. Lanterns. Books." He shrugged. "They should be able to connect the dots."

"How long?" Gapjaw asked.

"Let's do this tomorrow, middle of the night," Sanction replied.

"Sounds good," Safety nodded. "Looks like we have a plan."

SORTING POINT, THE DOCKS.
22ND ELISAR. FIFTH HOUR PAST DAWN.

The planks and piling thrummed with vibration from traffic. The Hammer perched at the edge of the raised road, looking down at the pier with his spyglass, ignoring the traffic behind and below. A massive ship had spent the better part of the morning making the final approach, and it had been secured against the dock for nearly ten minutes while customs officials conversed with the crew. The ship's low and wide construction, square sail, and buxom carved figurehead all suggested she was a Skovlan craft, full of hopefuls trying to make a better life in the port city that helped conquer their people.

Finally, a smile crossed the Hammer's face as his spyglass probed at the piling supporting the dock. A flicker of motion, a young woman emerged from under the dock and climbed carefully up to the side. As the flood of people began to flow down two gangplanks and onto the dock, she hefted herself up and rolled at the crowd, smoothly rising to her feet and joining the others arriving in Doskvol today.

The Hammer snapped his spyglass shut and dropped down to the ladder, climbing down to the dock-level street. The archway over the street read "Sorting Point" in three languages. He headed to the "Arrivals and Departures" building, thoroughly Skovlan in construction, a taste of home in a strange land. He had time, after all. The crowd leaving the ship had to present papers, go through delousing and property search, and gain temporary papers that would allow them to get work.

Pulling his flap cap brim low and shrugging himself back into his raised collar, the Hammer stamped into Arrivals and Departures as though he belonged there. Raucous cries echoed and rebounded in the tall space that was nowhere near capacity.

Waving off the barmaid, the Hammer took a seat at the counter where he could see the door. Then he scanned the room.

One corner had Hooks and Sinkers, a new Skovlan crew setting up on the docks north of the Menagerie. Twain, their leader, had cornsilk dreads and badly scarred arms revealed by his sleeveless vest. A number of others hung back, watching for potential recruits.

Ironborn's people had triple their usual numbers, partly because they filled both their usual booth and also took over for the Grinders;

where the Grinders normally held court here there were numerous small memorial gestures. The center table was covered with candles, and cross-stitch funeral gifts, small rocks and vials of sand from the homeland, and a number of small sculptures. Ironborn's second, Havid, sulked in the dimness of the back alcove. One crusted boot was up on the table, and at his side was the massive iron and horn hammer that helped make his reputation as a killer.

Up a level, leaning at the balcony, the Skov Amenders waited to review the newcomers for recruits. The Hammer felt somewhat easier that if one of their leaders, Corben, would be so brazen as to send his people somewhere as predictable as this that maybe the spies rounding out the crowd would be less interested in the Hammer. Immigrants fresh off the boat were more open to supporting the sort of reforms the Amenders pursued; they had not yet felt the boot of Doskvol against their necks, and change seemed like a reasonable thing to want.

The center of the room, nearer the door, was filled with those who had more exploitative use for the newcomers. Some of the agents had standards they unfurled with the basics of the jobs they were offering. To one side, the eeleries promoted a living wage to those who wanted to "work with animals." Off to the other side, Barrowcleft delegations offered work digging ditches for irrigation, planting, and harvesting in the radiant fields. Whitecrown's Academy had several departmental representatives all looking for strong healthy test subjects, lab workers, and laborers to support the studies of others.

Hours passed, over to the afternoon, then through its end. The Blind Hour settled in, fogging the windows, but it was the same at home and the Skovs were used to it. After the Blind Hour passed, the tavern activity peaked, and there were hundreds of Skovs present and willing to sing and drink and remember happier times.

One of the Skovs leaned at the bar, yelling over it. "Maybe I could sell your drinks!" she shouted in Skovic. She had a fresh face and close-cropped hair in a pageboy cut that looked like it had been self-inflicted with a dagger.

"You don't want this one," hollered the man who leaned in at her side. "She's trouble." He grinned, and looked her in the eye.

Niece blinked, and was completely shocked to see the Hammer here.

He took advantage of the moment to grasp her elbow and steer her away from the bar, out the side door by the kitchen, into the alleyway beside Arrivals and Departures.

"How did you find me?" she demanded in Akorosian.

"I remember the time Trellis said that of all of us, you could most easily conjure up a brand new backstory, if you came in through the Sorting Point again." He paused. "I assume you remembered too."

"Here I am," she shrugged, "brand new, zero history in the Dusk." She tried on her best smile. "How does it suit me?"

"I can leave you to it," the Hammer said, "if you want out of your past life."

"No, that's not it," she said quickly as she put her hand on his forearm. "I just—I didn't know what else to do." She looked him in the eye. "Rowan destroyed the Grinders."

"I heard about that," the Hammer said, sober.

"I got separated," she said, "and the Bluecoats, they captured my aunt just for knowing me. I've been a walking target before, but now, I feel like anyone I talk to can get me killed, and a whole circle of whoever is nearby. People I have talked to. People I might talk to." She looked over her shoulder. "The last time I felt this alone, I came to the River Stallions and they took me in."

"We need a plan," the Hammer said earnestly.

"I mean, yeah, sure," Niece agreed. "But what can we do?"

"We look out for ourselves, and each other, and claw back everybody we can to a safe place," the Hammer said. "Turns out Saint is in Ironhook."

"So is Ryha!" Niece said.

"Ironhook has lots of floors, and wings, and nooks. Lots of places prisoners can be put. We won't have time to search for them when we get in, so we need to consult the Central Exchange. That's where the wardens keep track of the prisoners."

Niece blinked. "How do we get in there?" she asked in a small voice.

"We need a plan," the Hammer said, confident. "We need Trellis. I have thought and thought, as I have seen them do. I have written things on small pieces of paper," he said, his brow furrowed. "I have replayed many stories in my mind, of how they do these things. But in the end," he sighed, "I am not a mastermind, or a planner. I can take down a fortification," he clarified, "and there are certain operations I am well suited for. But a rescue?" He shook his head. "I cannot think of a good plan."

"How do we get Trellis if everyone in the city is looking for him and he doesn't want to be found?"

"You can help me with that," the Hammer said. "Just three streets over is Ink Lane. They have many tattoo artists, but that is also where the city's newspapers and reviews are printed. We find one that advertises to radiant enthusiasts and maybe we code a message. Subtle enough to not draw the wrong sort of attention, but clear enough to reach Trellis."

"Sounds like fishing to me," Niece said, resisting the skeptical feelings that were overwhelming her.

"I found you, didn't I?" the Hammer replied with a crooked grin.

Niece thought about that for a moment, then nodded. "Alright, Mister the Hammer, we have a plan to find someone to make us a better plan."

"I call it progress," he said sagely, offering her the crook of his elbow.

They vanished into the steaming dimness of the Dusk.

RUNWATER CORNERS, CROW'S FOOT.
23RD ELISAR, SECOND HOUR PAST DAWN.

"This is it?" Red Silver said, unconvinced, eyeing the stone shell of a tower.

"This is it," Inkletta agreed quietly. She looked over at her cowled and shrouded partner. "You know how you reach out to your bat Nails. If you open up, you can feel it."

Red threw her a skeptical look, then relaxed, breathing out. A frown creased her forehead, and she opened her eyes at once. "Slit the Void Sea," she swore, "what is—that?"

"There's a spirit well below that tower ruin," Inkletta said. "The tower was built to conceal the spirit well, and almost immediately a bad storm threw so much lightning into it some of the stone melted." She shook her head. "That was about thirty years ago."

"And that's where we're going," Red clarified.

"Oh yes," Inkletta replied, expressionless. "The question is whether the well has defenders or not."

Red waited for a moment, then glanced over at Inkletta. "If it does?"

"We'll have a hell of a fight on our hands," Inkletta breathed. "You ready for that?"

"Yes, I'm ready," Red said through clenched teeth.

"Last I heard, followers of the Shrouded Queen were using this place," Inkletta said. "This particular cult to the Shrouded Queen believes she is incomplete under her shroud, so they send her a tithe of their best body parts to choose from to find completion." Inkletta grimaced, eyes still fixed on the tower. "Once rebuilt, she can reveal herself. She will cast aside her shroud and ascend into the mortal world, radiant and fully powered."

"Huh." Red pulled out her customized and silvered over-under pistols, squinting at one, then the other. "Well then."

"We want to keep this quiet," Inkletta said. "We only kill them in the presence of the spirit well. Their deaths will be absorbed or at least masked by the energy, so we don't have to worry about the Deathseeker crows tattling on our business."

"You think we can do this with just two people?" Red clarified, studying the tower.

"I know we can," Inkletta said, her voice hard. "Let's go." She pulled her spirit mask up over her features.

They crossed the street and ducked through the remains of a dilapidated fence, climbing the stairs to where the door to the tower hung to the side on one last hinge. They scanned the street briefly before turning to the stairs that led down through the ragged remains of the floor, into the utterly black pit below.

Red shook her glass orb, activating a dim glow. Inkletta rubbed at a tattoo glyph on the back of her hand, releasing a small spark of light that rose to head level and glowed, following her as she descended the stairs.

A moment later, Red holstered a gun and steadied herself with a hand against the wall as her breathing intensified. "I don't—this isn't—" she began.

"There," Inkletta said, gesturing at a glyph on the opposite wall. "If your will is not strong enough, you retreat."

"Yeah, about that," Red said, clenching her jaw. "I will keep going." She paused. "In a minute."

The darkness rustled below, there was the clink of metal on stone, hissing and whispers.

"Yeah, I'm good," Red growled, and she pushed past the landing, Inkletta at her heels.

They approached the bottom of the winding stairwell, the world they left behind a grayish patch of lesser darkness above. Two ragged men stood at the bottom of the stairs, each missing an arm. They were dressed in rags, but each wielded a vicious dagger. Behind them there was a crowd of the maimed, easily mistaken for the undead because of missing eyes, teeth, noses, and jaws, but all still painfully alive somehow.

A man stood up on something tall towards the back of the crowd, barely visible at the edge of their light. "You must leave now, for this place is sanctified to the Shrouded Queen and you do not bear marks of her worship."

"I need the spirit well, and you're in my way," Inkletta said, cool. "So let's have a clash and see who comes out on top."

The spokesman paused. "Just—just the two of you?" he said, bemused, gesturing between them with a finger.

Red Silver whipped both pistols out and up, snapping off a pair of shots, one into each of the door guards at the bottom of the stairs. As the mob registered her movement, she raised both pistols to point at the spokesman and fired the second barrels; he dodged one bullet as he twisted back off his raised block, but the other shot caught him in the chest and sent him flying.

Red twirled the guns and holstered them both, pulling out the long damask knives sheathed behind them, and she banged a kick across the first cultist leaping up the stairs. As he toppled, she parried a gaff hook planted on a woman's wrist stump that thrust at her torso, and whipped her other knife across the woman's face.

Inkletta took a knee and lashed down with her open hand, shattering a glass bottle. A swarm of twinkling electroplasmic viscera scattered, now free, and her spirit mask took on a sympathetic sheen of bluish light. The electroplasm flattened to discs, and as she recoiled, the discs tugged back with her fluid full-body gesture. The spirit well let out a noisy crack, and a jagged glowing line flared in the background; energy spun and twirled out of the crack, illuminating the corners of the room with unhelpful night-vision-killing streaks.

Red jabbed forward with her knives, but a short man with wild eyes clambered up on the stairs behind her and hurled himself into a grapple. She staggered down off the stairs onto level ground with the mob; they closed around her immediately.

Caught in the crush, she slithered down to one knee, her face locked in a teeth-baring grimace, and she slit tendons, punched her blades into joints, slithered the sharp end across load-bearing limbs. The press was too tight for them to effectively get a hold on her as those she injured screamed and staggered, and when a hole opened up she cut through it.

Then the twisting coil of energy connecting Inkletta and the spirit well flattened and burst, sweeping the room, hurling the cultists against the walls with bone-shattering force. The light from the breached well pulsed with a heartbeat as the injured spokesman stood once more on the altar constructed on the site of the well.

Now the spokesman was cloaked in dark energy, only partially visible in the shroud, only a pit where the face had been. *YOU INTRUDE* the avatar breathed.

"I need this site, your majesty," Inkletta replied coolly.

YOU SHALL NOT HAVE IT

Inkletta did not immediately respond, but instead she waited, watching the avatar. Breathing through her mouth as quietly as possible, Red snapped her pistols open and reloaded them, re-holstering the guns and gripping the gore-slick knives, still on one knee.

ALL THESE WHO ARE MINE MAY RISE AND TAKE ALL FROM YOU

"And if they do not?" Inkletta asked, quiet. "If you extend into our world on that scale and find only defeat?"

THEN YOU SHALL JOIN ME HERE

Inkletta switched to Hadrathi, the words slithering from her. "I was raised in the shine of this place, and within my bones are memories I did not make. Your stolen flesh is not tied to this place as mine is, and your borrowed power passes through a door I may close," she whispered.

DO NOT DARE OR I WILL FEAST UPON—

Inkletta sprinted past Red, leaping into the air and shoulder-checking the avatar; the impact resonated with a glassy crunch and flickered with a spiderweb of light as she struck something behind the Mirror. She let out a scream and recoiled as the spokesman avatar burst, spraying the whole chamber with crystals and gobbets of meat. The light winked out.

"Inkletta!" Red screamed. She scrambled to her feet, rushing to the steaming body of the Whisper, rolling her over. Red reached for the spirit mask and recoiled as it stung her fingers with something like heat; it sizzled on Inkletta's face.

"Come on, stay with me!" Red snapped, gripping the Whisper's slender wrist, groping for a pulse.

A hiss escaped Inkletta's lips, and she was utterly still.

MINISTRY OF TAXATION SATELLITE OFFICE ARCHIVE, SILKSHORE. 23RD ELISAR. HOUR OF SILVER, 3 HOURS PAST DUSK.

The plan unfolded like clockwork. A mass of rats drew attention to the routing office and its pneumatic tubes all through the archive building, now feeding oxygen to a rapidly spreading fire. The automatic fire suppression system turned out to be damaged by rats and without pressure. The mass of Ministry employees, the Bluecoats, the Brigade, and off-the-street volunteers all stamped around in the confusing maze of the high-security facility as the flames rippled behind the walls. Theft was rampant on all sides.

"That was easier than I thought it would be," Piccolo admitted as he stood on the roof of a Ministry building three blocks away.

"Mmm," Sanction replied, sitting cross-legged on a balcony, looking over four books. He straightened with a smile. "This. This is the one." He opened it, and the others gathered around as he flattened out a two-page spread with cramped family tree penned in. "There's Rowan," he said, triumphant.

"Well," Safety said slowly, "that looks like about fifty relatives."

"Too many to beef up security on all of them," Piccolo agreed.

Gapjaw stayed at the edge of the roof, watching the building burn, a satisfied smile on his face. "Feels good for something to go right, and for some senseless act of vandalism to destroy city records," he said through his peaceful smile. He heaved a deep sigh of contentment. The stain of light from the fire was countered by the smoke that blotted out half the neighborhood.

"I suppose we need to chew this over for a while," Safety muttered, squinting at the page.

"No, I've picked our next target. This one right here," Sanction said, stabbing at the page with his finger. "Let's hit him tomorrow."

"I like the new you," Piccolo said. "I like this workmanlike attitude that just gets the heisting done."

"Don't get used to it, I've got a life of decadence and debauchery waiting for me on the other side of this murderous vendetta," Sanction sighed, snapping the book shut. He looked at the other books. "Those could be expensive," he said, cocking his head to the side.

"Or they could give us away," Piccolo said. "They're almost but not quite the books we were after."

"And we're out of wiping paper," Gapjaw grunted, a grin on his face. "Tax documents seem like a natural for that."

Sanction just gazed at him for a moment, a smile growing on his face. "It's your ass," he shrugged, and he chuckled at his own joke. "Okay, let's get going. Tomorrow we're going to hit the University."

OUTSIDE THE PORT OF DOSKVOL, THE VOID SEA.
23RD ELISAR.

The engine chugged and the paddles spun, propelling the steamer across the glassy shoulder of the wave's swell. The shattered fragments of the sun pulsed in the sky like a dying campfire's embers, and below the sea was lit with constellations long-missing from the vistas above.

"M-master," gasped the helmsman, face contorted in pain, "the city—it lies—ahead," he gasped out.

A tall shadow stood at the bow of the steamer, contemplating the first jutting rock with a lightning tower on it as they approached. He stretched his hand out to the side, and the helmsman whimpered as he felt his life force connect to that hand. The tall shadow closed his hand to a fist, forcing life back into the helmsman, who wept aloud.

"I see that," Razor Wind murmured, "but thank you."

The Whisper closed his eyes, and licked his teeth, and breathed deep. There, ahead, in the city. He felt a flare in the curse, he felt the tug in the runes. A survivor. The last survivor.

"Patience, dear, patience," he murmured. "We're near the end now."

Somewhere in the city, a giant bat shrieked in dismay.

CHAPTER EIGHT

Commander Tarrant assembled Tarrant's Toolbox—code names for the four officers that managed the bloodiest work of the battlefields on Kronen's Point, the Alabaster, Icerock Narrows, and the Chord naval engagement.

The Awl was his assassin, the Hacksaw handled scouting and ambushes on enemy supply lines and stockpiles. The Prybar was a terrorist interrogator; the mention of her title was enough to loosen resolve among the Skovs. Then there was the Hammer, a war leader with a gift for crushing enemy formations and fortifications. By his third year at the front, if word circulated that the Hammer was headed for a fortification, there were even odds the defenders would pull back before he arrived, leaving their strong points empty.

Tarrant was arrogant and he felt success made him untouchable, so when he caught a bullet at Flatstone and his command was split up among rival commanders, they had little interest in preserving his tactics or his legacy. The Awl turned up dead, and the other three disappeared; since they operated with code names, they could still be in the military now for all we know.

— From the "History of the Skovlan Unity War, volume III"
by Hubert Cacrassi

A NEW PRISON.
23ᴿᴰ ELISAR. THIRD HOUR PAST DAWN.

He pushed against the darkness, and it slowly parted, tearing like silk that was only a breath in thickness. Beyond was a grayness, and so he pushed again, and it slid down the sides of his face as he leaned into it, towards the light, frictionless black caressing his cheeks as he forced his way upward.

His eyes snapped open, and the illusion of silken darkness twisted into a metaphor. He tasted the dead and metallic tang of chemicals in his mouth, and his consciousness flowed from his eyes down through his logy body, pushing senselessness before it, discomfort filling in behind.

Flares and ribbons of pain reported from the flesh to the mind, and he winced slightly, then blinked to refocus everything.

Tied to a chair. That's something.

His leg was bound up in a splint. Tight wrappings compressed his broken ribs. He looked down at himself, noting he had been scrubbed, stitched, bandaged, and dressed in silken pajamas with a robe for warmth in the drafty room.

He sat next to a table with a glass-chimney lamp that housed a chip of steady flame that illuminated very little of his surroundings.

Clearing his throat, he felt the soreness of his larynx and the ache at the base of his tongue. "Hello?" he rasped experimentally.

"So glad you could join me," replied a figure at the other end of the table, just beyond the lamp's range. "I was wondering how long it would take you to gather your wits."

"I may not have them all, but," he paused for a ragged cough, then a couple deep breaths. "I've herded some of them back into the pen."

"Do you remember your name?" prompted the shadowy host.

"Saint Suran, and I'm delighted that so far I've still got all my teeth," Saint replied with a crooked smile. "No bookmaker in Silkshore would have taken those odds." He cocked his head, regarding his host. "Most of the people I irritate tell me they want to punch me in the face. Sometimes they even specifically mention the smile."

"I've expressed my displeasure with your efforts sufficiently, I feel, and I'm ready to put that behind us. We have the future to consider, after all," the host said.

"Is Soapstone in that future?" Saint asked. "I'm afraid I may have offended him when we spoke last. Hurt his feelings." Saint was still smiling, but it wasn't a friendly expression.

"Soapstone has many things to handle, poor man, so I thought I'd help out and take you off his list." The host stood, rounding the table, moving into the lamplight. "We need to talk about your future, and I have the power over that discussion, not Soapstone." Lord Rowan smiled at his prisoner.

"That's good news," Saint admitted, "because just between us, I don't like Soapstone. He takes too much for granted."

"Yes, he does," Lord Rowan agreed. "That's why I'm taking over your case."

"Shall we handle this like a delicate dance where every morsel is revealed with a fresh turn in the mind game? Or is it time for cards on the table?" Saint asked quietly.

"Let's be frank," Lord Rowan replied. "I want my adept back. I want the River Stallions and Silkworms gone; nobody touches my operations with that kind of arrogance and gets away with it. I have bigger things to do and they are an irritation that's already lasted five days, which is the extreme outer limit of my patience."

"So I flip for you and get you your adept and betray my fellows, in exchange for either fantastic rewards or a shallow grave. That's the size of it?" Saint asked.

"I was thinking more along the lines of you advise me on the way forward from here, and depending on your usefulness, I decide whether or not to scrub your identity and give you a new one as a fixer in one of my many organizations," Lord Rowan replied coolly.

"Here I am trying to think big, and still not thinking big enough," Saint sighed. "You remind me why I've never had the knack for masterminding the big picture. I have to admire your plan." He shrugged. "Bringing me here. Now that you've done it, I should have expected it, but in Ironhook it was hard to put all the pieces together."

"You had no way of knowing your comrades would give my organization such a difficult time," Lord Rowan shrugged.

"I want to help you, I do," Saint said. "Tell me who you've killed or captured so far."

Lord Rowan paused. "I overestimated Soapstone's grasp of the tactical capacity of your people," he admitted. "We had some near misses, but so far they've eluded apprehension. I believe some of them are injured, but we have no confirmed kills. We have you, and Niece's great-aunt or something, from the homeland. A number of contacts, allies, and employees taken to Ironhook for questioning and to discourage support for the fugitives. They have lost access to their assets."

"Progress, I supposed, but... no casualties. That's bad," Saint said conspiratorially. "Survival only emboldens them, you know."

Lord Rowan narrowed his eyes. "I want Trellis and Sanction first. How do you make that happen for me?"

Saint paused for a long moment, then closed his eyes and shook his head. "I'm having trouble thinking," he admitted. "What do you think about untying me and letting me have a stretch? Maybe something decent to eat. Maybe a seat with a cushion."

Lord Rowan regarded him for a few seconds. "You know, of course, I have horrific inducements nearby."

"I do not doubt it," Saint said, eyes wide. "I don't even want to know what they are. I really appreciate this, as far as it goes," he said with a wince as he shifted in his bandages and restraints, "but there's a level of comfort beyond basic medical care that sinks into the soul itself." He tried on a smile. "We scoundrels are an adaptable lot, but one of the reasons I descended into this life of crime was for the luxuries." He nodded to Lord Rowan. "You know the value of the finer things."

"Let's do this," Lord Rowan said. "You can have an hour, a meal, some time with my string quartet, and a divan. Then we'll speak again."

Mischief crept into the corner of Saint's smile. "That will make you my third favorite captor ever," he replied. "Something to eat, then we'll figure out how to trap a spider."

UNDISCLOSED LOCATION.
23ᴿᴰ ELISAR. FIFTH HOUR PAST DAWN.

The music flourished once, then released into resonant silence. Saint lay on the divan, his injured leg up, his wineglass dark with a classic vintage, his eyes closed and a smile on his face.

"That's Tanalyse's Third," Lord Rowan said as he approached. "When he wrote it, his stepfather was critically ill, on his death bed. The terrified old man had asked his prodigy son to write a song that would carry him away to bliss, and protect him from the source of all fear." Lord Rowan shrugged. "Tanalyse did his best. What do you think?"

"The word 'uplifting' seems most appropriate," Saint murmured. "In the last movement piling arpeggio upon arpeggio, the broken chords climbing the octaves, the underpinning base chords fading like the shadow of earth as you climb past the clouds into light." He opened his eyes and pointed a frank look at Lord Rowan. "It's alright. You need a new violist, the current one gets lazy and turns some of that crystal to mush." He sipped his wine.

"Critics everywhere," Lord Rowan replied with sardonic amusement. "Now that you've shared your thoughts on the chamber music, perhaps you could share your thoughts on Trellis and Sanction."

"Absolutely," Saint nodded. "First off, there's too many places in a city like this where they could hide, so if you've got a reward out that's the best you can do. If you cannot find where they are, then the next goal is to figure out how they communicate. If they were all together they would have moved together by now, and you'd know it. So they're still scattered, and the main way they have to communicate that you cannot control is by taking out ads or bribing people to change minor details in the letterhead of certain publications. Ideally the daily publications, unless they're being careful. Really, you'll want to ramp up your spy network's focus on Ink Lane."

"Any particular publications?" Lord Rowan asked, raising an eyebrow.

"Bring me paper and a pen and I'll sketch out my first suspicions, if you want to bring a week's worth of every rag you can get I'll help you look them over," Saint shrugged. "Now, for Trellis you want an aristocrat's hobby paper on radiants and gardening. Something like that. For Sanction, focus on muck-rakers and reporters keeping watch on Ministry activity, ideally in Silkshore."

"These signals indicate what?" Lord Rowan asked.

"Possibly meeting points, or a 'stay away' signal, or indicating a drop. Lots of it is impenetrable because it relies on knowing inside jokes," Saint explained. "While I might be able to spot signals, and I think it's critical that we try that first, we should also line up a message of our own, to try and lure one of them into a trap. I think we should start with Sanction, as he's a former Ministry man and could be useful to the city once again once we get him on board. He may not be able to get very far inside Trellis's head, but he's our best bet for catching the wily old man." Saint sipped his wine. "And if he resists, or even if he doesn't, you can tell Trellis you're hurting him. Force the old man's hand. He's really very fond of Sanction."

Lord Rowan studied Saint thoughtfully. "What if I told you that wasn't good enough? Not fast enough?"

Saint put his glass down. "If you had Trellis here, he might be able to produce me like a rabbit from a hat in a street magician's act. Let's just say there's a reason that I was trying to join the Fairpole Grotto Council of Gondliers, then Trellis came out of nowhere and took it over. I'm not on his level. But I understand people, and I have a background with the team." He paused. "You want a better plan? Tell me everything you've done to get at them, and I can probably tell you which things will provoke which people to hit back, and how. When they hit back, *that* is when you get them." He shrugged. "I've been in jail. I'm out of the loop."

Lord Rowan's smile was genuine. "You are good, Saint, better than I expected," he said. "You knew what you wanted all along, to start figuring out a plan, but you waited until I pressed harder, before you countered, so really it's all about me helping you to help me." He shook his head. "I may not be able to trust you, but I can admire your work."

"I know you can't trust me, my whole skill set revolves around betraying trust," Saint said earnestly. "Still, I'm on your side here. The River Stallions are done, even if this thing was over right now and you walked away, because they provoked the aristocracy and someone will make sure they pay for it when they come out of hiding." He shook his head. "Working for you means not having to look over my shoulder, because I know what I can offer you and how badly you need it. Not for this manhunt, but for handling delicate issues." He paused. "You think I would have formed a crew and worked the criminal side of the fence if I had the option of becoming a shadow agent of the City Council?" he demanded. "You are telling me the price of my promotion is my old life, and that's a skin I'm willing to shed."

"That doesn't paint a pretty picture of your loyalty," Lord Rowan admitted. "Sounds like you'd jump at the next offer and sell out your new friends too."

"The key here is a *better* offer," Saint said, looking Lord Rowan in the eye. "Who makes a better offer than you?"

Lord Rowan regarded the scoundrel with the broken leg. "Who indeed," he mused.

Saint sniffed, and nodded. "You can decide what to do with me later," he said. "In the meantime, I'm all yours. So. What have you tried so far?"

EMPRESS OF GULLS' WORKSHOP SLOOP WRECK, TANGLETOWN, CROW'S FOOT. 23ᴿᴰ ELISAR. HOUR OF FLAME, 5 HOURS PAST DUSK.

The chamber was dim, lit only by two palm-sized braizers filled with glowing chips. A gnarled old woman in a heavy veil sat ramrod straight on her throne. It was made of driftwood and bone, woven together, forming branches up to the ceiling and roots down the stairs to the floor. Stripes of glyphwork and spells were daubed or carved across the room, and some of them were glowing faintly. Two barechested and handsome men were standing defensively before the throne; the tension in the room was high.

Three gentle knocks upon the door.

"Enter if you must," the old woman replied in Hadrathi.

The door creaked open, and a tall man ducked inside. "Greetings, Empress of Gulls," he said in accented Akorosian. "I understand you ease the vexation of customers who come to you with proper deference." He bowed low as several bands of spellwork brightened along the walls and floor.

"I like your manners," the woman on the throne said quietly. "You've brought a lot of power into my little workshop. How could I possibly help one such as you?" She struggled to keep her tone on the polite side of what those words could mean.

"I have sufficient power for my purpose," her visitor said. "I lack local context. I am following a beacon, but it has been obscured. I know that one such as you would know of significant occult happenings in this city," he said. "A curse was revealed five days ago."

The Empress of Gulls regarded the stranger. "What is your name, sir?" she inquired.

"I am Razor Wind," he answered, expressionless, his face only lit by the pulsing glow of spellwork activated by his presence.

"As far as I know," she said carefully, "we have no quarrel with each other."

"And I wish to preserve that state of affairs," he replied.

She studied him over for a few long seconds, and reached a conclusion. "Cursework was revealed at the Rowan Estate in Six Towers. It is the talk of the town, a celebrity medium's party was crashed by an angry ghost. I do not know the details, but it seems this must be what you seek." She paused. "Lord Rowan has a seat on the Council, and is one of the most powerful men in the city. He has offered significant reward for more information on the fugitive with the curse, he has made that plain by sending agents to all the places occult practitioners are known to gather."

Razor Wind narrowed his eyes. "I sense you are telling me the truth," he said, "and giving me something for nothing."

"On the contrary," she shrugged, invisible behind her veil. "You came with politeness and I answered with truth, those are gifts we both brought. I shall not ask a price for putting you further down this path, for I sense it will not end well for you. Nor can you turn from it." She tilted her head. "No, I will not ask for payment, I only ask that you continue on down your dark and gruesome path without involving me further."

"When this is over," Razor Wind murmured, "I will return to Ilysia, my home."

"I really don't think you will," the Empress of Gulls replied, something like sadness in her eyes.

He nodded to her, turned, and ducked out of her chamber.

ADRIFT IN DREAMS
23ᴿᴰ ELISAR. HOUR OF PEARLS, 6 HOURS PAST DUSK.

With a clink and slither, the surf made of broken glass ebbed. Above, there were again stars in the sky, as a giant wave of the Void Sea curled over the city in a vast arc, so the constellations in its depths were again overhead. The ground shuddered slightly as somewhere inland the earth struggled to chew something that would not yield and break, or perhaps flinched from a thousand piercings leaning this way and that as they stood up from the ground's ruptured flesh.

The Mistress of Tides wandered alone, far from the shore, among the wrecked ships and giant bones that littered the sea bed that was revealed by the withdrawal of the ocean to make the giant wave. Ghosts hovered at the edge of her sight, half-eaten by demons and twitching as they dripped electroplasmic viscera that twirled away ungoverned by gravity.

This dream was not unfamiliar, and she felt no fear.

Then she heard the tapping.

Tapping was new.

She counted eight taps and a pause for a few seconds, then five taps, then eight, a relentless staccato in her legato dreamscape.

That meant intrusion.

Effortless and disembodied, she traveled up the gouged riverbed to the Tangle, only to find it weirdly deserted and as inaccessible as a matte painting. The tapping was much louder, from Crow's Foot, which sizzled in a mottled glow, releasing clouds of black feathers up into the sky. They twirled and danced on updrafts that only affected them.

A few steps slid the Mistress of Tides through the chaotic tumble to where the glow started; she saw a pillar of flame, shivering, falling up through the broken Mirror and catching fire as it touched the mortal world, up from the broken ground. Within the fire a cloak shifted restlessly, trying to settle on its wearer, as though she was falling at great speed and the cloak was trying to sit on her anyway.

The figure in the flame had a stick with a nail through the end, and she tapped the stick against another stick so the nail peppered the ground with holes; eight taps, then she paused to rub the nail point against her fingernail, where some kind of ink had an unwholesome glow. She resumed her tapping marking the ground, and the cloak clawed at her to get a grip. Already she seemed infected by cosmic energy, worming into her flesh, lighting her up as though she was made of wax.

"Inkletta?" the Mistress of Tides whispered. Then she read the sigil on the ground—

—and woke screaming.

COLLEGE OF IMMORTAL STUDIES, CHARTERHALL UNIVERSITY, CHARTERHALL. 24ᴿᴰ ELISAR. FIRST HOUR PAST DAWN.

The massive Sparkwright Tower gusted a six-colored flame tapestry into the twilight of early morning, and smoke darkened the courtyard. The flare cast shadows behind the hand cart and the two cloaked men struggling to push it along.

"Let's see your pass," a bored guard said as the two men pushed their cart in range of the side gate into the courtyard. The guard grimaced. "What's that stink?" he demanded.

One of the men looked up with a servile grin. "Oh, we have a dead donkey," he said in a fawning tone. "This exotic herbivore is something sure to interest the dissectionists. We made an arrangement for sale, but a condition was we bring it to them." He bowed low.

The guard reached for the canvas covering the corpse, but the other man stepped forward. "Please," he said, eyes wide. "The tarp—it keeps the smell in. See?" he said with a hopeful smile, tugging a leg and hoof out for the guard to see. "Donkey." He paused, dead serious. "It was in the canal," he said, a catch in his voice.

"Okay, you win," the guard shrugged. "So, you can wait here while I get the check-in paperwork so you can sign or make your mark, and we can have an inspection of the goods." He paused, eyebrows raised.

"Isn't that the six eel expediency fee? For fast-tracking it?" the smiling porter said. "Our donkey is not getting any fresher."

"Sure, I can handle the paperwork for you," the guard agreed. "That's six apiece, and two for the cart." He jutted out his jaw. "Twenty eels, and in you go."

"Right," the porter said, his smile somewhat stiff. He made a production of counting out the eels, then handed a ratty bag of coin to the guard. "Thank you so much."

"Oh, thank *you*," the guard replied with a tone utterly lacking in gratitude. The two men heaved at the cart, and had it through the gate and into the courtyard.

They pulled up alongside the side door to the Physiker Academy hall extending from the College of Immortal Studies, and looked around; not many people about this early. They tugged the tarp to the side, trying not to gag at the smell, and Gapjaw grinned up at them.

"I told you the donkey leg was a keeper," he said, gesturing with the leg. It had a handle affixed to one end, and a tassel. "You never know when you'll need a donkey leg, that's what I said."

"I want a plan that doesn't involve rolling in stench," Safety grumbled. "Gapjaw, you're impossible to stand next to right now."

"Don't be a baby," Sanction said, tossing his hat in the cart. "Let's do this."

The three men mounted the stairs and opened the door, ducking inside and closing it to keep the cold outside.

"Took your time," Piccolo observed mildly, leaning against the wall with his arms crossed.

"It took longer than we thought to find the donkey leg," Safety said tightly.

"It was key to the plan," Gapjaw protested, brandishing the leg.

"Whatever," Piccolo said. "Third floor."

They headed to the stone stairwell, following the curve upward. "So this place is pretty well locked down, right?" Sanction murmured to Piccolo.

"Right," Piccolo nodded, "but our intel about Professor Stansby was right on. He's working away in his lab. A real early riser."

"Perfect," Sanction said through his teeth.

On the third floor, they strolled past the guard station where a guard slumped at his post, appearing to be asleep. Piccolo smirked at him on the way past, flexing his fist.

"I bet you already unlocked the professor's door," Sanction muttered as they approached the lab.

"I don't even need you guys," Piccolo shrugged. "I could have popped this guy by myself. Security isn't much," he added with a gesture back down the hall.

"We're not just here to kill him," Sanction said. "We're keeping an eye open for opportunity."

"I do that too!" Piccolo protested.

Sanction waved him back, then quietly opened the door and stepped into the lab, the other scoundrels at his heels.

The room was full of narrow tables with stools, and both walls had long counters jammed with shelves and folios. The lamps at the professor's work station barely illuminated the rafters above, and the flickering light was refracted and distorted in the various alchemical equipment down one side of the room, and specimen jars down the other side. The professor looked up, startled, a wine glass in one hand and a quill in the other.

"You!" the professor blustered in a tone that surely struck fear into his students. "This area is off limits before hours of instruction." He squinted. "You aren't in my classes, are you," he said as the first tendrils of fear brushed at him.

"No, Professor Stansby, we are not," Sanction said as he approached down the center aisle with Gapjaw at his back. Safety took one side aisle, Piccolo took the other. Like a pack closing in on wounded prey, they approached.

"What do you want!" the professor demanded, a querulousness in his tone that had not been there before.

"I'm going to kill you," Sanction replied quietly. "Or have him kill you, that's more likely," he observed with a nod to Piccolo. "If you plan to beg for your life, this is the time to do it." He was unreadable, his calmness chilling.

"What is this about? You want money? Drugs? Is this about a student's grades? You'll find me reasonable and relatively inexpensive," the professor said, hanging on to his composure if not his dignity.

"This sort of thing happen to you often?" Sanction asked, eyebrows raised.

"Not me, exactly; most people understand I am not to be touched," the professor replied. "But I hear about it happening to my colleagues."

"You didn't lead with that," Sanction said, stopping short of the professor's desk. "That you are not to be touched. Who offers you protection?"

"V-various former students made good," the professor lied, eyes darting from one threat to the next.

"I think you recognize us," Sanction said quietly. "Why not just say it? Why not just tell us that if we hurt you, the House of Rowan will come for us?" His tone hardened. "Take everything from us. Make us suffer before we die." He slammed his fist on the professor's table as he stared him in the eye.

"Killing me changes nothing," the professor said, his voice soft. He looked Sanction in the eye.

"False," Sanction murmured. "Killing you signals intent to the House of Rowan. There's no use leading with a threat. I need to be sure they understand that my course of action is set and I require persuasion to desist." He shrugged. "I plan to kill three or four of you before I even bother contacting Lord Cleith Armeide Rowan IV."

"I have money," Stansby said, faint. "I can get you five thousand eels now, right now, and another ten by the end of the week."

Sanction's eyebrows raised at that. "Truly a princely sum," he said. "How do you come by that kind of money? You aren't *that* connected."

Sensing a way out, Stansby risked a faint smile. "I—I have a black-mail operation," he said. "I have certain associates who keep an eye out for opportunities, then I take advantage."

"Tell me more," Sanction said, crossing his arms over his chest. "Seduction?"

"My targets tend to be shameless," Stansby said. "I poison them. I have access to a lot of poisons here, and there are some that have rare cures, that resist even supernatural remedies." He paused. "I use the Dolorous Crimson. It takes about a week to kill, which is plenty of time, and it takes an injection to dose the target. It isn't communicable." He paused, sizing up Sanction. "Any supernatural effort to counter it causes agony to the victim, actually tearing holes in their spirits while they're still in the body." He shrugged. "Plasmic bruising is green and white, blood bruising is black and blue and yellow, someone suffering from both gets pretty mottled."

"You have some here?" Sanction asked. The other scoundrels exchanged a worried look, but Sanction ignored them.

"Yes," Stansby said. He turned his back to them and used a key to open a safe. Piccolo and Safety leveled pistols at his back, but when he slowly turned to face them again he had a black lacquer box. He tilted it open to reveal eight vials of red and eight vials of green.

"Red to poison," he murmured, "green to cure." He paused. "This is the height of my life's work. Foolproof uncurable blackmail."

"You have documentation of this?" Sanction pressed. "Instructions to make it, and to make the antidote?"

"No, that's only one place; here," he said, tapping his head. "Insurance," he added with a smile, confidence creeping back into his demeanor.

Sanction narrowed his eyes. "The antidote right there in the safe," he said. "No." He looked over at Piccolo. "Hurt him."

Piccolo closed with the professor as Stansby's hands flew up to defend himself, but he was no match for the lurk. Piccolo snatched his wrist and twisted, pivoting the academic around and dropping him to one knee with casual pressure to a joint lock.

"Okay okay okay," Stansby gasped.

"Do it," Sanction said, cold, and Piccolo twisted. Something broke in Stansby's arm, and he let out a proper scream.

"Shut him up!" Sanction demanded, and Piccolo bounced the professor's face off the back of the table, startling him and cutting off his scream. Safety withdrew to the door, to watch the hallway.

"Where's the antidote really?" Sanction asked Stansby.

"Ch-chandelier," Stansby said, pointing with a shaky finger.

Piccolo looked up at the chandelier, an iron ring fitted with lamps hanging over the room. Releasing Stansby, he hopped easily up on the counter, sprang up the tottering shelves, and launched to catch the chandelier; as it swung, he tugged himself up on it, and pried loose an iron box hidden in the middle.

"We could have lowered it," Gapjaw observed mildly. "Showboat."

Piccolo tossed the box down to Sanction, and Stansby trembled as he scrabbled at the lock with the key. Opening the box, he revealed a row of black powder in glass vials, and also a small black ledger. Sanction took the ledger and opened it, observing the names of people and amounts of payments. The blackmail operation.

"Mix with water and drink," Stansby said, bitter. "So are we in business? Will you keep me alive for your mission of vengeance?"

"Ugh," Gapjaw said. "Who wants to babysit?"

Piccolo jumped down from the chandelier to a table, then to the floor, crossing to Stansby. He looked to Sanction.

"Kill him," Sanction said quietly, not looking up from the ledger.

The scoundrel nodded, slipping his knife out as Stansby's eyes grew round.

"I can make you—" the dead man struggled to promise before Piccolo's glove covered his mouth and the knife angled between ribs, right into the beating heart. Stansby spasmed, then died. Far, far away, an unearthly bell tolled once.

For a moment, all was quiet as Sanction regarded the powders and liquids before him.

"So we look for money before we go?" Safety prompted.

"Yes, we could use a war chest," Sanction said. He snapped the book shut, put it in the box, closed the boxes, picked them up, and headed for the door as lookout. Piccolo joined Safety in a quick examination of possible hiding places. There was a box of coin in the safe, and one of the drawers was full of small bags of pre-measured bribes. Hefting the moderate take, the scoundrels headed out, down the back stairs, and into the fog of morning.

CHAPTER NINE

I couldn't wrap my head around it. Teacher said it was not about the material world and the immaterial world, any more than ice melt flowing from a glacier was otherwordly. Matter and energy back and forth, life and death as different clothes for the same body. Demons were the waking of the elements into sentient shape, ghosts were the thoughts that outlive meat, breath is our reminder that energy moves in tides both in this state of being and in the next. All that is one single unknowable idea that is speaking out through you, even if you do not hear it. Your thoughts are not yours, nor are they real, but they are byproducts of your being that are as ephemeral as mist and as indestructible as color.

To me, just a mess of images and nonsense. So my cousin was accepted to train as an adept, and I learned to paint the charms and guide the boat. It's not a bad life.

I tell you this so you understand adepts are people who grasped the depths of their ignorance enough to fundamentally change how they see the world. They see life, and death, and existence in a way you never will. And Whispers... don't mistake them for people. Whispers have touched the root of the Real. When they deliberately alter their perceptions, the whole world shifts.

— From "Reflections on the Waterways: a Gondolier's Truths"
by Simael Trent

RUNWATER CORNERS, CROW'S FOOT.
24ᵀᴴ ELISAR. SECOND HOUR PAST DAWN.

Red Silver slumped against the crumbling plaster of the wall, motionless. She looked like the rubble of the shattered room, her listless eyes betraying no sign of life or thought as they pointed at the courtyard below.

Across from her, on the lumpen wreck of a mattress, Inkletta's body lay senseless and unresponsive. She was buried in deep shadow, the glitter of her rarely-seen spirit mask the only light that escaped the corner.

Red had carried the Whisper's body across the courtyard, and climbed up into this building, instinctively seeking a perch. Now she seemed to have nothing left. Even with loaded guns across her lap, she did not appear to pose any kind of threat. Her red-rimmed eyes were fixed and vacant.

A shadow flickered over the collapsed roof of the room, and a down-draft swayed the air as the giant bat flicked his wings and came in for a landing. He scrabbled for a moment on the loose tile of the busted roof, and peered down intently at Red with one eye, the metal ball in his other eye socket gleaming and polished in the colorless dim of mid-morning.

Red stirred. "I hope you've put some thought into what you're going to do when I'm gone," she croaked, her voice unexpectedly hoarse. "Stupid furball."

The bat pounced down into the room, then scrambled low across the floor, nose questing up under Red's arm, thrusting his head between the crook of her elbow and her torso, stealing a hug. The bat snuffled loudly up at her, anxious. Red tugged him over across her lap, leaning her face down into the strangely warm coarse hair of his shoulder. The bat's wing lay across her shoulder, and he vigorously licked her hand as she moved to pet him.

Her attention returned to the courtyard below. Bootfalls and clattering echoes from metal-shod wagon wheels signaled the arrival of a dozen Bluecoats escorting goat-drawn wagons marked with the insignia of the Spirit Wardens. They headed into the courtyard, the leaders barking orders to cordon it off. More Bluecoats followed to strengthen the defenses.

Red heard a cascade of pebbles from the other side of the building, and she flexed, shifting the bat off her torso as she rose to one knee. Pausing, she sifted the sounds, ignoring the echoing noises from the courtyard, straining towards more subtle cues from the side of the building. She heard floorboards creak in the room next door, and she soundlessly aimed a pistol in that direction.

A figure stepped into view, dressed in long robes with a hooded cloak. Red blinked. "Mistress of Tides?" she breathed.

The Mistress of Tides turned to face her, then crossed the floor quickly, pulling Red up into her embrace. "Oh, Red," she murmured. "Where is Inkletta?"

Red mutely pointed to the shadowed corner where Inkletta's body lay. The Mistress of Tides released her, stepping over to the body as the bat crabbishly moved out of the way and withdrew to a corner. The Mistress of Tides knelt, pulling her spirit mask into place under her veil and splaying her hand in the air over the body.

"She's not dead," the Mistress of Tides said quietly, "but she is far, far away. Deep." She shook her head. "Almost gone."

"How did you get here," Red muttered, her voice rough.

"Inkletta came to me in a dream last night," the Mistress of Tides said. "She drew me to this area. Today, as I got close, I followed the Bluecoat caravan to get closer. Then I looked for high ground," she shrugged.

"Then—then there's something left. She's not dead," Red demanded, pinning the Mistress of Tides with a red-rimmed stare.

"I think she's trapped on the other side of the Mirror," the Mistress of Tides said gently. "We will have to help her get back through and into her body. It is very important," she continued, putting her hands on Red's shoulders, "that you tell me exactly what happened."

"There was some kind of glyph that tested your mettle, so people wouldn't just, you know, wander down there. Under the ruined tower across the way. Where the—the spirit well is." Red shrugged the Mistress of Tides' hands off her shoulders, and rubbed her face with the back of her hand. "We had a parlay with this cult of cripples, the boss said the place was sanctified to the Shrouded Queen. So," she sighed, "I shot him, and we got into a fight, and Inkletta cracked their spirit well open, then the leader seemed to, I don't know, channel the Shrouded Queen or something. Inkletta threatened the leader, and jumped at the guy, and there was a bang, and he exploded, and her mask burned onto her face and—and she stopped breathing—" Red stopped, struggling to swallow.

The Mistress of Tides regarded her for a long moment. "There's often a little more banter," she murmured. "Sure this avatar form wasn't more chatty?"

Red winced. "Well it was all in Hadrathi, which is not my main—you know," she said. "And it was stressful."

"Try to think," the Mistress of Tides said.

Red closed her eyes, concentrating. "Okay, yes," she murmured. "The avatar threatened to extend into the world and kick her ass, and she threatened to slam the door on it, and that made the Shrouded Queen very angry and alarmed, then Inkletta just rushed her." She shook her head. "Inkletta said something about this place being in her bones."

The Mistress of Tides settled in where Red had been keeping watch, pulling her cloak up to vanish against the rubble. Red lay against the broken wall nearby, trying to catch her eye. "What's the next step?" she asked, finding the Whisper's veil totally unreadable. The bat slithered over and pulled himself half up on her lap, and she absently petted the back of his head as his ears swiveled and lay down.

"I do not yet know," the Mistress of Tides replied.

Red frowned. "So, the Forgotten Gods. Are they... real? I know people worship them, but—I guess I never took them seriously before."

"Are they real," the Mistress of Tides echoed. "This is not the right time to get into an exploration of what 'real' means. They are real enough to manifest dangers, and transmit hungers, and they are a kind of power that worshipers can take into themselves and use."

"So... Inkletta is wrestling a god?" Red asked in a small voice.

The Mistress of Tides chuckled. "As of last night," she said, "Inkletta was *winning*."

For the first time since she saw Inkletta struck down, a bleak smile touched Red's lips.

Piccolo stood, stretching, then he rubbed his face. He looked over at the rickety table where Sanction sat, poring over the book.

"Did you sleep?" he asked quietly, not bothering to look over at where Gapjaw and Safety still quietly snored.

Sanction looked him in the eye. "I need you to know what I'm planning."

"What, just me? Not everyone?"

"I don't want a debate," Sanction shrugged. "When the time comes, we've got to be clear, and if you and I are together, then the others will fall in line."

"Sounds like you're planning something naughty," Piccolo said quietly. "Or vicious." He shrugged. "Either way."

Sanction laid it out.

Piccolo got a distant look in his eye for a bit, then he nodded.

"What's all this—" Safety started, before he was interrupted by a giant yawn. He blinked his eyes into focus, then tried again. "What's all the whispering?" he demanded.

"Planning. We whisper because we're scoundrels, and we're up to something," Sanction replied, deadpan.

"That's true," Safety said, slowly rolling up from the floor to a standing position. "Ugh. Basements."

"Want to see the plan?" Piccolo asked.

"Of course," Safety winced, and he rubbed at his eye. "Plans are better than breakfast."

"Piccolo goes in and makes the stab with the syringe," Sanction said. "You've got the reins of the stolen goat cart, and Gapjaw is back-up. I'm holding back a few blocks away, and after the three of you are away, I go in and tell the victim what the situation is, then I melt away into the crowd."

"You are one of the most wanted people in this city," Safety frowned. "What makes you think you can get away?"

"Three blocks over you'll be ready to pick me up," Sanction said. "Here's the diagram for the first attempt. We can refine our technique as needed."

"I don't like you having no backup," Safety muttered as he looked over the precise charcoal drawing. "I don't like Piccolo operating alone either."

"This works if we pick the right setting, with minimal security and crowds," Sanction shrugged.

"We could certainly do that," Safety nodded, "if we had the time and manpower to scout the sites, spy on their schedules, deploy back-up gangs in case something goes wrong, or, you know the normal prep for a job like this. Instead, the whole city is looking to collect a flatteringly robust bounty on each one of us."

"He's right," Gapjaw muttered, sleepy, still laying on the floor.

Sanction spared him a look. "We do this fast, in and out. We're experienced in close quarters maneuvering. If we overthink this we lose our momentum. You want to live in a basement for the next five years?" he demanded.

"He's right too," Gapjaw shrugged.

"Go back to sleep," Piccolo said, irritable. He returned his attention to the plan. "We could have a couple breakaway contingency plans," he said.

"Well, think fast," Sanction said. "This afternoon, we stake out the location and do our scouting. Our second target will be here tonight; his habits are well known because he's untouchable. He'll have guards, but that's fine." He leaned back in his chair. "Make ready, my friends. Tonight we strike back with a blow that will sting Lord Rowan deep enough he'll remember us."

Gapjaw's snore spoiled the moment.

"That's a rift welder," the Mistress of Tides said suddenly, interrupting the long silence. "The Spirit Wardens mean to attempt stitching the Mirror back together where the spirit well cracked it."

Red blearily regarded the cobbled square below, the Bluecoats in defensive positions, and the Warden Initiates with their distinctive half-masks struggling with the equipment. Crates, cabling, some sort of grating apparatus.

"Is that good for us?" Red asked, irritated by how petulant she sounded.

"We are going to blow it up," the Mistress of Tides replied. "While they are getting into position, it's time for us to act." She rolled to the side and crawled away from the edge of the building, then rose to her feet in the shadowy interior. Nails the bat regarded her quizzically, and Red petted his head.

"You stay here," she murmured. "Backup. Backup?"

Nails let out one loud echolocating click, as loud as fingers snapping.

"Good boy," Red said with a faint smile. Then she followed the Mistress of Tides.

They followed the broken stairs down from the top floor, descending into the midday shadows, just beyond the Bluecoat cordon. Red froze as she spotted a figure seated in the alley behind the house.

"Relax, it's Neap," the Mistress of Tides murmured. They approached Neap, and the Mistress of Tides took him aside for a brief exchange too quiet for Red to follow. Neap nodded, then left on his errand, picking his way through the wreckage of the alley.

"What was that?" Red asked, nodding towards the retreating adept.

"Part of the larger plan," the Mistress of Tides replied. "Let's focus on our part."

Red shrugged and let it drop. "How do we do this?" she asked.

"I've been watching, and it looks like about thirty Bluecoats, ten Initiates, and one Spirit Warden. The local Bluecoat station is some distance away, it would take at least fifteen minutes for them to become aware of distress and send reinforcements, and I am not certain they would. This neighborhood has a bad reputation, Bluecoats only come here in force."

"We need to get Inkletta's body back into that basement, is that the—" Red paused as a crackle of gunfire split the quiet afternoon. She scrambled over to a gap in the walls around the courtyard, the Mistress of Tides at her heels. They saw Bluecoats and Initiates come up out of the ruined tower's basement, hauling bodies.

More bodies.

There were a lot of corpses down there.

"We are going to have to move fast and stay cool," the Mistress of Tides said tonelessly. "Can you do it, Red?"

Red's face twitched. "I'm so tired," she murmured. Then she cleared her throat and nodded. "But I can make it through this. Don't you worry about me." She looked over at the Whisper. "We need to get Inkletta back."

"Yes," the Mistress of Tides agreed. She pointed her veil at the sky. "Maybe twenty minutes until the Blind Hour. That is when we'll strike." She regarded Red. "Here's the plan."

RUNWATER CORNERS, CROW'S FOOT.
24TH ELISAR. TWELFTH HOUR PAST DAWN. THE BLIND HOUR.

Fog was creeping up from the river, rolling silently between the buildings.

"I like it better when I can see 'em coming," grimaced one of the Bluecoats. He turned up the flame on his lantern, peering into the layers of fog that drifted into the courtyard.

Nearby, the ritual circle was hastily scrawled on the floorboards with charcoal, candles lit on the points, and incense sent its questing columns of smoke up into the disruption of the light breeze as its flesh smoldered. The Mistress of Tides sat, legs crossed, back straight. One hand gripped a stray cat, and the cat's four legs all returned the grip on her forearm, claws sunk into her flesh so blood trickled from the wounds. Her other hand was locked on the cat's head; its eyes were desperate, its ears lay flat, and it growled its rage and fear as its claws flexed in her arm.

"With pain, and with blood, I focus you," she whispered in Hadrathi, her words seeming to push the incense smoke into shapes. "With death, I call you forth." She twisted hard, and with a crunch, the cat's spine gave. Energy sparked and twitched in the nearby spirit well, tumbling loose over the brim of the material world's effort to contain it. Feeling that energy flow loose, the Mistress of Tides deftly guided it, rolling up the stairwell, flopping over sideways into the corpse pile of cultists. A dark smile creased her features as she infused the energy into the bodies, flaring through the hydraulics of their muscles and searing energy through their electrochemical nerves.

"Come, Shrouded Queen," the Mistress of Tides murmured almost soundlessly. "See the gift I have made for you on this side of the Mirror."

The pile of corpses twitched, and one of the cripple corpses let out a loud groan. The two Bluecoats standing by the pile pivoted, alarmed.

"What's the big idea?" one demanded, unable to believe anyone would be so committed to a prank that they would climb into a pile of corpses. He drew his pistol, pointing it at the pile.

A corpse sat up, and he shot it.

Then another one sat up, and one rolled off to push up to all fours. One Bluecoat let out a hefty scream and bolted, the other emptied the other chamber of his gun into a twitching body, then swore loudly and tore his sword from its scabbard, laying into the corpses as they found fresh power.

The pile rolled at him, and several rising bodies at once lunged for him; however, his fellow Bluecoats were with him, and a combination of shot and bludgeoning put the bodies back down in more pieces than ever.

"I hate Runwater Corners," one growled, and he spat to the side as he reloaded his pistol.

"You aren't the only one," muttered the Bluecoat next to him, looking around. "Better check the perimeter positions."

"Note those who are missing, and do your best to tell if it's desertion or foul play," the sergeant said, his eyes on the corpse pile. "Meantime we have a job to do, and Spirit Warden backup."

"But it's the other way round, isn't it, sarge?" one Bluecoat piped up. "The Wardens have their mission here, and we're helping them out."

"We're dealing with a dug-in cult," the sergeant replied, flinty. "That's bad for everyone, and we all do our part to clean it up when it spills up out of the basements. Any more questions?" he growled, staring around the group. "Right then, back to it, stay in groups of three. Be careful so we all make it home." He nodded, and they moved to carry out his orders. "Everything alright up here?" an Initiate called from the stairs down to the spirit well basement.

"Just some pockets of loose energy," the sergeant replied. "You must be shaking things up down there." Then he turned away, regarding the fog-shrouded courtyard and the jumble of buildings surrounding it. "We'll keep it secure up here," he said, and he shook his head. Another wave of fog wiped out the view of the far end of the courtyard.

On the other side of the stairs leading down to the spirit well, the fog was underlit by sparks and plasm flares as the initiates worked to assemble the welder. One of the three Bluecoats looked down the stairs uneasily, the other two watched the fog.

"D'you suppose what they're doing down there is—wholesome?" one asked, his lip curled with disgust.

"No," the other two answered flatly in unison.

All three of them swiveled their heads towards a new sound in the fog; the halting grind of a metal-shod wheel against the cobbles. It was impossible to make out how far away the cart was as the sound rolled around in the fog.

One of the Bluecoats exchanged a look with the others, and raised his lantern, heading in that direction. "Who goes there?" he demanded.

"Blind Nelly," replied a quavering voice, "headed to market. It is market day, yes?"

"You picked the wrong day," the Bluecoat said, trying unsuccessfully to keep the sneer from his voice. "Go home, old woman." He saw the cloaked figure, and her wheelbarrow, but he stopped short when he saw there was a masked, unconscious woman sprawled in the wheelbarrow.

"What—" he started to say, but Red stepped out of cover and drove her blade right into his throat, a clean life-ending strike. The Bluecoat spasmed back, clutching at his throat, eyes wide; Red nodded to him, and he fell.

The lantern's glass shattered, and the flame whiffed out. Red ducked over behind the low wall, and the Mistress of Tides vanished back into the mist. Another Bluecoat came to investigate.

"Tocker?" he said, hesitant. "You okay?" He saw the wheelbarrow, unattended. His danger sense served him well, and he immediately took a step back, then turned to see Red one step away, daggers out.

He managed to get his gun out of its holster, but he could not pull the trigger; her knife drove up under his chin into his brain, and he keeled over as his knees buckled.

Enough sounds of death reached the third Bluecoat that he retreated down the stairs. "We may have some trouble up here," he announced.

Then the wheelbarrow crashed into him from behind, surprising him and knocking him off balance to topple down half of the flight, banging into the landing and recovering his balance. He shook his head and looked back up the stairs to see Red with her pistols out and the Mistress of Tides wrapped in silk and mist.

The basement had undergone significant changes since the Spirit Wardens had begun work. Now they all halted, looking at the newcomers. There were ten Initiates in the filthy shrine. They were bolting down the racks that somehow regulated the welder, and setting up power stations, and electroplasmic fuel canisters. The man in the center of the room was a Spirit Warden. He turned to face them, and they were close enough to see the etched prayers on his bronze mask, the talismans sewn into the plastron of his armor, and the custom plasmic bullets in his gunbelt.

"I dared hope this would lead me to some of Lord Rowan's scoundrels," the Spirit Warden confessed, a smugness suffusing his tones as the mask amplified and decentralized his voice so it came at them from all directions. "Those guns will do you no good."

"No?" Red retorted, focusing them on the bank of electroplasmic fuel canisters instead of any of the human targets.

"You would bury us all?" the Spirit Warden demanded.

"Make a move," Red said between her teeth. "Find out."

He cocked his head to the side. "You have announced yourself without attacking. A curious strategy, unless you're ready to parlay."

The Mistress of Tides trembled as she wrestled invisibly with a slippery kind of energy. She assumed a stance, and the Spirit Warden chuckled, a hollow and deadening sound.

"We are in a basement, you know," he said. "You think to call down lightning here?"

The Mistress of Tides finally lined up her energy and dropped to one knee, her palm slapping the floor, drawing a crooked bolt of energy from the ruptured spirit well that flashed with impossible brightness as it drove into the Spirit Warden's back. He was knocked off his feet, and Red pounced on him, jamming her gun between his jawbone and the base of his skull, below the strap that kept the mask on. She pulled the trigger, and the muffled crack pounded a bullet up into his brain; there was no surviving that.

"Get out," the Mistress of Tides said, her voice flat, her eyes invisible behind her veil. Lightning flickered along the edges of her garb. Red pushed up off the Spirit Warden's corpse and backed to the side, guns trained on the Initiates.

One of them put his hands up and edged towards the stairs, then scrambled up, past the Mistress of Tides. That one example was enough to resolve the moment, and the rest of them left also. The Mistress of Tides almost swaggered down the rest of the stairs, walking past the Spirit Warden's body without a glance.

"Won't they just get the Bluecoats and come back down?" Red asked in a low voice.

"The Bluecoats have their hands full," the Mistress of Tides confided. Just then, two of her adepts came down the stairs, supporting Inkletta's senseless body between them.

"Now for the hard part," the Mistress of Tides said, and she set her jaw. The adepts hefted the body over by the ruptured spirit well, and lay her down on her side. They retreated to the base of the stairs, and waited. The Mistress of Tides stood before the spirit well.

"I can sense your turmoil," she whispered in Hadrathi. "One of you will escape into these bones, and the other will be locked away. I call now to Inkletta, to abandon the Shrouded Queen and dive back into her blood."

Red glanced over at Inkletta. "Is there—is there enough room to get out?" she asked hesitantly.

"Yes, a wide crack," the Mistress of Tides murmured. "The lightning pushed it open wider."

A long moment of quiet lay between them. Red looked at Inkletta, whose spirit mask was a charred ruin, her face burned, no discernable breathing. At least her limbs had not stiffened.

"How will we know—" Red started, then she whipped her guns to orient on Inkletta's body, whose back arched as it gasped in an impossible amount of air. The spirit mask's charred remains sprayed off her face.

"Now, Inkletta!" the Mistress of Tides shouted abruptly, extending her hand. Inkletta's hand slapped into it, and she swung to her feet and down to the altar, on her knees, blasting it with some kind of energy as she drove her palm against the stone, the physical shape that hid the energy of the spirit well.

Both Whispers shuddered, then relaxed.

"It is done," the Mistress of Tides said, "and we got Inkletta back."

"You can tell just by looking?" Red asked, skeptical.

"I see things you don't," the Mistress of Tides replied. "Now we really must be going."

"Can you walk?" Red asked Inkletta.

"Yes, I believe so," Inkletta replied. She was hot to the touch. "I am still full of—of energy, let's say," she managed. Her balance returned at once, and she took a few steps.

"Let's get out of here," Red said through her teeth, and the three women headed up the stairs together, the Mistress of Tides' adepts behind them.

At the top, three cowled and masked figures met them in the mist outside the ruined tower.

"Payment as promised, your way cleared to take the electroplasmic canisters," the Mistress of Tides said to them. "Now we need to meet your boss."

One of the masked figures nodded gesturing for them to follow, trotting into the mist. The other two stayed by the tower.

"This is all according to plan?" Red muttered to the Mistress of Tides, looking all around.

"Pretty much," the Mistress of Tides nodded.

Red's mouth closed to a thin line.

Their guide led them up a staircase built into the side of a building, to a flat rooftop hemmed in on two sides by higher stories on the building. There, several more masked figures waited, along with the rest of the Mistress of Tides' adepts.

"You were successful?" one masked figure asked.

"Inkletta has returned to us, yes," the Mistress of Tides said with an incline of her head. "Now, you can have all the electroplasmic fuel canisters. I recommend you use one or two to collapse the tower ruin and keep the Spirit Wardens away from it."

"Is it sealed?" the masked figure demanded.

"Not forever, not wholly, but enough," the Mistress of Tides shrugged. "It is a slow trickle, and it is no longer active enough to hide deaths from the Deathseeker crows of Bellweather Crematorium. The Spirit Wardens should lose interest in the area."

"Good enough," the masked figure said. He threw some hand gestures at the others, and the three of them retreated in different directions off the rooftop.

"Were those the Wraiths? Tell me those were the Wraiths," Red whispered to the Mistress of Tides.

"Those were the Wraiths," the Mistress of Tides whispered back. "I had my adepts ask around, see who was upset with Lord Rowan's treatment of the gondoliers. Who might be willing to back a play to pour some sand in his sheets. I took a risk and involved the Wraiths, and as long as we keep it moving and do not give them any clues to sell to other hunters, we get away with it."

Red paused. "Do you figure they were gentle with the Bluecoats?" she asked.

The Mistress of Tides' veil was impossible to read. "Gentler than you, certainly," she replied. "Time to go."

Red nodded, and followed the Whispers and adepts off the roof, back down to the street, and towards the underground.

Behind them, not far away, a massive explosion rocked the earth, and the last remains of a long-unsteady tower finally crashed into the ruptured foundation.

CHAPTER TEN

It was the early 30s, the Sepulcherian Company of the Silver Nails had staked out territory in the Lost District outside the city's lightning barriers. The Severosian cavalry wanted haunted ground for training their horses to fight ghosts, and isolation to discourage scoundrels from tampering with their expensive horseflesh.

Like all the officers, Grainer was an adept. He was on an errand into the city when he saw a little girl, not even ten, chased by a ghost. He was ready to swoop in and save the day when he saw her take hold of the ghost and rip it open. When he found out she was homeless, he adopted her.

Silver is a noble metal because it does not corrode. It also holds enchantments well. When Grainer gave her the first of many silver weapons, she solemnly told him she wished her blood was silver too—enchanted and incorruptible. After that, he gave her the nickname Red Silver, like her blood could be pure too. She thought her blood was dirty and haunted. Maybe Grainer was too hasty to suggest otherwise. He had no way to know what her eventual betrayal would cost him or the Company, but even if he had, I don't think he would have loved her any less.

— From unpublished notes on Silver Nails and the Lost District by historian Garnel Taldorian

ROWAN MANSION. SIX TOWERS.
24TH ELISAR. TENTH HOUR PAST DAWN.

The wax cylinder slowly turned, and the wavering shadow of music emerged from the amplifying cone over the machine. Saint rested in the overstuffed chair, regarding the luminous painting of a field, imagined before the sky shattered and the sun's brilliance sank into irrevocable shadow. Radiant strands in the paint gave the textures a sketchy echoing effect, memory half experienced in a drowsing mind.

Lord Rowan pushed the door open and strolled in. "You sent for me," he said.

"Yes," Saint replied, not taking his eyes from the painting. "I found a message in the Ministry paper for the 20th, the masthead has a comma turned into a period. I think that was an invitation to meet, probably somewhere around Canter's Lowland. I'm not sure who placed it, but the message was likely aimed at Sanction. And on the 22nd, there's a message in 'Horticultural Dailies' that I'm pretty sure is designed to lure Trellis to the Vancell Gardens in Nightmarket." He spared Lord Rowan a look. "Pretty sure about those two."

"I can verify the one on the 20th," Lord Rowan said. "An assassin engaged them in Canter's Lowland."

"And he didn't make it," Saint added, half a smile on his face. "So that means there were probably a number of them."

"All it means is that they got lucky," Lord Rowan snapped. "The remains were found by a Leech named Workshop, who returned the corpse to us with most of his gear intact."

"Neither crew generally deals with Workshop," Saint said, "but we knew they wouldn't go to anyone they normally go to. At least we know they were hurt. Did Workshop give up any details on that?"

"The group that sent the assassin has particular feelings about having their people returned unmolested, so Workshop got a pass," Lord Rowan said through his teeth.

"You could send someone to charm it out of him," Saint prompted.

"Yes, that's a good plan," Lord Rowan agreed, "and my backup efforts discovered he closed up shop and relocated. He has not yet surfaced."

"Tough break," Saint said, furrowing his brow. "Who did you contract assassins with? I bet you can get some of the finest talent it the field. Have they already sent out a follow-up?"

"I did contract with the best, they have sent out a follow up, and it's just a matter of time; but I grow impatient," Lord Rowan said through his teeth, looking Saint in the eye. "I want this done!"

"Right, I'm with you," Saint nodded. "How about the lead on the 22nd?"

"We need to move on that," Lord Rowan said. "Any idea who we're looking for?"

"The more level-headed membership," Saint reflected. "Sanction and Piccolo are likely to think they can do things on their own, make their own plans. The others, though, they will probably feel like they are lost without a master plan. Really, Trellis... he's the only one that threatens you," Saint said as he squinted at Lord Rowan. "The others can make some noise, do some collateral damage, but success will make them sloppier and bolder. When Trellis makes his move, he's going to crack the bone."

"I can see how you would think highly of his efforts," Lord Rowan sniffed.

"Under Trellis I get to run my crew and be a big shot in Silkshore," Saint shrugged. "Under you, I get to become invisible and I can have anything I want." His smile was wide and bright. "Trellis is a danger, and I'm saying we go after him, so we can get on with my new and improved life."

"Alright, let's kill Trellis," Lord Rowan said. "What do we do?"

"If I know Trellis, and I don't, but I'm more familiar with him than most," Saint said, "he's been working out some kind of plan with contingencies and elaborate galleries so that no matter what parts don't work out, something gets through. That takes time," Saint shrugged, "and I figure at least ten days before he's ready to move."

"But he's somewhere in the meantime," Lord Rowan pressed.

"We have to lure him to us," Saint explained, "because this crazy son of a bitch might be hiding in an echo neighborhood that can only be accessed with a ghost key. He might be in a submerged wreck of a ship with a ventilation system under the docks. He could be in the servant quarters of your political rival. He could be in a secret room in the basement of the University library, coming out to study at night. The true story is probably weirder than any of these things. Lord Belderan, the Trellis of Barrowcleft, does not tell other people about his backup plans. They are elaborate, they are aggressively creative, and they position him to strike." Saint shook his head. "I say we go after his family. How many of them do you have in Ironhook so far?" He shrugged. "You know. Trump up some charges."

Lord Rowan was quiet for a moment, rubbing his chin, looking at the mass of newspapers spread out over the table.

"Lord Rowan?" Saint prompted.

"You may not know this," Lord Rowan said, "but Trellis was once the Unseen Hand, a high-level agent in the Hive. One way that he got there was by having a number of family members embedded in that organization. I do have the resources to target the Hive and push them back out of this business, but that would require rearranging my assets; it is an escalation I hope to avoid," he said as he stared at the table, avoiding eye contact with Saint.

Saint unhelpfully allowed the silence to gather weight.

"I'll send some agents to the Vancell Gardens," Lord Rowan said, abruptly turning away and walking to the door, where one of his seneschals waited for orders.

"The Hive," Saint quietly scoffed. "Do you want this guy, or don't you?" He drained his wine glass and smacked his lips with satisfaction.

OUTSIDE SAROOL'S HOUSE CUISINE, UNITY PARK, BRIGHTSTONE. 24TH ELISAR. TWELFTH HOUR PAST DAWN.

The crisp clatter of well-shod goats and metal-bound carriage wheels was the sound of affluence on the move. The plasmic light poles that had replaced the old coal-burning lamps laid out sharp shadows that barely flickered. The broad street around the hexagon of Unity Park was relatively clean, carriage drivers were more defensive than reckless, and there were few vantage points that did not include a Bluecoat on patrol.

"I am a fugitive, you know," Safety said under his breath as he furtively glanced around, a carter's cap low over his brow. "Places like this make fugitives all itchy." He paused. "Then caught," he added.

"Steady on, little one," Gapjaw rumbled, hanging on the side of the stolen carriage like an experienced porter, looking up at where Safety sat on the buckboard. "We have every likelihood this won't get noisy."

"You are almost always wrong about that," Safety complained quietly. "I think you just say it. You don't have any sort of factual base at all."

"I'm surprised they let babies cry here," Gapjaw reflected. "I would think it would be against an ordinance."

Safety squinted around. "I don't hear—" he caught himself, then scowled down at Gapjaw. "You are hilarious," he growled.

"Right?" Gapjaw agreed with a wide grin.

The carriage's sedate pace took it past the front of Sarool's House Cuisine, a magnificent five story restaurant that boasted the best Iruvian food in Doskvol as well as one of the most expensive facades ringing the park. As they rolled past, the carriage slowed, Gapjaw opened the door, and Piccolo took a long step to the curb, headed straight for the front door. He was dashing in his black suit and white shirt, his outfit balanced credibly between staff uniform and restaurant patron. He held a case tight to his chest. In moments he was through the door and melting into the crowd of patrons waiting to be seated, and the carriage continued rolling slowly down the street.

"I'm looking for Lord Swint," Piccolo said to the seating host as he smoothly cut to the front of the queue.

"Please wait your turn," the host replied from the far end of politeness.

"I am not a patron," Piccolo persisted, showing the small case he held, angled so the seating host could see it was cuffed to his wrist. "I am a courier with the Ministry and I have an urgent delivery for Lord Swint."

"I see," the host said, raising an eyebrow. He snapped his fingers, and a smartly dressed young woman stepped forward. "Second mezzanine, quadrant two," the host murmured, and the young woman nodded. She led Piccolo into the opulence of the restaurant.

The main floor was lit by candles, and tables had a bowl of oil at the center with a column of flame rising from its surface. The second floor did not have candles, but was instead lit by radiant plants growing from strategically placed planters, and from arrangements in the center of the table.

Passing through the fashion show of the main floor, the waiter and Piccolo reached the stairs, rising up to the higher mezzanine. The quality of light was different here, as it flowed through water. There were radiant plants, but most of the light came from giant walls and columns of water tanks that held living things bred to glow. They rounded the jellyfish tank, and passed a tank with small sharks. Skeletons shone through the complicated shark skin, projecting wrinkles and patterns on the inside of the water tank as the sharks moved, the brightest light coming from the ranks of teeth in their shadowless mouths.

A back alcove held a small party of six, with Lord Swint holding court. He looked up as Piccolo approached, noting his black outfit and case, and grunted to himself. "Please excuse me," the corpulent man said to his guests. His expression was somewhere between a scowl and a sneer, but it had the lived-in look of furrowed displeasure that was seldom shifted. His clothes were dark and expensive, as were his companions. He gestured greedily for the case, and Piccolo approached, putting the case on the table in front of him.

"Never a dull moment," Lord Swint growled as he pulled out his key. He prodded at the lock with the key, and it didn't go in. "What's this?" he ground out, his expression darkening.

"Let me try," Piccolo said, pressing the key at the lock and triggering the secret catch that opened it with his other hand. "There we are."

As Lord Swint picked up the envelope sealed with wax, Piccolo slid the syringe into the back of his upper arm, depressing the plunger.

Lord Swint jerked around to stare at him. "What are you doing? What was that?" he demanded.

"What—was what?" Piccolo replied, wide eyed with innocence.

"Get out of here," Lord Swint snarled, and he broke the seal and read the message as Piccolo vanished into the restaurant.

"That's... interesting," Lord Swint murmured, his face closing like a fist as he considered a mystery. "You lot stay here." With difficulty, he levered himself out of his seat. His two bodyguards also rose, and he waved them away with irritation. "Just going to relieve myself," he grumbled, and he waddled towards the back of the mezzanine.

Once he entered the dim tiled space, lit only with lamps, he squinted around. "Lord Hesanath?" he growled.

"He's not here," Sanction replied, stepping out of the shadows. "That was a ruse to get you here so we could talk." He paused. "I could have sent you a note, but I wanted to be sure you understood your situation. I wanted absolute clarity," he said, something in his paleness and the softness of his tone that gave weight to his words and prickled the back of the skin on Lord Swint's neck.

"Cheeky bastard, I could have you whipped for this," he grunted.

"You are going to die," Sanction replied. "All of us are, sooner or later, but you've got maybe a week. Your death will be horrific," he added, raising his eyebrows. "You will scream with pain until you drown, your lungs full of filth."

Lord Swint stared at him for a moment, then reached into his coat and pulled out a surprisingly large knife. "You try it, runt. You just try it," he rasped.

"It's done," Sanction shrugged. "Remember that pinch, when you got the note?"

Lord Swint blinked, then blinked again. "Bullshit," he roared.

"Dolorous Crimson," Sanction said. "It undercuts your life energy, and the body breaks down.

Lord Swint seemed to inflate with rage. "You will not make it out of here alive!" he roared.

"I like my odds better than yours," Sanction replied with a wintery smile. "The Rowan family is about to have a number of expensive funerals."

"Guards!" Lord Swint shouted, taking his eyes off Sanction for a second.

When he turned back, Sanction was gone. Of *course* there were back ways out of the restrooms.

Lord Swint gripped the counter top as his two bodyguards raced in to join him. Glaring at the mirror, he blamed nerves for the peculiar dizzy spell, as fear bloomed through him.

ADRIFT IN DREAMS

The boy dressed in white ran along the dim gray hedge. The broken crimson sky leaked darkness that pooled in shadows, across the colorless shoulder of the lawn. Ahead the ball bounced and rolled as though possessed of a mind of its own. Laughing, the boy with golden curls followed, but the metallic sheen of his hair was flattened out to paleness in the lived memory of the dream.

Like quicksilver the snake crossed his path, and he felt the same dip in adrenaline he had as a child, the same tightening, the same moment of fear. However, this time, he was not alone.

Slowly, he broke with the dream's script, turning to find a fresh-faced young man standing behind him dressed in lightless robes. The pale young man smiled.

"I thought we should meet," he said. "I am the Razor Wind, a Whisper. And you are Lord Cleith Rowan, yes?"

"Are—is this my dream?" the boy asked hesitantly.

"Please permit me to be bold," Razor Wind said with an indulgent tone. He gestured, adding dozens of years to Rowan, shifting their meeting room to a study in the main chambers of his rooms in Whitecrown. Snow drifted down outside as Lord Rowan now had wine in his glass, and Razor Wind stood before him with a matching glass.

"My chambers are warded against intrusion like this," Rowan said with a frown.

"The ancestral home's protections are better than those in your lodgings in Whitecrown," Razor Wind shrugged. "Besides which, I am no ordinary talent." He sipped his wine.

"Do you mean me harm?" Rowan asked, eyes on the dream image of Razor Wind.

"I don't care about you at all," Razor Wind replied. "Six days ago you had a party. A curse was revealed at that party, somehow. I need to know more."

A slow smile spread across Rowan's face. "I am willing to help you, if you will help me. I am trying to locate the person I think you're after, as well as that person's associates. I am looking to kill them."

"I will kill the one with the curse," Razor Wind said, "but I care nothing for the rest."

"Very well," Rowan nodded. "A young woman, she goes by the name Red Silver, and is a scoundrel working for the River Stallions. My considerable assets are focused on finding her and her allies. It will not be long," he said, "but if you get to her first, then by all means, do what you must. I would like you to tell me when it's finished, if you would."

"Fine," Razor Wind replied. "What do you know?"

"She is a hunter and a sniper, skilled in gunplay," Rowan said quietly. "She is bonded with a bat that helps her scout. She is friends with two Whispers, Inkletta and Mistress of Tides. Her curse was revealed at a séance contacting one of my ancestors, a master of the occult. He chose to ride her flesh, then felt the cage of curse runes affecting the body, and burst out. That shredded the ritual that hid her, and as far as I know she has not been seen since," he said.

Razor Wind watched him for a moment. "No clues, no further suggestions for where I might find her?" he asked.

"If I knew more I would have her already," Rowan said. "I do have some more life details, background color, information on her associates, that sort of thing."

"Make a copy, bundle it up, and leave it with the barkeep in the Gyroscope," Razor Wind said. He paused. "Are you the sort of man who remembers your dreams?" he asked quietly. "Or do you think this will slip away?"

Rowan watched him for a long moment. "Time will tell, I suppose," he said.

"Regardless, you gave me what I need to keep going," Razor Wind shrugged.

"We could be partners, you know," Rowan said quickly. "I have a contingent of Whispers, but you are extraordinary. We should meet. In person, you know. We might be able to work something out."

Razor Wind almost smiled. "I'll consider it," he said, then he stepped back out of the dream, leaving Rowan alone.

Lord Rowan snapped awake, blinking, and sat up on the settle in his study.

"Dammit," he muttered to himself, looking over at the hall to the more heavily-warded bedroom. He let out a deep sigh, rubbing at his eyes, then rose to his feet, crossed to the desk, and began quickly writing down everything he could remember about the dream.

SURBAN ESTATE, BRIGHTSTONE.
24TH ELISAR. HOUR OF PEARLS, 6 HOURS PAST DUSK.

A low rumble of thunder woke the sleeping man; his eyes twitched open to see the silhouette of a silent man standing over him. The sleeper scrabbled towards his bell pull, but his arm was expertly caught and twirled around into a lock, and a syringe stuck him in the chest. Then the shadow pulled back. Another man stepped forward, this one not wearing a mask, half his face lit by the glare of the plasmic lamp outside.

"Lord Surban," he said quietly.

"What—what do you want?" the noble sputtered.

"I want you to know that you're going to die, in about a week. You've been given an injection that makes that inevitable now."

"Alright," Surban said, sitting up in bed, rubbing at his wrist. "Alright, I see. Now we negotiate, yes?" He shrugged. "You could stab me, but instead you stick me with something. Give me a week to live. So you want something." He squinted. "Tell me."

"You will suffer," Sanction murmured. "Your panic will rise. You will spend money on treatments. Your feeling of helplessness will be underscored by mounting agony. You will gather your loved ones to you, and they will mourn your loss. You will extract promises, and settle unfinished business." Sanction paused. "That is what I want. And I'll get it," he shrugged.

"That's not reasonable," Surban said, puzzled. "You have gone to some trouble to put yourself in a position of dominance over me. Why not use it?"

"I am using it," Sanction murmured. He paused. "Your half-brother is Lord Cleith Rowan."

"Ah," Surban said with a nod.

"He is destroying my life, and that's not without consequence," Sanction said.

"He hates me," Surban said. "You're doing him a favor."

A bleak smile touched Sanction's lips. "He is a nobleman and you are his blood. Internal divisions tend to be minimized when the family as a whole comes under attack." Sanction shrugged. "And if I'm wrong, then you will be a message that I am serious. Your pain and death are still useful. Sooner or later, I'll get to the family members he does care about."

"For what it's worth, you might want to aim your efforts closer to the Leviathan hunting ships. He idolizes the uncles and cousins that run the ships themselves. Me? I'm into education and art," he said with a wry smile, "and that's never been something that enthuses my dear brother."

"We'll see," Sanction replied with a hard smile, and he stepped back, following the other shadowy figure out of the bedroom.

Surban regarded the single drop of blood on his skin from the injection, and heaved a deep sigh.

MATHER OUTFITTING COMPANY, THE DOCKS. 25TH ELISAR. SECOND HOUR PAST DAWN.

"I'm kind of tired of stealing carts," Safety confessed, rubbing at his eyes in the early morning light.

"Nobody cares," Gapjaw shrugged, sitting on the buckboard next to him. "Puffs?" he offered, brandishing a paper bag still steaming with the roasted mushroom caps inside.

"I don't even like these," Safety scowled, taking the caps. "Too much garlic."

"Don't you worry, I'm taking notes, to submit to 'Maybe Someone Cares, Daily' in case you might make the front page." Gapjaw grinned, chewing with his mouth open.

At the other end of the alley, Sanction and Piccolo looked across the street at Saltford's, a massive stone bank. The lamp posts down its flank supported several hanging corpses.

"So I guess the message is, 'don't try to rob the bank,'" Piccolo muttered.

"More to the point, if you do, no one can help you," Sanction nodded. "Good thing we're not robbing the bank."

"Not yet, anyway," Piccolo shrugged. "When all this mess is over, I want to go back to proper heists." He sniffed. "Always did want to rob a bank."

"Stay hungry, my friend," Sanction replied with a dangerous grin. Then they rounded the corner, mounting the boardwalk and heading through the main doors, into the Outfitter.

The Outfitter supplier started out equipping ships for voyages, and over the centuries morphed into a high-end fashion shop for those in the shipping culture. The framed pictures, paintings, and displayed tools conveyed the story as well as projecting a certain style to attract captains, ship owners, and those who made their fortunes on the Void Sea. Sanction and Piccolo followed the wall of windows towards the suits and the tailoring area.

They veered off as they got closer, because there were half a dozen competent bodyguards lounging around waiting while Lord Grainbalt was fitted for a suit by the tailor. He stood on the dais, mirrors on three sides, chalk marks sketched on the fabrics draped across his powerful form to customize the expensive suits so they fit him perfectly.

"Maybe don't sass talk this one," Piccolo said through his teeth, eyeing the bodyguards from a safe distance behind a rack of sealskin boots.

"You've got the right idea," Sanction agreed. "I'll back you up, just in case." He handed Piccolo the syringe. "Good luck."

"This isn't as easy as it looks, you know," Piccolo frowned.

"That's why we trust the task to an expert," Sanction shrugged with a winning smile.

Piccolo sidled around the side to the tailor's station, and when the little man came in to get fresh chalk, Piccolo stepped out of nowhere and put a knife against the old man's ribs.

"I am going out with you," he whispered. "I am your assistant for the next few minutes. I have friends nearby. If it goes poorly for me, it goes poorly for you. Nod if you understand."

The tailor nodded. Piccolo sheathed the knife. "Now," he said, "how can I look convincing?"

The tailor draped a white cloth over his shoulder and handed him a box, then headed back out, Piccolo at his heels.

"—can still make it to Farzia's for lunch with Captain Bowdare, right?" Lord Grainbalt said to his dashing, broad-shouldered assistant.

"It's going to be tight," his assistant shrugged, "considering we had to get the fitting in now."

"Well the gala is in two days," Lord Grainbalt said, "and Mr. Cayanno is the best, aren't you, Mr. Cayanno?" He chuckled at the tailor, who bowed deeply. "I'm not so effete that I need everyone to come out to my manor, not yet. I can still remember working for a living," he said with a sneer that cast doubt on how serious his light-hearted comment was. "You change your money, don't let your money change you."

Several of his entourage agreed heartily, none of them going so far as to applaud. He smiled at them, benign, as Piccolo pretended to measure his feet for shoes.

"Hey," Lord Grainbalt said, frowning down at him. "Watch the pins."

"So sorry," Piccolo said with a quick nod, glancing at the tailor then taking his box and heading to the back.

Sanction watched the tailor; would he reveal that he had been coerced, and therefore put Lord Grainbalt at risk? Or would he pretend nothing happened, and avoid being involved in whatever just happened? The tailor carried on as though everything was normal, and a few minutes later, Sanction and Piccolo were in the cart as it rumbled away along a dockside street.

VANCELL GARDENS, NIGHTMARKET.
25TH ELISAR. FOURTH HOUR PAST DAWN.

"Too soon to get discouraged," the Hammer muttered to Niece. He swigged his opaque green drink, glancing furtively around. "We're fine."

Niece heaved a sigh. They sat at a table in the area where the manual laborers shuffled in, an ever-shifting roster of people capable of work and desperate for pay. Soon, a foreman would be along to look them over and evaluate their ability to move the heavy planters, bags, and equipment of the nursery. This was not a place to get curious about anyone else's life story.

"The signal has run for two days," Niece said under her breath. "I think he must have missed it."

"Or he's watching us right now," the Hammer shrugged. "We don't know. We *can't* know. But what I do know for sure is that we need his help." He took another swig. "So we wait."

"What are you drinking?" she demanded, staring at his glass, the liquid oozing slowly down the wall.

"Superfood," he replied reflectively. "All mushed up. I think there's octopus involved. Kelp, for sure."

"How is it?" she asked with a wince.

"Enhanced," he grinned back, tugging the lapel of his tattered work coat open to reveal a now-empty flask.

She rolled her eyes. The dim hum of conversation was soothing, and the four story nursery had open space for about a third of the building, all the way up, and raised beds with seedlings of radiant plants on every floor. The front door had a bar and grill to one side of the lobby, the manual workers penned up on the other side behind a screen of plants. The first round of workers had already been picked up, and it would be an hour before the next round was hired. She struggled to make peace with waiting. Then a conversation at the bar across the foyer caught her attention.

"Crooked," the patron insisted, slapping his hand on the bar. "Too much sybariam makes the little plants... the little glowy plants... they come up crooked. *Crooked*. Poor little plants." He shook his head. "I'll have one of those superdrinks," he said.

"Look, pal," the barkeep began.

"Just making a point about the *crooked plants* and how you gotta tie them up with silk string," the man insisted, using the outside-voice loudness of a drunk. "Or they never grow straight."

"That's great, keep it down," the barkeep said with a frown.

"Too much sybariam?" Niece said, standing at the man's elbow. "A common enough problem. Do you tie the seedlings to poles?"

"You can do that," the main said, eyeing her, "but it's a better idea to tie them to a trellis."

"I thought as much," she nodded. "What do you say we get out of here?" She offered him a winning smile.

"Yeah, let's do that," he replied with something like relief. "Keep the superdrink," he said to the barkeep, and he led the way out. The couple headed out into the darkness of the morning streets, the Hammer unobtrusively pacing them.

"What do you know?" Niece asked under her breath.

"Just that I was to make an ass of myself and talk about crooked plants until someone asked me how to prop them up. And to talk about silk string," the man replied in a somewhat petulant tone. "I didn't ask for this, alright? This woman came in and gave me instructions, in exchange for clearing up a little problem that's none of your business."

"This sounds sufficiently elaborate," Niece murmured to herself. "And what do we do now?"

"I take you to an alleyway and get paid," the man shrugged. "Then I go on with my life."

"Sounds like a plan," Niece nodded, wondering how many layers she'd have to penetrate to meet up with Trellis. "Some people are just paranoid," she muttered.

A shadowy figure trailed at a distance, blended with the morning traffic.

Chapter Eleven

You hear them gloating about trailblazing new technologies. They crow about their methods of discovery. It's foolish. They batter open a metal door and pretend the bone door was never there, or that both doors do not lead into the same house. Have they forgotten that this city is five centuries older than its lightning towers?

We harvested Leviathan blood, we emptied ghosts, we drank from the rivers behind the Mirror. We paid a cost for it, and we learned what was safe and what was not, and we had respect. They move too fast, take too much, and ignore all warning signs. The energy they treasure is not defenseless. There will be consequences.

— From the Whisper Grizelda Slake's personal correspondence to Nalia Finn, her apprentice

ROWAN MANSION, SIX TOWERS.
25ᵀᴴ ELISAR. FIFTH HOUR PAST DAWN.

"What," Lord Rowan said flatly, looking up from his paper.

"It's your guest, sir," the servant said. "He is requesting employment records from three of the asylums of Brightstone."

Lord Rowan squinted at that information, then put his paper down on the table, rising to stride from his dining room, down several hallways, to the guarded door. One of the guards saw him coming, unlocking the door and holding it open for him. Lord Rowan strode into the makeshift opulent cell.

"What are you thinking about?" Lord Rowan demanded, standing before Saint, crossing his arms over his chest.

"I've got it!" Saint replied, his face flushed and his eyes bright. "I know where your adept is stashed! Or, very nearly," he admitted. "Safety had some contacts with former rail jacks, and if we can find a new employee hired around 840 who has a background protecting the trains, then we can see if one of those people was promoted to a position of authority. To a position that could hide an adept in a posh oubliette and keep the prisoner out of all human contact until those scoundrels returned to pick him up. It's *perfect*," he insisted. "They would not even need to check on the prisoner, so even if they were found they could not be followed to the site. Food, water, shelter, security, anonymity; these houses are where the families secure their mentally unstable embarrassments."

Lord Rowan frowned thoughtfully. "How many of the scoundrels do you think know where Leslin was hidden?"

"No more than two, maybe just Safety," Saint said. "This is your chance to get the jump on them and rescue your adept before they have a chance to leverage him." His tone was eager, and he trembled. "Be careful though, don't tip your hand or the adept may suffer, and possibly die." He shook his head. "This rescue is going to have to be fast and complete. Plus, you have a chance to lay a trap for when they eventually go to check on him."

"If this lead works out and we retrieve Leslin, that's significant for your future," Lord Rowan said. "You are sure it is one of the asylums you noted to my servant?"

"It has to be," Saint replied, sure. "Inkwine, Soluvian House, or Half Moon Sanitarium."

Lord Rowan shrugged. "I hope you're right," he said. "For your sake." He turned and strode out of the room, barking orders, putting together an expedition. The door locked behind him.

"Oh, I'm right," Saint murmured, thoughtful. He winced, and touched his taped ribs.

TEN FRINGE CORRIDORS, NIGHTMARKET. 25TH ELISAR. FIFTH HOUR PAST DAWN.

"This is it," their guide said, distaste obvious in his voice. He faced the Hammer and Niece. They stood in a broad alleyway almost a dozen feet across, built up almost a dozen feet on each side. "My contact told me to bring you here and leave you." He glanced around, then shrugged. "Good luck," he said, and he pulled his hood lower over his face, turning away and vanishing into the murky shadows.

"Yeah, this feels like a Trellis plan," Niece said under her breath as she scanned the ragged walls flanking the alleyway.

"Think we were followed?" the Hammer asked, resting one hand on the butt of his pistol.

"Maybe. Or maybe local predators picked up our scent." She frowned. "We walked through a kind of stone maze to get here. What's the deal?"

"Oh, the Ten Fringe Corridors are a mess," the Hammer said easily. "Two noble houses and a guild contested ownership over the course of two hundred years, building up the whole region to a height of maybe seven or eight stories. About thirty years ago, the City Council ruled that the parts belonging to each faction that were built on land they did not legally control had to be pulled down and returned to their rightful owners, with the owner paying removal costs. There is about a ten block area savaged down to, or nearly to, ground level. All those little basements, alleyways, walled in areas," he said with fluttering hand gestures, "all exposed to open air as whole buildings were reduced to rubble and carted across town." He shook his head. "The City Council does not tolerate being tied up in this sort of legal challenge without making sure everybody bleeds." He almost smiled. "We're standing in the basement of what was a bookstore, next to a butcher shop, under a warehouse, under a dance studio, next to a townhouse mansion." He shrugged. "Or something. The looting around here, and the contracts from one faction to hinder or hurt the others, made this choice hunting for a while."

"How long do we wait?" Niece sighed.

"Until we have a better idea for catching up to Trellis," the Hammer shrugged. He slid down a wall, feet tucked in near him, and he leaned on his knees.

The first snowflakes fell.

"Fantastic," Niece muttered.

Time passed.

The Hammer blinked. "Rain?" he frowned, and he touched at his face. His fingers came away bloody, and his eyes widened as he looked over at Niece. She turned to look to him, and she flinched as red drop-lets spattered her forehead.

Both of them reached for weapons as they saw a dozen figures standing in the alley, some in each direction, some between them, flickering into view.

"Wait," one grated out. "You see us because we include you in our stealth ritual. We have been here waiting." The figure who spoke wore a ragged cloak, and a face mask with a beak made of what appeared to be wingbones, now looking like clenched teeth as they were woven together. Disk-like goggle lenses hid all feeling.

"Stealth ritual," the Hammer echoed.

"You should follow us," the spokesman said.

The Hammer looked over at Niece, and nodded.

"Our pleasure," she lied.

The group pulled back several dozen feet, then hesitated, and the spokesman looked back.

The shadows on the far end of the alley flexed, and a woman prowled out of them, a pale blade in each hand as she probed the shad-ows with her eyes, stalking forward soundlessly. She flexed one hand, and the blade vanished. She pulled an amulet from her pocket, and whispered to it in Hadrathi, and it pulsed like a tiny sunrise in her hand. She flexed her grip on it, and it levitated, then tugged to the end of its chain, orienting on Niece and the Hammer.

"Quickly," hissed their guide, who led the ragged mob down the al-ley quickly. Behind them, the assassin pulled out a handful of powder and spread it in the air; it gravitated around the shadows where the stealth ritual had cloaked the tattered strangers. The assassin hissed her annoyance, and closed in on them fast.

Running with the others, the Hammer and Niece followed broken steps into a basement, through a hole sledgehammered in the wall that led to an unfinished alley between basements, past two other open-ings, then taking a turn to go down more stairs to knee-deep water, slogging through at speed.

Niece stopped suddenly, the shrouded mystery guides moving around her effortlessly. The Hammer stopped too, turning to look at her.

"Hammer," she said, her voice brittle. "These people." She pointed at crossed saws mounted over the doorway they scrabbled through. "Limmers."

"I know," he ground out. "But we're going with them. Find the nerve." His voice had no mercy, and no harshness. He reached out his hand, insistent, and she put her hand in his. He pulled her along, and the last of the limmers fell in behind them as they clambered through the doorway under the crossed saws.

They found themselves in something of a wind tunnel, a steady wind causing the shrouds around their guides to flap, drying them quickly. The spokesman turned to them, offering each one a medallion.

"Tune to it," he demanded.

The bone flake was black, and carved with an unfamiliar symbol. The Hammer closed his eyes, took a deep breath, let it out slowly, then pointed a level gaze at the bone. He tied all his senses to his sight, then focused, unfocused, and refocused, allowing the medallion to drift in the mid-range, until it seemed to choose a depth where all its details were clear. He felt the sensation in his chest, and knew he was tuned to it. He reached out with his free hand, and Niece grasped his hand. Together, they saw the door in the wall that had not been there before they tuned to it. The door opened, and they entered, along with their escorts. The door closed behind them without a trace.

The silence pressed in on them until their ears rang with the pressure. They followed the broad stairs down to the eerie shadows of the wide circular platform. The ceiling released a kind of time-lapsed frenetic glow from shapes around black symbols that seemed to squirm under direct scrutiny. The walls were textured with alcoves, the alcoves were filled with urns.

"Welcome," said the imposing figure standing across the chamber. His armored shoulder pads settled over his shroud. His craggy face held a depth of wisdom, rage, mirth, and pain that telegraphed more than the usual handful of decades of life.

"We did not come for you," the Hammer said, stepping forward, his hands out to the sides.

"Yet you did. We expected you," the old man said. "Trellis asked us to take you in one way, and release you another." His craggy smile held many flavors. "He suspected you'd be trailed by one of the city's best assassins, and he was right."

"You don't look worried," the Hammer said.

"I am not," the patriarch replied with a slight shrug. "I am Father Crolaange, and these are my people." He raised his hands to take in the group, and most of them shrugged their hoods back, took down their hats, lowered their masks, and otherwise relaxed somewhat.

"We did not mean to bring you trouble," the Hammer said.

"Trellis asked us to wipe trouble from your back trail," Father Crolaange said. "He has contributed to our privacy through the years, and we are happy to share some of it with you." Again with that distressing smile. "If the assassin comes in among us, then we will feast on her."

"Seems fair," Niece said through her teeth.

"Come, let us get more comfortable," Father Crolaange said, turning. He led his people through the door on the opposite end of the burial chamber, the Hammer and Niece in tow.

"We might be on the wrong side of the Mirror," the Hammer murmured to her, rubbing at his chest. "We've gone through a door. We're between."

"This doesn't feel like near death," Niece frowned.

"Death is not the only way to cross the Mirror," the Hammer replied, his voice low. He blinked, then frowned. "Your hand."

She looked down at her hand, and saw a pulsing black shadow under her skin. "Okay, what," she said, her flat voice harsh.

One of the escorts turned. "That? You've been tagged, the assassin is tracing the trail you leave in the aether. Fear not. We will purify you." He smiled, revealing several missing teeth. "You will come beneath the gaze of the Fallen Star, and you will be cleansed."

"Neat," Niece said through her teeth, balling her hands into fists to hide any tremors that might haunt them. They continued on together through the oddly luminous dark.

LOWER COURTS, JAYAN PARK, CHARTERHALL. 25TH ELISAR. EIGHTH HOUR PAST DAWN.

The shrill whistle cut through the background of crowd noise, and the packed bleachers seemed to shift as the crowd resumed their seats. Reserve players, referees, coaches, and support staff lined the long sides of the playing field, fences flanking the goals centered on the shorter ends. Tall towers with three foot columns of flame surrounded the field, illuminating the players, casting muted shadows in all directions.

Stands were built between the towers, allowing plenty of bleacher space for the fans. Below the stands was a mass of litter and debris, as well as several trysts where spectators slipped away for some semi-private encounters. It was deep in those shadows that Piccolo met Sanction.

"Okay, here we are, the others are with the stables," Piccolo said, sullen.

"We're almost done," Sanction replied, steady. "One more after this." He paused. "This one is the hardest. It's a child, number 48 on the Lightning Eels team."

"You've got a plan?" Piccolo demanded.

Sanction watched him for a moment. "No qualms? You know what we're doing here."

"No qualms," Piccolo scoffed. "That spoiled little turd is a larval aristocrat. Let him hatch and he's right up there with the rest of them."

"Okay," Sanction nodded. "Everybody who gets close to the teams is personally known and vetted by the security officers, and the only exception I could come up with on short notice is the medic on duty. He's out sick, and they've got a backup medic who is currently in the locker room. One substitute looks much like another, so if you have his credentials you should be fine."

"This is a lot of work for me," Piccolo noted, brows drawn. "I feel like I'm doing it on my own."

"I did some groundwork and I'm backing you up if it goes wrong." Sanction paused. "But it won't. You are Piccolo. You have a rep," he said with a wry grin.

"Yeah, hear me roar," Piccolo muttered. "I'm calling it, though. I do this, I pull it off, and you owe me one." He looked Sanction in the eye, serious.

"Yes, I can live with that," Sanction nodded. "Now go do what you do."

Piccolo nodded, then climbed the back of the bleachers. From an elevated perch, he surveyed the layout of the compound, then he slid down and dropped off the poles, strolling along the sidewalk.

He passed the guards at the front gate, veered off to the public restrooms, then sidestepped the main door and leaped, catching the lowest eave and pulling himself up to the first rooftop. Some quick climbing maneuvered him around to the alleyway between the fence at the short end of the field, and the back of the bunker room. He homed in on the back employee entrance, and knocked vigorously.

A moment later, he heard shuffling, and the loud snick as the lock disengaged. The door started to open, and he kicked it hard, sending the person on the other side flying back. He was inside, the door snapping shut behind him, and as the dazed medic struggled to rise he slung a punch down at the surprised woman.

"Sanction, you may have overlooked a detail," Piccolo frowned, looking down at the short, round, very female medic. He sniffed, refocusing. "Lucky for you, I'm that good," he said grimly to no one in particular. A moment later he wore her comically short and loose jacket, and had her credentials in hand. He picked up a bag of medical tools, heading for the exit to the sidelines.

"Hey," said a man stepping out of an unobtrusive side corridor. "Who are you, and how did—" was as far as he got. Piccolo tossed the medical bag up, and as the man's eyes widened and he caught it, Piccolo stepped into a driving blow to his torso. The man flew back into the wall, rebounding, and Piccolo neatly snagged the back of his head and pivoted, sending the unfortunate man sideways and airborne to bang into the opposite wall. Three rapid punches to his head subdued the athlete.

"Looks like an assistant coach," Piccolo said, straightening his jacket. He picked up the tool bag as his victim shifted and groaned, and he moved quickly to leave the locker room and get on the sidelines.

Light on his feet and moving with purpose, Piccolo avoided those who were yelling and waving their arms. He maneuvered around those who sat and ducked through shouted conversations. The noise of the fans made conversation almost impossible. He closed in on the coach for the Electric Eels.

"Number forty eight!" he shouted to the coach. "Between plays, pull him in! Bad news from home!"

The coach frowned, then nodded. On the field, the Lightning Eels snagged the ball, then made a bold play directly into the jaws of the Ironcats, fancy footwork tugging a hole open in the line so one player could slip through and drive towards the goal. The backfield was not having it, and the Eel managed to jump over the sliding tackle, but lost control of the ball, which was redirected towards the other end of the field until it disappeared under a mass of player bodies. The whistle blew, and the coach signaled for 48 to come to the sideline.

A sweaty ten year old child trotted to the sidelines obediently enough as the field reset, and the coach waved him over to Piccolo, who leaned in close.

"Good game, kid," Piccolo yelled, holding eye contact. "When they ask, blame Lord Cleith Rowan. Got it?"

"What?" the kid demanded, then he jumped and pulled away from Piccolo, rubbing the back of his arm. "Hey, who the hell are you?" he shouted. "Bye, kid," Piccolo shrugged, tossing the syringe aside. He turned and walked fast, moving towards the fence that separated the sidelines from the bleachers.

"Hey, stop that guy!" the kid yelled, pointing at Piccolo. Not only did his teammates take note, so did the Bluecoats and House Guard stationed around the bleachers.

Four enthusiastic kids jumped at him, snatching fistfuls of his clothes, gleeful at the opportunity to interfere with an adult. Frowning, Piccolo reached into his pocket and pulled out a canister, snapping the top off so it jetted out a spray mist; he aimed it at one child at a time, and they fell back clawing at their faces as the chemical burn flared through their nerves. Now bigger guards were closing in.

Piccolo could not restrain a feral grin as he bounded up and raced along the rail fence, a width less than his footprint, with fast-pedaling grace. Only two guards were able to reroute to pursue with a chance of catching him. One lunged, and Piccolo jumped out of range, his landing on the railing wobbly but keeping him moving as the last guard loomed up.

Close enough. Piccolo shot him point blank, aiming for a leg, and the Bluecoat went down with a spastic gasp. Piccolo launched off the railing, dropping almost twenty feet and landing in a somersault, popping up at a run through the light crowd that was looking around in confusion as the crack of the gunshot resounded. A ten foot wall separated the lower green from the roadway, but he saw the head and shoulders of someone standing on the roof of a carriage, and he sprinted towards the wall, jumping to kick up and snatch the ledge, pulling himself up to be cut on the defenses along the wall's crest.

Still, the carriage was there, with one last tug Piccolo heaved himself over most of the broken glass embedded in the wall and dropped, trailing a little blood. He rolled into the carriage with Gapjaw and Sanction, the door snapping shut behind him.

"Did you get him?" Sanction demanded.

"Yes," Piccolo yelled. "Let's go!"

The carriage rattled off, merging with the traffic, vanishing into the city.

"So that's the plan," Lord Rowan said to the big man sitting opposite him in the parked coach. "Sanders, you take Belton in as your brother, looking for a discreet place to stash your grandfather where no one can figure out his location. Stress the need for security, find out what he's got, then get him and an orderly at gunpoint. Hurt the orderly first, to make him comply. Find Leslin. Bring him out here."

"Yes sir," Sanders replied. "Does Director Jesrael survive this?"

"There are other secrets in that house that we do not want to expose, I am sure," Lord Rowan shrugged. "Only kill Jesrael if he makes you." He glanced at Saint, who sat next to him. "Once Jesrael is compliant, get Leslin. You know him, make sure he comes out in one piece."

"Yes sir," Sanders replied, and he opened the door, stepping out, followed by his partner. As they headed up the stairs to the looming mansion, two wagons behind the coach opened up, and a team of elite warriors fanned out, following the property lines to surround the building.

"You are a dead man if Leslin is not in there," Lord Rowan said quietly.

"I'm not worried," Saint shrugged. "It's a good plan, it's their plan, and you'll get your man back."

"Why did you wait until today to tell me about this?" Lord Rowan demanded.

"I didn't even know they took your adept until you told me, less than two days ago," Saint retorted. "I was staring at those papers so hard looking for clues, I realized I needed to step back and take in the whole picture. I realized I hadn't been thinking about an adept hostage at all, and I spent all last night turning it over in my mind."

"Any other insights emerge?" Lord Rowan asked, unreadable.

"Nothing you'll like," Saint shrugged.

Lord Rowan waited.

"The survivors are going to be angry," Saint said as he squinted out the coach window. "They won't try to kill you, unless they all get back together. And even then, there's enough of a mean streak in that group that your death may not be enough to answer for what you've done in pursuing them." He looked at Lord Rowan. "They're going to try to hurt you," he said.

"How?" Lord Rowan asked quietly.

"What do you love?" Saint shrugged. "Your Leviathan hunting boats, your captains, your income, the loyalty of your people, your friends, your alliances and enemies on the City Council, your favorite cooks and tailors. You're trying to wreck their world, and they know yours is too big for all of it to be untouchable. This is going to be a horrible combination of pettiness and bloodshed, if they are pushed far enough without being killed." He shook his head. "The River Stallions crashed your party. The Silkworms are known allies who let them, and are also a controlling interest in Silkshore. I get why you picked those two as targets. If anyone in Silkshore is positioned to protect the River Stallions, it's Trellis." Saint sighed. "You and Trellis are both aristocrats, you both have things you love that you can't protect, and you both think you're so smart and powerful you should have your way." He pointed a frank look at Lord Rowan. "This ends in fire."

"None of that is new," Lord Rowan observed.

"You're pinched," Saint shrugged. "You can't hire new people, because they might be applying for the job just to get close to what you're trying to protect. Who can you trust? A question that's always with you, but now lays its steely blade next to your beating heart. You're worked into everything, and that gives you a lot of power, but you can't withdraw to safety. Even if they do decide to kill you, they've got two Whispers. They have a sniper. One of the best lurks in Silkshore. They can steal all the money they need to fund their operations. If they want you dead, then your window to stop them is closing." Saint rubbed at his eyes. "I need you alive," he confessed, "because my old life is over no matter what, and I'm betting it all on your gratitude, or sense for opportunity, either one."

Lord Rowan narrowed his eyes. "There's something more," he prodded.

"Well, yes," Saint winced. "Your life never goes back to normal either. They've been your target for, what, about seven days? I have no idea how many crews, gangs, houses, guilds, and consortiums you've pissed off in your rampage to get at them. Your peers will look down on your efforts here. People hungry for what you've got will think maybe now you're weak. Perception of the might of House Rowan is shifting as these scoundrels survive out there, and as you break the rules of usual practice to chase them. Maybe House Rowan recovers, but I get the feeling you don't," Saint said, looking him in the eye.

Lord Rowan watched him for a moment, cold. "You've been honest with me," he said, "so hear this. From your point of view, this all makes sense. But from mine? I have untapped resources you cannot even guess about in your wildest dreams. The depth of power that I could bring to bear has not begun to be exerted. My eventual victory is certain. Things like opinion on the street may affect power in some paltry ways, but I have all the power I need to win this and come out a victor." He paused. "With or without you."

Lord Rowan rocked forward, opening the coach door and stepping down. The door slammed behind him as he strode up to the mansion, two guards falling in step with him.

A few minutes later, elite warriors came down the steps supporting Leslin between them as he cried out with hysteria, dressed in white pyjamas and a house robe. Lord Rowan followed him, flanked by guards. Sanders and his partner dragged Director Jesrael, and some orderlies trailed along at a safe distance.

Leslin was loaded into one of the troop wagons, which filled in behind him as guards clambered aboard. Lord Rowan stopped to have a brief conversation with Director Jesrael, who hung his head like a whipped cur.

As Lord Rowan approached the carriage, Jesrael looked up and saw Saint's pale face in the window. His eyes widened, and Saint saluted him with a twisted smile. Then Lord Rowan was aboard, and the carriage jolted into motion, leaving the mansion behind.

"The tide has turned," Lord Rowan said to Saint, baring his teeth in a smile. "I have my adept back, so it's time to turn this around and finish off the resistance."

"Right there with you," Saint replied, echoing Lord Rowan's smile.

ARBORSIDE CONDUIT, BRIGHTSTONE.
25TH ELISAR. HOUR OF SONG, 2 HOURS PAST DUSK.

"I thought that was just a story, you know; fiction," Gapjaw said as he peered down into the canal. "They do actually perfume the water here."

"Cleanse it, too," Safety agreed. "Sanction was telling me about how the Brightstone canals are different than the rest of the city." He turned to where Sanction stood brooding by the low wall, a few steps away from the carriage. "Right, Sanction?"

"Yes," Sanction replied in a distant voice. "Three levels of algae rakes and a lock mechanism to control what gets into Brightstone, the canals are half depth so cargo cannot be transported here, and there are crystal nuggets called sparkles that aggressively kill anything in the canal. So here, as elsewhere, don't drink the water." He squinted up at the clouds. Snow swirled down around them as they waited, but none of it gathered on his restless shoulders. "Piccolo should be back by now."

"He'll make it," Gapjaw said, and he resumed peering into the water. "No kelp, no eels, no corpses." He shivered in the chill night. "Hardly a canal. They should call them water features or something."

They all perked up to note Piccolo striding towards them across the street, his shadow long with the burning plasm lamp post at his back.

"How did it go?" Sanction asked.

"Easy," Piccolo replied, "or at least I make it look easy. Dressed as a nurse, got some knockout pills, tucked her in to bed, and injected her." His jaw flexed. "So what's next?" he demanded.

"We deserve a break," Sanction said, "and we've got to stay sharp. We disappear for a day or two, rest up, get our wits about us, then see how our plans are coming along."

"I don't hate the sound of that," Safety admitted. "What did you have in mind? We can't go anywhere we'll be recognized."

"I've got a marker to call in," Sanction said with an airy shrug. "We can actually relax for a day or two, then get back to it."

"Are you going to contact Rowan first?" Gapjaw asked. "Tell him what's happening?"

"He's so smart, let him figure it out," Sanction replied with a dangerous grin. "Now, who's up for some spores and wine?"

Moments later, the stolen carriage rattled off along the level, curated street, leaving a cold silence in its wake.

CHAPTER TWELVE

Rail Jacks protect trains from the clouds of starving ghosts in the wasteland between cities. Most trains have a post behind the engine compartment, called the safety seat, where one of the jacks can study the engineers for signs of mental pressure or possession. If an engineer is victimized, the jack can intervene. It's a good 'watch and learn' post for rookies.

So this kid is still an apprentice jack, and he's in the safety seat, and one of the engineers has allergies. First time he sneezes, the kid overreacts and fries him with the hook. Gives the poor bastard the shakes for life. So they put the kid up walking the train for the rest of the trip, and he saw a reflection he didn't like in the goggles of his partner, fries him with the hook. By the second trip, he had a rep for massive overreaction, posing more of a threat than the dangerous surroundings.

Some say he never had the nerve to be a rail jack, but his uncle was Speeder Zeke, and everybody's heard of that crazy bastard. So, he didn't get run off the rails, but he earned the nickname Safety, and people knew to keep an eye on the zap-happy twerp.

— From "Tales on Rails: Oral Histories of the Elevated Trains"
unfinished publication notes

SAILS ALLEY, CROW'S FOOT.
25ᵀᴴ ELISAR. SIXTH HOUR PAST DAWN.

Red Silver's eyes lazily drifted open. Above, she saw charred timbers, the flank of a battered and ancient building, and above that a torn mat of clouds half-covering the broken embers of the sun. Mid-day. She slowly dragged herself up to a seated position, her skin burning and crawling, her flesh a mass of bruises and aching.

"How did you sleep?" the Mistress of Tides asked, her veil in place, her back against the wall as she rested.

"Pretty well, considering we're in the most haunted corner of Crow's Foot," Red replied as she stretched. "You?"

The Mistress of Tides shrugged. "I sleep better where it's haunted," she murmured.

"Right," Red Silver grunted, hauling herself to her feet. "Inkletta?" she asked, looking over at where the other Whisper was bundled in a cloak, motionless on the ground.

"She'll be alright," the Mistress of Tides said. "Her fever has been diminishing now that she's encased in flesh again."

Red Silver squinted around the burned out ruin of the former basement, now exposed to sky, tucked into the curving and cramped quarters of the deep alleyway. "Now that we have Inkletta back, and I've had a good night's sleep, I realize I have no idea what to do next." She absently rubbed at the runes along her forearm, and they sizzled slightly, smoldering.

"I suspect Inkletta's plan was to hide your signal in the shadow of a spirit well, make you difficult to find, perhaps provide some insight into undoing the curse," the Mistress of Tides said. "It may not be that easy."

"That fiasco was easy?" Red Silver retorted.

"You are hunted by a cocky Whisper, and we need to figure out how to deal with him. Hiding you is at best temporary," the Mistress of Tides said.

"Okay," Red Silver said, reflexively checking the ammunition in her pistols. "What else should we do? Aim for an assassination?" She snapped a pistol shut.

"I think all roads end with you dead, or him dead," the Mistress of Tides said, pitiless. "So yes, one way or another, he dies."

"Killing a Whisper is just like killing anybody else, just, you know, you have to keep at it a little more. Right?" Red Silver shivered.

"More or less, usually," the Mistress of Tides said. "There are cheats like having ghosts with you that flow into your body if it loses consciousness, or catalytic rituals that can project your consciousness to the other side of the Mirror to transform you into a powerful specter upon death. Those are both abrasive to your life, before you die. In this case, if you mix in a depth of occult training and familiarity with demonic lore and power, this Whisper might have a bigger bag of tricks. There's no way to know," she shrugged. "Our end result is going to need to have a level of savagery to tear this creature apart."

"Yes, well, wearing clothes and using metal weapons doesn't make us civilized," Red Silver said quietly. "I'm ready to shed blood and rip spirit to free myself of a lifetime of terror."

"We need to choose our ground for a confrontation," the Mistress of Tides said. "My first instinct is the Forgotten Quarter." She paused. "I may know some areas there better than a stranger would."

"Whatever the plan, as long as both Whispers agree with it I'm on board," Red Silver said through her teeth. "Especially if you can see a way I come out of this alive."

Both women looked over to where Inkletta stood, her eyes smoldering white as she stood, trembling.

"Inkletta?" the Mistress of Tides said, uncertain.

"Here it comes," Inkletta whispered.

Then Red Silver started screaming.

CROWNWIND COURT, SILKSHORE.
25TH ELISAR. SIXTH HOUR PAST DAWN.

Razor Wind followed the landlord up the rickety steps, through the door, into the precarious loft at the top of the uneasily stacked tower. The landlord turned, looking at him, trying to hide his discomfort.

"You have some privacy here," the landlord shrugged, "and a cheaper rate, since the one who lived here before fell afoul of the law, and no one wants to give the Bluecoats a reason to look twice. Except you, it seems," he said with a wide and insincere smile.

"Red Silver's things are still here," Razor Wind observed, his eyes traveling over the rumpled bed on the floor in the next room, the pile of crockery, a crooked spice rack with bullets stacked in it, the Skov bayonet hanging on the wall.

"Sell 'em to you cheap," the landlord said, trying the smile again.

Razor Wind rustled past him, stalking through the rooms, looking around. He paused, then came back to the entry way/kitchen/dining room/parlor where the landlord waited. He held a long rifle.

"She loves this object," Razor Wind murmured. "Will you help me find her?"

"Ah," the landlord said, "I really don't want to get involved."

Razor Wind let a moment settle between them, gathering weight as the wind blew and the bones of the tower shifted.

"If you don't want to help," Razor Wind murmured, "then you have to tell me no." His whole posture shifted as he looked the landlord in the eye.

"A-anything for a f-friend," the landlord said, reluctantly taking the rifle from Razor Wind.

"Good man," Razor Wind nodded. "Thank you."

The landlord blinked. "Now what?"

"Just hold that pose," Razor Wind replied. He pulled a bottle from his cloak's interior, uncorking it and pouring powder in a circle around the landlord; he casually kicked the rickety table out of the way, the chairs clattering along. Tossing the empty bottle away, he pulled a tube forth, twisting the base so a sticky cylinder extended. He knelt, making a mark on the floor, then he rose and followed the circle, kneeling to make another mark.

"This is not a good way to get the apartment," the landlord said, distraught and baffled. "You can't just—"

"I can," Razor Wind interrupted. "Be quiet and wait your turn." He stuck crystals in the gluey material marking the floor, then stood back. "This is a delicate ritual. Requires a focus object and a human sacrifice." He nodded. "Thank you for that, by the way."

"A-a-a what?" the landlord said, his instinct to fight or flee hampered by greed and civility.

Razor Wind took a long step back, dropping into a deep stance, and the landlord could not even scream as his spirit was torn from every fiber of his living body, dragged out and concentrated into the gun, then sent spiraling through the roof up into the sky.

"Show me," Razor Wind whispered in Hadrathi. "Show me where she is." He waited, his eyes half closed, focused on the energy.

Meanwhile, the landlord's corpse twitched uncontrollably, then began to peel. Meat slopped off the bones, thudding in a wet pile, the top half of the body revealing wet shining bone. The bones clicked and snapped, reforming, making a new shape.

"I didn't call for you," Razor Wind said, standing up straight.

The new skull flexed, crunching out a muzzle and a row of spines, the ribs spreading and growing together. "I do not require you to call me," the top half of the skeleton intoned. "We are allies, after all. Neither owns the other."

"Have you come to help?" Razor Wind asked calmly, sweat standing out on his forehead.

"Just wondering why you do not use the tracking sigils I taught you," the demon replied, polite enough.

"The tracking ritual is twenty years old, give or take," Razor Wind replied. "I do not wish to loosen the pattern in her flesh by tugging on its foundations. Instead, I want to pour more energy into it, to bolster its signal."

The demon bucked its chest, hopping its skeletal legs out of their meat columns so the last of the landlord's corpse squelched down in a filthy pile. The bone limbs popped and twisted into recurve legs, the ankle climbing half the shin to form long splayed footbones.

"Planning to stay a while?" Razor Wind asked, cocking an eyebrow.

"In a way, I never left," the bone demon's new body growled playfully, speaking by resonating bone to create sound instead of shaping air with wet organs as humans do. "Now, you pitted your life force against the family line for Selraetas blood, so both could not endure. You slaughtered many upon many, and arranged for the deaths of more.

My ledger indicates there is only one left." The alien skull creaked as it deformed to present a hideous grin. "How could I not want to watch this?"

Razor Wind observed him for a moment. "You'll want to wear at least some meat, if you want to walk about the place. Probably cloth too." His smile was not kind. "I don't think the people of Doskvol are ready for your naked truth."

"No one likes truth," the demon agreed airily. "Not even you."

"But I can endure it," Razor Wind countered, "and that's what matters."

"Sure," the bone demon shrugged. "Now, say my name, give me a better foothold. I'll put on some meat," he added, almost patronizing.

"Elziraan," Razor Wind said, "please put something on."

The skull grinned, then snatched the pile of gory meat that had once been the landlord, swinging it around like a sheet so it spread and slapped on the new bone frame. A sound like a million needles swallowing down a charcoal tube shook the apartment as the demon knit a new look, then it stretched, in roughly the shape of a skinny man. Cloth followed shortly, draping around him in a very private hooded cloak.

"You are still a master," Razor Wind admitted. "My own fleshcrafting is not nearly so expert."

"It's a matter of practice. Takes thousands of attempts to be any good at it," Elziraan said, almost dismissive. His voice was muffled, and his lips did not move; the bone he used for speech was now under flesh.

"So," Razor Wind said, "are you going to help me track Red Silver?"

"Maybe if you use runes," Elziraan sniffed. "This spirit work is distasteful."

"Fine." Razor Wind focused all his concentration on the spirit bound in his ritual. *"Show me."*

The bound ghost dove into the city, screaming, until it was destroyed.

"It's a start," Razor Wind said through his teeth. "She's in Crow's Foot." He snatched the rifle and brushed past the door, leaving the gory apartment and vanishing down the stairwell.

"Ah, Doskvol, always awash in drama and intrigue," Elziraan resonated, leaning his hands on the windowsill and taking in the crooked shadows of the city's rooftop mosaic. The demon chuckled, then hopped lightly out the window and vanished into the darkness.

SAILS ALLEY. CROW'S FOOT.
25TH ELISAR. SIXTH HOUR PAST DAWN.

They ran. Sometimes stumbling, sometimes leaping over debris or low walls, they tumbled and raced down the alleyway. The Mistress of Tides skidded to a halt at the top of stairs leading down to the riverside market that flanked the ruin where they had been squatting.

"Go!" Inkletta shouted, pointing, and the three women scrambled down the stairs and pushed their way into the alleyway, following Inkletta as she deliberately chose a route through the shops and beggars. She hurled herself at an ornately carved wooden door that reluctantly groaned open under the impact, and they dashed inside, slamming the door behind themselves.

"Damn!" Red Silver shouted. The net of cursework on her skin flared and sizzled, energy unfurling from her chi meridians. "What was that!"

"It was a ghost *and* a ritual," the Mistress of Tides said through her teeth. "Somehow your attacker may have penetrated your identity, found an object you care about, and weaponized all that with human sacrifice."

"I smashed the ghost, but the energy fell into your curse at close range," Inkletta said. "You're bright as a star right now. That's why we're here." She gestured at the thick-walled shrine.

"Rock won't help," the Mistress of Tides frowned.

"This is a shrine to the Closed Eye," Inkletta countered. "They may be willing to share the favor of their patron with us. We need to close an eye," she said, still breathless from the sprint.

A shuffling sound attracted their attention, and they looked to the shadows in the shrine, where a man and woman stepped into view, into the dim light from the market that came in through holes in the dome above. The man had an eyepatch on his right eye, the woman had an eyepatch on her left eye.

"We are the guardians of this shrine," she said. "Your grounds for asylum?"

"Instincts of the Shrouded Queen," Inkletta said, regal in the moment.

"We long for her favor as well," the man said. "Come with us, and we will confuse all sight that follows."

"All sight," the woman added tonelessly.

Inkletta and Red Silver exchanged a glance, then followed, the Mistress of Tides right behind, and the shadows were empty again.

BENEATH THE GAZE OF THE FALLEN STAR.

They walked for what felt like forever, the stone beneath their bare feet smooth and uneven. Finally the blindfolds were reverently removed, and they stood before a stone tub set in the floor, slowly bubbling with dark liquid.

Niece glanced over at the Hammer, noting he was as naked as she was. She had not expected to see the gnarls and patchwork of scars across his arm, back, and leg. He looked over at her, but with a level unashamed gaze that aimed for her eyes and met them, offering reassurance as fierce as the curls of hair on his solid chest. Niece felt herself blush, and hated the inconstant blood that betrayed her embarrassment.

Father Crolaange soundlessly rounded the tub, holding a glass tube of glowing liquid in one hand and a small cup in the other. His mask was in place, so he was inscrutable in the darkness.

"Enter into the baptismal chamber of your own free will," Father Crolaange intoned. "You will be cleansed, all other energies driven from you but those of your native life. You shall then receive the blessing of the Fallen Star if you are found worthy, and if you are not, then you will suffer greatly before passing beyond reach of all that life touches."

The Hammer cleared his throat. "Am I touched by any alien energies, Father?" he asked.

The mask pointed towards him. "You are not. All that pollutes you is shame and regret. You do not need baptism to wrestle those."

The Hammer's brow furrowed. "I don't need those washed away," he said. "They are part of me. I earned them, and I don't like to think who I would be without them."

"That is between you and the Fallen Star, should you enter the waters," Father Crolaange replied.

Niece stared at the blotch under the skin of her hand, and saw herself trembling.

Startled, she looked over to see the Hammer awkwardly lowering himself to sit on the stone rim, then slosh down into the dark liquid. It slid away from his skin like water, leaving no stain or residue. He shifted, then gingerly settled on a submerged seat. He bowed his head, his nose almost touching the surface.

"Dammit," Niece murmured. "Damn it." Then she locked her jaw, stepped forward, and squatted by the pool, sliding a leg experimentally into the liquid.

The pool had a shadow of chill, and a breath of warmth, multi-textured with ribbons of current. She lowered herself in to half-submerge, and looked over at the Hammer. He raised his head as she felt the liquid flow around her. Her jaw shivered.

"You're a goddamn rock," she whispered to the Hammer.

The faintest smile shifted his features. "That's just about what I thought about you, when we met," he said. "Still do." He shook his head. "Here we go."

Father Crolaange tilted the cup, and a single impossibly large drop of liquid slid from it frictionlessly, plopping into the tub.

Then everything changed.

NIECE'S INTERFACE

She groaned with an intense binding that resolved into a bloom of sensation, more intense than an orgasm. She felt herself burst in the moment, ribbons of her thought and presence unfurling forwards and backwards, rippling the entire thread of her existence as her lifespan trembled with the presence of the Fallen Star.

She felt the dark majesty that loomed all around her, and realized that they had met before, when she hovered near death; again she tasted her mortality pressed flat against the Mirror on the edge of passing through, and the dark Leviathan that breathed upon her and sent her back into the world of the living.

An eye opened, resolving from a blank orb to an impossibly detailed iris. The iris had a thousand pupils open and shut within it as though the eye breathed reality like air, or water. Each hole was as thick as a tree, waxing and waning with age, the crusted bark protecting a slow compacting of sediment into rings of time and distance lived.

One pupil flexed, and she felt the day she was born and the death of her mother, and that experience was pulled into the Leviathan's impossible monstrous life force through the power of this baptismal moment. A deeper slit within the eye flexed, and she touched her own death—she experienced it, the sights and smells of the final moment searing along her bones.

All things that made up her whole world drifted, her lifespan and everything in it a mote in the sunbeam of one lazy blink of the eye for this engine of life force as it drifted through the foundation of the world.

For a wild instant she was adjacent to the awareness of the Leviathan. Her whole timeline burned with a single split-second of emotion; the thing she now touched had no need of struggle, but had always enjoyed its presence.

In that instant, she touched that ocean of living energy, and it touched her. A singular awareness amplified through her own. She bore a trace of undying Leviathan blood that connected her to the assassin that followed her, and the awareness slid through the connection, lightning following its own path through the world. Somehow, she knew the assassin was at this moment breaching the shrine using a ritual, entering, knife in hand.

She was a conduit for a thread of energy, a passing microsensation for the Leviathan that encompassed her birth, life, and death, and continued on to touch the living energy of the assassin that tracked her. Like a rivulet of water meeting the sea, the assassin's boundaries vanished, and all life force was one. She transmitted the casual flash that annihilated the assassin utterly.

The trailing passage of that stray thought fired Niece back into her body, where she wept like a child in the crystalline clear water, feeling the mortal amputation of being stuffed back into the confines of human senses and flesh.

Eventually the feeling of water on her human flesh, the fragile slop not made to glide through the crushing depths below, was too offensive to endure. She tried to climb out of the pool. Father Crolaange gripped her, pulling her out, and she lay on the stone shivering, hating the weakness of her comically disposable body.

"The assassin must be dead, then," Father Crolaange murmured. "She foolishly connected herself to you with undying blood; your experience followed the connection, tapped into the Leviathan's presence. Did you feel it?" he asked, his white teeth too square and strong in the dimness.

"Oh, that, and more," Niece said, shaky.

"Those experiences are for you, and you do not have to share them with anyone else if you do not wish to do so. And yet they are not secrets either. The Fallen Star is beyond us so far that there is no way we can betray it. We lack consequence," he said, his expression compassionate and bleak.

"I understand so much less than I did," Niece whispered.

"That's good, that's good," Father Crolaange soothed. He sat by her, looking around at the uneven cave. "You see it now, do you not?"

Niece blinked rapidly, then looked around, seeing the gentle glow of the walls across most of the cave's interior surface. They were bright to her, but shed no visible light. She frowned, then realization dawned, and her eyes widened.

"There it is," Father Crolaange said, watching for the moment in her eyes, his smile returning. "You see it now."

"How—how is—this isn't possible," Niece whispered.

Father Crolaange gazed around the shrine. "We are within the Fallen Star's skull," he said. "Over six hundred years ago we sacrificed a dozen humans a dozen times. There were other casualties, of course, it was over a hundred and fifty deaths. The bay ran red with blood, and that ritualistically concentrated life energy lured in the Leviathan. It beached trying to get to the sacrificial site, and that's when we descended upon it." His eyes were distant.

"We had crosscut saws, axes, buckets, stretchers, carts... we attacked with abandon to harvest as much flesh, hide, bone, and blood as we could. But the greatest matriarch the clan ever had, Stars Forever, led a concentrated effort. She wanted the brain of the deathless demon. Over sixty of the best limmers hacked away for ten minutes, heedless of arterial sprays or glandular secretions. They hooked mighty cables to the skull, slitting hide and cutting muscle, and the Fallen Star recoiled into the gory surf but left behind most of its skull." He gestured at the uneven cavern, and now the dozen eye sockets were visible from the inside, as well as the upper teeth on the far side, the strange shapes resonant with power.

"Even I do not know how they moved this shrine sideways, adjacent to the Mirror but on neither side," Father Crolaange confessed. "Those with the gift can concentrate here and catch stray thoughts from the Fallen Star, and a few of them recover. This is not terribly useful power, but it lures us, and we do penance and apologize and grieve for what we have done, even as we exult and are elevated by what we now touch."

"What's going to happen to me?" Niece asked in a small voice. "Will I go insane, or—or attract demons?"

"Who is to say?" Father Crolaange shrugged. "That is between you and the Fallen Star. How you respond to the dreams. What you push away and what you pull closer." He looked her in the eye. "It's dangerous. Of those who harvested the skull, two survived, and they never recovered. Of course you know the first Whispers were created from limmer lineage, as exposure to Leviathans changed them forever."

"That's one story," Niece agreed.

Father Crolaange cocked an eyebrow, his smile wry.

"Can't disbelieve it," Niece confessed.

The pool splashed, and the Hammer's wracking sobs drifted out. Niece vaguely began to care that she was naked.

"Thanks for your help with the assassin," she said, struggling against focusing on the most inane detail of the exchange.

"If you need to tell someone," Father Crolaange said, "you can tell me. While we're alone. Before the world returns to you."

Niece looked him in the eye. "This must happen a lot. People touch a god and have to unload some impossible idea."

"Only with the survivors," he shrugged. "Few people can talk about it at all once the world closes in. They aren't sure what they saw, or experienced." He paused. "This is your chance to say it, and make it real."

"Okay," Niece said as the Hammer struggled, coughing and choking on his sobs. "I saw my death. The Fallen Star was there, at my death." She paused. "It was... bittersweet."

Father Crolaange took her face in both rough hands and gently kissed her forehead. Then he rose, and moved to the side of the chamber, returning with robes as the Hammer crawled out of the pit.

"Are you going to be alright?" Niece asked, kneeling beside him, putting her hand on the scarred map of his back's hide.

"I'm a r-rock," he stuttered.

She patted his back as he trembled. There was nothing further to say.

DORVALE ESTATE, BRIGHTSTONE.
25ᵀᴴ ELISAR. HOUR OF SILVER, 3 HOURS PAST DUSK.

"I don't think they'll invite us in," Safety muttered under his breath.

"Right, we sneak in, they never know we were there," Sanction agreed.

"Doesn't sound like much of a party," Gapjaw observed.

"Do you trust me, or don't you?" Sanction asked, eyes bright, a rakish grin perched on his face.

"I'm too tired for games," Piccolo said shortly. "What's the plan."

Sanction glanced at the other rogues, all standing in the shadows between the glare of plasmic lights that lined the streets. He saw the shadow of fatigue in their features, the bandages, the slouching postures. He nodded. "You'll like this, I promise," he said. "We need to get to the stables. Follow me." He slung his heavy back pack up to his shoulder, and crossed the street.

Sanction approached the wall and jumped up, catching the top, pulling himself up as the others also approached. Safety gave Gapjaw a leg up, Piccolo ignored his injuries and scaled the wall effortlessly. They dropped into bushes, and waded out to the curated path.

Sanction jogged along the path, pack bouncing, the others keeping pace. He pulled a silver whistle from his coat and blew it soundlessly a couple times, then pocketed it once more.

"Dogs?" Safety asked.

"Something like dogs," Sanction said with a grimace. No one asked further questions.

They reached the stables, which had the musty smell of abandonment and damp. Sanction went to the last stall on one side, and probed at the wall for a few seconds until they heard a click. He opened the secret door, they followed him into darkness, shaking glass orbs to activate the bioluminescent algae inside. Passing the lamps and torches, they descended down an old stone staircase as the door closed behind them.

They crossed a wide room, thick with dust, and Sanction confidently continued across the grayed out carpet as though he knew the way. Through the door on the other end, and they were in an underground boathouse.

One side of the room was occupied by massive lock machinery designed to elevate a boat out of the space, up to water level outside. The scoundrels stood on a platform with stairs down into the water, a pool that separated one side of the room from the other. Across the pool there were cranes designed to pull a boat out of the water to drydock.

In the channel of water down the middle of the room, a compact but luxurious yacht lay motionless and silent, mast stepped down, tied to the stone on both flanks.

"He called it his funeral barge," Sanction said quietly, "and when he died I kept an eye out to see if anyone mentioned it or put it on the market." He turned to the others. "This underground yacht was the secret escape for one of the first supervisors I had in the Ministry, Doctor Halsek. He brought me here to celebrate my promotion and his retirement; said he had lots of wild parties in his youth but as time wore on he just wanted the privacy."

"This is all very touching," Piccolo said, flat.

"Alright, follow me," Sanction said, arching an eyebrow and smiling. "You lot are tough to impress."

"It's because we're so damn good," Gapjaw shrugged.

Down the steps and across the narrow stone, they reached the gangplank up onto the yacht. Once aboard, they were immediately aware of the opulence of the silken cushions, the fine wood and its engraving, and the attention to decoration and quality even for the wet bar built into the prow of the yacht.

"It was never intended to be out in the weather," Sanction grinned as Safety tugged one of the hexagonal bottles out of its custom cut holder and squinted at the contents.

"Blood and bone!" Safety said. "This bottle is worth a couple dozen eels easy." He peered more closely at the label. "Almost three hundred years old," he said, almost reverent.

Sanction moved into the dark interior, and moments later they heard a sparker flare, and the whoosh of oil. A central column lamp glowed to life, and mirrors carried the light to reflect over the whole yacht, bringing its forgotten decadence into full view.

Paintings on the walls and ceilings. Deep pile carpets. Cushions on everything. A cabinet of musical instruments and sheet music—even a harpsichord built into the wall. Everything had a touch of plush and artistry.

"Okay, better," Piccolo shrugged.

Sanction slung his heavy pack to the ground and opened it. "Food and water," he said with a proud gesture. Then he spread his hands to take in the whole yacht. "Also wine and drugs." He stepped over to a cabinet and opened it, revealing a massive set of minute compartments, nooks, shelves, and drawers. Opening one, he pulled out a tin full of dust.

"A little bit of everything, I suspect," he said as he looked at the dust on his fingertip.

"This is amazing," Gapjaw said, looking around. "So you figure the people in the house don't even know it is here."

"I'm not sure anyone but me knows," Sanction shrugged. "So it seems like a good hideout. And we were in Brightstone anyway."

"Okay," Piccolo said, "so you can plan your day. I'm going to get some sleep, then get drunk, then get stoned, then get some more sleep. Then, and only then, can we talk next moves."

"For once," Sanction replied, "that's my plan too."

CHAPTER THIRTEEN

Balancing the city's power with structure is impossible. Structures are occupied by individuals of varying passion and ability. Attempting to stabilize power through laws and rules is like trying to balance a gladiator match by throwing more weapons and armor into the ring. The power of Doskvol has always been its bloody hunger. It is hunger that propels the powerful towards more power, and it is hunger that motivates their enemies to drag them back from it. The only real check against the power lust of the rulers is the power lust of those they rule.

If humanity ever does curb that starving ambition, then the inevitable transition from rulership by mortals to rulership by vampires will accelerate. Vampires have the long view, and experience, and a hunger no mortal can match. So far the main resistance to this inevitability has flourished in the vampire's blind spot for the current moment. They get lost in future machinations and lose sight of unanticipated changes right before their eyes. The sharpening gift of mortality focuses humans and keeps the churn of power fresh, even when contained in ancient lines of aristocracy and tradition. Lo, before us is a new generation, and right behind it another. New faces, consumed in the oldest game.

— From "Six Inevitable Truths of Rulership"
by Lady Crolucia VenVaskell

SHRINE TO THE CLOSED EYE, SAILS ALLEY, CROW'S FOOT.
25ᵀᴴ ELISAR. SIXTH HOUR PAST DAWN.

"Quick and quiet, down the stairs, to the left," the man with the eyepatch said as he pointed down the crooked stone steps.

Inkletta led the way, followed by Red Silver and the Mistress of Tides. The foul miasma was almost a mist, they could feel it accumulate on their skin as they bustled down the stairs into the shabby and crooked sub-basement. They saw another corridor to the side, as well as an opening on the left with stairs leading further down, the entry framed by a metal cage door that was currently hauled up to the ceiling on a pulley and chain.

"Down the stairs?" Inkletta called back to the couple that followed them down the stairs.

"Quick and quiet," agreed the woman tonelessly.

Inkletta set her jaw, sensing that it was too late to reconsider their course of action. She headed down the stairs, blinking, and a cough slipped out as she struggled to breathe the foul air. The others followed, and the man and woman were right behind them as they entered an uneven chamber with wavering walls, variously compressed by the impossible weight of buildings above. One side of the chamber had a long wooden table, with a jar of crawling and glowing beetles on it. The other side of the chamber had another metal cage door frame, the door raised up by a chain.

The old couple caught up, and the man shook his head slightly. "We will go beyond where eyes follow," he murmured, "but we must be ready, we must be prepared." He looked to the woman, and she turned to the corner of the room, opening a shadowed wardrobe that had been dragged and battered long before ending up in this forgotten chamber. She pulled out long black robes.

"No time to be shy," the old man said with the first hint of intensity. "You are pursued. Put your clothing and gear on the table and put on the robes so you might be ready."

"Confuse all sight," wheezed the old woman, her one eye glinting in the light. "Confuse all sight that follows."

The scoundrels exchanged a glance, then stripped down quickly, pulling the black robes on. They were surprisingly silky, almost elegant in their plain simplicity.

"I keep the mask and veil," the Mistress of Tides said in response to the old man's unspoken question as he looked her over. He shrugged, then nodded to the woman.

"That way," she growled, pointing at the cage door and more stairs down. "Sanctuary from sight."

Red hesitated only a moment, then headed down the stairs. She paused, wincing.

"Shoes? Boots, sandals, something?"

"You will not need them," the man replied with a nod. "All is well."

She headed down the stairs, grimacing against the growing stench. Inkletta followed, and the Mistress of Tides brought up the rear.

As they reached the edge of the light glowing down the stairwell from above, they saw the glint of reflections on water. "There's no boat," Inkletta said.

Behind them, the grating clanged down, the old couple swiftly locking it in place.

"What is going on?" Red Silver demanded, rushing over to the stairs to glare up through the bars.

"A baptism of forgetfulness," intoned the old man, scratching at his filthy eyepatch. Beyond him, the woman shuffled up the stairs as the man continued. "We will hide you so you are never found. We will build your leftovers into the walls of the shrine when you have slipped between the lids of the Closed Eye, and join your mysteries to the single worthy Mystery beyond." He grinned, his face pouching unpleasantly, showcasing several missing teeth. "For a week we have prayed for sacrifices, and you have been sent to us. Praise the Mystery."

They felt a dull clang and thud through the stone, and with a burbling rush that disturbed the surface, water began pumping into the pool from somewhere below.

Red Silver took a step back on the stairs, suddenly aware of the scratches on the stone around the almost horizontal cage blocking the stair exit to the chamber above. She stood where the sacrifices drown. Her eyes were drawn to the dark gaze of the cultist who stood watching, waiting, and she viscerally felt the weight of the past, the times this death scene had played out over and over. Somewhere behind the cultist's eyes his lust had concentrated so keenly his face was expressionless, unnecessary, forgotten as he was alive to the imminent desperation and drowning.

Reeling from the moment, she turned her back on the cultist, descending the stairs towards her only hope. "Now what?" she demanded of the Whispers, unwilling to waste another moment on their captor.

"We must be calm," the Mistress of Tides murmured. "This is not where I drown." She turned, regarding the pool as it swelled, each net of ripples pushing further across the stone. "I will look into this." Fearless, she waded into the pool, then dropped out of sight.

"Can you do something about the cage door?" Red Silver asked, before locking her jaw so it would not tremble.

"Maybe," Inkletta shrugged, "but my gear is on that table."

"You didn't keep any tricks?" Red Silver asked, eyebrows raised.

"Not like you do," Inkletta shrugged, and she touched at the dark ink on her arm. "I've got some surprises stowed in my tats, of course." She looked to the water. "Let's give the Mistress of Tides a chance first."

The water was ankle deep and rising faster. Through the cage door, they saw the bland-faced woman with an eyepatch rejoin her man, but she was transformed by an eagerness now, and she rubbed her hands together as she stared through the bars at them, her expression twisted by anticipation so intense it nearly robbed her of reason.

"However this goes," Red Silver said through her teeth, "we come back and settle up with them, yeah?"

"Yeah," Inkletta agreed.

The Mistress of Tides descended into the turbulent water. Her heartbeat was a subdivision of the slow tidal rhythm of the world, so the machine-pumped current was an offense to her blood. She brushed the chin of her spirit mask, and it sent out a moonlight of energy released from a slowly decaying soul anchored in a diamond stud under the smooth bone eye covering of the mask.

She curled down like a comma of life, punctuating a pause between phases of being, and below her there was a deep pile of bones cleaned to glowing purity by the dark mass of crabs that shifted and scuttled, unsure of what the light could mean. Some were already riding currents up the walls, preparing for the meat they would clean.

And there, before her, ancient Imperial construction. Probably the wall of a sewer pump house, forgotten centuries ago as the tides of construction and condemnation washed over the face of the neighborhood in their ceaseless round.

Her lungs burned as she continued to be impossibly heavy in the buoyancy of her flesh, sliding around the current to reach the wall. Its grating was old, corroded, an embodiment of how centuries of dark currents and corruption could weaken the resolve of anything.

The Mistress of Tides let her hand drift into the current coming from the pipe. She listened carefully, tuning out the crisping crush of her heartbeat as it sucked her blood, desperate for oxygen. She sensed the ancient pump mechanism, the depth of the water on the other side, the pressure that longed to equalize and fill the foundations of the whole block. She sensed the flickering of their chances to survive, the magnitude of the danger they now faced.

Releasing her weight, she twisted into the current of inrushing water, propelled up and inward. She emerged through the surface, from death to life, and the water flowed down her like a last shedding of memory. The water was now waist high. The others hid their moment of relief upon her return, their doubt tinged with shame.

"No clear exit," the Mistress of Tides said. "I can take another look."

"We are running out of time," Red Silver said, subdued. "Inkletta?"

"I can get us through that grating," Inkletta said. She coughed a little, and slung her shoulder-length mane of hair around to the side, grabbing it into a column and squeezing water out. She shook her head like a wet dog. She snorted, then glanced at the others, something wild in her eyes.

"I'm going to need some room," she said in a rough voice. They backed away in the deepening water.

Inkletta focused, not breathing, then hyperventilated, then focused again. She raised her forearm, and clamped her palm over a tattoo, then let out a shout as she raised her cupped hand, dragging plasm through the Mirror where her skin served as its surface, a tiny gate to where she contained a spirit on the other side. In a violent spasm of her arm she yanked the plasm through in a luminous torn arch of energy above her. Focused, she let out a sound like a scream, but breathing in, and the arch twirled and twisted down into her nose and mouth, lighting up her flesh so her bones were shadows in the glowing wax of her meat, and her tattoos were grainy and dim on the surface.

Lunging forward into a stance, she unleashed a shriek that forcibly ejected the plasm mixed with the air of her life force, shaped by her bone and flesh. The energy plumed forward like a jet of flame, sluicing through the metal of the grating and striking the cultist, sending him flying back. Stretched too thin, the surface area of the energy burst, and a massive explosion rocked the cellar.

A moment later in the concussed darkness, the Mistress of Tides' mask shed light into the swirling sediment in the air. A dim luminous residue clung to the bars; Red Silver sloshed forward and banged the grating with her forearm, and the profoundly frozen metal snapped even as the cold bit into her arm. Ignoring the pain, she struck twice more, then stepped up through the broken bars into the chamber, sparing only a glance for the remains of the cultist; frozen, burned, and burst, it was a sloppy mess spread across half the chamber.

The Mistress of Tides supported Inkletta up out of the water, and Inkletta dropped to her knees and heaved, vomiting up some glowing leftovers. Red Silver retrieved her gear, stripping out of the wet robe and dressing in her dry clothes. She brought the Mistress of Tides her effects, and Inkletta slowly stood, rubbing the tattoos on either side of her throat.

"That was pretty badass," Red Silver said.

Inkletta nodded, and threw a handful of hand signs. Then stopped, a shadow of emotion crossing her face, and she just pointed at her throat.

"Right, takes some time to recover," Red Silver said, and Inkletta nodded. Then she took her effects from Red Silver and began pulling them on over her wet robe.

Moments later the scoundrels headed up the stairs only to find the next cage door also locked in place.

"Fine," Red Silver said through her teeth. "Let's check out the other exit." They headed back down to the sacrificial chamber, sidestepping the pieces of the cultist, and followed the corridor into darkness.

DANSE PARK, PAPER STREET, NIGHTMARKET. 25TH ELISAR. HOUR OF SONG, 2 HOURS PAST DUSK.

The dapper young limmer led the way, followed by the Hammer and Niece. They emerged from a cellar door under a pub, but the cellar did not connect to the pub. Up the street, offal tossed from the second floor splatted down in the gutter, and a passer-by swore; down the street, a busker slowly played a squeeze box while watching the crowd go by, his hat at his feet, not overly cluttered by coin. Across the street, a walk-up food counter perfumed the night with the smell of battered shrimp and fish, and fresh-baked shroomloaf.

"This feels like a dream," Niece said through numb lips.

"You'll sink back to the level of the real before long," her guide assured her. "I'm Niles, by the way. Congratulations on both of you making it back into the world, you bucked the odds." His smile was sharp and lean, and he used the head of his cane to knock his top hat to a jaunty angle before he led them out to the street.

The Hammer said nothing, but followed.

Niece grasped at Niles' sleeve. "What—where are we? What's going on? I don't know what we're doing." She stopped walking, and rubbed her face. "So goddamn lost."

Niles also stopped, and took a long moment to light his cigar with a plasmic sparker. He squinted at Niece.

"This is an understandable reaction," he agreed, "since you've been way out beyond today, and now you're back in the thick of all this nonsense," he said with an airy gesture at the street. "But you're not god damned, see there?" He gestured towards the park at the corner, and the black statue looming in the shadows. "That's the Night Queen, Nightmarket's adopted patron goddess. She'll look out for you," he said with a crooked grin. "You will also note you're dressed in nice clothes, respectable like. That's because you're scholars now," he continued. "You are planning to attend a symposium. Fancy, eh?" he said as his grin straightened but an eyebrow cocked. "You have an invitation to an invitation-only meeting of the minds to study one of the city's problems. It's an academia sort of thing," he shrugged.

"And here?" Niece asked.

"Here to meet your contact, who has been paid to take you to the symposium." Niles shrugged. "That's all I know. Father Crolaange is involved in this to do a favor for some mysterious buddy he has from years back, going to some effort to manage a handoff from one cutout contact to the next." He shook his head. "Too much cloak and dagger for this simple fellow."

"I get the feeling you're all about the cloak and dagger," Niece said, squinting at him like he was giving her a headache.

"Oh, I am," Niles agreed. "I'm your man for confidence artistry and a spot of knife work, all charisma and animal magnetism, but this is next level. Codes and nested plans. I'm exhausted just thinking about it." He paused. "Onward?"

"Onward," she agreed wearily, threading her arm through the crook of the Hammer's elbow and guiding him along with them. He stared at the cobbles, frowning, and kept pace.

They passed the fenced in park with its stone trees imported from the deathlands, rounding the corner to Song Street. A light snow began to fall as they approached a shelter by the road, for drivers to use when waiting for a fare. Several coaches stood ready, and Niles looked over the drivers and chose one.

"You must be Mr. Welker," he said. "I've got those scholars for the symposium. You were told I was coming, right?"

"Right," the driver sighed. "Up you go." He paused. "Luggage?"

"Sent ahead," Niles said with a false and charming grin not intended to fool anyone.

The driver shrugged and mounted the cab, and Niece climbed in with the Hammer right behind her. Niles slammed the door and waved as the cab pulled out to the road, leaving him behind.

"Hammer, I hate to ask, but... are you okay?" Niece asked as they jolted along. She tried to catch the Hammer's eye, and he reluctantly looked up at her. He was haunted. "What happened to you in there?" she murmured.

He gazed at her for a long moment, then shook his head, and his eyes dropped back down.

Niece watched the scenes of Nightmarket slide by, then they rattled across a bridge into the sooty shadowscape of Coalridge. A cascade of sparks fell by them, glowing and dying, as the road led them under the elevated light rail. Light touched at the skyline from many different angles, above and below. The view shifted texture, all velvet and chalk as the sooty lanterns hung here and there shedding enough light to reveal the skeletal vandalized plasm lamp posts.

Fresh jolts and rattles punctuated the trip as the carriage passed over rails that led to the old train station, before Gaddoc Station dominated all train travel. The hulking shadow slid by the window, and the carriage continued on towards the rippling sheet of darkness flowing past the banks. Before long, the carriage ground to a halt by the Ironworks docks, in the shadow of a manufacturing bay where welders assembled plates destined to serve as a ship's flank.

Niece reluctantly disembarked, looking around for the next step. The Hammer climbed out next to her, and looked up at the driver. He pointed his whip at The Estates Dock, then applied the whip to the goats, who let out an ill-tempered bleat and hauled at their straps, dragging the carriage away.

Niece and the Hammer followed the paving and steps down to the dock, where they saw a steam launch moored on the pier. Its captain was seated on a bench, reflectively smoking a pipe, but he jumped up as they approached.

"You are Dr. Rillkin's subject matter experts, I take it?" he asked. "Very good! I was not sure when you'd show exactly. I trust your travel was pleasant?"

"Yes," Niece said.

The captain paused for a moment, then nodded. "Well, good then. I'm Captain Reyburrow, and I'll be taking you to the symposium now." He cocked his head to the side. "No luggage?"

"No," Niece said, trying to smile.

"Well, no problem, welcome aboard," he said as he bowed, gesturing at the gangplank to the stubby boat. "We'll have you there in no time."

"That's such great news," Niece said. She boarded the boat, the Hammer at her heels.

The engine room flared as coal was shoveled into the furnace, and the launch belched steam before nosing out into the current, its one big wheel at the back churning away in the dark water.

"One of the services I offer is some small talk," the captain said to Niece. "We exchange pleasantries, I point out the landmarks. Even on this grim stretch," he said conspiratorially, letting her in on the joke as they plowed towards the left fork of the river. "On your left, the world-renowned incarcertatory facility, the grandest gaol, Ironhook Prison. On your right, the workhouses and factories of Charhollow." He paused. "You've got a lot on your mind," he observed.

"So much," Niece agreed, staring out across the water, seeing nothing.

"You?" the captain said, turning to the Hammer. The Hammer just shook his head, and looked down. "Very well," the captain shrugged. "I'll leave you to it."

"Where... if I might ask. Where are we going again?" Niece asked.

The captain glanced at her sideways. "You're headed to meet Dr. Rillkin, at the symposium." He paused. "Strangford House, on the island."

Niece squinted a minute, then a small smile emerged. "Thank you, captain," she said. She leaned back in her seat, and seemed to relax.

The rest of the journey passed in relative quiet, the engine's rhythmic thuds churning the paddle wheel, the water sloshing past, grim silhouettes and constellations sliding by on either side. Ahead, finally, the island loomed. Its massive walls and buildings were much better lit than those on either shore. Servants were waiting for them as the launch chugged to a rest by the pier.

"Greetings," one of the servants said with a broad smile. "You are here for Dr. Rillkin?"

"Absolutely," Niece agreed, crossing to the pier with the Hammer at her side.

The servant hesitated. "No luggage?"

"No," Niece replied, more sharply than she intended. "We just need to see Dr. Rillkin."

The servant smiled once more, and with a grand gesture, turned and led them along the pier, up the stairs, and through the massive door of a side entrance.

"The symposium is well underway, but Dr. Rillkin is a rather eccentric scholar," the servant said. "He's been given use of the Mastiff Library, on the south side, for his research. His summaries have provided Lord Strangford with considerable satisfaction, so I imagine that's the impetus for his special treatment," the servant explained. "He asked for you two to be brought to him here to accelerate his research, I hope you're ready for some heavy lifting. He's quite the scholar, as I'm sure you know."

"Quite the scholar," Niece agreed.

"I did not catch your names, however," the servant said, pausing by a stone archway with a mastiff's head carved into the center.

"Probably for the best," Niece confided, putting her hand on his forearm for a moment. Then she led the Hammer down a flight of stairs, into the library and all its bookish smells.

To the left, there were two long rows of freestanding shelves as well as the shelves built into the wall. Windows filled the long wall overlooking the river. Across that dark expanse, the coastline of Silkshore glittered. To the right, there were several study tables, and a couple overstuffed chairs were arranged in front of a massive fireplace with a stone dog on either side. The tables were piled with books and paper, the clutter of research. Also, a rangy old man smiled and opened his arms.

Niece took three steps and wrapped her arms around Trellis, hugging him tight, assured by the reality of his physical form. She let him go and stepped back, blushing, and Trellis shook hands with the Hammer.

"I'm so glad you made it," Trellis said with a broad grin. He was dressed in a fine shirt and breeches, wearing slippers and a smoking jacket, his hair combed and his face clean-shaven. He looked rested, hearty, and relaxed.

"You look none the worse for wear," Niece observed.

"As hiding places go, this one is choice," Trellis agreed. He crossed to the doors and hauled them shut, barring them. "Now we can speak somewhat freely," he said. "As far as I know, any observation would be somewhat limited here. That's one reason I chose it."

"So what's the word?" Niece demanded.

"Please, sit," Trellis said as he settled on one of the chairs before the fireplace. "I'm far more interested to know what news you bring," he added as the others sat.

"Sanction and Piccolo decided to go on some killing spree to hurt Lord Rowan, stabbing some of his kin. Aristocrats are pained by losing blood relatives, that's the idea," Niece said. "The Hammer didn't want to do that, so he found me where I was trying for a cover as a recent immigrant, and we put the notice in the paper, to look for you."

"I see," Trellis nodded. "And the others?"

"I have no idea," Niece shrugged. "The Hammer said that Sanction and Piccolo had Gapjaw and Safety with them, so hopefully they're still together. But the Whispers? Red Silver? I wouldn't know where to start." She hesitated. "The Hammer found out Saint is in Ironhook, and my aunt Rhya is too. We were hoping you could come up with a plan to get them out."

Trellis let that stand between them as he looked into the fire. "Yes," he said after a moment. "We will certainly get them out. And keep them safe," he clarified. He looked over at them. "It is good to see you two again," he confessed. "Thank you for enduring my security precautions to get you here."

"Generally no problem," Niece said, something evasive in her eyes, "except for Crolaange. The, uh, cleansing."

"Yes, about that," Trellis said, shifting in his seat. "I don't know what they told you, but the fact of the matter is, we have some business that was mutually beneficial some time back, and I know they have little use for money or aristocratic threats, and besides they could eliminate any tracers. I hope they didn't get too melodramatic."

"The Hammer went through the baptism with me and hasn't said much since," Niece said in a small voice. "I don't know if he ever will again. What I experienced was pretty intense. I have no idea what his experience was."

Trellis leaned back, a distant look in his eyes. "Long ago, I found my purpose in a similar situation. It changed my life. These—alterations in perceptions. They can be very influential." He looked the Hammer in the eye. "Maybe it will just take some time."

"How much time do you think we have?" Niece asked.

"That is a tricky equation," Trellis replied, rising and facing the other two. "We have four days, that's the ultimate answer."

"Awfully specific," Niece replied, eyebrows raised.

"That's the next meeting of the City Council, 29th Elisar," Trellis replied. He turned his back on them, walking over to gaze out the window at the light snowfall over the river. "There are six members of the Council, and currently Bowmore, Clelland, and Rowan are aligned against Strangford. They want to remove the house from the Council and transfer control of the Leviathan hunting fleet to the Ministry of Preservation, as an energy concern that affects the safety of the city."

"So you came to Strangford to hide from Rowan, since they're political enemies," Niece said.

"Additionally, Strangford has this symposium going on, scholars predicting where the best Leviathan hunting will be in the coming season," Trellis said. "So, I had a cover, and there was sufficient bustle for me to reach Lord Strangford and have a conversation without drawing the attention of spies. Of which there are, naturally, a pile." He glanced over his shoulder at them. "Try not to talk to people, or risk your cover as my subject matter experts."

"Of course not, Dr. Rillkin," Niece replied with an arched eyebrow.

Trellis smirked. "For the benefit of the spies, I'm having an affair with Lady Strangford, so she slips in here for a few hours now and then and we give each other updates on the state of our plots. That's how the gossip explains the preferential treatment I get; for example, my own library," he said with a broad gesture. "As I am sure you know, Lord Rowan can't call a truce, so we must bring him low. Also, we lack the resources to do that without just assassinating him, and if we kill him we've got bigger problems than we do now—and our problems now are substantial."

"I don't like your plan so far," Niece confessed.

"That's not so much my plan as the boundary of my plan," Trellis shrugged. "My plan involves Strangford, obviously, and also Dunvil and Penderyn, the last two members of the City Council. If Rowan's alliances go awkward or disintegrate, there's fallout there that benefits those who are not part of the alliance. Rowan was pretty heavily leveraged politically before he overreacted to a threat and surged against his normal limits. Destroying him is not the issue," Trellis continued, strolling over to the desk and choosing nuts out of a bowl, filling his hand one by one, attentive to his task. "We could kill him, we could have him killed; that's amateur posturing. Most of those pathways have lethal blowback; we would accomplish our objective and that satisfaction would have to warm us in the grave."

He turned back to the others. "Instead the objective must be to defuse the wrath of the elite and to neutralize Lord Rowan specifically. Let us not lose sight of our bonus objectives of regaining as much of our lives as possible, and discouraging others from coming right at us as Rowan did."

"I'm glad this is all easy for you," Niece said, as neutral as she could manage.

"It is delicate surgery, but I am a surgeon; that's my training, my task, and my passion," he shrugged. "I looked at Lord Rowan first, to learn about his strengths and weaknesses. Then he is removed, and I study his context; his alliances, his enemies, his opportunities, his persistent troubles. Then my gaze widens to the forces that make his victories and his defeats possible, to consider what they need from Rowan and what they want from him, how he has hurt them and how he has helped them. A few stark opportunities emerge through that process," he shrugged, and he ate a nut as though it was a singular morsel of delight.

"But you need some operatives," Niece realized.

Trellis pointed at her. "Precisely," he said. "Proper scoundrels, prepared to carry out the work. Experts, professional ne'er do wells." He smiled. "I think it's about time we got the crews back together."

Something unclenched in Niece's chest, and she realized she was smiling too.

"Yeah," she said. "Let's do that."

◄══┐ CHAPTER FOURTEEN ┌══►

It is a hard thing to be mastered by one who does not love you. This is true for politics just as it is in families. The final blow in an indifferently abusive relationship was the Immortal Emperor's decree that plasmic refinement would center in Lockport, a city that had a ten year legal wrangle among its chiefs to grudgingly allow the first cannery for its fishing fleet.

In less than a year, the city famous for scrimshaw, canny fishing expertise, and white cliffs was overbuilt to five times its size. The original city was a neighborhood, surrounded by massive refineries and military installations. Slippage and accidents released slicks of undying blood still writhing in demonic agony that left people changed; the mist released by refinement sometimes left a twist of deathless misery and rage in the fog. The cliffs turned black.

It was enough to send the Skovs to war. Over two thousand Skov refugees poured into Doskvol, the closest port, during the war. Even more came after Skovlan lost.

One of them was a sixteen year old winsome lass whose uncle (Hutton) ran the Grinders, a Skov gang of Lockport refugees. Her first week in town, an Akorosian thief stabbed her in the gut. Her own people reported her dead as she lay nursing a mortal wound, and when it looked like she might survive, they tried to kill her; mere facts should not defuse an act of war, even if it is only a gang war. She escaped, found the criminals who attacked her uncle and her people, and offered to broker peace. She could manage it because she was Hutton's niece; in an underworld driven by wealth and relationships, it was the "Niece" part that stuck, and her name was lost behind it.

She survived dislocation and assault, and chose to try and build a new home with diplomacy among dangerous criminals. She had Skov immigrant credentials, and local grievance, and she used that to bolster credibility among Skovs, giving her authority to counter claims she was nothing more than a mouthpiece for the native criminals. She was smart, and tough, and a nat-

ural networker. She had an instinct for turning loss into power. Of course she became a target.

— *From "Roots, Grudges, and Blood: the Skovlan Influx"*
by Cyriun Talvadge

ROWAN TOWNHOUSE, WHITEHALL.
25ᵀᴴ ELISAR. HOUR OF SILVER, 3 HOURS PAST DUSK.

Saint sipped at his tea, looking out through the slightly warped glass at the dimness of the evening street as a bell chimed the hour in the nearby square. The compressed algae log in the fireplace hissed as another chunk crumbled off, burned and spent. Saint winced slightly, and pulled out the bottle of pain-killing powder from his vest, opening it and tapping a bit into his tea, then stirring it in with a spoon so it dissolved to the pleasing sound of silver clinking on thin ceramic.

The side door opened, and Leslin stood in the doorway, once again dignified in his dark suit. He stepped into the room reluctantly. He was pale, his eyes dark, and a look of revulsion unsettled his features. Saint could not miss noticing the knife depending from his belt. Leslin said nothing, his thumb tracing over the spirit bane charm he held, his eyes locked on Saint.

"Good afternoon," Saint said experimentally.

"I understand you are the architect of the intrusion into Lord Rowan's unveiling," Leslin said, steady. "You led the scoundrels that took me."

"Yes," Saint replied.

For a long moment, they watched each other. Saint spoke first.

"For what it's worth, I went to investigate. My orders to the crew were very specific; they were not to take anything." He shrugged. "It's hard to find good help."

"I'm supposed to believe you weren't there to sabotage the project?" Leslin sneered, emotion driving the mockery as he struggled to stay cool.

"We had no idea what the project was," Saint replied quietly. "You overestimate our spies. We were there to try and find out what Lord Rowan was doing, and why it was causing such a stir among better informed criminals." He paused. "That was enough ambition for us. That was information we could sell. I thought we were being ambitious just trying to get in." He sighed. "Turns out we were," he said with a gesture to his braced and bandaged leg.

"Your forger," Leslin said abruptly. "He sold us the information of your cover identity. We knew you were coming."

"Huh," Saint said, a distant look in his eye. He shrugged the moment off. "I was caught before the presentation. Here's the thing," he said, leaning forward with a wry grin. "I *still* don't know what Rowan's secret project is."

Leslin stared at him a long moment, then barked a laugh. "This is the future," he said, extending his hands to the sides so his wrists slid further out of his sleeves, revealing black disks embedded in his flesh. "I am the key to an electroplasmic security system that even Whispers cannot sabotage. I can manipulate the energy moving through an interconnected system. I can see through mirrors, shock through contact plates, speak through resonators, and lock down doors." He shrugged. "It's the future. I am the future."

Saint cocked his head to the side, his mind racing. "That must cost a fortune to power," he said.

"That's the best part," Leslin replied, warming to the subject in spite of himself. "Ambient collection. The condensers are calibrated to draw energy directly from the Ghost Field, boiling it down and storing it for use. Refined electroplasm is only necessary for backup, in case there is a problem. Or in case the background is sufficiently depleted, which is a real likelihood over time."

"Are you serious?" Saint said, eyes wide. "That—with collectors like that, the lightning walls will be obsolete in a generation!" he said breathlessly.

"If that!" Leslin agreed, caught up in the moment. "With dedicated factories and the necessary security, we could begin implementing these systems, starting with aristocratic bastions in the city core and moving out. And the possibilities for customizing, I mean, it becomes possible for a private individual to create a relatively safe space outside the city ring."

Saint shook his head, searching for words, then he looked Leslin in the eye, pointing at him for emphasis. "You, sir, you are a pioneer into a future of human liberation," he said, something like awe in his voice. "This changes everything. Agriculture? You could make a new form of radiant irrigation. War? Oh ho!" he said, enthusiasm getting the better of him.

"Long range weaponry," Leslin agreed, leaning forward. "And if the enemy deploys plasmic weapons? They just reinforce our reserves!" His smile revealed a missing canine, recently knocked out. "We unbalance the battlefield to force foes to come at us with primitive weapons while we fight with *lightning*."

The door opened, breaking the spell, and Lord Rowan entered the room with a bemused look at the two men waiting for him.

"Leslin," he said quietly. "Are you feeling better?"

"Much improved," Leslin said, cooling down, tugging the front of his shirt into alignment. "Thank you sir. Thank you for coming to find me."

"Indeed," Lord Rowan said, standing behind the chair at the head of the table. "We have Saint to thank for narrowing down the search to uncover your hiding place." He paused. "I'll understand if you don't want to thank him personally," he said, unreadable.

A woman came through the door behind him, dressed in wine-dark vestments with a red collar. Leslin immediately rose to his feet and bowed his head, looking down at the table; Saint struggled for his crutches.

"As you were, gentlemen," the woman said, forestalling further pleasantries with a gesture.

"May I introduce you to Mother Talitha Grine, based out of Brightstone," Rowan said with an ambiguous smile. "Mother Grine is on loan from the Church of Ecstasy to offer immediate access to church resources in the continuing effort to round up the fugitives."

Mother Grine smiled, her too-red lipstick in stark contrast with the almost yellow paleness of her features. Her eyes were dark and magnetic, her hair cropped close to her skull. She had a peculiar grace, an almost alien beauty. Her age was difficult to guess; no longer young, but deeply vital.

"I understand you've been helpful," she said to Saint.

"I like the idea of a future," he replied with a broad smile. "I'm all for tidying up the last details of my past." He looked to Rowan. "I'm doing my best to pay my debt to society."

"He's been very cooperative," Rowan agreed, turning to Mother Grine. "I think we may need to use him as bait." Saint shrugged agreeably.

"Does the church have any leads?" Leslin asked.

Mother Grine ignored him, speaking to Rowan. "I see your prisoner here, and it reminds me. When you pulled this one out of Ironhook," she said with a gesture towards Saint, "you did place an assassin impostor, yes? I assume they will attempt a rescue sooner or later."

"Already done," Rowan agreed.

"I see your adept here, and it reminds me," Mother Grine continued. "We've talked about the more traditional methods, but it just now occurs to me to ask what kinds of ritual magic you used to attempt to track the fugitives." She almost concealed her distaste.

"Well, we have access to the adepts sanctioned by the Spirit Wardens," Rowan said, "and I've hired a number of freelancers, concentrating mainly on the Tangle, in Crow's Foot." He shrugged. "They have been unsuccessful. I get excuses about hiding by spirit wells, or in places protected by rituals, or not having enough of their physical form or loved objects." He shook his head. "We've got a pile of physical material from these scoundrels, dredged from their friends and known hideouts. Even the fastidious among us leave something behind."

"I'm not entirely startled that your ephemeral efforts have failed to yield concrete results," Mother Grine replied, pointedly not looking at Leslin.

"We also hired some specialists," Rowan said, more quietly. "A guild of problem solvers. Twice they have managed to get a tracer on one of the fugitives."

"But not capture them or kill them on the spot?" Mother Grine said, eyebrows raised.

"One leads to others," Rowan shrugged. "My priority is Trellis, Lord Belderan. If the others can lead me to him that's my most efficient path."

"How does one rid oneself of a supernatural tracer such as what these assassins use?" Mother Grine asked directly.

Rowan looked away. "I'm not sure," he said distantly. "Every method they suggested seemed a long shot or an insane risk." His thoughts returned to the present, and he reasserted himself. "We can talk about the hunt later. For the moment, I've come to check on you," he said to Leslin. "We have some delayed appointments for showcasing our test environment to some key supporters." He paused. "How are you feeling, Leslin?" he asked.

"Very little permanent damage," Leslin said through his teeth, unsmiling. "I am ready to run the system, sir."

"Yes," Rowan said firmly. "I knew I could count on you."

"If I may," Saint said, "I ask that I please be allowed to come along and see this in action." His face shifted with a ruddy shine of admiration. "When I heard about this innovation, I was deeply intrigued."

"Yes, your curiosity certainly served you well," Rowan said, dry, eyes pointing to Saint's splinted leg.

"If this can do what Leslin says it can," Saint replied seriously, "all that suffering is a small price to pay to be part of it."

Rowan took that in for a moment, then turned to Leslin. "Any objection to this scoundrel who masterminded your abduction coming along to your workplace?" he asked sardonically.

"Maybe we should have him close by so we can keep an eye on him," Leslin replied with the barest of smiles, struggling back towards banter. He looked over at Saint. "It's fine with me."

"Right then," Rowan said. "Let's go."

CANDLE STREET, CROW'S FOOT.
25ᵀᴴ ELISAR. NINTH HOUR PAST DAWN.

Finally, they leaned back against either side of the indifferently built tunnel, the darkness relieved by an oval of dim light crosshatched by a grating between underground and the streets. They heard the babble of voices, the clatter of wagons, the bleat of goats. Finally, the stench of the underground was interwoven with the stink of civilization.

"So we're almost out," Red Silver muttered. "What's the plan when we reach open air?" She absently rubbed at one of the glyphs on her forearm, and the reddened flesh around it hissed almost inaudibly as the glyph glowed like an ember under gentle breath.

Exhausted, Inkletta shook her head and gestured a signal with her hand; she had nothing to contribute.

The Mistress of Tides hesitated fractionally, then folded the veil up from before her face, and tugged the hat off, dropping both in the tunnel. She pulled the spirit mask from her face, and looked the others in the eye.

"We go to the Empress of Gulls. She will hide us for the night. Long enough to rest. I trust her, even if I trust no one else we will pass on our way to her."

Inkletta and Red Silver exchanged a glance, then looked back to Mistress of Tides.

"It's a bold plan," Red Silver said, "but we're with you."

The Mistress of Tides smiled, and Red Silver shook her head.

"I'm just really not used to you having a face," she said with half a smile.

The Mistress of Tides patted her shoulder. Then they turned and followed the tunnel, shoving through the often-sabotaged grating and vanishing into the street traffic.

The Hammer slouched in his chair, chin on his chest, eyes sightlessly watching the fire. Niece didn't bother suppressing the jaw-cracking yawn that flexed her whole body. She glanced blearily over to where Trellis had moved out of sight, bustling around in the library.

"I could sleep for a week," she said quietly.

Trellis returned to the table with a slim case, snapping the lock catch releases and tilting the case open. "There we are," he said reflectively.

"Secret weapon?" Niece asked with half a smile.

"Yes," Trellis replied with a tone of supreme satisfaction.

Niece hefted herself out of the chair and strolled over to take a look as Trellis began unpacking the case onto the table. Looking at the bundles and packages, she frowned.

"Is that—are you serious?" she said, trying to control her tone.

"Indeed," he replied, hands busy.

"This makes me *very* uncomfortable," she said, picking up a finger-sized stuffed doll with tufts of hair on its head, a fingernail clipping stitched on its torso, and oily smudges rubbed on it. "This one is mine, Trellis."

"If it makes you feel any better, I've never used it," he shrugged, pulling out the other sample containers and arranging them on the table.

"Those are essentials!" she said, pointing at the small neatly labeled boxes. She put the focus doll down, picking up a box and opening it to see the dusty material inside.

"Essentials are easier to use for ingredients, easier to store, they keep their potency longer," Trellis shrugged.

"Trellis, you've made these—you can have a ritual lock on any of your crew!" she protested. "And the River Stallions!" she added, louder, looking over the names on the boxes.

He paused, looking up. "Well, yes," he replied. "Of course," he said, orienting on her, a curious cast to his features. "You came to me because you knew I'd have a plan. I'd be prepared. Yes?" He looked at the case. "This is part of my preparation. And now you're glad I did this extremely creepy and threatening background work, because tonight we'll have a ritual where I can reach into the dreams of your crew and mine, and coordinate our next move." He looked back at the case and its contents. "I put this one together after the Gratitude Festival, got most of the ingredients after many of those present were stunned senseless with celebration." He smiled fondly. "I've got an adept that helps me with the essentials ritual."

"So... how many cases... people to target, and backups for us—" Niece struggled to form the mass of unpleasant inquiry into specific questions.

"Please stop," Trellis said pleasantly, returning to his work.

"Yes, you're right—of course you're right," Niece said, feeling a touch of numbness. She nodded. "Let's focus on the task at hand."

"There's my girl," he smiled.

PIER 18, NORTH HOOK ANNEX, THE DOCKS.
25TH ELISAR. HOUR OF FLAME, 5 HOURS PAST DUSK.

The carriage rattled to the side of the sparsely populated thoroughfare. Leslin and Rowan's elite agents, Sanders and Belton, got out on one side of the carriage. Saint struggled to free himself of it and end up on his feet, trying to manage his splinted leg on his own. He had no crutch. Impatient, Belton took him by the elbow and roughly pulled him out of the carriage, and dragged him towards the sally port into the warehouse with a grip that offered equal parts support and coercion as Saint staggered and hopped.

The warehouse was flanked by stairs down to the sea level, and a dock that extended out, modestly sized for ships and smaller boats. Its weather-beaten colorless exterior did not advertise contents of interest, but almost every building at the docks was designed to deflect attention.

The door into the warehouse opened into a cage twelve feet long and wide, with a low ceiling and another door on the other end—this one controlled by the plasmic system. Leslin unlocked it, leading the way into the dimness. He flipped a breaker switch, and electroplasm lighting glowed before shining, illuminating the space.

Smaller structures filled the big open space of the warehouse; sample walls, doors, living areas, and storage rooms filled the warehouse floor with a counter-intuitive maze.

"The control room is upstairs," Leslin said as he jogged up the metal staircase bolted to the wall. "Bring him, will you?" he called back to the guards, who exchanged a look. The guards hefted Saint, one clamped on each elbow, and followed.

The top of the stairs led to a catwalk that ended in a boxed-in control room. The ceiling of the control room extended heavy cabling down to fuse boxes below, which were connected to reserve electroplasmic tanks. The cables continued down out of the control room, along the wall of the warehouse until they reached its floor, then snaking into the simulation environment. Leslin smiled in spite of himself as he started the system, adjusting the control panel opposite the dimly glowing reserve tanks, then looking to the far end of the control room where the throne waited, its cabled helmet off to the side on a stand.

"I need to have this ready for Lord Rowan and his guests," Leslin explained as he adjusted the settings. "He's going to run a demo. And you get to watch," he said with a grin, sparing a look to Saint.

"I can't wait," Saint grinned.

Leslin's smile faltered. "You know, at some point it seems likely we will be luring your former friends here, under one pretext or another. I figure at least one of them will die down there," he said, pointing at the maze.

Saint looked him in the eye. "I was crippled and thrown in Ironhook for daily torture," he said, his voice even. "Getting crisped in one go seems a mercy to me."

Leslin studied him for a moment, then shook his head. "You've got a cold streak, Saint," he said. "Now let's get this started." He moved to the throne and sat, his wrists connecting to the plates on the arms of the throne with a clack. Sanders followed, settling the helm on Leslin and getting him adjusted.

"I know you're going to try something," Belton said frankly to Saint, arms crossed over his chest. "Maybe escape, maybe assassination, maybe theft; who knows," he shrugged. "When you do I'm going to be there, ready to kill you." He cocked his head to the side. "I am ready to kill you right now," he added.

"Maybe I'll surprise you," Saint replied with a winning smile.

"That's my point. You won't," Belton said flatly.

"Well, at least we have some common ground," Saint said, looking out over the maze.

"We really don't," Belton retorted.

Saint looked over at him with a wry smile. "I can't wait for this to be over," he said.

Belton blinked, then shrugged.

"Fair enough," he said.

In the maze below, mirrors flickered and locks snapped open and shut, lights dimmed and flared, and one man's will flowed through the empty rooms and corridors.

EMPRESS OF GULLS' WORKSHOP SLOOP WRECK, TANGLETOWN, CROW'S FOOT. 25TH ELISAR. HOUR OF PEARLS, 6 HOURS PAST DUSK.

The door creaked open, and a handsome shirtless man peered warily out of the well-lit chamber at the three hooded and cloaked figures waiting outside.

"The Empress of Gulls sees no one without an appointment," the man said in a pleasing baritone.

"I bear a message from the Mistress of Tides," the hooded figure in the lead murmured.

"Wait," the man frowned, closing the door.

"Really? You bear a message?" Red Silver said sardonically.

"Well, I do," the Mistress of Tides shrugged. "If we are sent away, then my relationship with the Empress of Gulls is not what I thought it was, and it is best I not confess to being within range of easy capture."

"You are really smart," Red Silver replied.

"It's true," the Mistress of Tides agreed.

The door creaked open again, and the man stepped aside deferentially. The Whispers and Red Silver passed him almost soundlessly before the door closed behind them.

"I expected you earlier," said the elderly woman on the throne, her posture proud and erect, her features hidden behind a heavy veil. Knobbled hands were restless on the arms of the throne, touching at its interwoven driftwood and bone. "I trust you knew this place would be safe for you."

"Too many people know you would offer me safety," the Mistress of Tides replied quietly. "The world needs you in it more than I need a temporary respite. We face grave danger from many sides."

"Yet here you are," the Empress of Gulls replied.

"Vigilance is unlikely to be eternal, and even if I am spotted here, there are ways out." The Mistress of Tides paused. "We must hide Red Silver's curse, and I know of few places that could shelter us from scrying, seeker rituals, or prying eyes for a night. We need a little time to figure our next move."

The Empress of Gulls regarded the inner walls of the workshop, where bands of ritual protections were softly glowing, and several had already flaked off the wall, disintegrated. "That's quite a curse," she observed. "Razor Wind was here looking for you."

The trio of visitors said nothing.

The Empress of Gulls smiled behind her veil. "I told him there was a disturbance at Lord Rowan's party, and off he went to investigate." She paused. "He was very polite, and one of the most evil creatures I've ever seen." She shook her head. "The power in him. It radiated in waves. Yet I sensed his own death among the others he carries. He draws near to it."

"Are we safe here?" the Mistress of Tides asked quietly.

"Yes," the Empress of Gulls replied without hesitation.

The Mistress of Tides switched to Hadrathi. "Then let tomorrow bear its share of troubles."

"For tonight, we stand tall," the Empress of Gulls said with an audible smile, finishing the ancient verse.

The long room seemed bound together with light, buoyant against the storm-lashed background of endless waves of shadow. However briefly, the weight of vigilance eased back, and the scoundrels drew a deeper breath.

"I don't know about you," the Mistress of Tides said, "but I need a drink."

MASTIFF LIBRARY, STRANGFORD HOUSE, OVERLOOKING CHARHOLLOW. 25TH ELISAR. HOUR OF FLAME, 5 HOURS PAST DUSK.

Trellis consulted his pocket watch. "Very nearly the Hour of Pearls, when today dies and tomorrow is born," he murmured to himself. He looked over at the table. "Are we ready?"

"Nearly," replied the bald man, tightly wrapped in a strangely designed robe, liberally decorated with bangles and jewelry. He turned his kohl-rimmed eyes to Trellis, strangely morose. "The ritual is prepared, and I need heat and breath on both sides of the Mirror."

"That's our cue," Niece said, somewhat nervous as she sat at the table. The Hammer sat beside her, and she took his hand, and the chilly hand of the ritualist.

"So, you're a proper Whisper, right?" she asked hesitantly.

"Yes, you may call me Evergreen," the Whisper replied. "I was once an adept, until I first encountered a Leviathan close up."

"Fascinating," Trellis said, his tone contradicting the sentiment. He sat down and joined hands with the Hammer and Evergreen. "You are prepared to connect these dreams all into a singular space, right?"

"Yes," Evergreen nodded. "You will be able to instruct them, or hear from them. Communication can be difficult, so do not assume you can interpret a statement—ask for clarification unless you understand clearly."

"What should we do?" Niece asked.

"You concentrate on your breathing," Evergreen said. "In through the nose, out through the mouth, keep it as steady as you can. Feel the life force of the others in the circle. Hold up that life. Then the spokesman should be empowered to concentrate on his role for communication." Evergreen looked at Trellis. "Any questions?"

"Let's do it," Trellis replied, grim.

Evergreen nodded, then lowered his head and centered his energies. He began speaking the ritual in Hadrathi. First naming the earth, the sky, the sea, then naming the gates through which they communicate, then Doskvol's most ancient Litany of Place. An aggressive weight gathered in the consciousness of those in the ritual, and they did not resist it.

Together, they slid out of the world, tumbling down among the dreams.

ROWAN TOWNHOUSE, WHITEHALL.
26ᵀᴴ ELISAR. THE HOUR OF SILK, 7 HOURS PAST DUSK.

Saint gasped, choking on his own yell, spasming and thrashing in the bed. He managed to drag himself upright.

"Help!" he shouted, hoarse. "Help me! We gotta move!" He struggled to get out of the bed, shouting as loud as he could.

Two guards arrived first, wild eyed.

"Get the coaches ready! Get the troops ready! Get moving!" Saint bellowed at them, but as one guard stared at him the other looked around warily.

"I said get moving!" Saint almost screamed, hauling himself up. "Get me Rowan! Get me that church lady! Anybody!"

As Saint tried to drag on a house robe, Rowan appeared in the doorway, his expression dark. "What's the matter, Saint?" he demanded.

"Trellis!" Saint gasped. "I know where he is!" His face was pale and sweaty, his jaw slack, his eyes painfully wide. "Ritual, talked to us in our sleep, in dreams, set the meet!" He hurled his boot to the ground, unable to work the buckles in his panicked state. "We need to get there now!"

Rowan was already moving, barking orders, and the whole household lit up in the deep of the night as servants and soldiers raced around preparing to move.

"Six Towers!" Saint shouted. "Mistshore Park!" The first riders raced to the stables. "Six Towers!" Saint bawled as loud as he could. "Get to Mistshore Park!"

Ten minutes later he was swaying along in the carriage, along with Belton and Mother Grine. Lights strobed by from the massive electroplasmic torches illuminating the bridge as the carriage swept past them, and beyond that, the surface of the Void Sea was a glitter in profound shadows below. The close-fit bridge paving and the craftsmanship of the carriage provided a ride smoother than most boats could manage. Nevertheless, Saint clutched at the handle on the wall as though his life depended on it.

"This is an odd moment for you to bet your life on an outcome," Mother Grine said, bloodless.

"I'm cooperating as best I can," Saint gulped. "Aren't you permanently on Lord Rowan's elbow for these things?"

"He's on horseback pretending to be a guard," she replied with a dismissive wave. "I'll reconnect when we arrive."

"Seems you took your time to offer help," Saint observed.

She cocked an eyebrow at him. "We assumed he had the situation in hand. The church asked me to provide support when it seemed he might need it."

"It was the Inkwine raid, wasn't it," Saint mused. "The Inkwine Center for Refocusing. He got too close to somebody else's secrets." Saint nodded. "When he rescued Leslin."

Mother Grine frowned. "You misunderstand my role," she said. "I am here to offer support."

"Yeah, like I don't know Cleith Rowan's uncle is Elder Dracha Rowan, who is the head of the Church of Ecstasy," Saint said. He shook his head. "Maybe family support is evaporating. Maybe this isn't even about the church." He grinned as his face lit up with a sudden insight. "I bet you're here to monitor the situation for the rest of the family!" Saint winced. "Ouch."

"Keep guessing," Mother Grine said, expressionless. "See what happens if you hit a nerve."

"Hey, I need Cleith to come out of this a winner," Saint shrugged, eyeing Mother Grine. "I'm just trying to get a sense of the lay of the land. The Rowans need friends. They need Trellis to disappear." His eyes were earnest. "I'm doing my best to help you," he said.

For a long moment, she studied him. "You are a good liar," she mused, then she shifted restlessly. "That's not fair. You are stunning. You are a real talent." She cocked her head. "Still. You lie."

Saint looked puzzled. "Huh. What do you think is giving me away here?" he asked, almost petulant.

"You believe it," she replied, something vague in her tone. "When you are completely honest, there is always a part of you that does not trust yourself. You do not believe in absolutes. Not until you must. You only open the gates of true sincerity to drive a message through them; you have no use for real truth in your own life."

With a bone-jarring clatter, the carriage crossed the threshold of the bridge, where it reconnected with the paving on land. Saint held on tight, watching Mother Grine.

"I guess we'll see," he said.

She leaned back, satisfied, and her eyes glittered as she watched Saint's every move.

CHAPTER FIFTEEN

When the Gates of Death were shattered, and the Immortal Emperor rose, the entire field of theological enterprise was obliterated. Speculation about higher powers and the afterlife seemed in poor taste. Still, humans need to organize their inner lives, and as they sought a new balance, religious veneration followed two main paths.

The Immortal Emperor lent support to the refocused worship of the mystery of life, seated in blood and bone and air, and recognized the new Church of Ecstasy of the Flesh. If religion must create an "us" and a "them" then all those living could be the "us" group, and those refusing to leave upon dying could be "them." This did not create the hoped-for unity, but did provide a workable state religion with mysteries, rituals, structure, and costumes.

The other path was to worship things beyond understanding, and personify them. Humans once gazed at the stars before the sky broke; they drew pictures between points of light and gave them names and stories, granted them authority over their lives. So too with the Forgotten Gods, drawn from fragments of stories, inexplicable experiences, or the dreams of the mad. The point is to have secrets that allow people to love, fear, belong, and sacrifice, all without undue interference from the object of worship.

Living flesh minds its own business. But at some point, when the faithful whispered to the nothing, the nothing started whispering back.

— From "Findings of a Heretic Scholar"
by Fr. Dunswether Kakel

MISTSHORE PARK, SIX TOWERS.
26TH ELISAR. HOUR OF WINE, 8 HOURS PAST DUSK.

The carriage rolled around the circle drive at the south gate to the park, passing the six horses that stood with wide eyes and sweat-lathered flanks, three guards holding on to their bridles and reins. Saint squinted at the animals, as he had rarely seen horses close up. Their tiny heads, massive necks, and spindly legs were strange proportions to eyes accustomed to the draft goats that hauled most of the city's loads. Horses were rare and expensive, but had the incredible ability to amplify the speed of one or two people at a time. Scouts were already in Mistshore Park, looking for support for Saint's insistence that Trellis was here. Saint bit his lip, feeling sweat trickle down his ribs, his heart beating no faster than usual, but perhaps a bit harder.

Belton yanked the door open and pulled Saint out; the scoundrel hopped and staggered, then was hefted upright before Lord Rowan, who pointed a flinty stare at him.

"It is the Hour of Chains," Rowan said quietly, "which seems fitting enough. Still two hours until dawn." He turned his back on Saint to regard the gate. "Perhaps the darkest hour of the night."

One of Rowan's scouts easily clambered up the gate and vaulted over it, landing neatly and striding over. "Sir, I spotted a couple scoundrels doing some spade-work near the temple," he said.

"Digging?" Rowan echoed, his forehead creased. "Alright, did you see anyone else?"

"There was a light burning in the boathouse by the river, someone was moving inside. It was a woman, and she appears to be alone."

Two more wagons rolled up in the meantime, and a dozen armed men and women disembarked to form a loose crowd, their expressions grim under the merciless light of the lamp posts. Lord Rowan turned to them.

"Alsan, take your men to the boathouse and secure it. Don't let anyone destroy anything that might offer clues as to what they are about here. Bolt, take your men and bring me back these diggers and whatever they're burying or digging up. Go." He crossed his arms over his chest, and a troubled expression surfaced as his agents expertly snapped the gate lock and rushed into the park, moving fast and relying on the ambient light trickling into the shadows of the park from the street and the slightly luminescent clouds.

Mother Grine stood at his side, gazing at the darkened park. "It has been years since you rode a horse in the city," she observed, "and as far as I know, never at that pace." She regarded Saint. "He has motivated you," she said.

"Of course Trellis would use dreams to contact his people," Lord Rowan replied tonelessly. "It's the sort of crooked move that is consistent with his capabilities and creativity. Also, Saint has been right so far, all down the line. I would be a fool to let my pride blind me to this opportunity. Besides," he said, turning to look her in the eye, "if he fails, he is entirely within my power. So there's that."

"Unless it's a trap," Mother Grine replied, raising an eyebrow. "Here you are with hardly any guards."

"I have you," he shrugged, "and not one of my agents has your record."

Mother Grine threw a sharp look at Saint, suppressing her flash of irritation before it surfaced. "This is not about me," she said to Lord Rowan.

"It really isn't," he agreed, his patience thinning as he watched the gate.

She watched him for just a moment, then nodded to herself. "I will pray for their blood to quicken, then, to bring about their success."

Saint briefly rubbed at his face, and turned to Belton. "I don't suppose you have a smoke," he murmured.

"Do not ask me to give you fire," Belton replied quietly, "or I will light your lying ass up."

"This ongoing hostility is wearing on our friendship," Saint pointed out.

"You have not yet seen hostility," Belton shrugged.

Four guards surrounded those waiting for news, along with two holding the reins, several drivers, Lord Rowan, Saint, Belton, and Mother Grine. Even with almost twenty goats panting and stamping, and half a dozen horses, it seemed a small knot of life in a pool of light, isolated. One of the goats belched up a cud to chew, unaffected by the tension settling into the people who waited.

Some agents returned, dragging along a couple struggling scoundrels. Other agents in the group held shovels, and one of them carried a modest locked box. Bolt thrust one of the diggers forward, and the dirty man offered a quick and pained bow to Lord Rowan.

"Yer Lordship," he wheezed.

"What were you doing in the park," Lord Rowan demanded flatly. "It's closed at night. You were trespassing. Breaking the law."

The agent with the box put it down right next to the dirty man, who gave it a very worried sideways look. "Just looking for a little extra, you know, odd jobs," he whined. "No one gets hurt, see, just a little landscaping." He shrugged. "No harm done?" he said, a verbal wince.

"And you?" Lord Rowan demanded of the other digger, a grungy young woman.

"I carry the shovels," she replied. "I help dig." She blinked. "He's the boss," she added, pointing at the man, who offered a painful crooked bow as a terrified reflex.

"How did you come to be here?" Lord Rowan demanded. "Who hired you?"

"Some fella, we live just down the way and were in the Tapped Out, just there, and he offered us a little coin to bury something, pulled it off the wagon and had a key for the park, showed us where, told us he was a groundskeeper and it was all up-and-up, and we didn't ask no questions," the man said.

The other group of agents approached, escorting a battered old woman smoking a pipe. Her expression was as closed as a fist, and she puffed on the pipe as she strode towards them. Lord Rowan turned his attention to them.

"Yer Lordship," she said, dropping a shallow and insincere curtsy. "What's the meaning of all this?"

"She's the caretaker for the dock," Alsan said, holding up a much-creased official-looking document. "As for why she's here at night when the park is closed, she said she was paid to do it; irregular, but within her mandate."

"Why," Lord Rowan demanded.

"This fella came up in a steam launch with some friends, and picked up some of his friends, and they sent for some locals to bury something in the park, then they took off," she replied, her chin jutting out. "They said no names, and I agreed, because who needs the botheration."

"You don't know who they are?" Lord Rowan pressed. "No names perhaps, but descriptions? Ever seen them before?"

"Never seen 'em. Sure there was a big fella with a mean look and a pretty Skov girl on the launch, they met with this dandy and some rough men; one was fat, one was a killer, the other one was boring. There were three women in cloaks and hoods; one had a veil, one had tattoos all over her face, one of them—she had marks on her face, and I think they might have glowed."

"Was there an old man?" Lord Rowan demanded, his expression darkening.

"No," the woman replied, and she worked her pipe so the bowl glowed as smoke puffed out her nostrils.

"When did they leave? Which way?" Rowan demanded.

"Downriver, maybe ten minutes ago," she replied.

Lord Rowan looked to his best riders. Five of them swung up on horses and dashed off. He turned to Alsan. "Break it open," he said.

Two swift blows with a rifle butt snapped the lock off the lockbox, and Alsan slowly tilted it open from the side. He pulled out a waxed leather folio that provided a level of waterproofing. He undid the clasp, and opened it up, revealing stacks of neat papers.

Lord Rowan put out his hand, and Alsan gave him the papers. "This can't be right," Lord Rowan said, brow furrowed as he saw his personal seal and signature on the first one. And the second. The third. "What is this?" he demanded, coldness blooming through his blood.

Mother Grine put her hand on the papers, and Lord Rowan hesitated only a moment before releasing them. Her eyebrows raised immediately as she scanned the opening lines.

"This is a forgery," Lord Rowan said with some heat. "I have never seen those letters before."

"It's a damn good job," Mother Grine replied, reading.

Lord Rowan channeled his flash of frustration elsewhere, turning to his agents. "You two, check the tavern and see if anyone else knows any more. You lot, upriver to Nightmarket, see what they know. You, to the point guardhouse, see if anyone was monitoring traffic who remembers the launch, try and track it back to its origin." He rounded on the caretaker. "What was the launch's identification number, you are required to track that for every landing."

"Indeed I am, unless the launch is the personal vehicle of a nobleman deployed for the purpose of pleasure or resupply, and I was assured it was Lord Belderan's official yacht collecting his friends for a party." She dug a letter out of her pocket. "It's got his seal and everything," she said, "so I didn't insist just because Lord Belderan was not present." She looked Lord Rowan in the eye. "I cooperate with the aristocracy as fully as possible, m'Lord."

Lord Rowan stared at her for a moment, then rounded on Saint. "Where are they going," he demanded. "They are back together. Where would they go."

"Honestly," Saint replied, spreading his hands as he shrugged, "Trellis has had a week to figure out the answer. There's no scenario for this, not that I know."

"Guess," Lord Rowan said between his teeth, fear igniting his anger.

Saint looked him in the eye. "Trellis doesn't trust me," he said. "He didn't wait. The others got here, and he took off. That tells me he knows he's trying to outsmart me too, now," Saint shrugged, "and that's a game I cannot win. But if I had to guess?" He paused. "The Lost District. Outside the lightning walls. Out of reach." Saint gestured towards the darkness of the river, and beyond it the flaring walls of light on the far shore. "He's an expert in radiants, he's got connections with the occult underground, and he's picking up a couple powerful Whispers. Safety used to be a rail jack. And don't get me started on Red Silver."

Lord Rowan turned to Bolt. "Get this update to our guild friends," he said in a low voice, "and tell them I want to know where these people are by midday. Got it?"

"Sir," Bolt replied, and he swung up onto a wagon and took the reins, slapping them across the hindquarters of the goats so they let out a bleat and took off at a brisk pace.

"The prisoners, sir?" Alsan asked.

"Let them go," Lord Rowan growled with a dismissive gesture. He turned to Mother Grine. "Take this fool back to the estate and wait for me there." He mounted the last horse, wheeled it around, and took off at a trot.

"Looks like I might need to work out my future with you," Saint said frankly, looking Mother Grine in the eye.

"You really are shameless," she said, almost caught off guard.

"What has shame done for me lately?" he shrugged.

"Into the carriage," Belton growled, giving him a push.

NORTH HOOK CHANNEL, DOSK RIVER. 26TH ELISAR. HOUR OF ASH, 9 HOURS PAST DUSK.

"Good to see you safe," Gapjaw said as he hugged Niece from behind, not caring that she was at the steamship's helm. "You too, big fella," he said over her shoulder to the Hammer, who smiled slightly.

"What's this I hear about a curse?" Sanction asked, leaned back against the hull as the steam launch shuddered downstream, the lightning wall along one side of the dark waters and the sleepy shore of Six Towers on the other.

"There was a séance at Rowan's party," Red Silver said, "and it activated this curse I have carried. Called out to this dangerous Whisper, Razor Wind, who is hunting me."

"What did you do to him?" Safety asked.

"I was born," she replied, bitter. "Look, he has a grudge against my family and he swore to wipe us all out. That's all you need to know. This curse tells him where I am so he can meet his stupid goal."

"We've been poisoning Rowan's relatives," Piccolo said. "You know, get his goat by wiping out some of his bloodline." He shook his head. "Red, you must be a noble, because they're the ones who care about blood relations. When nobles cross you, it's the thing to do," he shrugged. "Kill off the family."

Red Silver stared at him for a long moment. "Taking the death mark off you was the dumbest thing we ever did," she said through her teeth.

"Now that's just hostile," Piccolo observed.

"First, I am well pleased to see you all," Mistress of Tides said, cutting in. "Second, let's stay focused on the problem at hand. Does Trellis know about Razor Wind?"

"I don't think so," Niece replied. "From what he said of his plans, I think they are all about Lord Rowan."

"Then we have two problems to solve," the Mistress of Tides said. "We have to get out from under Lord Rowan's attacks, and also do something about Razor Wind."

"Can't you Whispers just have a big three-way ghost fight and you take his ghosts away then somebody shoots him?" Piccolo asked with interest.

"Maybe," the Mistress of Tides replied, "but from what I understand he is very powerful. Also, he has blended his studies of electroplasmic manipulation for rituals and ghosts with studies of demonic glyphs. There is an elemental underpinning to his power, and I am not sure what he can do."

"Sounds like we need to track him before he tracks us, then we ambush him. If we can't find him, we bait a trap and take him out," Piccolo shrugged. "This is all basic assassination. No master class here."

"Rowan is the trickier puzzle," Sanction agreed. "Sounds like Razor Wind is a lone operator. No one will avenge him if he disappears. With Rowan, if we don't handle this very carefully, even if we win we lose."

"Yes, let's focus on the *important* problem," Red Silver said, bitter. The glyphs on her face flared slightly as her heartrate sped up.

"Easier, not more important," Sanction soothed. "Piccolo is clumsy, but what he means to say is that he's confident we can protect you from Razor Wind. We're just less sure of our plan to protect all of us from Lord Rowan."

"Right," Gapjaw said. "The only thing making it hard to deal with this rogue Whisper is that we can't throw money around, talk to our contacts, set up the situation, get some gossip going so he'll find out where you are, that kind of thing. It's hard to hide and also set a good trap." He looked at Piccolo. "Right?"

"Yeah, that's what I meant," Piccolo said, unrepentant.

Red Silver looked squarely at each of them, then turned to the Mistress of Tides. "Is it too late to go back to the Tangle?" she demanded.

"We're going to see Trellis," the Mistress of Tides reminded her.

"I swear by my blood, one more man tells me my problem is no problem, I'm drawing steel," Red Silver muttered.

"Where *are* we going?" Safety asked from his position huddled against the frame of the door to the cabin.

"First we spend a few hours getting good and lost in river traffic and mooring at a few docks. Then, on to our destination. You're going to *love* it," Niece said, grinning as she adjusted the helm.

Meanwhile, Inkletta pointed a level gaze at the Hammer, and he looked her in the eye. Neither spoke. Still, it seemed they were alone on the launch together.

"That's the Constellation," Gapjaw said reverently as they maneuvered in the shadow of the Leviathan hunting ship. "This is one of Lord Strangford's biggest hunters."

Dawn tilted touches of light through the thick clouds, the broken sun struggling to provide something to the shadowed world as night drew to a close. The launch chugged alongside the flank of the ship, a wall of metal that rose far above the Void Sea. The wall had been battered and dented, and bore huge swaths of replaced plating; the overall effect was formidable, a barrier that could hold back the end of the world.

The launch lolled in the waves as it nosed past the mighty sword of the hunter's prow, a blade of metal soaring up out of the uneasy sea. The launch's engine noise reverberated between the Leviathan hunter and the massive dock. The wood and steel of the dock were built up to the height of the deck, where massive cables secured the ship in place. There were several sub-levels below that, down to the waterline. The launch sloshed alongside a lower deck, and Safety and Gapjaw leaped over to the structure to tie off the launch and lower a gangplank. As the crew clambered off the launch and onto the dock, a man with a slouch hat and high collar, wearing the garb of a sailor, grunted at them as he passed and climbed down onto the launch. They untied the little steamboat, and he heeled it about, making his way out to the channel.

"So, Trellis is somewhere in a nearby warehouse?" Safety said.

"No, we're going on this ship," Niece said, nerves in her voice, her eyes lively with something like excitement. "This is where we're meeting Trellis." She turned, leading the way up the ramps and stairs, and the others followed as they kept an eye on the shifting shadows.

Two thirds of the way up the hull there was a shaft on the adjacent dock that was open to the sky, and a massive platform covered with crates. It was surrounded by a net which was attached to a hook at the end of the cable reaching up to the crane far above.

"This is us," Niece said, climbing the netting to hold on near the top. The other seven scoundrels surrounded the netting and held on, and Niece used her fingers and her mouth to make an ear-splitting whistle. A grinding sound followed, then the net juddered and shook, rising up through the dock, up into the raw winds of the early morning. They held on, most covering their faces and gripping the rope for all they were worth as the crane jolted to a stop, then pivoted for what seemed like forever. Eventually they descended again, down through the open deck plating, into the ship. Niece, Gapjaw, the Hammer, Sanction, Safety, the Mistress of Tides, Inkletta, and Piccolo had arrived aboard the Constellation.

Shaken and relieved, they let go of the netting and glanced around the gallery hold, built into the upper level of the ship between its outer hull and the massive tank at its center where the still-living Leviathan blood would be deposited by a successful hunt.

"I must say, this could be our cue to take up smuggling," Gapjaw said, shaking his head. "Port authorities are supposed to monitor this sort of thing."

"They did," Niece replied. "They checked the crates and so forth, then took a five minute break when we docked. And here we are," she said with a gesture.

A voice rang out, harsh in the almost entirely metal environment. "There you are. Follow me." The sailor turned his back to them, and they followed into the corridor, lit by tubes of algae high up along the walls that glowed when the ship moved. Its constant shifting on the uneven support of the sea kept the halls dimly lit day and night.

They did not go far before they took a turn and ended up outside a map room. The sailor rapped a pattern of five knocks, glanced over his shoulder, then walked away from the crew. The door wheel spun, unlocking. The door opened to reveal Trellis silhouetted against the light inside.

"About time," Gapjaw said gruffly, pushing his way in as Trellis stepped to the side with a bemused smile. The others filed in, and Trellis shut the door behind them with a clang as they blinked against the brighter light, adjusting.

"I am *so glad* to see you," Sanction said, containing his grin.

"I suppose you already know about Red Silver's problem," the Mistress of Tides added wryly, gesturing at the metal walls.

"First of all, I am thrilled that we're together again, Silkworms and River Stallions," Trellis said effusively. "Second, yes I am aware of Red Silver's problem, and one of the best-warded locations in the city is the interior of a Leviathan hunter. When you hunt demons, protect secrets, and run a wildly profitable enterprise, you can afford the best etheric protections. This is one of the ship's map rooms, where they keep archival maps of constellations and calculations for moving on the Void Sea." He gestured at the broad table, the chalk boards, the lamps, the deep pigeonholes and shelves at the back of the room. "This is a good place to talk about our plan."

"If you knew about Red's condition, why not tell us?" Niece asked, trying to stay calm. "And what is the condition?"

"We're together now," Trellis said, "and it is time for outlining the situation and charting our way forward. Rather than go over these things over and over for the benefit of one group after another, we will discuss the whole thing here; where we've been, and where we're going. Please, everyone, have a seat."

Inkletta sat at the table, and rapped on it with her knuckles. "Saint," she croaked.

"Where is Saint," Trellis nodded, now the only one still standing. "He has been captured by Lord Rowan. Niece's Aunt Rhya also. We must keep them in focus as part of our plan."

Sanction leaned forward. "If you know about Red Silver's problem already, that saves time. What *is* our plan?"

"We are concerned with three points as we look to our objectives," Trellis replied, picking up a silver stylus with chalk exposed on one end. "The center of our efforts must be Lady Naria Clelland, representing her family on the City Council," he said as he sketched out her name. "Secondary to that, Elder Dracha Rowan, the head of the Church of Ecstasy in Doskvol. The third focus is Razor Wind," he said as he clicked out the third name on the board.

"Uh," Gapjaw said, "Where's Cleith Rowan?"

"We do this right, he's out of the picture," Trellis replied without looking at Gapjaw.

"High level summary," Sanction requested politely.

"You need the key context for some of this," Trellis replied with a small smile.

Safety snorted. "They aren't good at context," he said. "Saint tried to explain what we were doing with the Rowan job to them, that maybe we shouldn't antagonize a Council member. Some of them retained 'don't steal anything' but we still pulled off a kidnapping, and here we are."

Trellis faced the group. "So did we learn something from that?" he asked.

"Enh," Gapjaw shrugged.

Trellis smiled, almost in spite of himself. "Humor me," he said. "Six families have representatives that form the City Council. We have Naria Clelland, Milos Bowmore, Cleith Rowan, Holtz Dunvil, Stavrul Penderyn, and Wester Strangford." The chalk clattered as he neatly printed each name.

"Now, Clelland has formed an alliance with Rowan and Bowmore, centered around seizing control of Strangford's ownership and influence with the Leviathan hunting fleet and shifting energy oversight from the Council to the Imperial level." He drew a bracket grouping Clelland, Rowan, and Bowmore, and put an "x" next to Strangford.

"That makes no sense," Sanction said, puzzled. "Why would the Council give up power to the Imperials? The Council is focused on keeping control of city issues firmly within city jurisdictions; losing control of the Leviathan hunters would make the city vulnerable to a higher level of Imperial interference. If the fleet base relocated to another port, or the profits flowed between cities instead of pooling here in Doskvol, that would be catastrophic for us."

Trellis nodded. "Clelland plans to use her success in shifting the energy to Imperial control to get herself named the Imperator of Doskvol, a new position where she represents Imperial interests in the city. Then her family still wins and the city still keeps the wealth. For now," he shrugged. "As Imperator, she would have oversight of the Lord Governor, the Ministry of Preservation, and the Imperial Military. Currently, the City Council technically reports to the Lord Governor, but more realistically stands as a buffer between Imperial edict and city cooperation. They have enough power to force the Lord Governor to negotiate if something unpopular is dictated to them, unless it comes with significant resources and muscle."

"I've missed this," Piccolo lied to Gapjaw, who nodded knowingly.

"Still," Sanction pressed, "this is a huge gamble for Clelland. Why reduce the Council's power instead of taking over the fleet and redistributing that power, assuming this attack on Strangford is not personally motivated? Weakening the Council doesn't make sense. If Strangford was looking to broker his power at the Imperial level, sure, take his bargaining chip. But why does she want to take it then give it to the Imperials?"

"I wondered that too, at first," Trellis nodded approvingly. "So I looked into it. All this started because the founding families who serve as the City Council are disqualified if they reach a point where there are less than five heirs available at one time who can accept the authority should disaster strike."

Trellis paused, but the room reflected confusion back at him. He continued. "The Clellands have traditionally been very strict about their genealogical records, refusing to recognize the bastards of the line that survived their attempts to trim off the loose ends. They are traditionally pretty sour; they struggle to maintain marriages, much less produce viable heirs. They have wealth, and influence, but there are exactly five left who meet the criteria to be on the Council, even in name while a steward conducts business. If Naria Clelland tries to get the rule changed, odds are good that the increased attention to this minor rule in the bylaws means rivals will step up assassination efforts."

"Kill the bloodline," Piccolo said, nodding sagely.

"So she wants to keep power for her family by shifting it out of the Council's rules, and up to an Imperial scale," Sanction said. "She is willing to put the entire city at risk to protect her family."

"Aren't we all?" Trellis shrugged. "Now it's one thing for her to want to cash in Council power to protect her family, but how does she get the others involved in acting against their interests?"

"Yeah, how?" Safety said, interested in spite of himself.

Trellis continued. "It's no secret that Bowmore hates the Skovs and wants punitive laws in place to check their power, making them second class citizens or taking their citizenship where possible," he explained. "She told Bowmore that if she was Imperator, he could be Lord Governor; she would have more power in Doskvol, but that would give him the official position needed to participate in legislation at the Imperial capitol, Ilyria. At home, Clelland's family controls the Bluecoats and he would control the military, so they could finally resolve some of those tensions and get down to making money from subjecting the military to local corruption in a way the current Lord Governor resists."

"And Rowan?" Sanction asked. "I can't believe he would support stronger Imperial influence in Doskvol."

"The Rowan family certainly would not," Trellis agreed. "But Cleith Rowan is obsessed with his new security technology. He believes he can use it to change the world. In Doskvol he encountered nothing but bureaucratic restrictions on his research and implementation, and he has run out of patience for scientific and political caution. He wants to build his equipment to scale, and with support at an Imperial level he can mass-produce the equipment, increase his research, and implement across cities instead of estates. He is a man with a dream," Trellis said sardonically, "and Clelland has promised him everything he needs to realize it."

"Penderyn and Dunvil have stayed out of it so far, from what you said," the Mistress of Tides said. "Do they know Clelland's motive, and her goal?"

"Hard to say," Trellis replied. "They would certainly not approve of the Council sacrificing power to the Imperials. It is possible Clelland tried and failed to tempt them. We cannot approach them directly, as they do not welcome interference in Council business even if it is to their advantage. This must be handled delicately."

"So we manage Rowan family politics," Sanction said, "and get Elder Dracha Rowan on the Council instead of Cleith. Dracha is with the Church of Ecstasy, he won't be tempted by Cleith's probably-heretical technology."

"Right," Trellis nodded. "With internal politics in the Rowan family readjusted, Cleith loses the resources he needs to hunt us with brute force, and we can negotiate internal checks so his own people make him back off, so we can return to our lives."

"What about Clelland then?" Safety asked. "Why is she a focus?"

"She's building coalitions and shifting power," Trellis replied. "I don't like what she's up to. That is normally not enough reason to interfere, but if we are going to get the Rowan family and the rest of the Council to encourage Rowan to back off, we're better positioned if we've done them some kind of service. I'm sheltering with Strangford, and his family is the target of this effort, so I owe him as well."

Sanction shook his head, looking at the names on the board. "How do we do this?" he asked, almost rhetorically.

Trellis smiled broadly. "Silkworms, please stay. The rest of you are welcome to go to the barracks across the hall, they're unoccupied while the ship is at anchor. By tonight, we should have the details worked out for our next steps."

"And for my problem?" Red Silver asked quietly.

Trellis looked her in the eye. "We will solve your problem or die trying," he replied.

Red Silver looked over at Piccolo. "That's how you do it," she said with a small tight smile.

"Yeah, Trellis does everything better, he's the smart guy, I just stab people, bla bla bla," Piccolo said, rising and stretching. "Get some sleep." He made a mock serious face. "Or die trying."

"That'll do," Trellis said absently, regarding the chalkboard.

Then there was shuffling as the River Stallions rose and headed out, the Silkworms had a light breakfast, the chalk stick adjusted, and the planning got underway.

CHAPTER SIXTEEN

Maybe fifty years ago a traveling zoological attraction suffered fire and shipwreck off the coast of Ankhayat Park, in Silkshore. A monster the owner called a "river horse" got loose. It was massive, twice the size of the heaviest ox, with giant jaws full of blunt teeth. Irritable as hell. The local gondolier-based enforcer gangs cornered it for capture, and it resisted. There were lots of deaths—including the river horse. The toughest gondolier gang working for the Fairpole Grotto Council at the time was the Clamdiggers. Selman, the leader, was looking to update their image.

He mounted that monster's skull on the wall; fleshless, it looked as fearsome as a dragon. He changed the name of his gang to the River Horses.

Twenty years later only the old-timers remembered the story, and the skull was one trophy among many. Denyek was in charge, he had his mistress paint a tribute to the gang. She made this beautiful mural of a white horse in the river. Even that was old and outdated fifteen years ago, when Sunset had a falling out with the leader and decided she was going to start a proper crew, not just thugging for the gondoliers anymore. If they were river horses, her crew would be River Stallions. She got her crew matching tattoos based on the mural under the Cox Street Stables. They never looked back.

— From "Iconography of Dust: Stories Behind the Stories"
by Tadger Bleek

NEAR THE CONSTELLATION, THE DOCKS.
26ᵀᴴ ELISAR. ELEVENTH HOUR PAST DAWN.

The afternoon smear of dim red clouds textured the sky, and the dark city hosted an endless mosaic of light as though its souls glowed. Structures provided shadow by every lamp, candle, algae orb, and plasmic torch. Omnidirectional and overlapping darkness layered in among the colors and flavors of illumination that pushed back against the eternal blindness beyond its borders.

The door to a rooftop dining area banged open, and a cloaked figure stalked out into the open, glaring around. "Well?" he demanded.

"This hunt is making you surly," the narrow demon resonated with poorly concealed amusement. He sat at an almost comically small round table, a shot glass of thick coffee on a saucer before him. "You sacrificed to a ritual so you could finish your hunt for the last of the Selraetas line yesterday. But she was too fast for you. Slipped away somehow." He picked up the coffee cup, holding it delicately as he regarded the single wisp of its steam. "I ordered this to share, I have no use for it," he shrugged.

Razor Wind hesitated for half a second, then seated himself opposite the disguised bone demon, taking the coffee. "Thank you," he gritted out.

"I hate seeing you like this," Elziraan confided, his lips unmoving and no breath moving through him. "I'm bending some of the more flexible rules, and I've tracked down your quarry myself. Her bones are tied to mine through the ritual, the one you paid to create, the one that connects us. So, I had only to look within, and I located her with little trouble." He waited, his unnervingly almost-human eyes watching Razor Wind.

"I am, as always, in awe of your competence and generosity," Razor Wind said as though it didn't sting at all.

"This time, I go out of my way because of our abiding friendship," the demon said with careful enunciation in his resonance, curling his lips back so his teeth could be heard more easily. "If I locate her for you again, you'll have to pay for it."

Razor Wind watched him closely. "You mean to tell me where she is?"

"I do," the demon nodded. "She is there, aboard the Constellation." He pointed at the Leviathan hunter's silhouette, a blank gap in the map of star-like points of light under the Void Sea where the massive ship docked, providing its own skyline. The lamps of the dock were inadequate to light its vast flank, and its deck was currently unlit. "That's why we are meeting at this charming third story café." He stretched his legs. "For dramatic effect."

Razor Wind rose at once. "I will not need to find her again," he murmured, glaring at the ship as though he could bore a hole in it with his will alone. "She dies today." His fists tightened. "Now."

"Are you sure that's wise?" the demon buzzed. "That ship has defenses. Crew. It is designed to endure the wrath of a Leviathan." He paused. "You are no Leviathan," he pointed out.

Razor Wind had already turned away, and he strode into the building without a backward glance.

Elziraan shivered with glee and rocked his shoulders, settling himself into comfort. "Just like that," he hummed to himself, then he rose and stepped over the railing, dropping into the shadows of the alley and vanishing into the city.

*

Razor Wind strode towards the Constellation's dock, his boots clacking on the cobbles as he made no effort to be subtle. There was little traffic so close to the high-security ship. He was conspicuous, with his billowing robe and cowled cloak. Two of the Leviathan hunter's crew stepped out of a guard house, one holding up his hand.

"Sir, you are entering a restricted—" he stopped short as Razor Wind pinned him with a smoldering stare that seemed to drive the words back into a tangle in his throat, and the other crewman's eyes narrowed as he drew a pistol.

Razor Wind gestured at the armed crewman's wrist, and the crewman's bones tugged out to straighten his arm, pistol pointing at his fellow; the trigger jerked as the arm reached its fleshy limit. The other man was hurled down by a point-blank gunshot.

Razor Wind clapped his hand on the man's forearm, and the survivor gurgled as his ribs locked; he could not draw or expel air, and he staggered back in agony and desperation as Razor Wind turned his back on the dying man and strode onward.

Attuning to the defenses of the Constellation was trivial for a talent like Razor Wind, and he saw the giant plate-like glyphs etched into the various layers of metal along the ship's flank. Etheric vision saw them as interlocking shields that contained and preserved the energies within them, repelling demonic incursion into their space. Not even hesitating, Razor Wind strode to the edge of the dock, and dove cleanly off, plunging through the surface two stories below, air plumed around him as silver streamers of bubbles. Pivoting under the surface, he saw the giant reinforced glyphs protecting the hull line of the ship, and the glyphs angled to intersect with the primary protections. They were generations old, and they had been rebuilt many times. It was simple enough to see some places where the reinforcement had not been perfect; he swam to one of those stressed seams, and wriggled through. Once inside the projections, he kicked up towards the surface, and burst through. Taking a deep breath, he squinted up the wall of the ship's flank.

Focusing, he put his hands flat on the hull, as though listening carefully, his head tilted to the side as lank black hair hung around his face. Above, the hue and cry spread as his victims were discovered, and a quick search spread out looking for him. He felt the material he needed close enough at hand; the cleaning efforts were thorough, but never complete, and the crew had left weapons for him in their ship.

A few drops of undying Leviathan blood drifted down towards him, and a couple thread-like streams wriggled down the hull. After a few minutes, he had collected a ball of blood almost the size of his fist, slowly rotating in the air couched in his concentration. He cupped the ball in his palms, and it responded instinctively to his demonic pact, connecting with him and flowing over the backs of his hands, over his fingers, growing out to impossibly sharp claws. His smile was bright and deadly as he began climbing the metal, his claws giving him easy purchase on the armor plating.

The gap between the glyph protections and the hull eased out to a wider space towards the top railing, and he jumped away from the metal wall and shaped the shredded slurry of ghosts that swarmed in his orbit, providing a supernatural boost that landed him on the deck with a decisive clack.

The captain's identity was clear, as all others were deferentially pointed towards him and he also had the most impressive hat; a plume of feathers and a spray of bones enhanced the hatband's reptilian strip of skin, and the brim was improbably proportioned. Razor Wind easily identified the harpooner, a hard-bitten woman with a scarred face and shaved head, and the lead Whisper, a heavy-set masked figure in robes and chainmail with a bandolier of glowing orbs. Six adept ritualists were also in the consultation, variously armed and armored, but all tattooed extensively. Razor Wind had their attention, as well as nearly a dozen tough Leviathan hunter crew that jogged over to intercept the intruder.

"This can be simple," Razor Wind said, his tone clarifying that he had no real hope the crew would cooperate. "I'm here for the criminal known as Red Silver. Give her to me and I will go. No one else has to die." He opened his hands, feeling his skin swarm with the itching of contained energy.

"I like your style," the captain admitted, "and your initiative. I'm Captain Darfalle. You looking for a job?"

Razor Wind felt himself smile. "I really hope I don't have to kill you," he said. "You've got spunk." He shrugged. "This is no time to get caught up in the demands of honor and hospitality. Give me the girl and I am gone." He subtly shifted the ball of his foot, refocusing his balance, the inky demon blood gauntlets shifting and squirming on his hands.

Captain Darfalle looked him in the eye. "Hospitality matters now most of all, or it never really did," he said. "Now it's your move." He paused. "Good talk."

The adepts pivoted to face each other, and softly chanted a familiar ritual; Razor Wind saw the swirl in the Ghost Field as they began to gather energies to feed to their Whisper and the harpooner. The harpooner bounded into their circle, standing in the middle, as the Whisper stalked across Razor Wind's facing, headed for his flank, watching him closely. The captain withdrew behind the crew members, who focused themselves to activate their spirit bane charms, which glowed in the Ghost Field like penetrating, irritating lights. Razor Wind saw movement in the cabin of the ship's tower, and saw the bridge crew looking down; he felt them shift some of the runes, readying activations that could be used to stun or repel Leviathans. He had nothing that could stand against that kind of power.

"For so long," he whispered to himself in Hadrathi, "I have contained my frustration and focused on a hunt." The frozen core in him that ached for killing swelled out of his bones all the way to the back of his skin, and at last he was made of murder. All the warning he offered was a curt nod to the Whisper.

Razor Wind felt the pulse of energy darting under the deck, controlling the glyphs that burned behind the Mirror. Jamming his demon-blood claws into the deck, he focused his will into that simmering control layer, and contorted the signal to trigger a stunning blast that invisibly and silently roared up around the Whisper; the startled man was staggered, but the blast tore off a layer of protection instead of burning him out of his flesh.

Recovering with the speed of a warrior, the Whisper drew a gleaming femur from a quiver at his side, running his finger down the line of burned runes so they glowed. As Razor Wind rushed him, the Whisper snapped the bone, releasing the prepared ritual. Plasmic energy shaped by the ritual drove a brutal wedge between the front and back of the Mirror, painfully tearing Razor Wind's energy presence apart from his physical presence as time shifted to move differently for a few seconds behind the Mirror; the rupture would be fatal for any attuned mystic, and viciously inconvenient even for a demon.

Razor Wind raised his fists and interposed the undying Leviathan blood of his gauntlets in front of his own life force, and as that blood was torn to microdroplets with a piercing scream in the Ghost Field, Razor Wind landed right in front of the Whisper and snatched his shoulder.

An inhuman whistle of agony escaped the Whisper as he tried to scream, his bones growing finger-length thorns into and through his meat, in a pattern radiating from the shoulder Razor Wind gripped. Releasing the hapless and dying Whisper to collapse squirming on the deck, Razor Wind rounded on the adepts and harpooner.

The harpooner flung her spear with killing force, the energy summoned by ritualists twisted around it so the point would penetrate any defense, locked on to Razor Wind's lifeforce with an attack meant to puncture the hide of a Leviathan. Razor Wind's arm whirled, gathering all the shredded ghosts that surrounded him and jamming them into a single point of energy as he pivoted out of the way. The harpoon's lock was confused, staying focused on where he had been and slamming through the ghosts as Razor Wind closed with the ritual circle.

The crew opened up with firearms, and several of them had plasmic ammunition. The bullets and bolts rattled and sparked from the last of his amulet-based defenses, and one caught him squarely in the shoulder. Hurled off his feet, he slammed down on the deck plating, rolling over as best he could, disoriented by the force of the blows. Her footfalls battering the plating, the harpoonist charged, and leaped at him with her other spear held high; the blade was made of Leviathan bone, it was an ancient and vicious weapon oozing with death.

Razor Wind thrust a stiff-fingered gesture at her, and she felt her anklebones twist as they flew out behind her; too late to correct, she banged down onto the deck forearms first, crying out to defuse the impact. Razor Wind rolled over, leaving a smear of blood on the deck, drawing a bone dagger from his sleeve. As the harpoonist scrabbled back, struggling to rise, he lunged forward and jabbed her with his blade. She let out a cry as she fell back, and the knife gleamed as it remained embedded in her life force. Razor Wind hauled back on it, roaring, and it peeled her life out of her flesh so a corpse toppled back from his attack.

Razor Wind took the glittering knife in both hands and slammed it down on the metal plating so it shattered, and the bursting explosion of the blade shards filled with fresh life force disoriented the ritualists and the crew for a few seconds. That was too long.

Snatching the lethal Leviathan-bone harpoon, Razor Wind wasted no time in jamming it into a ritualist, then levering that corpse off to the side as the rest of them lost control of the energies they were pooling. Razor Wind made a swift encompassing gesture, attuning immediately to the energies they had painstakingly distilled, still attuned to the ritualists. Pivoting, he pulled his arm in close, and together they screamed as some of their life force was yanked loose by their connection to the etheric swirl he had commandeered. The energy that tore out and drifted to him was partial life force, the basic stuff that could coalesce into a ghost, ruptured out of a living thing. Again he had a shredded mass of ghost energy in his orbit as the ritualists stumbled and collapsed, badly injured by his theft.

Captain Darfalle had enough, and as he charged his spirit bane charm glittered with a penetrating light that blinded the etheric senses and drove energy away before his rush. Razor Wind barely got a glimpse of the etched cutlass the captain wielded as the vicious cut swept at him. Yanking the harpoon up to block the blow, Razor Wind was dismayed as the cutlass shattered the brittle bone of the piercing weapon; still, the loss bought Razor Wind a moment, and he did not waste it.

Snatching the captain's baldric, Razor Wind barked a cry of pain as he attuned to the spirit bane charm and drove his life force at it; one would shatter, and the protective amulet gave first, snapping random pains through both the captain and the Whisper. The captain fumbled at Razor Wind's throat, and as the Whisper knocked his hand away, he didn't see the other hand that jammed a dagger into his chest. Razor Wind reflexively stumbled back, startled by a cough of blood. The captain had just a moment to snarl a satisfied grin before Razor Wind snagged his wrist and twisted his hand off the haft of the knife, driving his weird demon-gifted power into the captain's body.

With a distressing slitting burst, the captain's skull fired out bone spines; he was dead in an instant, his brain punctured, and as his corpse staggered, his head looked like a gory sea urchin, spines of bone protruding in all directions. Razor Wind let out a hysterical cackle as he dropped to one knee and the captain wandered a few steps before collapsing.

The crew stared, unbelieving, and Razor Wind glared at them as he slapped his hand on the captain's leg and pulled off a wad of flesh as though the captain's body was made of snow. Dragging the dagger out of his chest, Razor Wind pressed the handful of stolen meat on his chest, shivering, his force of will forestalling the crew's next round of attacks. Razor Wind rose to his full imposing height, no longer bleeding.

"Anyone want to go fetch Red Silver for me now?" he asked, holding out a palm under a trembling witchlight that grew stronger as it drew the ambient life energy from the killings into a concentrated form. No Bellweather bells had chimed in this fight, the glyph walls contained news of deaths to this pocket of the Ghost Field.

The deck shifted slightly as the water under the ship moved, and Razor Wind realized the glyph protections for the ship had been powered down from the bridge cabin. The remaining crew on the deck raced for doors to get into the ship, and he turned, sensing a massive shift in the energies of the Ghost Field.

He saw a glittering wall of water, already higher than the deck of the Leviathan hunter, starlight glinting in its opaque depths, impossibly poised—

The wave hit the ship, crashing it against the dock, splintering the support structures adjacent to the Leviathan hunter and driving it sideways into the land with a jolt. The inexorable mass of water powered over the deck, scouring everything from it, flushing into the docks. The energy filling the water swept it over the pilings and the walls, sluicing across warehouse fronts, runneling down alleyways, spraying through buildings as people let out brief cries of dismay before the disorienting slosh battered them out of position.

The wave hit full extension for a surreal moment of balance, then dragged at the docks, clawing people and debris along its slithering wake as its bulk raced down the new paths of least resistance back towards the briny shoreline.

Reeling from a sudden impact with a building, Razor Wind was unable to marshal his defenses in the blinding gush that shot him over the docks, whacking into invisible obstacles, tumbling loose as the wave retreated back to proper depths. He barely felt the bone-numbing cold of the water, but his scourged senses were alive to the fury that simmered in the water around him, searing his fresh-stolen energies away. He was not alone. Lungs burning, he twisted to see the serene figure, oddly visible in the debris-clouded riptide, her robes appearing white and dappled by a pale flavor of moonlight that had not been seen since the Gates of Death broke, her veils arrayed around her in the weird weightlessness of the deep.

He realized she had been working this ritual as he confronted the crew of the Constellation. He realized that her tempest did not come from the sky. It came from the sea. And here, now, she was willing to shatter the docks and risk her survival to stop him.

Struggling to pull his concentration together, he was distracted by his bucking and flexing lungs dying without air. He had no sense of how far under the water he was. He could not guess how close to shore he might be. Desperation wormed through him, setting his blood on fire. There was a hatred in the water, and it squirmed up his nose, into his ears, compressing around his chest as bloody bubbles were forced out.

For the third time in his life, Razor Wind chose not to die.

Reaching deep into the living meat inside his bones, he flexed his life force through the Mirror, into the Ghost Field, and unfurled skeletal wings that swept the vastness of the riptide and kept every dying breath they touched. The burning that coursed through him intensified, fed by energies beyond his own. He sensed the Mistress of Tides teetering on the edge of her capacity, badly overextended by her ritual, now alone with the deadliest Whisper of the age.

Razor Wind gathered the drift of torn life from the riptide and fired it at the surface without loosing his grasp; the energies surrounded him once again with the half-formed screams that saturated the background of his entire adult life. He shattered the surface with his flesh, and as he gasped air in, power flowed with it.

The Mistress of Tides had done what she could, and she would offer no further resistance. He turned from her, back to the battered docks and the city lights beyond.

Red Silver's curse burned bright, he tasted her blood.

Razor Wind slashed through the water, against the riptide, a swarm of death lending him strength as he closed in on his prey. She had nowhere left to hide.

*

The Constellation's escape launch nosed up to docks far enough away from the killer wave to be undamaged, even though the uneven surf still expressed the disrupted ocean's displeasure. As the Hammer and Gapjaw climbed out and secured the lines, Safety stared at the ongoing gush of water from the violated docks back into the sea.

"Damn," he murmured.

"Indeed," Trellis said crisply, abandoning the helm and springing over to the dock, helping Inkletta over as Niece and Piccolo followed. Sanction and Red Silver carried cases and sling bags with some gear. Safety took the helm, nodding to Gapjaw and the Hammer to cast off again.

"See to it you bring the Mistress of Tides back to us safe and sound," Trellis said to Safety.

"You got it," Safety agreed, and he cranked the engine in gear and sent the launch thrashing away from the dock, curving back out towards the sea, on an intercept course with the rip tide.

As the others watched the launch steam away, Trellis cleared his throat. "Well," he said, "I know all of you are not enthusiastic about the next few steps, but I ask you to trust me." He paused. "There are still a few ways we come out of this intact."

"I guess," Sanction said, his voice tight as he avoided Trellis's eyes.

"At any rate, you have your orders," Trellis continued, a touch of frost in his tone. "You know how to get in touch, and we've got a lot of work to do." With that, he picked up his bag, and headed up towards the crowd that was gathering to point and stare at the wreckage down the way.

The scoundrels split up and followed their own pathways. In the near distance, the slightly dented Constellation righted itself, leaning away from the shattered dock with a rumble and a shower of timber.

*

Inkletta followed the shadows of the alleyway, her spirit bane charm in hand. Her senses explored around her, like a tongue rubbing along teeth to find the flash of pain from breached bone. She felt the unsteadiness rising in her as her consciousness expanded into what was waiting for her in the Ghost Field.

No one else needed to know about this.

The corruption was felt more than seen, like a hairline fracture, and she let the odd flash of pain lead her towards its source. Soundless, she prowled through the litter of the alley, and stepped over a sense-less drunk. She was close, now. Close enough to be very, very careful.

She climbed up on a barrel, jumped up to catch the eave of a lean-to, and pulled herself up to climb the steep tiles. From there, she found the ladder that granted access to the roof three stories above, and she managed the climb as quietly as she could. The dark presence she followed seemed to swell as she approached.

Finally she straightened, standing on the decorative crenellation of a former noble's penthouse that had been converted into shipping offices. The view of the ship and the broken docks was spectacular, but it did not take her breath away as cleanly as the slender man shape that watched her speculatively.

"If you're here to fight," the demon said, "your best hope is that you can get a shot in while I'm trying to decide what horrible death to give you."

"We aren't here to fight," Inkletta replied, feeling a resonance in her voice and wondering if the demon could feel it too. "I'm here to take something from you."

The demon flashed a grin, revealing bones that were more artistically creative than accurate representations of human teeth. "That's rather a lot of attitude!" he retorted. "Now I'm curious. What do you want?"

"You've got a bone, don't you," Inkletta murmured, feeling her senses wash through the demon's shape. "Something from Selraetas. Something from her skeleton."

All trace of amusement dropped out of the demon's demeanor. "Who are you?" he demanded. Then he narrowed his eyes. "*What* are you?"

"You're going to want to stay out of the rest of this," Inkletta heard herself say, still able to shape the conversation somewhat as she felt herself slipping. "Destruction waits at the end of Razor Wind's hunt."

The demon's legs croaked and clicked into lean, recurve shapes, and long piercing spines punched through the back of its forearms as a muzzle stretched the meat it wore on its true face. "Threats?" it growled.

"I keep my word," Inkletta whispered as she slipped away behind the thing that flowed through her into the world, pressing past the Mirror more easily near the demon that thinned the barrier.

The demon let out a bark of rage and fear as it faced the Shrouded Queen, and it lashed out with a bone spike loaded with elemental power and death, tugging at the skeleton of the Shrouded Queen's host. All the attack did was form a connection, and the cloak swiftly engulfed the demon, rubbing at it from all sides as it let out a startled shriek.

Unbearable pressure, for just a moment, then a crunch, and something yanked loose.

Released, the demon scrabbled and slid back, then pinwheeled its arms as it hung over open space and fell from the roof.

SO MUCH MORE TO HARVEST

"In time, my Queen," Inkletta breathed unsteadily as she returned to herself. "In time."

Her hand opened to reveal a small molar, pulled from the demon; instinctively, she knew it belonged to Red Silver's mother, and connected to her bloodline.

"Let's see you track her now," she said to the demon's absent shadow. Then, feeling suddenly vulnerable, she too vanished into the dark city.

CHAPTER SEVENTEEN

The Sanctorium in Brightstone was designed by the Immortal Emperor himself during his last visit to Doskvol, nearly five centuries ago. He was in Doskvol for a realignment, as a number of civic and religious structures had become wayward and required his personal attention to prevent a civil conflict that could have been on the scale of the recent Unity War. The death toll from the brief trials for heretics and dissidents ran up into the hundreds, and the bones of the executed were worked into the foundations of a monument erected in honor of the Immortal Emperor's visit.

The Gates of Death, rebuilt; the Sanctorium was intended to echo the impression of the supernatural barrier that was shattered over eight centuries ago. The Immortal Emperor tasked the founding families of the City Council with building the Sanctorium to conform to certain parameters, funded by Imperial coffers. This gift to Doskvol provided a place for its citizens to purify themselves of the traces of death that creep into life through age and incorrect thoughts, and to oversee the ritual destruction of rogue spirits. Catacombs below protect the remains of flesh without life, ashes of the notable contained in expensive urns, more eternal than memory.

The Founding Families have spiritual authority as well as temporal clout, because the Immortal Emperor laid upon them the mantle of policing the boundary between life and death while offering guidance and instruction to the living. They are stewards of the gates of life and death. They choose what endures and what is silenced forever. If they were merely people, like everyone else only with money, a reasonable person could conclude that their influence outstrips their authority. But if they are gatekeepers for this city's soul-saddled flesh, we owe them everything. As I am sure you know, they seldom hesitate to collect.

— From "Six Foundations for Revolt" by Concerned Citizen

The ancient wooden door creaked open, swirling the stale, sacred air of the preparation chamber. Several lamps burned low, shielded from the draft by glass chimneys. The gnarled old man silently entered the room, footfalls vanishing into the deep pile carpet. He stood before the dressing table and its various trays, bowls, and boxes. He sifted his thoughts, then he began working jeweled rings off his thick fingers.

"Thank you for seeing me," the man behind him said quietly.

The old man's instincts were shaped by the weight of his authority, rather than by an animal survival reaction. He cocked his head to the side, then slowly turned, squaring off with the young man in black standing unobtrusively by the brocade drapes. Both men allowed a long moment to spin out, wordless and thoughtful.

"I would say you have me at a disadvantage," the old man said, "but you really don't." He turned back to the dressing table, putting his ring on one of the posts on the side of the jewelry box. He started working on the next one. "What do you want."

"I regret to bring City Council and family business into this holy place," the intruder said with a gesture, "but this seemed the easiest way to get an audience without other ears in your business. There are developments afoot that you will want to know about."

The old man's face hosted a wisp of smile. "The Sanctorium has excellent security," he said as he put another ring down. "So I'm told. This is your idea of easy?"

"Security will always rest uneasily with secrecy," the intruder shrugged, "and we cloaked ourselves as actors in confidential transactions." He paused. "We're very clever."

"You must represent Sir Belderan, the infamous Trellis of Barrow-cleft, and his Silkworms. Yes?" the old man said, unlatching the collar on the half-cloak, purple with red brocade and jewels, sparkling like living blood through flesh.

"I do," the intruder agreed. "Elder Rowan, I have stolen this moment, but I wish to purchase an audience."

"With coin?" the old man said, his voice neutral. He continued methodically putting his ritual costume on the dressing mannequin in the corner.

"No, with an antidote. There, on the table, that black box has a counter to the Dolorous Crimson afflicting a number of your family members. There is only one cure, that's why it is so effective for blackmail."

Elder Rowan turned to face the intruder, his brow drawn low and his mouth set. "You think that's enough for me to allow you to leave here alive?" he growled.

"The antidote is a gift from Lord Strangford," the intruder continued. "This gift prevents a number of murders in your family line. I don't think that's enough to buy my safety, just to secure an audience. You may benefit from listening to what I have to say." He watched Elder Rowan, unreadable.

Elder Rowan turned to the box, and tilted it open, seeing the jars and bottle and neat parchment rectangle with the names of victims printed clearly. He snapped the box shut, paused for a long moment, then stepped over to a small table and lowered himself into a chair. "Very well," he said.

The young man sat opposite him. "I am Sanction, and as you already observed, I'm here on behalf of Trellis," he said. "As I am sure you have already guessed, I'm here to talk about your nephew, Lord Cleith Rowan."

"I cannot wait to hear this," Elder Rowan said, deadpan.

"You know your nephew has made quite an impression on the city," Sanction continued, looking Elder Rowan in the eye. "You have reservations about his security technology."

"No reservations that rise to the level of being visible outside the family," Elder Rowan replied shortly.

"Cleith's obsession has made him vulnerable, and through him, your family and the City Council," Sanction said. "He has lost his balance, and the other families know it. Clellan is building a coalition, and she worked through Bowmore to bring the Rowan family on board by offering some dock space Bowmore controls for Cleith to build his prototype without having to go through bureaucracy and approvals where other factions could slow the process unless given concessions. Then there was his grand unveiling, and that unfortunate business where his adept was spirited off."

"Unfortunate," Elder Rowan echoed.

"The response was not proportional," Sanction shrugged. "Cleith—"

"Lord Rowan," Elder Rowan interrupted.

"Apologies. Lord Rowan has involved the Lord Governor, using the navy to firebomb a Skov community; between the Skov reaction and the military protests and the papers yelling about it, that's made more noise than it was worth. I cannot begin to estimate the cost to the family of his stunt with the Ministry's Lending Commission gutting the Fairpole Council. He flexed all the City Council's muscle elsewhere in the Ministry too; razing the High Six garden and authorizing a Spirit Warden compound on the site cashed in a *lot* of favors and goodwill, I'm sure. Then there's the arrangements with Iron Hook and the costs to persuade those responsible for prisoners to accept risks on behalf of the family to give the Rowans their way within those walls. I cannot imagine what had to happen to obligate Lord Rowan, his family, and even the government to employ the caliber of assassins he—"

"Quite," Elder Rowan said sharply.

Sanction studied the old man, who waited.

"The point being," Sanction said slowly, as though feeling his way across very thin ice, "Lord Rowan has raised the family's profile over the last week or so in some very unhelpful ways, investing Rowan influence and wealth in projects that may not serve the family well. If you choose not to get involved, we are on the edge of the situation deteriorating even faster."

"Why."

Sanction nodded. "Lady Naria Clelland plans to take over the Strangford family's Leviathan hunting fleet, and trade city control of the fleet and the fuel to the empire, in exchange for an imperial title in the city. She would erode the City Council's influence in Doskvol in exchange for advancing her family's interests on a bigger stage. Lord Rowan is currently her ally and supporter. If he gets his way, the City Council would have a local Imperator to contend with in matters of city governance." He paused. "Imperator Clelland."

Elder Rowan leaned back in the chair, light glinting off his eyes in the dim room. "You have given me a lot to think about," he said. "Assuming that is true."

Sanction's eyebrows raised slightly. "Alright, then there's the matter of the letters," he said, a new hardness edging out some of the deference in his tone. "Trellis did some digging to try and find some angle to defend himself and his people from *Lord Rowan's* aggressive suppression. He came across some correspondence between *Cleith* and the *South Point Rowans*." Sanction gave Elder Rowan a few seconds to interrupt, and when he didn't, Sanction continued. "Your grandfather's legacy is scouring the adepts and mystics out of the family, driving them away from the church. Your father spent his life consolidating the Church's influence, and you did too. If the Rowan family allows trafficking with the dead—"

"Let's not belabor the point," Elder Rowan snapped, eyebrows low. "Lord Rowan has responded to those allegations, he says it's all forged."

Sanction let that stand between them for a moment. "It's possible," he agreed. "I also heard a theory that only one side was forged. Or that several copies of the forgery were made and another box of letters could surface at some point. The point, at the risk of *belaboring* it, is that your nephew is refining technology that runs on *ghosts* that requires *adepts* to function." Sanction shrugged. "I see why you don't want to exile him, but there is a reason he didn't build his prototypes on any of the Rowan properties in the city; what does it take for him to overreach the family's tolerance? Maybe it's time to think about who represents the family on the City Council. If the South Point Rowans do return, for whatever reason, you'll be dealing with that for the rest of your life." Sanction met Elder Rowan's stare eye to eye and did not waver.

Elder Rowan leaned back in his chair, then sniffed and allowed a small chuckle, glancing off to the side. "You sure got sassy there at the end," he muttered, almost to himself. "I do appreciate a little backbone, but I will not tolerate insolence." His jaw shifted, and he looked Sanction over, thoughtful. "Be frank. What do you want."

"Basically we want a clean slate," Sanction replied. "One step along that path is you replacing Lord Rowan on the City Council. You are not honor bound to hunt the Silkworms or the River Stallions. You are respected among the Rowans and the other families, no one will raise an eyebrow. Lord Rowan's honor gets smudged, but he is not publically shamed—or hurt. Still, you can hang any bad blood on him as your predecessor, and you can be a peacemaker and share that glory with the Church." He paused. "Other changes are happening behind the scenes with the City Council and the Six Families," he added. "If you join the City Council with an eye to letting bygones be bygones and keeping power in the city, we're going in the same direction."

"You and your people have had a rough time," Elder Rowan observed. "You are telling me you have no interest in vengeance?"

CHART ROOM, ABOARD THE CONSTELLATION, THE DOCKS. 26TH ELISAR. FOURTH HOUR PAST DAWN.

"What?" Sanction exploded, leaping to his feet, vibrant with fury as he stared at Trellis.

"This isn't negotiable," Trellis said, mild. "We are giving the antidote to Elder Rowan. A gift."

"You don't understand," Sanction snapped, banging on the table for emphasis. "That jackass Cleith does *not* get away with this. What he did—we answer that in blood!"

"His worst offense was to make you feel helpless," Trellis replied. "Understandably, as fugitives, we want to hit back. We want our tormentors to feel that helplessness, that fear. And, as a fugitive, that was a good move," Trellis shrugged. "But now we're not fugitives. We cannot afford to think that way. We are architects of the future, and the future has different demands than the moment, or the past." He paused. "This is where we decide who we want to be. Whether we want people to see us as unpredictably violent and vengeful, or whether we want people to see us as integral to handling solutions to their problems. Assassination redistributes problems, it doesn't solve them."

"Bulldozing High Six. Only the Immortal Emperor's Sacred Blood knows what's happened with your house, with our family members, with our money and property, our friends interrogated or jailed, probably some of them are dead, and you want to play architect!"

"I like this," Trellis said, his head cocked to the side. "I mean, we must never do this in front of the others, but the honesty, the passion; it's refreshing."

"Dammit Trellis!" Sanction shouted.

"Right," Trellis nodded, "here's the thing. Life is transactional in a crooked market. There are costs, and you take what you can in exchange for all those losses and trades. Sometimes you get some bargains, sometimes you lose it all. If you're going to throw a tantrum when the stakes get high or you feel unfairly treated, then I'm going to send you back to the Ministry." His tone held no heat or coldness, just an implacable quiet conviction.

"Oh, is that so?" Sanction snapped, struggling for something better to say.

"Patience," Trellis soothed. "I failed out of the Hive and had to spend over a decade trying to make peace with what I did before you and your cousin came along and wanted to start up a new criminal crew. Now look at where we are." He smoothed his jacket. "Trust me. Relax through this pinch point. See what's next. My plans rely on incorporating the creative initiative of my allies. You created this fantastic leverage point, poisoning Rowan's relatives." He looked Sanction in the eye. "Let me use it," he said softly.

Something in Sanction folded, and he leaned his elbows on the table, put his head down. "Damn," he muttered.

"I need you to make peace with this," Trellis said briskly, "because you're the one who will sell it."

Sanction barked a laugh.

"This conversation started with a reprieve from a death sentence for a number of Rowans," Sanction replied. "We got in over our heads. Survival is insolence enough," he replied with a hint of a smile. "We are a pragmatic sort; we'd rather have influence and a reputation as problem solvers. There is little profit in bragging rights for getting away with irritating the aristocracy."

"Sure," Elder Rowan said. "I make no promises, and I owe you nothing. I have decided to let you leave," he added, echoing Sanction's slight smile. "Unless there is anything more."

"Just some theft," Sanction said, rising and smoothing the front of his black suit. "My associates have been helping themselves to some customized costumes that are only available here."

Elder Rowan shook his head slightly. "In service to this master plan, I suppose."

"Yes," Sanction nodded. "We live, you serve on the City Council, and its influence is protected."

"No one dies," Elder Rowan said, examining his fingernails, "and the vestments are back here tomorrow."

Sanction hesitated for only a moment. "Agreed," he said.

"Get out," Elder Rowan sighed, fluttering a gesture at Sanction, suppressing a smile. Sanction bobbed a quick bow, then quietly let himself out the side door.

Elder Rowan gave Sanction a couple minutes for a head start before he pulled the bell rope. Moments later, one of his security officers opened the door and knelt before him.

"I need to speak to Mother Grine," Elder Rowan said vaguely. He focused on his guard. "Then we must discuss my security arrangements."

The steam launch lolled in the long swells of the sea, its engine chuffing and clattering as the paddlewheel built into the stern churned away. Lanterns hanging from the sides of the cabin, the post on the prow, and posts on both sides of the stern put a dim flicker of light across the scene. The weak light seemed almost brilliant against the inky darkness of the sea and the roiling mass of clouds above.

Safety gripped the helm with his metal hand, and his eyes were half-closed as he rested his palm on the veil draped across the console. He breathed in and out, feeling the swell of the ocean and its alien apathy towards land-dwelling life. He felt the endless wind, its scope majestic and beyond noticing the energy that shaved off onto the water and drove it into waves to cope with the overflow. The sea was restless beneath the refracted moon or moons that hid in the billowy cloudbanks.

Again; he felt the thought, the life glow, like a sipped breath as a drowner connected with the air for just a moment. He winced slightly, trying to drift at the flicker of life like a balloon trying to find wind blowing the right direction.

He had no idea how much time had passed, but he was sore and exhausted by the time he throttled the launch back, drifting alongside the pale form floating on her back in the sea. He dove off the launch, reaching her in a few strokes, wrapping his metal arm around her and kicking back towards the launch. He threaded her arm through a pair of buffers on the hull, then pulled himself out. Pivoting, he dragged her up into the launch, kneeling and putting his ear to her mouth, searching for breath.

did he get away

The Mistress of Tides barely formed the words. Maybe she breathed them, maybe she thought them loud. Safety sat back on his heels, gazing down at the waxen face the Whisper normally concealed behind veils. Her eyes were dark, bruised by exhaustion, only open a slit.

"As far as I know he's pursuing Red Silver," Safety said. "I came looking for you right after you summoned that wave."

She almost smiled. *did it work*

"Everyone got back to shore, split up, headed out to do mischief." He rolled to the side, leaning back, savoring the sensation of urgency draining out of him. "You've done your bit for the cause. We're headed back to Lord Strangford's island, he'll give us some protection until this is over." He paused. "If Trellis is right, we're almost through."

almost through

Safety watched her narrowly for a long moment. "Are you out of danger?" he asked, trying to keep the demand out of his tone.

just... need rest

Safety pulled out a blanket and tucked it over her, but there was little more he could do. The launch heeled around in the surf and battered its way back towards the lights of the city skyline.

PIER 18, NORTH HOOK ANNEX, THE DOCKS. 26TH ELISAR. THE HOUR OF SILVER.

Razor Wind stared at the weather-beaten colorless exterior of the warehouse. The sally port hung open, darkness within. He squinted up, and against the purple mess of clouds above he saw the silhouette of a bat, banking in a curve over the building. He focused for a moment, tugging a hot sensation out of the nearby rune markers; he could almost feel Red Silver's yelp. So close. After all these years, she was so close.

He paused for a moment as unsteadiness shivered through his bones. The flesh patch over the stab wound in his chest was holding his lungs, air, and blood apart for now. The mostly-deflected bullet injuries oozed a foam of blood, brine, and plasm, but posed no immediate danger. He felt a weariness from rapid spirit work and fighting, and from the battering he received in the tempestuous killer wave. Still. His prey had no more allies, no Whispers, no Leviathan hunters. He could sense her ahead, and sense her isolation. She was alone.

Drawing in a deep breath, he exhaled weariness and damage, feeling the shredded life force swirling around him pull in to fill the abscesses left behind. He had few defensive objects of power left, and he had endured a lot to get here, but the lure of the end drew him on. He pushed ahead, crossing the street like the shadow of a vulture, closing in on prey that might as well be dead already.

The confidence that hurled him headlong aboard the Constellation had temporarily deserted him. Ignoring the open door, he shuffled down the stairs along the warehouse flank, around to the dock area. There was a door there, and a flex of his knife popped the simple lock on it. Noiseless, he ascended the staircase inside by the loading dock. He could see in the dark easily enough, his eyes had long ago adjusted to pick out detail on both sides of the Mirror without relying on light.

From the back corner, he saw some tall propped-up structures like the set dressing for a play viewed from backstage. He also saw the cage built around the front door, and stairs that led up to a catwalk that ended in a box-like upstairs overview office. There were low lights and shadows in the office, and he almost smirked; an obvious trap laid by a desperate sniper. He ignored the cabling and stubby pylons, though he felt the simmering energy of the tanks of refined plasm.

Prowling around the side, he looked into the tangled maze of supply rooms, out-of-place furnished drawing rooms, hallways, even a room designed to look like a cellar. Several walls had mirrors mounted on them.

Sensing for his prey's life energy, he furrowed his brow as he felt her signal coming from the maze of fake rooms, equipment, and storage space. He looked up to the office again, and saw a little shadowy movement. A quick moment of concentration reinforced that there were no Whispers or ghosts or demons up in the office, and he didn't see any snipers. Just the buzz of plasmic energy tanks.

Razor Wind burned the last of the shredded life energy drifting around him, shaping it into shadows that he wrapped around himself to deflect the eye. Crouching, he moved into the maze, treading by the verge of a runner carpet in a strangely typical game room transplanted into a warehouse.

A loud clack resounded through the warehouse, and several plasmic lights glowed dimly for a couple seconds before flicking and powering on with their unwavering burn. Lit from several angles, Razor

Wind felt his shadow melt off, and he rose to his full height, defiantly staring at one of the lamps.

"Come get me, you bastard!" a tinny female voice shouted, reverberating through a number of speakers. *"I am done running!"*

"Yes," Razor Wind breathed. "At last, yes." He drew an obsidian knife with a chipped blade out of a sheath in his sleeve. Twirling the knife once to set his grip, he stalked into the polyglot maze in search of his quarry.

SHINING MANE PUBLIC HOUSE, BRIGHTSTONE. 26TH ELISAR. HOUR OF HONOR, 1 HOUR PAST DUSK.

Soapstone did not look up as the public house door opened and shut; it was a busy night. He focused on the scrawl of his notes, and the pint of foamy alcohol that wasn't doing much to give him flavor or a buzz. Tucked into a corner booth, he was undisturbed by the general chatter and camaraderie that flowed as freely as the beer, generally of the same indifferent quality.

He paused, and looked up as he caught the smell of the man who stopped by his booth. He frowned at the fat man with curly hair and numerous scars (and low-tide fragrance) who patiently awaited his attention. Soapstone summed the intruder up in a flash. The thatch of untended facial hair, the dark bags under the intruder's eyes, and the whiff of alcohol radiating from the man's breath and clothes was more than enough to form an impression.

"Go away or I'll have you thrown out," Soapstone said dismissively.

"We could do that," Gapjaw agreed, "but here's my counter. You behave yourself long enough to get a message from Trellis—" he gestured to forestall Soapstone's reflexive reaction "—and I walk out of here." He shrugged. "Or I shoot my way out of here, I leave either way. The question is whether you want to hear what Trellis wants to tell you. Or find out the hard way," he grinned. His hand rested on the butt of his pistol, and his confidence was unnerving. He tossed a charm on the table with a clatter; Soapstone immediately recognized the one Trellis took from him in the carriage seven days ago.

"What's the message," Soapstone demanded, his tone flat and his mind racing.

"Pretty simple," Gapjaw shrugged. "The warehouse where you are testing the security system. Yeah, get there quick and warm it up. Sometime in the next hour or two you'll have the best chance ever to test it out. Just keep a low profile and pay attention. Also bring along a rep from the Church, seeing the system in action will change their minds about backing it, you bet," he said, adding a wink for good measure.

"What, some kind of trap? You think I'll just do what you say, fugitive?" Soapstone snapped. Gapjaw squinted at him, hearing the embarrassment and anger under his tone.

"I should go," he said. "Tell someone else. Make a move, though, if you want. If I report back that I shot you, I don't think I'll get in trouble." He paused, reflective. "I've been wrong before," he confessed.

"I will get you," Soapstone breathed, furious. "All of you."

"Nah," Gapjaw grinned. Then he pivoted, putting his arm over the shoulders of a passing barboy, who shrugged him off with irritation; by then he was halfway to the door, then out.

Soapstone didn't wait another moment. He was on his feet, notes forgotten, racing out the side door waving for a cab.

PIER 18, NORTH HOOK ANNEX, THE DOCKS. 26TH ELISAR. HOUR OF SILVER, 3 HOURS PAST DUSK.

Pausing for only a moment, Razor Wind touched the cold pommel of the knife to his forehead, feeling its dark thirst, and he sifted his thoughts and feelings to isolate the deep bond he had with Red Silver's curse. He opened his eyes, and they were traced with red glyphs; he peered at the walls around him, and saw her limned-out shape ahead and to the side in a crouching position. Narrowing his eyes, he padded towards her, down a hall and across a storage area with spare equipment.

The floor seemed to tilt abruptly, and Razor Wind dropped into a wide stance and focused. Odd. He expanded his senses, peering into the Ghost Field, then flexed back into a recoil; as he opened his senses they fell out of him, like swimmers jumping into a drained pool. He felt a trickle on his upper lip, and wiped at it. The blood on his sleeve was bright. He felt the crispy dryness of sinuses in winter, the blur of eyes too dry for tears. Panic whispered into his tightening lungs as he realized he could no longer see Red Silver.

Razor Wind's instincts still worked fine; he leaped to the side, behind a crate, and the bullet meant for him blasted a chunk out of the front of the box. Like an echo of the gunshot, clatters resounded through the warehouse as all its exterior doors crashed shut and locked.

"Just us now!" Red Silver shouted, tight with fury. The patter of her footfalls slithered through the maze as she relocated.

Razor Wind's smile sent blood streaking down his cheek. "I have seen your death—so many times!" he shouted hoarsely. He pulled back, turning to a door and rattling the handle; it did not open. Peering at it, he felt the energy running through its lock, a flavor like nothing he had ever sensed before. He touched his fingertips to the metal, drawing at the energy, but he jerked back, stung.

"For years," Red Silver's voice echoed, "there were so many questions I had. So many things I wanted—no, *needed* to tell you. But now? Tonight?" She switched over to a microphone somewhere, her voice becoming brittle and omnipresent. *"Here's what I realized. You are a bully and a coward, and hunting me makes you feel big. That's when I realized I just do not care what you have to say."* The speakers crackled off.

"Me—I'm the bully," Razor Wind repeated, almost to himself. He found a door that was open, and cautiously stepped into a replica of a kitchen. "All this started because of bullies in your family—bullies who took *everything* from me."

"I bet you are the only one left in the world that cares," the speaker snapped. *"I'm done talking to you. Nothing that happened to you justifies what you did to me. We're done."*

Razor Wind slunk through the kitchen, ducking glances out the windows; there a living room, there an alley, there the back of a wall.

"You mean nothing," he rasped, "beyond what you represent to me. All you ever were was a loose end. When I tie you off, the whole world starts over."

Movement; he glimpsed her in a mirror reflection and turned to face it, taking a big step to the side for cover. The mirror wavered, and he realized it was manipulated somehow—

A bullet thundered into his back, flinging him forward to his knees and palms, the knife clattering away. His bones were wrenched with the shock of it, and all the plasmic life force had had drawn in, even the emergency flesh patch—all were dry, brittle, a rattle of dead leaves. He drew his will together to rise imperiously—his will collapsed, and he was face-down on the rough stone.

Gavrita Elena Soskitu Selraetas emptied her pistols into him.

Red Silver reloaded.

Chapter Eighteen

Grainer was always too soft hearted. I told you he adopted this street rat in his last posting, when we camped in the Fallow Stables in the Lost District. Grainer let his stray bring in another stray; she had this stinky blanket wrapped around a Solusia bat pup the size of my fist. The locals put out poison that blinded the mice and other vermin so they starved to death. This bat pup ate poisoned vermin, it was dying.

I insisted she abandon the pup or go live somewhere else until it was all over. I was outvoted, but I put my foot down. If we could hear, see, or smell the thing it had to go.

It would start scratching on its wooden box and I would yell "Claws!" Imagine this slip of a girl scolding me on my language, insisting that her bat had wingnails (like fingernails), not claws. Whatever, right? So I would yell "Nails!" and she'd tend to it and shut the damn thing up.

Grainer called in a favor with the vet captain, who dosed the pup with medicine so it just lost one eye. Once it was clear the pup was going to live, I think Grainer's brat gave it a flowery name too stupid to remember. Everybody called it Nails. If it's still alive, it would be pretty big by now.

— From Zyxa Fen's unpublished notes
on the Sepulcherian Fourth Company interviews

PIER 18, NORTH HOOK ANNEX, THE DOCKS.
26ᵀᴴ ELISAR. HOUR OF SILVER, 3 HOURS PAST DUSK.

"Yes!" Lord Rowan shouted with a wild gesture as staccato gunfire flared in the maze. He pivoted, looking to Leslin. "That was a proper Whisper, and the ambient suppression—the latent plasmic energy—denied access?"

"Yes," Leslin replied, his face hidden within the interface hood. "The Whisper tried to drain the Ghost Field ambience for his own use, and it was dry. His own energy bled out into our systems as he attempted plasmic manipulation."

Lord Rowan smiled as he turned to the dark-robed churchmen, the house guards, and Saint, all standing in the confining space of the warehouse control room. "You saw it, a live test. Combat conditions. A rousing success."

"Congratulations," Saint said with a nod.

"We'll pick up the killer," one of the guards said, ignoring Saint. "The exits are locked down as you instructed, should be a simple enough matter."

"Go," Lord Rowan agreed with a nod, and all the guards but his two bodyguards and the one at Saint's elbow headed out of the office.

"Lord Rowan," Leslin murmured, "Mother Grine has arrived and wants to come in."

"Certainly, allow it," Lord Rowan nodded. "I'm keen to find out what was so critical she had to go to a meeting with the church instead of coming along to witness this."

Leslin concentrated, manipulating the locks on the front door while simultaneously reconnecting reflected light, transmitting a reflection from a mirror in the maze to cast its wavering image on a mirror in the control room.

Lord Rowan watched, fascinated, as Red Silver reloaded her pistols and looked up, alert to the approach of guards from several directions. She put her pistols on the ground, and two damask knives, and raised her hands up and to the sides as guards eased out of concealed positions, weapons trained on her.

"Tell them to bring her here," Lord Rowan said to Leslin, who murmured the words through concealed resonators near where Red Silver was captured. Lord Rowan turned to the office door, where Mother Grine entered.

"Well, Mother Grine," Lord Rowan said, his enthusiasm covering a sharp edge. "You can ask your priests here, my security system hampered a Whisper to the point where a pistol shot killed him. It works.

All this is going to work," he added, sweeping his hand over the vista of the test maze below. "How did your meeting go?"

"I have news for you," she replied coolly.

"Can it wait? I'm in the middle of something here," Lord Rowan said, nodding towards where the guards were capturing Red Silver.

"Certainly," she replied, expressionless.

He paused, and looked at her sideways. "I'm likely to be busy later too," he said. "What is the news?"

"You might prefer to hear it in private," she said.

"Or you could just tell me," he replied.

"Very well," she shrugged. "Elder Drachma plans to represent the family at the next Council meeting on the 29th. He wants to know if you are going to oppose him."

Lord Rowan stared at her for a long moment.

"Perhaps this *would* be best handled in private," he said through his teeth. He shot a glance at Saint's handler. "Get him out of here, take him and the other prisoner back to my quarters." He looked at the priests, who nodded and withdrew.

Saint said nothing, but a smile filled his whole face in spite of the pain from his leg as he was prodded down the stairs.

MASTER WARDEN'S ESTATE, WHITECROWN. 26TH ELISAR. HOUR OF FLAME, 5 HOURS PAST DUSK.

Two Spirit Warden Initiates strode down the carpeted and paneled hallway, three robed and cowled figures following them. They came to the inner foyer, with a massive desk in front of double doors. Two guards stood in the shadows, and the man at the desk looked up at them, expressionless, one of his eyes lost behind an eyepatch.

"What business brings you here?" he asked quietly.

"Our Brethren came to the front gate, they are here for access to the Library Within," the door guard said.

The man behind the desk evaluated the guests, his eye lingering on the elaborate brocade symbols and piping on the robes. "Well then," he said. "First Servant, you honor us with your presence, especially at this late hour. How may we serve?"

"I require access to some of our unique documentation," the old man in the cowl said through his teeth. "I understand that neither of us is happy that I'm here right now, but this is an urgent and sensitive matter."

"Of course," the man behind the desk nodded sympathetically. "May I see your Writ of Scope?"

The old man produced a scroll from his robes, made of finest paper, with a black waxen seal. "I have it here," he said, "but before I give it to you... we need to talk." He eyed the initiates and guards significantly.

"Give us the room," the man behind the desk said, and the initiates and guards reluctantly filed out. The man behind the desk stood. "I don't recognize you," he said to the old man.

"I never come down here," the First Servant shrugged. "I send my assistants. You know Darvo and Bayan." He paused. "If this issue was any less sensitive you'd be talking to them tomorrow morning."

"All this is in the Writ of Scope?" the man behind the desk asked.

"If you want this, I'm happy to give it to you," the old man said as he looked at the scroll in his hand, containing his emotions. "That's how I'd rather do this. But it isn't that simple."

"Oh?" the man behind the desk said, arching an eyebrow. "Complicate it for me."

CHART ROOM, ABOARD THE CONSTELLATION, THE DOCKS. 26TH ELISAR. FIFTH HOUR PAST DAWN.

"Say we get through the Sanctorium security like you're proposing, say you and Inkletta steal the specific robes we're looking for," Sanction said. "Even if you find a super-rare Conceptual Warden uniform, even if you find one with the Bounder patch so Whisper energies aren't a deal-breaker, even if you find a First Servant—look, even if everything goes your way there, the next part is never going to work.

Nobody breaks into the Master Warden's Estate. Nobody even tries. The defenses—"

"Are designed to keep intruders out," Trellis nodded. "We won't intrude. We will be part of the Church's functioning. We will be part of what the defenses are designed to protect."

"You can't just play dress-up and walk in," Sanction insisted. "There are protocols, passwords, credentials—"

"And those things are to protect the higher echelons from the lower echelons and outsiders. Sanction, my boy," Trellis said with a certain breeziness, "we are relying upon audacity here. The whole plan hinges on perception and dignity." He looked down at the table, carefully rolling an expensive sheet of parchment into a scroll. "Given the choice between protecting their image of power or their treasures, the Church will choose its image every time. The perception of power is what makes the treasure possible, because if people think you are purchasing your position then they'll consider competing with you. If they think you are beyond their reach, they won't lean in."

"One false move and we're done," Sanction said between his teeth.

"Same as most other plans," Trellis shrugged. "I've studied the protocols, traditions, and culture of the Church extensively for over forty years. I've impersonated high-ranking priesthood before. We'll be fine if you stick to your part. Besides, stealing the uniforms is not as difficult as you think. There is a special chamber in the Sanctorium where they keep model uniforms, so they have a reference to make sure new uniforms are consistent. You'll never find it if you don't know where it is."

"And you know where it is," Sanction said, his voice flat.

"I've done this before," Trellis said with a small smile.

"I envy your confidence," Sanction said, struggling to stay calm.

"Security is like armor," Trellis explained. "Plates to protect sensitive spots, except when you need a range of motion. Joints are difficult to armor. So," he shrugged, "we aim for a joint."

"How?" Sanction demanded.

"The Church has secrets," Trellis replied, his voice distant as he warmed a stick of wax over the candle. "They must protect those secrets. But who can you trust?" He shook his head. "Secrets require protection. Especially when a simple rumor can twist out of control and do untold damage."

"So?" Sanction asked.

"So we are part of Church business that cannot endure even a rumor," Trellis said. He looked Sanction in the eye. "You know the Ministry inside and out. Let me handle the Church."

He sealed the parchment roll with black wax, and pressed an official Church seal into the hot plastic shape.

MASTER WARDEN'S ESTATE, WHITECROWN. 26TH ELISAR. HOUR OF FLAME, 5 HOURS PAST DUSK.

"As you observed," Trellis said, "I am a First Servant. I am in support of the Doctrine Committee. This is my Steward, and a Conceptual Warden," he said gesturing back at his companions. "Our instructions from the committee are to review a few specific details from a very sensitive document. I insisted that my search should follow the protocols, but the chair of the committee, in consultation with his supervisors, requested an exemption of policy based on Internal Research protocol." His jaw flexed. "Our research is our own business. There's no benefit to hinting at what our discussions may hold for the future, or what our deliberations are reviewing. Inspiring speculation. You know," he shrugged, conspiratorially.

"Internal Research protocol," the man behind the desk said, expressionless.

"I'm with you," Trellis nodded. "I don't like handling these things in the shadows. If we need to look at our own documents, we don't have to explain why. I pushed the committee to leave the decision in your hands. I've got a Writ of Scope," he said, holding up the scroll. "I'm happy to turn it over to you." He paused fractionally. "The committee would prefer you not need it. Not for this." He nodded at the ledger on the desk. "I know you have to log every visitor, and note every reviewed document. You're accountable." He looked the man behind the desk in the eye. "The committee would prefer to relieve you of your responsibility to document the request, and go instead with a visual recognition and authenticity check if challenged."

The moment of silence between them seemed to play host to the echoes of all those who died to protect the Church's secrets.

The man behind the desk looked away, then turned and opened the double doors with a key from his sleeve. "Let's get what you need, and put this meeting behind us," he said, almost too quiet to hear.

Trellis smiled, and moved forward.

The walls of the Library Within were a minimum of an arm's length deep, solid stone reinforced with iron. Inside, the air smelled of old books and glacially slow decay. A single table and chair were on a circular stone dais, with rays of bookshelves pointing out in every direction, the shadows overloaded with ancient lore and documentation. Trellis seated himself without hesitation, the Steward and Conceptual Warden flanking him.

"What are you after?" the one-eyed librarian asked coolly.

"The Bellweather architectural plans," Trellis replied, calm.

The librarian frowned. "Those are on file with the City Council," he said.

Trellis looked him in the eye. "The *original* plans," he murmured.

The librarian watched him for a moment, then abruptly turned and vanished into the shadowed aisles.

CHART ROOM, ABOARD THE CONSTELLATION, THE DOCKS. 26TH ELISAR. FIFTH HOUR PAST DAWN.

"Okay, so we need Penderyn support for this new coalition you're talking about," Safety said. "That all sounds great. What are we going to offer her? There's no way we could scrape together enough money to capture her attention. Is this a blackmail thing?"

"No blackmail," Sanction said. "The Penderyn family likes the artifacts, the strange supernatural materials that can inform their research. With their wealth and power, they can pursue anything we'd be able to get our hands on—for the most part. The biggest gap in their power is that the Spirit Wardens are vigilant and rightly consider the Penderyn family a threat."

"Let's be clear," the Mistress of Tides said. "You are proposing we rob the Spirit Wardens of a valuable artifact just to curry favor with the Penderyn family and the Circle of Flame leadership."

"We don't have time for a lot of research, and this is one I've been thinking over for a few years," Trellis said with a shrug.

"What's the target?" Piccolo asked.

"Architectural plans," Trellis replied with a wolfish grin.

"What, to find secret passages or something?" Piccolo said, looking confused.

"When the Bellweather Crematorium element of the compound was added, after the shattering of the Gates of Death, the architect who conceptualized the tower that now houses the death bells and the Deathseeker Crows designed the structure *after* he was driven mad," Trellis said. "His soul was riven, and he was haunted by his own ghost, while alive. His original plans were descriptive and symbolic, with some codes on them. The Spirit Wardens took care to 'recopy' the plans and sanitize out a number of elements. Seeing the original might lend insight into how the death bells work, or the Deathseeker crows. There may be answers that raise more questions, secrets so well hidden we don't know how to ask the right questions. This is precisely the kind of gift that will soften the Penderyn family to align with our man Strangford."

"I'm not saying this is impossible," Sanction said slowly, "but it is wildly improbable."

Trellis shrugged. "You underestimate the clout of the Church leadership. The Wardens are generally well conditioned to let protocol slide if the one demanding the breach is of sufficient stature."

"We steal some weird stuff," Piccolo said, shaking his head.

The librarian emerged from the shadowed stacks with a box. He put it on the table, and stepped back, looking to the Conceptual Warden.

The box was painted with symbols and sigils, and had four screws that were also carved with runes and painted with a strange blue substance. The librarian watched closely as the Conceptual Warden looked at the box; it was warded and coded, secured with Warden rituals.

Under the metal mask, Inkletta let her eyes drift, unmoored, as she reached out with her other senses and poured her malleable consciousness into the intricate little puzzle. She felt the sensors and triggers, the energy construct anchored to glyphs and enchanted paint. With the patient sensitivity of cuttlefish tendrils, she took in the whole puzzle, then attuned to it, flicking her fingers and snapping all four locks out of the way.

His features did not reveal the faintest hint of surprise as Trellis matter-of-factly removed the lid and took the architectural plans out of the box. He paused, looking at the librarian.

"Perhaps a few steps back?" he said dryly.

The librarian crossed his arms over his chest. "No."

"Suit yourself," Trellis muttered. The Steward at his side opened a bag and pulled out a leather-bound book and stylus and handed them to Trellis, who opened to the ribbon bookmark, then began toying with the folds on the puzzle of the architectural plans, looking for one specific area as the Steward and Conceptual Warden took several respectful steps back, moving off the dais.

"Is this going to take long?" the librarian asked Trellis.

"Almost done," he murmured, not looking up.

"I don't know how we do this," the Mistress of Tides said, leaning on the rail and looking out to sea. "Trellis can plan to get in far enough to touch the plans, but... there's no way to get them out. The Library Within secure boxes block access through the Ghost Field, and the items in them bear a glyph, and the box will not seal unless the glyph is inside, so switching out documents won't work." She looked at Inkletta, who leaned on the railing next to her. "Any plan that requires force or triggers an alarm is an automatic failure because the rest of the defenses of the Library Within and the Master Warden's Estate activate and there's no muscling around or squeezing through all that mess. It's quiet or not at all."

"We know a lot of tricks, between the two of us," Inkletta rasped. "We'll figure it out."

"Where do we start?" the Mistress of Tides asked, reigning in her frustration as best she could.

"We can make a decoy to copy the glyph if pressed against it, that should fool the box for maybe a couple minutes," Inkletta replied.

"Okay, that's good," the Mistress of Tides said. "You know the librarian is going to look over the plans before putting them back in the box."

"Right, but we could arrange for something with sharp timing." She looked at the Mistress of Tides. "I've done a fair amount with object transposition, I can set up a ritual to manage it within certain boundaries. But the warding in that compound, anywhere in the walls, is going to be significant. And inside the library? I'm not sure I'll be able to manipulate the Ghost Field at all."

"What about something small?" the Mistress of Tides said. "If we could align a fake with the plans, and then Trellis could copy the glyph signal onto our fake, and it could be swapped out with the original after it is verified but before the box closes and cuts off transposition..." she trailed off.

"That's a *lot* of 'if' right there," Inkletta observed. "Plus a ritual to make a ready-to-copy glyph, a ready-to-swap decoy, and some kind of mask to hide the energies in case they get searched. And, in the moment, split-second timing on a ritual while observed."

"Plus," the Mistress of Tides reflected, "we cannot set up the ritual for the transposition ahead of time because the defenses of the compound would deactivate active rituals. And anything we start inside the Library Within is likely to trigger defenses there. The librarian is going to be alert and probably have resources to see through an illusion if it isn't perfect—and we don't have time for perfect."

For a long minute, the Whispers were quiet together, gazing out over the strangely empty skyline, a rumpled vault of shadow above the sea, an alien view for those who lived in the tightly stacked city.

"I'm not ready to tell Trellis we cannot figure this out," the Mistress of Tides said.

"We need another day," Inkletta shrugged.

"He said he wants to do this tonight," the Mistress of Tides sighed. "I just don't see how."

Inkletta suddenly stood up straight, her mind racing.

"I think I have an idea," she muttered.

MASTER WARDEN'S ESTATE, WHITECROWN. 26TH ELISAR. HOUR OF PEARLS, 6 HOURS PAST DUSK.

The librarian raised his eyebrows. "Finished, are you?" he said as Trellis shuffled his notes together into his book, putting it off to the side.

"Yes, thank you," Trellis said with a distracted look, as though processing some distressing idea.

"Very well," the librarian said, picking up the architectural paper puzzle, glancing over it, checking the glyph on an unobtrusive flap. He pulled a monocle from his belt and attuned to the document, seeing through any illusions, and he nodded to himself and put the monocle back in a pouch on his belt. He slid the plans into the box and closed it; with a whir, the locks reset themselves.

"Thanks," the steward said gruffly, clapping the librarian on the back. "You've done us a great service."

"Mm," the librarian replied with a frown. "Let's go."

They left the Library Within, and the librarian closed the door with a very final-sounding "click" of the lock, then turned to face them. "Let's see your bags and pockets," he said.

The two guards stationed in the antechamber stepped forward, and Trellis raised an eyebrow.

"No," he said. "I'm not submitting my person and my documents to this kind of rough search. Nor my entourage," he added.

"I've let you in without an official record," the librarian retorted, "and you'll do me this courtesy to thank me for taking the risk."

"I owe you nothing for your risk," Trellis replied, cold. "We are both in service to the committee, and this is what they've asked of us. My risk equals your own. If you think you're doing this for me, then let's log the visit right now."

They were interrupted by steps, two Initiates leading a priest down the hallway. The priest pushed past them as they approached the entry.

"First Servant, master, I come bearing an urgent message from Mother Grine," Sanction said breathlessly. He paused, and blinked. "Did you go in the Library Within?" he asked, awe in his tone.

"No," Trellis replied, his tone chilly, not even bothering to glance at the librarian. "What is your message?"

"She requires your presence at once, master," Sanction replied.

Trellis looked over at the librarian. "Is our discussion of security finished?"

"Yes," the librarian said, unwavering. "Yes it is."

"Then I'm off," Trellis replied. "Swiftness of blood."

"Swiftness of blood," the librarian and his guards echoed.

Then down the corridor, out the side door, to the waiting carriage. Every second they felt a raised alarm rushing towards them from inside, but it did not catch them before the carriage jolted off, the goats bleating aloud as the whip fell liberally to get some speed out of them.

"Please tell me you got it," the Steward said to Trellis.

"Right here," Trellis smiled, pulling the plans out of his tunic.

"How?" Sanction demanded, clearly impressed.

Inkletta tugged the metal mask off. "A glyph that would copy any glyph it touched, in with Trellis's notes," she said, her voice still hoarse. "He found the glyph on the plans and copied it, and added another glyph we prepared. When the librarian's monocle attuned to the document, they connected, and I could trigger the ritual to switch the monocle and the plans. I did the switch between when he put the plans in the box and when he closed it, and the Hammer distracted the librarian while Trellis plucked the plans from his monocle holster. We strolled out, and you showed up to discourage a closer look." She leaned back. "Easy."

"And," Trellis added, "the glyph in the box was not strong enough to last more than a few minutes in the box's defenses, so by now there's an alarm and they know they were duped."

"So they'll be after us," Sanction said, grim.

"Not at all," Trellis shrugged. "They would have to admit that they were robbed, if they were to take action. And they cannot be sure it was us. Once we turn this over to Lord Strangford, then the Church will not bother with us, they are not that petty. Unless we go around bragging that we stole the original architectural plans of Bellweather Crematorium from the Master Warden's Estate." He paused. "Don't do that," he clarified.

"You're just brimming with wise advice," Sanction said, arching an eyebrow.

The carriage rattled off into the cramped shadows of the city.

CHAPTER NINETEEN

In one of his various writings on church doctrine, Dr. Solcunias reflects on how the aristocracy bent doctrine on the Church's Habitation Anchor to match their needs. He identifies that as a decision that moves many of the faithful from the search for understanding to a more cynical search for who benefits from the outcome of these theological decisions.

The Habitation Anchor precept is a way around the binary division of the world into matter, which is good, and energy, which is bad. A personality, memory, or concept (energy) anchored to a physical form (like a book or a person) is acceptable to the Church. The Felswift Report was a theological study that interpreted the Habitation Anchor precept to allow vampires to be acceptable by the church, so long as both the host body and the inhabiting spirit had been faithful to the Church in life.

That report opened the way for dynastic hives of ghosts to be legalized as long as the ghost was anchored to something Church-approved, and the wealthiest families took advantage of installing them; it was a real fad for about fifty years. Also, that's how Lord Scurlock and a handful of other vampires got the Church off their collective backs. As an aside, I must mention Dr. Solcunias died of a sudden illness about a month after his blistering repudiation of the Felswift Report came to light.

*— From notes taken in Dr. Hills Vancell's
lecture on Scholarly Structures and Pursuits*

CLELLAND NORTHSHORE TOWER, SIX TOWERS.
26ᵀᴴ ELISAR. HOUR OF THREAD, 4 HOURS PAST DUSK.

Steam wisped from the bald man's pate as he huffed, jogging up the cobbled street pulling a two-wheeled cart with two slim figures seated under its canopy. Wheels rattled along the uneven stone, their noise echoing from the impassive faces of the mansions flanking the empty roadway. The elegant rickshaw slowed in front of one of the mansions, and the runner rested the tongue of the cart on a waist-high support, stepping aside to steady it. The two cloaked figures stepped down.

"Wait for me," one said to the runner, and the cloaked pair turned away. They approached a dark mansion, the lights around it extinguished and broken. It seemed to be an island of shadow in a sea of struggling illumination.

"Remember what I said," one man said to the other, his jaw tight. "Keep your mouth shut. Mulled wine and trance powder. Let's take one last look at you." He thumbed a catch on his cane, and the goat head handle snapped back as a pin stuck out the front. A crackling loop of energy arced between the head and the pin, providing a flickering blue light that locked the shadows into complete darkness and lit up the two men.

The man with the cane wore a silk top hat and matching iridescent overcoat with a half cape, his blouse beneath pressed and scented with an Iruvian wrap pattern. His eyes were outlined in kohl, and greasepaint rendered his slender face and high cheekbones skull-like.

The other man shrugged his stylish cloak back over one shoulder, revealing his gauzy blouse and tight hose, a fanciful demon-head codpiece drawing the eye. His hair was stylishly tousled and reinforced with some kind of product, his cheeks were rouged. Bright red lipstick reshaped the shape of his lips. Silvery eyeshadow and blood-red mascara and eye liner resonated with his lips, an arresting color scheme against the silver and rose of his features. He airily brushed at his feathered hair. His fingernails were painted black with white stripes. Beneath the blouse, his long and lean muscles were evident, along with the shadow of hair and nipples. He raised his chin to showcase the length of his neck, which was scented with musk, the lines and planes of his throat accented with expensive makeup applied with a deft hand.

"Do I look good enough to eat?" Piccolo asked, a sardonic undertone to his simpering.

"You are a suicidal madman and you need better friends," the man in the top hat said between his teeth, snapping the cane head shut. "But yes. You'll do. Stringier than her normal fare, but you've got spirit, and I think she'll like that for a few minutes." He shrugged. "Then you're dead."

"I'm suicidal?" Piccolo retorted. "You're the one who decided becoming a pimp chef for vampires was a career with a future." He shrugged his silky cloak back over both shoulders, raising his hands to the side. "Better spritz me again, Zingzh."

Zingzh produced a glass bottle with a bulb sprayer, and squirted a mist into the air. Piccolo walked through it, chin up, and swirled his cloak around a few times. "I don't smell a thing," he said.

"It's human adrenaline and extract of passion," Zingzh muttered. "My own recipe. Gets her all juiced up and ready to play. Or feast. Depends on the night she's having, I guess." He pocketed the bottle, and gripped his cane with both hands. "Remember, you promised. She doesn't get hurt, and I don't know anything about your plan. A duped innocent," he growled.

"I won't give you up, but she's not stupid," Piccolo said. "I can't promise she won't take it hard that you brought me in." He squared off with Zingzh. "Not like you get to walk away if you betray me. Even if I die. Unless you want to go up against the rest of the Silkworms."

"Keep it light," Zingzh replied with a thin smile that accentuated his skull-like appearance. "Nobody is making threats here." He paused. "You ready?"

"Walk in the park," Piccolo shrugged. "Let's go."

They mounted the uneven stairs to the broad paved frontspiece to the house, and approached the door. Zingzh pulled a key from his lapel pocket and slotted it into the massive lock on the front door, wincing slightly as he muscled the heavy key around. The door unlocked with a loud clack, and Zingzh shouldered the door open.

As they walked into the echoing tunnel of the main entry, Piccolo reflexively noticed there were half a dozen locks on the front door; only one had been engaged, so Zingzh was obviously expected.

The entry corridor had the spicy rotten smell of old death, and even in the deep shadow the old sprays of blood along the walls were still discernable. Piccolo did not even shiver as he walked through the very spot where dozens, maybe hundreds of people had died over the centuries. The left wall had a faded family tree delicately painted on the plaster, and it had not been updated in many generations; it slowly decayed, a portrait of more prosperous times. The opposite wall was decorated with alcoves. First for a doorman, then a guard, then a shrine to the Church, then a houseboy. All were drifted with debris; papers, clothing, broken furniture, discarded weapons. Possibly corpses.

They reached the central vestibule, a massive round chamber with two balconies on the house side and an elaborate multi-level chandelier suspended in the center. The mosaic floor drifted towards colorlessness under a layer of grime, only the footpath worn smooth across it showing the faint glint of metal inlay among the stones, a glimpse of its grand pattern. A restless breeze tightened their skin as they reached the center of the chamber, feeling eyes upon them but resisting the urge to look around more carefully.

Zingzh faced Piccolo and put his hand on his shoulder, and Piccolo responded to the pressure to droop down to a kneeling position. Zingzh pulled ring of absolution from his inner pocket, a circlet of fingerbones cut down and strung together in a stylized carved spine with bone beads at five points to represent the limbs and head. Zingzh whispered the Prayer of Five in Hadrathi as he touched the circlet to Piccolo's forehead, each cheekbone, and chin. Piccolo obediently raised his hand, and Zingzh used the sharp beak of bone on the bead representing the head, and gave him a shallow cut. After a moment, Zingzh gathered blood on the beak, and painted a circle on Piccolo's forehead.

Piccolo was now ready for death.

Zingzh kissed the top of his head, then abruptly turned and strode down the entryway, letting himself out the heavy front door. He locked it behind himself, the noise of the bolt shooting into place resonant in the open chamber.

Piccolo waited on his knees, patient, sensing the subtle breezes as air drifted around in the cavernous chamber. He did not hear or see anything, but an intuitive sense within him trembled at danger, tightening his skin, and he needed no further evidence to know he was not alone.

"I consulted Lord Strangford to see what was keeping Dunvil neutral in all this," Trellis murmured, almost to himself as he consulted the chalkboard on the wall. "I've got some temptations in the works to bring him around to accepting a power shift on the City Council, but... there's some sensitive information that Clelland controls that could be damaging to Lord Dunvil. Or someone in his family," Trellis sighed. "Apparently a few years ago Dunvil and Clelland went a few rounds, and dug up some secrets, but they were both successful to the point where they called a truce. If Clelland is desperate, and of course our plan will make her desperate, she may pull some kind of stunt to try and force Lord Dunvil to back her. We want to neutralize that tactic before it is employed."

"Blackmail is tricky," Sanction winced. "It's one thing to get it and deploy it, but defusing sensitive material on someone else by robbing a blackmailer is not generally smooth. High risk, and we do not have a lot of time."

"Of course you're right," Trellis replied mildly. "You should start us out by listing what we'll need."

"Sure," Sanction said. "You need to know who holds the blackmail, how they protect it, where they hide it, whether it's a single object like evidence or it's a secret that you can't neutralize through theft. Is it the kind of thing where the victim of blackmail will try to kill anyone who has interacted with the material, or is it possible to get some gratitude out of the effort?" He shifted uneasily. "If you know all that, then your methods are informed, and you plan it like any other heist."

"Let me paint you a picture," Trellis said. "Skannon Clelland was a tragic figure. Forceful will, brutally possessive, high maintenance. Almost four centuries ago she was a darling in the Clelland family, and her arranged marriage would help secure their legacy. However, she has a torrid affair with a lesser light, an aristocrat from a somewhat diminished house. She loved his beauty, his voice, his starry eyes." Trellis paused. "I read some of her poetry about him," he added, deadpan, "so I've already suffered for the cause."

"We're all grateful to you for that," Piccolo said with a raised eyebrow, "but that matters how?"

"He left her," Trellis said, "and she flew into a rage. Unable to bear her reprisals, he slit his wrists and died. Wracked with remorse, and unable to face a future bereft of his beauty, she swore it must stay in the world. So she committed ritual suicide while his body was packed in ice, and her acolytes assured she rose as a ghost. She inhabited her victim's body, and merged with him for all time." Trellis paused. "She became a vampire by intertwining her ghost and his corpse. She preferred his beauty to her own, so now she sees him in the mirror."

"I thought vampires didn't have reflections," Piccolo said.

Trellis looked to the Mistress of Tides. "The curse of union affects them differently," he said. "They have different ways to move, to feed on life energy, different supernatural senses, different... expressions," he said with a vague gesture. "Anything to add?" he asked the Mistress of Tides.

"They are invisible behind the Mirror," the Mistress of Tides said. "They are the most powerful predators we know. Their weaknesses are difficult to exploit, and their strengths..." she shrugged. "They are formidable."

"I don't like this picture, and this plan is a terrible idea," Sanction said bluntly.

"Skannon Clelland is covered by the Felswift Report, the Church has her on record and has allowed her existence and put her off limits to the Spirit Wardens. Her lair is one of the old Clelland properties in Six Towers. She has a quiet existence away from the public. Far as I can tell, she has no servants and is the only thing that moves in the estate's bounds. She guards the family's hoard of secrets."

"You want to sneak in to a bored vampire's lair?" Piccolo asked directly, eyebrows raised.

"I don't think that would work," Trellis said. "So I expanded my search."

"Because you figured this was coming," Sanction said, rolling his eyes.

"Sooner or later," Trellis shrugged. "Using Strangford's contacts, I discovered there is a supplier that brings victims to Skannon. Home delivery, hot fresh prey. As it turns out, Strangford has some leverage over this supplier, Master Zingzh."

"So what, we poison this thing?" Piccolo pressed.

"That's more of a backup plan," Trellis said. "I had something a little more subtle in mind."

CLELLAND NORTHSHORE TOWER, SIX TOWERS.
26TH ELISAR. HOUR OF THREAD, 4 HOURS PAST DUSK.

Piccolo barely felt the exquisite sharpness that touched at the back of his silken cloak, slowly sliding down through it with no resistance at all as the fabric parted. The cloak fell from his shoulders, and he shivered slightly, uncomfortably conscious of his hammering heart and the rapid slither of blood all through his body, sluicing through his flesh, bathing his bones, pulsing under the soft skin that held the world away from his interior workings. He felt an intolerable echo, as though something nearby was thinking so loud he could overhear it.

"Fear not these shiverings," cooed a voice with a feminine cast through a male register. "Your body tries to grip itself tight, flex its workings to make heat and trap it inside. Your mind does the same, when the temperature drops."

"How can you tell?" Piccolo asked, his voice more even than he felt. "How can you tell the difference between fear and excitement?"

A throaty chuckle replied. "I like you," the voice purred. "I can tell the difference because I have centuries of experience in isolating and combining the flavors of how you feel, what you think, what you do, how you live, and how your body is a catalogue of everything you've been or ever will be."

"Huh," Piccolo said. "I live in here, and I can't always tell the difference. I guess I don't have centuries of experience."

"Less than three decades," the predator said dismissively. "Not enough time to really learn anything."

"I feel like I've learned some things," Piccolo said. "Mostly the hard way. Some lessons over and over." He paused. "I want to see you."

"I did not tell you that you must remain still," the predator replied. "Only your fear told you that."

"Well, sure, my fear and also Master Zingzh," Piccolo retorted. "He said I couldn't move until you said so."

"Are we arguing?" the predator mused.

"No, I just don't like feeling misunderstood," Piccolo replied. He rose to his feet, effortless even after a period of kneeling. Turning, he saw the predator halfway across the vestibule, and another shiver rippled through him; he was not used to trying to track other people in his space and getting no cues at all about their position.

Skannon's stance was, at first glance, an akimbo and fashionable pose. Piccolo immediately knew better, seeing Skannon with a knife fighter's instinct. He sensed the alien looseness and power suffusing the attractive shape before him. The body's position and arrangement was an afterthought that could be rearranged in a moment's subconscious whim. The lean male shape was draped in a silk robe, otherwise unadorned, hair woven into intricate braids and knotted. Handsome, sure, but the eyes instantly revealed the lethal energy that animated the long-dead form, and the hunger saturating this thing defined its identity more than anything else ever would again.

"We have disagreed twice," Skannon observed aloud, "and that's twice more than most of my guests. You've been spiced but not drugged, and your scars are earned by action more than punishment." Her eyes narrowed. "Why are you really here?" Her voice took on a depth of sibilance and resonance, filling the chamber with its quiet menace.

"My cover story is that Master Zingzh wanted to give you a spicier dish," Piccolo shrugged. "I got some exotic suggestions of things to try to get and hold your attention. I need you distracted for a while."

"To what end?" Skannon asked, arching her eyebrow.

"Nobody sneaks into a vampire's lair while the vampire is bored," Piccolo replied. "But if you're busy, then maybe some thieves have time to find the good stuff."

"Seems odd you'd commit suicide without even trying to persuade me of your cover story," Skannon said, oddly neutral.

"You can taste my scar tissue," Piccolo said, and he shook his head. "The people that sent me underestimated you, they don't really know how sharp you are. I'm not that guy. When I'm wrong, I don't double down. I change my plan."

"And what's your new plan," Skannon soothed, as patronizing as an adult consulting a child about what the child's artistic scribbles and shapes could possibly represent.

"I've heard some rumors, and I bet you haven't. I know who sent me, and if you kill me outright you won't. You want to keep track of your enemies, and I bet that's hard to do in here. Alone," Piccolo said, gesturing around the room, trying to keep the tremble out of his hands. "I was hired to work against you, sure, but I'm dumping the contract right here." He paused. "I don't want to be your enemy."

"So how does this work now?" Skannon asked, slowly circling Piccolo. "You want to extract assurances before cooperating?"

"I've seen my hand of cards, and I'm beginning to see how much better yours is," Piccolo said. "My best bet is to aim for your goodwill and hope for the best. I don't have a lot to negotiate with here, I'm in over my head." He paused. "I was told you were this inbred relic that wanted to take its time with meals, all bored and lonely." He looked at Skannon. "You're a goddamn force of nature."

Skannon watched Piccolo, unreadable. "Who sent you."

"Remira Welker. She's a fixer, sent me in here to get what I could for her to sell to other blackmailers. She's riding high right now, her reputation got a major boost after she got the Book of Seven Slayings notes out of your stash."

Skannon frowned. "She didn't get the Book of Seven Slayings notes out of my stash," Skannon said, something sharp under her tone. "It's right where I left it."

Piccolo hesitated for a moment. "I'm not going to disagree with you a third time," he shrugged.

CHART ROOM, ABOARD THE CONSTELLATION, THE DOCKS. 26TH ELISAR. SEVENTH HOUR PAST DAWN.

"But that's a published book," Sanction said. "Is there a special edition used for a book code or something?"

"No," Trellis replied, considering his audience. Piccolo, Niece, Gapjaw, and Mistress of Tides were in the chart room as others split up to work on other plans. "We are not after the book, we are after the notes. See, the Book of Seven Slayings is presented as a scholarly work pulling from restricted information that the author could access but the public cannot verify. It was a passion project for Dursella Dunvil, and that book reinforced the hard-hitting Dunvil reputation as law and order enthusiasts in this century, using aristocratic access for the common good. However, rumors circulate that several sources were invented wholecloth or adapted past the point of faithfulness to reinforce the story. This kind of blackmail serves our purposes well, because it's a physical object that provides leverage instead of information alone," Trellis said, "and we know such a revelation would be very damaging to the public impression of Dunvil honesty."

"So, there's a vault or something?" Gapjaw said with a vague gesture.

"The estate was built by paranoid aristocrats," Trellis replied, "and it is filled with secret doors and hidden spaces. Also, most passages have adjacent spy passages, so if the aristocrat feels threatened, there are murder holes littered all through the place to trap and destroy intruders."

"So we have zero chance of finding any hidden blackmail," Gapjaw clarified.

"And it gets worse," Piccolo prompted, an educated guess.

"Because vampires are invisible in the Ghost Field, they do not trigger attacks from dartus weed," Trellis agreed. "Dartus weed shoots paralytic darts. So there are indoor cultivated patches that will disable unwary intruders until the vampire finds them."

Piccolo rubbed the bridge of his nose, and continued making a "go on give me the rest" gesture with his hand.

"And according to my sources the blackmail materials are cursed," Trellis continued with a small smile.

"There it is," Piccolo sighed.

"So much as touching them will trigger one of a variety of unpleasant side effects," Trellis clarified.

"Is that what I'm there to do?" the Mistress of Tides asked. "Blunt the vampire's dangers and disable the curse on our target?"

"If possible," Trellis nodded. "My first thoughts revolved around using your abilities combined with Piccolo to infiltrate the house, but like all the Great Manses, it has some heavy glyph work and ancient warding, dating back to when aristocrats still used massive human sacrifices to power the protections on their residences."

"What are your current thoughts?" Gapjaw asked. "And do we have supper plans?"

"Oddly related questions," Trellis mused. "We're going to force the man who supplies the vampire with people to devour to take one of our people in to con the vampire."

"I bet I know who gets to be bait," Gapjaw leered at Niece, who frowned.

"That's right, me" Piccolo grinned, pointing at himself with both hands. "Juiciest honeypot in both crews." He crossed his arms with a wide grin.

Gapjaw blinked. "Okay three things," he said. "One, this is a terrible plan. Two, what the hell am I going to be doing while Piccolo is getting killed? And three, I still want to know about our supper plans."

"My defenses are intact," Skannon snapped. "You and I are alone in here. Maybe the rest of your team recognized their folly before they came in."

"Maybe so," Piccolo agreed easily. "Probably."

Skannon stared at him for just a moment, then was by his side, snatching him and tossing him at a third story alcove and ledge across from the balconies. Piccolo rushed through the air and tucked in tight, banging into the wall and dropping on the narrow ledge, almost sliding off. He braced himself, heart pounding, body reeling from the impact, and saw the vampire dash away from the vestibule into the house interior.

"Closer than I'd like," he said through his teeth, and he quickly adjusted his position on the ledge, ignoring the drop, tugging off his sash. He ripped one end to free the bone grapple hook inside, attached to the heavy silk cable woven back and forth in the sash material.

His second toss snagged the chandelier.

*

Niece struggled to focus, the room swimming apart before her eyes as her senses bucked towards unraveling. She still felt the golden liquid in her mouth, numbing her face and throat, her teeth invisible to her senses. No one was supposed to ingest this much silence at once; the senses would collapse under the effect. Unless she handled dosing herself very carefully. Holding the alchemy in her mouth, she struggled to breathe, unable to feel or hear her own heartbeat.

In the room below, the vampire bolted. Niece dropped from the ledge, the rope playing out through the carabiners with what should be a roaring buzz, but there was no sound as she plummeted, slowing her fall enough to scramble loose of the harness when she reached the floor. She took off at a run, sinuses blooming with raw nothingness, her face sliding apart as her mind scrabbled down into her body in search of sensation.

Still, there was no sound as her boots rammed into the paving, and no vibration escaped the supernatural divot in the Ghost Field that the alchemy spun out of her battered consciousness.

They raced through the corridors and side rooms of the house, Niece giving everything she had to keep the lithe vampire in sight. Silence rolled with her, putting such pressure on the Mirror that multiple senses slid into an emptiness radiating from her meat and bones.

Niece had no idea how long the chase ran, down stairs and through a cellar, dropping into a false ceiling and from there into a vast wine cellar, into the cramped office by the double-wide stairs leading back up into the house. The vampire entered the office, swept one book from a shelf full of logistical journals, and snorted.

Then Skannon stopped, lost in thought, and focused. Scanned the surrounding area. Niece slid between two hulking tuns of wine, pulling the silence in as tight as she could so the distortion itself would not give her away. There was hardly enough of the potion left to coat her tongue now, but she felt profound disconnection from her distant-seeming physical form.

After an impossibly long matter of seconds, Skannon sniffed, frowned, and put the book back on the shelf before dashing back the way she came.

Niece gave her to a count of five, and raced towards the office. She pulled the silence in all the way to her bone marrow, brandishing a spirit charm and focusing to line it up with her perceptions and the Ghost Field. As they merged, she sensed the various cold energy fogs drifting out of all the cursed material in the office.

I'm sure, she thought, staring at the unmarked book spines, *that it is one of these three.*

She put her fingertips on top of three books, and tilted them out of the shelf, tucking them into her bag as she felt the reverberating shock of curses latching into her.

*

Like a sailor ascending old-fashioned rigging, Piccolo darted up through the baroque ironwork of the massive chandelier, wriggling up through the lights, squirming between internal supports, sending a shiver through the whole structure in his mad upward climb. He saw the small hole that had been blasted into the roof by a silent explosion, but he heard nothing even as a rope slid down from the roof above the hole.

Piccolo reached the massive chain that supported the chandelier as Skannon arrived once more in the vestibule. Skannon screeched in fury, bounding up in a mighty flat-footed jump to snatch the base of the chandelier. As the vampire swarmed up through the interior, Piccolo launched from the chain to catch the rope, twirling over the lethal vastness of space.

He could spare no attention to look down as he climbed hand over hand. His muscles burned, his ribs and spine ached, sharp pains raced through him, his hands were freely bleeding, but he drove up the cable to squirm into the hole in the roof as the jangle of metal in the chandelier accelerated impossibly.

Piccolo almost panicked as he got one shoulder out of the hole, then the other, pulling himself up through the gap, aflame with the expectation that a grip would close on his leg and tear it off; then he was out, rolling forward, and he heard the crack of a nearby rifle and the blaring hiss of plasmic ammunition; a burst of energy lit up the night behind him as he sprinted down the curve of the dome, dropping to slide when it got too steep to run across.

From the ledge around the vestibule dome, he dropped to the ridgeline of the chapel, then down that slant roof to the guardhouse wall by the inner courtyard, then down to the burial ground—

Too late, Piccolo heard the distinctive hissing spit of dartus weed.

*

With a small cry of frustration, Niece hurled her shoulder again at the unresponsive hidden door. Too late, she realized it was barred from the other side, which meant—pivoting, she raced back towards the door she had come through, only to see it snap shut and lock. She stood panting, trapped. A view slot ground open on the door, and she saw one luminous wicked eye on the other side.

"You are brimming with magic," Skannon whispered, "a fortune of alchemical enchantment. You are only half real. *You will melt in my mouth*," the vampire breathed.

"Th-through the d-door?" Niece stammered, still unable to feel her heart beating.

The lock snapped open again, and the door drifted out of the way, revealing the tall, handsome vampire on the other side. "Oh, little kitten, you have brought me such a treat," the vampire murmured, gliding into the murder hole with her victim.

"I thought you were after—after the other one," Niece managed.

"I was," Skannon replied, and she gestured at her neck, which had a burned crater blown out of it. "As I was considering my next move, I felt a disturbance. Those are not for you," she admonished, her chin tilting towards the bag of books. "You are cursed, and me? I am simply part of the luck that curse brings you."

"So the others? They get to escape?" Niece protested.

"Maybe, for now, if they're very lucky," Skannon shrugged. "Leaving the estate is not as easy as it sounds." Her eyes narrowed. "But you? You stole from me. And also marinated yourself quite thoroughly in some unexpected delights." A smile filled the monster's face.

"And you can drink in some of this cursework too," Niece frowned. "It's connected to my life force."

"I had almost forgotten the burn of potent spices," Skannon replied, and she stepped into the light from the globe out of reach up above. She extended her long, muscular arms. "Thank you so much for this," she whispered to Niece.

Skannon's forearms trembled, then their flesh slit as skin parted, peeling back over tendon, muscle, bone; the interior of the vampire's forearms was slick. Niece's perceptions blurred so all she could sense from the vampire was the starvation of the feeding wounds. Her blood rushed to her front and left her giddy and light-headed, pooling towards that endless thirst.

Niece cried out as invisible force cut her forearms, the skin curling back, bright blood spraying up into the air and falling towards Skannon as though she was the center of all gravity.

"No!" Niece screamed, and she jammed her hand into her jacket and pulled out a fist-sized intricate medallion circled with pale gems; she focused hard, aiming the medallion through the shower of blood between the vampire and the prey. Niece felt her blood sluicing out, felt the cold inert stability of the spirit bane amulet, felt the vampire's energy in the Mirror between the Ghost Field and the breathing world; the amulet attuned to her perception, and snapped shut the space between the world of flesh and the world of spirit.

Skannon snarled, her forearms closing with a wet slap, the unbearable singularity driving her starvation back as light dispels shadow. Niece ran at her, screaming, and Skannon staggered back, her too-keen senses filled with burning; she could not react fast enough as Niece darted by her, slamming the door and barring it, then turning to stagger away as fast as she could manage.

Only then did Skannon realize she was locked in the murder hole. Roaring, she drove a single blow into the door, exploding it into flinders, and she raced after the thief.

Another barred door. Another. Furious, Skannon ducked through a secret passage, moving swiftly to flank the intruder, who did not know the layout as well as she did. Headed to the east moat gate, most likely; Skannon would arrive first.

The vampire stood between the secret sally port on the shore of the courtyard pond, and the unremarkable stretch of wall that contained one of the better-known secret doors in her estate. Sure enough, the door opened, and Niece stumbled out, gripping the spirit bane charm in one hand and the bag of books in the other, badly weakened by blood loss. Scents and flavors streamed from her like pennant flags fluttering brightly on a decorated holiday; the silence potion, the spirit bane charm, her anxiety, her youthful ferocity, the cursework still sinking through her layers towards her core.

"You almost made it out," Skannon taunted Niece, her voice intensely patronizing—the click and blast gave her a fraction of a second to react, but guns were still new enough that dodging automatically was not yet ingrained. Instead she pivoted to see what the noise was, so the plasmic shot hit her square in the chest, hurling her off her feet.

Niece looked up to the wall, where the tree grew too close to it, allowing a scoundrel to make it up with relative ease. Gapjaw snapped another shot off at the surprised vampire, and this time she did dodge, but she was off-balance. Gapjaw held the rifle in one hand and drew a pistol from his belt with the other, blasting away with plasmic rounds that tore into Skannon's shoulder.

Wasting no time, Niece stumbled at the wall, and Gapjaw kicked the knotted rope he had been securing off the ledge; Niece climbed as fast as she could as Gapjaw dropped one pistol and drew another, firing off two rounds in close succession. He didn't get a clean hit, but he did send the vampire reeling. He tossed his rifle down on the outside of the wall, then grabbed the rope and leaped off the parapet. His weight was substantially more than Niece's, so the rope banged past each knot as he went down and she dragged upward.

Niece was almost delirious as she ducked at the parapet and rolled over the crenellation, dropping over the other side as the enraged vampire flung a stone that exploded to shrapnel on the wall behind her.

By the time Skannon raced to the sally port and flung it open, the scoundrels had crossed the street and dashed down the quay to where their boat waited; they nosed out into the canal, Niece piloting the boat as Gapjaw grimly stared along the backtrail and reloaded custom ammunition.

They were clear.

Niece was sobbing with pain and dislocation, it was too much to handle. She experienced a sudden flash of a scene of carnage, and looking down, realized she had just murdered a number of people; shaking it off, she tasted the acrid bitterness of the cursework firing through her system and spasming into hallucination of a murderous ghost loose in her flesh.

Gapjaw whuffed at the receding shoreline like a territorial guard dog watching intruders retreat. "That could have gone worse," he said, and he kicked at Piccolo's unresponsive leg. "Right, Piccolo?"

The paralyzed scoundrel stared at him, expression slack, but eyes still somehow capable of expressing hostility.

"Dartus weed?" Niece demanded. "Is he alright?"

"He'll be fine, we'll all be fine, we'll get those curses weaseled off you with our Whispers when we get back," Gapjaw said with confidence as he finished reloading his rifle. "I just want to point out that the honeypot here," he said with a nod to Piccolo "and our magicked-up thief," he nodded at Niece "both ended up needing good old Gapjaw to pull them out when the vampire was closing in." He sniffed. "That should put a stop to jokes about being the lookout and getaway driver."

His self-satisfaction had not prepared him for Niece to pivot and throw her arms around him, hugging him tight as she bawled into his shoulder.

He awkwardly patted her back as the boat drifted in the canal, so surprised that he forgot all the jokes he had prepared about taking advantage of Piccolo while he was painted up and scantily dressed.

Probably just as well.

CHAPTER TWENTY

Look, if you don't have an academic theory to push or an image as a proper grown-up expert to defend, it is perfectly reasonable to accept the common understanding of how Doskvol got its name. The Skov kingdom built the mine and called it "The Skov's Coal" and that translates to "Doskovol." The extra "o" in the middle was dropped along the way to common usage.

Pinning down the origin of the nickname "Duskwall" is even simpler, as it stems from a single point of misunderstanding compounded by lack of correction. In the 380s, the Dagger Isles were expanding their trade routes in lock step with their improved shipping hulls and rigging schemes. Under the Sail Sultan, Lord Masaath, a daring cartographer named Sirinaav Kraylatha was given a golden statue with the dimensions and likeness of each of his family members in exchange for an authoritative map of the Void Sea and its interruptions. His occult charting techniques were fiercely accurate, in contrast to his grasp of Akorosian. He wanted the Dagger Isles charts to be unique, so he bypassed the Akorosian name for the port (North Hook) and penned in "Duskwall."

People normalizing that nickname are signaling that they were influenced by the criminal underclasses. The nickname only got purchase among those who dealt extensively with Dagger Isles nautical types, and the main reason to do that was the smuggling of luxury items.

— From "Disambiguating Scholarly Speculation in Akorosian Linguistics" by Professor Lativan Smek

CITY COUNCIL CHAMBERS, DOSKVOL CIVIC PALACE, CHARTER HALL. 29ᵀᴴ ELISAR. FOURTH HOUR PAST DAWN.

"So conclude our meditations," intoned Father Rowan.

"It is so," the City Council murmured in unison. Their stillness dissolved into a moment of adjustment, ordering their papers and small books, glancing around the room, clearing their throats. Only six of them were seated around the massive table. A scribe sat in a dedicated alcove with a hidden back door, three security guards stood watch with soundproofed helms, and one cowled man relaxed on the opulent bench set into the wall five paces behind Strangford's seat.

The Members wore stylized costumes, based on sere black legal robes but elaborated with stoles around their necks that were embroidered with their various accomplishments and achievements in the Church, and vests bearing their family crests.

Bowmore stood, his mane carefully tended and curled back over the mass of his shoulders. He picked up the City Scepter. "As we transition to discussion of allocating public resources, we have an opportune moment to acknowledge our newest and returning member, Father Dracha Rowan. Welcome, I am confident you will continue to reflect your family's commitment to the betterment of the city."

"Thank you, Lord Bowmore," Rowan nodded.

"Also, Strangford, looks like you've got a mystery guest," Lord Bowmore continued, gesturing towards the cloaked man.

"Indeed," Strangford said. "I have a proposal for reallocation of some public resources and I brought along my expert and consultant so if there were detail-oriented questions he could serve as a resource, and also so his efforts would align as closely as possible with the will of the Council." He gestured, and Trellis lowered his cowl, revealing his features. He smiled blandly, projecting the very soul of a boring aristocrat. "This is Sir Belderan, he has decades of experience with Ministry issues."

"Welcome," the Members murmured with various levels of disinterest. Only Clelland fixed him with an icy stare that he pretended not to notice.

"Let's hear it," Bowmore said shortly, handing the Scepter to Strangford, who rose to accept it.

"My proposal creates a new port. You received the initial brief," Strangford said, his low register resonating in the room. He paused. "Until very recently, there was an alliance here in the Council among its Members, seeking to remove dynastic rights to manage and direct

Leviathan blood collection on behalf of the city. I am pleased to report that we have settled the matter and found other solutions. Now, before we continue, I acknowledge that nothing can happen on this taxable scale without approval from the full City Council and all of its members." He paused, and no one spoke, though Clelland deliberately crossed her arms.

"You may reasonably wonder what I get out of supporting this project," Strangford said. "The hunting fleet could use more dry-dock space and construction facilities. Our current facilities are overextended by the need for repair and refitting. I promised my people I'd figure something out," he shrugged with a winning smile, "and this is my solution."

"It is expensive, for a beginning," Rowan murmured, shifting position as his eyes roved over the briefing documents. "The defensive lightning wall does not protect the site of the old North Port."

"Correct, and for several reasons of practicality and enmity. All that is behind us now as we face the future," Strangford said. "We can raze that haunted territory and rebuild with modern techniques."

"The old North Port is a threshold between our city and the Death-lands," Bowmore observed mildly. "How do you plan to assure its safety if we fill it with living blood again?"

"I have had some strategic discussions with Lord Cleith Rowan," Lord Strangford said modestly. "The main driver he had for stepping off the Council is his research into the Ambient Defense Systems. He has conducted successful tests and tapped a number of sponsors for further development. What better test than to have a reclamation project to deploy the systems against the hazards of the Deathlands?"

Rowan cleared his throat. "Yes, Lord Cleith Rowan did not want a perceived self-aggrandizement or abuse of leverage through membership on the Council to taint his research and its value. I have agreed to relieve him of Council responsibilities so he may focus his attention where it is best used."

"And," Clelland cut in, "I suppose the profits go to the Strangford house?"

Strangford looked to Dunvil, who smiled broadly.

"I have an appropriate work force for this sort of thing," Dunvil said. "Ironhook penance labor will clear the way and handle heavy lifting for the refurbishment, taking the brunt of the risk. Combining my initial investment and the history my family has with running North Port, I have agreed with Strangford's plan, which outlines Dunvil oversight for taxation and operation."

"So of course you're in favor of this tremendous undertaking," Clelland muttered.

"Of course," Dunvil soothed. "Think of what this could do for revitalizing taxation and stimulating the economy. Adding a second major port will create vast opportunities," he shrugged, and he did not need to spell out how much contraband and crime would swarm through such a relatively low regulation environment, further enriching those who knew how to tap those schemes.

"Member Rowan," Clelland said, turning to the old man, "Do you have any concerns about the theological implications and risks of your nephew's bold new technology?"

"This is an ideal test," Rowan said. "The stakes are low, and witnessing the operation will give us opportunities to test its efficacy and also provide live testing encounters. The laws are clear with what we must do in order to adjust the current lightning wall protection. We need the law to be clear again. We are developing something new, and this is the way to do that responsibly."

Bowmore snorted. "This is good for Rowans, Dunvils, and Strangfords, I can see that. The rest of us have little reason to buy into this—this distraction," he said, tossing his notes on the table. "Penderyn. You have opposed every change to the status quo. Nothing to say here?" he asked, voice sharp.

The trim man sighed. "Of course you're right," he said. "Except in this case, I saw the plans and they are quite persuasive. Integration of the old and new, with the City Council leading the way, is just the sort of boost in morale that we need right now."

Bowmore stared for a long moment, and Penderyn bore the scrutiny with a quiet and unreadable smile.

"So that's it?" Clelland demanded, her tone flat.

"Almost," Penderyn agreed, looking through her sheaf of notes. "Ah. I did have a thought of how we could signal our commitment to the restoration of our local antiquities," he said. "I propose a rider to the contract to restore the port to taxable condition. Its profits will contribute to the upkeep of the High Six." He lowered his papers, looking at all the other members except Rowan. "Seems there was an impromptu Ministry action that re-allocated the site of the High Six to serve as the foundation for a new Spirit Warden stronghold in Silkshore." His eyebrows raised. "I think we can agree that is not what's best for Doskvol," he said. "With the damages already done before demolition could be halted, a reliable income stream will preserve this treasure for generations to come." He shrugged. "We must defend it against rash action," he said.

"Unbelievable," Bowmore said through his teeth.

"Well we cannot do it without you, nor would we," Strangford said. "You've got a key role in all of this."

"Oh, is that so," Bowmore retorted, eyebrows and shoulders up.

"I was reflecting on your vision recently," Strangford agreed. "You have been looking at the bigger picture, how the Empire and its policies affect our lives here. I did some research, and there's no reason you could not be appointed as Lord Governor of Doskvol, and also serve on the City Council. You could be a unique bridging figure to streamline our governance."

Bowmore tried to look reflective instead of stunned. "Such a thing is out of reach unless the City Council supports it," he said with an airy gesture.

"Penderyn and Dunvil are with me," Strangford said, "and I'm with you." He looked Bowmore in the eye. "Let us agree to put bygone struggles in the past and focus on what we want for the future. If you were to accept appointment as Lord Governor, with our backing, we could finally accomplish real reforms with the military presence in Doskvol."

Strangford rose to his full height and pointed the scepter at Bowmore. "You could centralize control of both the Bluecoats and the military. Think of what you could do with that kind of authority."

Bowmore looked at Strangford, then Penderyn. "You would support me?"

They nodded, and Rowan rapped the table. "I would as well, young Bowmore," he said. "It's past time we had more local influence with the Lord Governor."

"Oh, me too," Clelland said through the distaste in her mouth. "Of course I'll help out. My family's investment in the Bluecoats is at least as great as yours," she said diplomatically through a pained smile, "and you cannot keep the order within their ranks if you cross me."

"I think you mean, if we disagree," Bowmore replied, mild.

"Of course," Clelland agreed, too angry to blush. "This seems like a well-considered plan. Aside from facing certain failure without my support with the Bluecoats. Surely there is incentive for me to lend my support," she added, struggling to keep the acid out of her voice.

Strangford nodded. "Naturally we want to make sure all of us rise with the tide," he said, placating. "Each of the families has significant investment and relationship with upper echelon leadership in the Bluecoats. In fact, that could jeopardize an appearance of neutrality, of checks and balances in this endeavor. Working together, we can establish a new district, populated by handpicked leadership and their preferred subordinates, and they can get the funding and support they need to heroically reclaim a part of our heritage from the Deathlands. You could shape that new district's Bluecoat force, create the culture and focus you want that's got the least influence from other city factions as it will be new and defending a very lucrative area."

Clelland watched him for a long moment. "That's not much," she said.

"And, of course, civic pride," Strangford added, a hint of chill in his tone. He shifted his stance. "Naria, I just don't see you standing in the way of something that's good for the whole city."

She surveyed the rest of the Members with a glance, then smoothed the scowl from her features, and smiled brightly.

"I'm in," she said. "For the good of Doskvol," she added.

The approving vote was unanimous.

ROWAN TOWNHOUSE, WHITEHALL.
29TH ELISAR. TENTH HOUR PAST DAWN.

Belton dragged Saint into the long parlor in Lord Cleith Rowan's chambers, thrusting him ungently forward to stumble before the nobleman. Red Silver followed them, with two more guards behind her. The prisoners were dressed in basic clothes, shirts and pants and slippers.

Rowan listed to the side in his chair, clearly on the worse end of a high-spirited exchange with a vast quantity of alcohol. He blearily glared at his prisoners, rolling up a parchment as an afterthought.

"Well, our little disagreement has come to a plateau," he said, his voice raspy. "You are free to go, and put this behind you." He gestured at them imperiously.

"Disagreements have at least two sides," Saint replied mildly. "You can't just dismiss this, we aren't square. Not yet."

Silence descended into the room like a gusting wind, and everyone stared at Saint.

"Pardon me?" Rowan said with exaggerated enunciation, controlling his first response.

"You're off the Council, and that's a fine thing," Saint continued, "but you did a lot of damage to us in a very short time. You've got a lot to answer for, and I need some more of your clout to put a few things right. Then we'll go." His expression was completely matter-of-fact.

"You dare," Rowan said, his expression darkening.

Saint took a step forward. "Are you about to threaten me?" he demanded, looking Rowan in the eye.

Rowan's hand spasmed around the parchment, and it crumpled. "What do you want."

"Just some odds and ends. We can work it out if you lend us Soapstone, and Belton here," Saint said with a gesture at his guard. "I've grown accustomed to his assistance when I walk. Oh, and some new clothes; we can't be seen trotting around in these rags." His smile was bland.

For a long, long moment Rowan stared at Saint and considered his options and their consequences.

"Take Belton and go," he ground out at last.

Saint bowed deeply, shuffled in a tight pivot, and headed out, this time with the others following his lead.

Rowan waved one of his agents over. "Sanders. Find out how he knew I was off the Council," he hissed, eyes fixed on the freed prisoners as they filed out.

"Yes m'lord," the agent replied, and he withdrew through a side door.

Provided with an opportune moment to reflect on decisions made and unexpected outcomes, Lord Rowan instead poured himself another glass of wine from a very dusty bottle.

SHINING MANE PUBLIC HOUSE, BRIGHTSTONE. 29TH ELISAR. TWELFTH HOUR PAST DAWN.

"Soapstone," Belton called out as he approached the booth in the public house. The lawyer glanced up, then scrambled to his feet, tugging the small pistol from his waistcoat as he saw Saint and Red Silver with only one guard.

Saint breezed past his spoiled dramatic entrance, and approached the lawyer. Now he wore a silver and blue silken suit with shiny buttons and a dramatic overuse of drapes and folds. Behind him, Red Silver had a new greatcoat over a durable leather outfit that included thigh-high boots. They smelled of new clothes.

Soapstone looked to Belton. "So they're released, then?" he demanded.

"And they've got errands to run," Belton agreed, his rage frozen and his face chiseled into a sculpture of displeasure.

"Which very efficiently brings us to you," Saint said, bland. He gestured with his new black lacquer cane, its silver head sculpted to the likeness of a snarling horse-head and mane. "We went to your offices to discover you'd knocked off for the day, and Belton here was familiar with your habits and figured we'd find you here. I trust you've got the supplies for some official correspondence?"

"I do," Soapstone said warily.

"Good, because you've got four letters to write, and then we're off. Assuming you can clear your calendar on behalf of Lord Rowan?" Saint inquired.

"Of course," Soapstone said, still disoriented. "What kind of letters?"

"Two to send and two to carry, so we had best begin," Saint said.

Red Silver stepped forward into his space. "Let me free up your hands," she said, snagging the half-forgotten pistol from his grip. "Tiny thing," she observed, looking it over, "but cute enough. Got a knife?" She looked him in the eye as her deft touch slid around his side, pulling a knife and sheath from the back of his waistband. She glanced at it with a critical eye, then nodded and tucked it into her coat. "Thanks," she said with a brilliant smile.

"We appreciate your generous gifts," Saint agreed. "And you want us to move on. So let's do this."

Soapstone gritted his teeth, sat down, and opened his satchel.

ARRIVALS AND DEPARTURES PUBLIC HOUSE, THE DOCKS. 29TH ELISAR. HOUR OF HONOR, 1 HOUR PAST DUSK.

Soapstone stared out the window of the jolting carriage, sullen. Saint and Red Silver sat quietly, opposite the lawyer and the guard. Finally the carriage slowed to a halt after a difficult navigation around the more ramshackle end, where immigrants landed to go through Sorting Point. Just beyond, the vast bulk of the five story public house towered in the night. Arrivals and Departures bustled with Skovs.

"I really don't want to do this," Soapstone said under his breath.

"Nobody cares," Saint replied shortly, opening his carriage door. "Belton?" he said, eyebrows raised. The guard stepped out, and offered his elbow, supporting Saint out of the carriage. Once out, Saint wrapped a scarf around his features.

Red Silver slid out on the other side, and glanced back at Soapstone. "You need a hand too?" she demanded.

"I'll be fine," Soapstone snapped, stepping out, "when this is over."

They closed in on the pub and passed the tangled knots of dirty Skovs standing around the entrance subtly vetting everyone who walked in.

Red Silver approached the counter with Soapstone. She unsubtly glanced over him and tugged his purse loose, examining its contents with a critical eye, jogging the bag so it jingled. She pulled out a couple coins and tossed them at the barkeep as she pocketed the rest. "I'm looking for Clef," she said.

"He's with the Haymakers," the Skov replied, jerking his head towards the back corner. Several torches had been lit in addition to the candles and lanterns of the pub, and the low throb of rhythmic drumming was underscored by Skovs clapping as some dancers performed in a cleared space. A blanket had been stitched with the crude representation of a three pronged trident impaling hay, draped from the balcony above the corner; Red Silver was glad she knew what it was supposed to be before she saw it.

Red Silver led Soapstone into the Haymakers space, and Belton escorted Saint after them a dozen paces further back.

"Which one?" Red Silver demanded of Soapstone, who thought better of pretending he didn't know. He gestured at the giant Skov leaning against a pillar at the edge of the clearing, and Red Silver steered them around to his periphery. He looked down at them, and genuine surprise registered as he recognized Soapstone.

"Who the hell are you?" he demanded, failing his effort to avoid sounding defensive.

"Good evening, stranger who I am just now meeting," Soapstone gritted out. "I have come with good news for you."

"Oh, good," Clef replied, unsubtly leaning back and lowering his hand to the haft of a nasty war club leaned up against the wall.

Soapstone produced a sealed letter from his waistcoat. "You have an appointment with the Ministry," he said.

"Everybody quiet!" Clef shouted, dimming the merriment and drawing all eyes. "It's loud in here, I don't think I heard that right. Try this ear," he said, leaning towards Soapstone.

Now on stage, Soapstone glanced around. "That's right, it's your lucky day," he yelled. "The Ministry has appointed Clef as their new consultant, assigned to help negotiate disputes between Skovs and the Ministry. Your important bloodline is known to the Ministry," Soapstone said, redirecting his comments to Clef, "and your nobility will help clear up misunderstandings caused between cultures."

Clef searched his face for a moment, then snatched the letter and peeled it open, breaking the waxen seal. He handed it to a hard-bitten woman at his side, and she glanced over the text. "This has Rowan's seal," she said in a low voice. "Stipend, housing, office." Shocked, she looked up at the big man. "It's real."

Clef rounded on Soapstone, unable to shake his suspicion. "Why."

Soapstone gestured a nod towards Saint, without breaking eye contact. Clef turned his head first, then his eyes flicked to the mysterious and expensively dressed figure at the edge of the circle. Saint let the drama sizzle for a moment, then he lowered the scarf over his features, looking Clef in the eye. He saw recognition, then something like panic, streak through Clef's thoughts in quick succession.

"Everyone mourns the Grinders," Saint lied easily, and he looked around the assembly of angry Skovs. "What happened to them should have been prevented. All the failsafes broke down, every check and balance was swept aside. We need more ways for the leaders of Akoros and the leaders of Skovlan to meet, to talk through problems so violence is not the only recourse." Saint returned his attention to Clef. "We are all here together, yes? When bad things happen, we can try to make a better future... or we can indulge our brutal instincts and live in the bloody aftermath forever." He let that hang for just a moment, then he played to the crowd.

"You listen to Clef!" he yelled. "Now the Ministry will too!" He brandished his cane, and the Skovs let out a roar. Using his cane as a baton, Saint slashed to the side, and the noise dimmed. He looked back to Clef. "If, of course, your chief will accept!"

The spotlight swung to Clef, and he knew what to do with it. He took a step, rubbing at his beard, lost in thought. Then he planted his fists on his hips, looked at Soapstone with something like defiance, and shouted, "I accept!"

The crowd mobbed him, more drink and food hustled out, and it was all Soapstone could do to get the big man's mark scrawled on the appointment letter. Then the Akorosians managed to extricate themselves from the crowd, back towards the entrance.

Before they escaped, a hard grip clamped on Saint's arm. He turned to see the tough woman who read the letter, and he absently noted he would need to find out who she was.

"This offer, with the Ministry—what the hell is it," she demanded in a low tone.

"Peace offering," Saint replied, matching her tone and intensity. "What happened to the Grinders was awful. Nobody wants a war. And Clef? He's got the noble blood, the back story, the support of the people. He can make a real difference. I want us to be done with revenge," he concluded, almost a hiss. "*Both* of us."

She slowly nodded, releasing his arm, and vanished back into the crowd.

"One more stop," Saint muttered to Soapstone as they left.

Niece and Safety stood in the shadows of the armored courtyard, arms crossed over their chests, heavy coats mostly concealing their heavy load of body armor, guns, and blades. The massive gates to the public road stood open, and this high-walled enclosure was the last stop of released prisoners. Half a dozen guards stood on the walls, ignoring the light snow, staring down at the pair who had come to Ironhook in the deepening night.

Releases only happen in the daytime. Everyone knows that.

Still, they waited.

A bobbing lantern approached up the road, and four more people approached the Dancing Gate. One of them had a word with the door guard to the main portal before heading into the enclosure.

"Niece! Safety!" Saint called out, waving to them as he led the others into the courtyard. The two scoundrels trotted over to join Saint, Red Silver, Belton, and Soapstone.

"I could not believe your letter," Niece said breathlessly. "I figured it was likely a trap, but Trellis said we should go; he didn't seem worried."

"This is the last errand we need Soapstone for," Saint said, "much to his relief. Just tidying up some loose ends, right?" he said, turning to the lawyer. "You sent the list ahead."

"I did, I sent the list. All of your known associates that we brought in for questioning." Soapstone did not meet his eyes.

"We're just waiving charges for things like resisting arrest, poor behavior in prison, related crimes revealed in the capture, that sort of thing," Saint pressed.

"I was very specific, Rowan requested a discharge but not a pardon," Soapstone said sharply. "They all get to leave, but if they broke the law that's not scrubbed out."

"You know what they say," Red Silver said. "In the Dusk, no one is unwanted." Her smile was sardonic, but lacked some of the sharpness she was famous for.

Distant echoes clattered, then the massive metal gate leading out of Ironhook ground open, slowly parting. Several guards stood aside, and a crowd babbled and staggered out of the prison; dozens of people, pale and smudged with grime, left the walled confines of the prison.

Saint came forward, addressing the crowd. "We have wagons out-side the gate if you have trouble walking, and we've got a barge at the dock to take you to Charhollow. From there we have a number of cabbies waiting, they'll take you anywhere you like. We'll put you up if you need food and a place for the night. You are free!"

Red Silver recognized fences, informants, scoundrels with other crews, gondoliers, suppliers, and a cross-section of the infrastructure that supported criminals like the Silkworms and the River Stallions. Haggard and battered, the prisoners headed for the wagons.

Niece was among them, eyes darting from face to face until she found what she was looking for. She wrapped her arms around Rhya, who let out a chuckle as she hugged her kin close.

"I knew they'd never get you," Rhya whispered.

Later, on the barge crossing the Dosk River, Rhya and Niece sat together. Niece held her hand tightly, watching Belton and Saint move around networking, Red Silver camped out keeping an eye on Soap-stone. Niece looked to her aunt.

"This is why I do it, you know," she said. "Why I chose to throw in my lot with scoundrels." She squinted at the prisoners. "So I could have leverage. Strength to defend my people. If you're alone out here," she added, shaking her head, "you just get snapped up." She looked to Rhya. "You got hurt because of me. I could never fix that mistake with-out help. I'm not sure I can fix it now."

Rhya put a leathery hand aside Niece's face. "Little one," she said, "don't you worry about me. I half expected some crazy prison rescue attempt, and I was worried about that, because it's been years since I was any good at climbing or running. This plan seems a lot less likely to get you spitted on a sword," she said with an approving nod.

"If all this business of scoundrelling has taught me anything," Niece said, "it's that criminals are just the dimmest echo of common people trying to get away with the kind of murder and theft the aristocrats wield as their birthright."

Rhya laughed outright, tickled by the idea. "So you plan to become an aristocrat?" she demanded.

"I'm still young enough to marry," Niece teased, dropping a shoulder. "But no, that's lazy. You don't need to *be* an aristocrat if you can force them to do things *for* you."

"Ai! When did you get so wise?" Rhya said, trying to catch her breath. "There is nothing left to teach you!"

"Let's not get carried away," Niece said through a smile.

"See? You already know the last and best lesson!"

They cackled together as the barge shouldered across the river's current. It seemed like forever since either had managed a real laugh, and they made the most of it.

Across the barge, Saint eyed Belton critically. "Not too late to kill me you know," he shrugged.

"It is only too late when you're dead some other way," Belton said through his teeth. "Or, blood rebel, I die first." He cocked his head to the side. "We'll cross paths again. You're a terrible person and sooner or later I'll get leave to end you."

"See, that's what I like about you," Saint said with a finger waggle, the lace at his wrist bouncing. "Like a dog with a steak draped over his nose, waiting for the command to go at it. Your loyalty and self-control inspire me."

"I'd rather you not think about me at all," Belton frowned.

Saint regarded him for a moment. "I could use your help," he said, blunt. "I will pay better and give you fewer orders that rub you the wrong way. Though I would still prefer you not kill me." He smiled.

Benton squared off with him. "You are unbelievable," he said. "I am loyal to Lord Rowan and the North Hook company. My life's work is protecting this city from predators and parasites."

"Well, think it over," Saint shrugged. He paused, struck by a thought. "So which one am I?"

"Parasite," Benton growled.

"I can live with that," Saint said with a smile.

Saint glanced at the shoreline, then squinted at the sky. The released prisoners could be home by midnight. Their ordeal was almost over.

CHAPTER TWENTY ONE

History lends a veneer of inevitability to the past. Education is a large part of this, as we are taught in a context of getting answers correct, memorizing key facts that mattered about the outcome, and naming influential figures. As I prepare young minds for politics, I present history across two sides; what could have happened, and what did, in the end, occur. I feel it is critical for the minds that will shape our future to understand that the swirling mass of successes and failures upon which decisive events rest could have produced other outcomes that would seem equally unavoidable. I teach them to distrust certainty, interrogate inevitability, and consider alternatives. Only then can the news of the day connect with interpretation of the past—only through the diaphanous veil of 'what could have been.'

— *From "Six Essential Techniques for the Indispensable Tutor"*
by Professor Ara Dalaasia

FLAP-FLAP TAVERN, BARKUL MARKET, SILKSHORE.
31ST ELISAR. FOURTH HOUR PAST DAWN.

"So yesterday was two weeks since this all went sideways," Saint sighed. "That damned party at the Rowan Estate." He shook his head, rubbing at the brace on his leg.

"Terrible," Gapjaw agreed, slugging back some brew. Saint looked at him sideways, noting that the pale foam around his mouth matched the graying in his hair more than ever, and for a moment he indulged the bloom of mortality that shivered his skin.

"We were never going to make it as a marathon, it had to be short-term," Saint reflected. "Trellis said it was safe enough to be out and about now, but I have to wonder, considering. Do you think the assassins were called off?"

Gapjaw let out a thunderous belch, and splayed one hand on his waist coat. "Sure," he shrugged. "You invoked the man himself, the Trellis of Barrowcleft, so you can try to keep up your end of the conversation with *him*," Gapjaw retorted. "He'll walk through that door any minute, and it will be *your fault.*" He shook his head sadly at the notion, and finished his stein.

Almost in spite of himself, Saint glanced at the door, only to see the flickering light reflected on its tinted glass interrupted by a silhouette. "No way," he breathed.

Trellis opened the door and strolled in, brushing snow from his narrow shoulders. Glancing around, he spotted the scoundrels at the end of the bar, and approached.

"Thank you for meeting me today," Trellis said, settling on a stool. "I thought we should debrief our escapades a bit."

"You scheduled through Gapjaw?" Saint said, half amused.

"He was the only one at your base when Piccolo dropped by, and he said he knew the where and when of your recovery drinking," Trellis shrugged. "Looks like he was right."

"Almost always," Gapjaw added with a sage nod.

"But you didn't tell him about it," Trellis clarified with Gapjaw.

"Never know when he might be squirrely about something and not show. I relied on his habit and thirst. He's not over his ordeal of being tortured almost to death and reamed by one of the most powerful men in the city. Me, I suspect he'd limp even if his leg was fine; everybody that gets repeatedly interrogated that deep and hard walks a bit funny." He grinned at the other two men, who did not grin back, so he imitated a sex act with his fingers. "You know, *interrogate,*" he clarified.

"Got it," Saint said shortly, and he deliberately turned to Trellis. "I don't know how many people in Doskvol could have defused a situation that volatile," he said. "Congratulations are in order."

"Thank you," Trellis nodded. "Now that I can move freely again I checked into how things went with Rowan, and I hear you did a superb job of playing the hand you were dealt."

"Ugh," Gapjaw grunted. "Too much. I'm out. Sporecaps to go," he said to the barkeep, who nodded.

As Gapjaw headed for the check-out and door, Saint gazed into his drink. "Thank you for sending me updates in dreams," he murmured. "That really helped me handle Rowan." Trellis tightened his face in a wintery smile. "Handle Rowan indeed. No one will ever know if you were betraying us or carrying out a con." He paused. "I suspect you don't know yourself," he mused. "But it doesn't matter," he said as he gestured to the barkeep. "You do your best work when you're pursuing your best interests. And that is what we needed from you." He looked Saint in the eye. "Your best work. I think we got it," he shrugged.

"No hard feelings?" Saint said, unable to make eye contact.

"None," Trellis said decisively, clapping him on the shoulder. "We all have extraordinary capacities, and rising to find their limits always bears some unsavory costs." He nodded to the barkeep as he took his drink. "Now we carry on."

"I won't tell anyone you've got a merciful side," Saint muttered, unable to fully conceal his relief.

Trellis let his gaze simmer down to a similar but wholly different expression. "Who would believe you?" he asked softly.

CANAL COORDINATION OFFICE, CENTRAL LANDING, THE EASE, SILKSHORE. 31ST ELISAR. FIFTH HOUR PAST DAWN.

The brief pat-down finished up, and a scowling gondolier handed Sanction his case of papers back. Turning away from the guards, Sanction seated himself at the table, facing a mass of gondolier leaders who stared at him. Trajan stepped forward and sat down opposite Sanction; he did not have papers.

"You called this meeting," Trajan said. "A bold move. We want to talk to Trellis."

"I am here on his behalf," Sanction said, "to explain the new-found advantages of your situation."

"New—advantages?" Trajan said explosively. "I know the Worms have been in hiding, but—this catastrophe is beyond generational!" he snapped. "Didn't you hear? The Fairpole Council might as well have been wiped out! Our livelihoods now dandle at the fingertips of the very people that we have had to resist for centuries, this is in every way a defeat for us! What can you possibly say to that?"

"The Silkworms want to make it right, and we've got some leverage to accomplish that," Sanction replied quietly, deliberately drawing down the tension in the room.

"You are going to buy our boats back, hm?" Trajan demanded, cranking the tension right back up as he slammed his fist on the table and stood. "The Ministry used the Lending Commission to buy over three quarters of our boats. Rowan bought them at sale price and hired their former owners to pilot them, and now we rent what we once owned!" he shouted. "The Worms did that to us!"

"Rowan did that to you," Sanction corrected, "and we will now turn that tragedy back into a comedy." He looked Trajan in the eye, and the agitated man bit back his first response, and reluctantly sat back down.

"Tell me," Trajan demanded.

"The Ministry of Preservation makes decisions about the waterways through the Canal Coordination office, which the gondoliers pretty much run even though it is an extension of the Ministry's governance. However, they have not been appointed to positions within the Ministry, because they are businessmen who have a conflict of interest; their boats are directly affected by the policy." He paused. "When Lord Rowan flexed his muscle and bought you out, that represented a massive expenditure that has of course attracted the attention of the Lending Commission at various levels. If aristocratic interference is moderated, and it has been, then the easiest way for the Ministry to deal with this use of funds for questionable purposes is to shuffle those involved in the implementation into different areas in the Ministry; no one wants firings or trials to draw further attention. Now that you are not boat owners, then it's time for you to choose out some of your best minds, and I will see to it that the Silkworms get appointments for your representatives."

Sanction stood, looking around at those in the room who were no longer certain in their anger. "You built up your power with the Fairpole Council because you had no recourse to official response defending your efforts. Vigilante action and collective response compelled a measure of attention to your needs. The government was iron-clad against you, and you could not get representation. Now the government has overextended in taking what was yours. They have left themselves vulnerable, and we will see to it that you get representatives *within the Ministry*. Once that happens, there are transfers, promotions, committee service; you will have the opportunity to infiltrate the bureaucracy."

Trajan stared at him. "You mean—you mean a seat at the table," he murmured. "The Ministry." The idea grew behind his eyes, lighting them up.

Sanction looked him in the eye. "You've been focused on the Ministry taking your boats. I'm offering you the power the Ministry used to take your boats."

Across the table, Trajan stood, emotions tumbling behind his eyes for a long moment as Sanction waited, composed.

Trajan thrust his hand out. "We'll get you a list of names," he said, and he nodded decisively.

They shook on it.

HIGH SIX RADIANT GARDEN, SILKSHORE. 31ST ELISAR. SIXTH HOUR PAST DAWN.

Trellis stood on the disrupted jumble of fresh-tilled earth where his favorite bench had stood two weeks before. He regarded the glittering, misty mess sprawled out in a vista below. It comforted him somewhat that he was still backlit by the mighty radiant oak, which had several bright gashes around its trunk where the first efforts to cut it down safely had experimented before the demolition was cancelled.

The Hammer followed the path up the hill, closing in on Trellis, who glanced over at him.

"Well," Trellis said quietly. "I'm surprised to see you here. Not usually your scene," he said with a vague gesture. He rubbed at his face. "There isn't much left, but... we'll get it back."

"I know you will," the Hammer said, hoarse. He looked around the wreckage. "This... feels right to me. Feels like I do," he said, tapping at his chest.

Trellis looked at him sideways. "You are ready to talk about it?"

"Maybe never," the Hammer rasped. "But you understand somehow. I feel it."

"I had a similar experience once," Trellis said, unfocused. "My perspective was altered forever. My sense of how things fit together, what's important. They were pulverized. I had to start over."

"Yeah," the Hammer said. "That's it."

For a while, the men stood, not looking at each other, nor particularly paying attention to the work crews and angry goats trying to rearrange the wreckage of the radiant garden's grave.

"What did you lose," the Hammer mused aloud.

"My humanity, I think," Trellis replied with an easy shrug. He turned to the Hammer. "You?"

The Hammer shook his head, struggling for words. "I lost... I lost my guilt. My... my pride. Everything I learned before and during the war. Everything that I thought mattered about what I did, or did not do." His face was slack, too shocked for tears. "None of that matters at all now," he whispered. "I need it to matter, or... what's left?"

More time passed as the moon attempted to climb into the broken sky and crossed its fault lines, refracting into three pale globes pushing at the gauzy clouds sealing the sky away from the earth. The moon and her dimmer sisters threw wild shadows.

"You resist the chaos of that void," Trellis said quietly, "or you do not. You are made of an order that defies that chaos; your lungs breathe within a capacity and a rhythm. Your heart beats. Your wounds seal on a timetable, your limits rise around you and provide their own kind of definition. You go from being trapped in your thoughts and experiences here," he said, tapping his temple, "to the basic construction of *what you are*. And that's here," he said, tapping his chest over the senseless repetition of his throbbing heart.

"And if I cannot find meaning there?" the Hammer asked quietly.

"Stop looking for meaning," Trellis said, shaking his head. "The worst thing you can do is to find meaning that can live side by side with that touch of demonic perspective." He managed to catch the Hammer's eye. "Decide on a purpose, however basic. Let that serve as your foundation." Trellis surveyed the wreckage once more. "If your foundation is sturdy enough, you can rebuild anything." He leaned back against the radiant oak.

The Hammer wrapped his arms around his torso, gripping himself tightly enough he could feel the beating of his heart.

"RIBBONS" EEL SHOP. SILKSHORE. 31ST ELISAR. ELEVENTH HOUR PAST DAWN.

Safety left the warm confines of the tiny shop, secure against the chill in his new greatcoat. He suddenly halted as he reached the edge of the street, seeing two priests standing in his way on the sidewalk. Pivoting, he saw two more, and Mother Grine between them.

"You must be Safety," she said.

"It's possible," he replied, planting his fist on his hip, between the gun holster and knife sheath.

"Don't embarrass yourself," Mother Grine shrugged. "I was looking for Saint, but got bored, and you'll do. I have a message from Elder Rowan."

"By all means, share," Safety said with an expansive gesture, trying to draw eyes away from his other hand by all the weapons.

"Let us be frank," she said. "You know there were assassins tasked with your destruction. The River Stallions and the Silkworms. You know how seriously they take their contracts."

"Yes," Safety said, reflexes at peak suspense.

"We have arranged for them to agree to kill you with time," she said. "The seconds and hours that pile up into days, years, decades. Time itself will kill you, surely, and they have contented themselves with that timetable. You will no longer have to watch your shadows for this particular threat."

"That's... unexpectedly generous of you," Safety said.

"It was an expensive gift, so make the most of it," she shrugged. "Don't look into it further. If you attempt to identify the assassins that came for you, or their organization, then you earn a swift death all over again." Then, turning, she walked away.

To Safety, her departure felt like something ending. He could not help but smile.

TRAINING CHAMBER, MAURO OVERVIEW, SILKSHORE. 31ST ELISAR. TWELFTH HOUR PAST DAWN.

Acolytes had cleared the remains of the meal away, and now the three women at the low table shared tea as they relaxed in the spherical room, feeling safe for the first time in a long time.

"At some point we need to work out damage control," The Mistress of Tides said coolly. "I have alienated a number of Spirit Wardens, and defied their arrest attempt. I will have to make peace with them somehow." She shifted position. "I also irritated the Head Whisper for the Fairpole Council. I'm not sure that's a relationship I care about repairing."

"The only thing I care about is the bone demon," Red Silver said. "It's still out there, and we killed its favorite Whisper."

"Don't worry about that," Inkletta said quietly. "I found the bone demon, it was connecting to you through a molar it tore from your mother. I retrieved the molar from its bones and sent it away."

The other two women stared at her for a long moment.

"There is no way you could do that," the Mistress of Tides said.

"True and false," Inkletta said, trying her best not to be evasive. "We are now talking about damage control. Before now we were in the chaos of planning and pulling heists, trying to stay alive and push through to our objectives." She paused. "I did not come back from the Runwater Flats spirit well alone."

"What do you mean?" the Mistress of Tides asked, her voice as level as she could make it.

"I connected with the Shrouded Queen. I wanted to fight, and I think she did too, but instead we... we more like *struggled*," Inkletta said, looking away. "She is incomplete, and I know what that feels like. In the time we battled, we also connected." Inkletta pursed her lips. "The Shrouded Queen wants me to harvest what she's missing, and she wants me to become an avatar in this world." She shifted. "I let a taste of that power out to ambush the bone demon, and to sense what part of him connected to you, and remove it. I don't think he'll be back; he mostly cared about his pet Whisper, who is dead now."

"And... you like the feeling," the Mistress of Tides pressed.

Inkletta's shrug was a bit helpless. "How could I not?" she said. "I grew up in the shadow of that spirit well. The Shrouded Queen inhabited it, she's infused by it, she... she *feels like home* in a way this goddamn city never will," Inkletta said with a gesture.

"Hey, as dark and confusing as this is," Red Silver said, putting her hand on Inkletta's forearm, "this is my chance to repeat what you said to me. I'm there for you, and we'll figure this out together."

"Together," the Mistress of Tides agreed.

"None of us expected to get through this with no scars, no debts," Inkletta said. "This is the damage that I took. I did not expect all of us to make it through this in one piece. I am grateful we're all alive," she said, "and I think we can figure out how to deal with a goddess's favor one way or another."

"You may be bound beyond debt," the Mistress of Tides said seriously, "but so too are we." She took Red Silver's hand, and Inkletta's hand, closing the circle.

GADDOC RAIL STATION, NIGHTMARKET.
31ST ELISAR. HOUR OF SONG, 2 HOURS PAST DUSK.

Sanction looked over the ticket again, worry suffusing his features. "Rutherford is supposed to be on this train," he said to Piccolo, who looked dashing in his crooked cap and impeccably neat new suit. "I would have thought he would send word, using the wire, from a previous station." He looked up again at the still-empty platform. "You don't suppose—"

"Aaaah, he's alRIGHT," Piccolo managed. "Just relax, you neurotic beanbag. Your husband is fine, he's on the train and the *train* is *fine*, and *everything is okay*, dammit."

"Of course," Sanction agreed, putting the ticket back in his coat. "You're right, of course. All is well. No need to be alarmed."

Sanction fidgeted.

"Do you—" he began.

"That was eight seconds!" Piccolo yelled.

Sanction checked with the wire office six more times and creased the ticket receipt and itinerary enough that the page cleanly parted along the fold. Piccolo did not murder him. Eventually the massive train chuffed into the station, the doors opened, and the crowds exiting the train mingled with the crowds assembled to meet them.

"Check again!" Sanction said, sharp, as Piccolo shrugged mid-crowd. Flustered, Sanction slipped past the guards near the engine and hauled himself up the ladder to where the engineer and conductor were having a conversation.

"I need to know about a passenger," he said, out of breath.

"Excuse me," the conductor said, his tone scolding more than his words could, "but we do not share that information—"

"I'm with the Ministry looking for an important guest from Iruvia," Sanction interrupted sharply. "He's not supposed to be on this train, I'm trying to keep things quiet so we don't end up in a shootout. Now, the assumed name is 'Rutherford.' Anyone of that name on this train?" he demanded.

Not quite convinced, but persuaded that he didn't want further trouble, the conductor consulted the list. "No one of that name, sir. We had one, but he cancelled before the train left."

Without another word, Sanction pivoted, left the engine, dropped to the station tiling and strode towards the exit. Piccolo fell in beside him.

"He's not there, I'm telling you for sure," Piccolo said.

"The conductor said he cancelled his ticket, wasn't on the train," Sanction replied, struggling against the wall of anxiety that rose like a murderous wave in his chest. "Rowan's reach could easily extend to Iruvia; I didn't want to contact Rutherford because the activity could be traced, but if they did, if they've got him, if they—" "You need to settle down before you start this war up again," Piccolo said seriously, one hand slipping subconsciously to the cosh tucked into his belt pouch. "What if he's going to be late and he sent you a message? It could be waiting at home!"

"Yes—yes, let's go home," Sanction said, painfully eager as he broke into a run. "There could be a message!"

Piccolo did his best to keep up and not render Sanction unconscious.

Half an hour later Sanction swung up out of the gondola at the quay, racing up the stairs and striding down the sidewalk towards his row house by the river, Piccolo right behind him. As they passed a darkened bridge support archway, they heard the distinctive click of a pair of pistol hammers cocking. They pivoted to see a tall shadowy figure aiming guns at them from cover.

"Rutherford?" Sanction said, trying to wrestle his desperate hope and his cold analytical senses into something like parity.

"What's the all-clear?" the shadow growled.

"Watercress," Sanction blurted. "The counter?"

"Pleats," Rutherford replied, visibly relaxing as he lowered the pistols and stepped into the light. Pale blonde stubble glittered on his cheeks under the plasmic lights, and he wore a rugged sailor's outfit. His hair could use a trim, but he had the same weary half-smile that defined him to his friends.

Sanction bounded forward and wrapped his arms around Rutherford. "Oh, body and blood, I missed you," he said. He thrust Rutherford back at arm's length, eyes furious. "What was that about, dodging me at the train station?" he demanded.

"I got word you all crossed the City Council," Rutherford said unapologetically. "For all I knew I was going to be a game piece in some skullduggery. So I cashed in a favor, got a ride on a fast ship, and arrived last night instead of taking the train." He glanced around. "Word on the street was that you more or less settled with the City Council, but I couldn't be sure." He clapped his hand on the back of Sanction's neck, looking him in the eye. "Nobody uses me to get to you," he said, hoarse.

"You scared the hell out of me," Sanction breathed, honesty unbecoming on him, as it rendered him somewhat child-like.

"Oh, because I went picking fights with the biggest dog in the city?" Rutherford replied, sardonic. "We can compare our sins later." He looked Sanction in the eye, steady.

"That's my cue to get the hell out of here," Piccolo shrugged. "You already sweep the house?"

"Of course," Rutherford said, pulling Sanction to his chest and talking over his shoulder.

"Then I'm done here. You kids have a great time. Stay out of trouble. Don't kidnap anybody," Piccolo grinned.

As Piccolo strolled away, Rutherford put his forehead on Sanction's forehead. "It's great to see you again," he muttered.

Sanction wrinkled his nose with a grin. "You smell like a dirty sailor," he said. "I guess I'll keep you all the same." He took a step back, and threaded his arm through the crook of Rutherford's elbow as they headed home. "Slick move back there, dodging all the potential points of engagement to get an isolated meeting. We'll make a scoundrel of you yet."

"Hah," Rutherford chuckled. "You don't have to be a scoundrel to know Doskvol is a dangerous city. Gotta keep your wits about you," he said. "Always with the contingency plans."

"I love it when you talk dirty," Sanction said with a wry grin. "C'mere, you." He led Rutherford up the stairs and into the house, and the door lock clicked into place behind them.

THE INCIDENT

DATE	PLACE	EVENT	CHAPTER
18 Elisar	Six Towers. Rowan House.	Saint and Red go to Lord Rowan's party, along with Gapjaw and the Hammer. • Gapjaw and the Hammer have a run-in with Captain Strank in the North Hook House Guard. • Saint is identified and captured. • Red is in a séance and channels the ghost of Shaw Rowan, who activates her curse, and she flees in desperate pain.	1
18 Elisar	Six Towers. Rowan House.	• Gapjaw and Hammer sneak through the house to the Mirror Chamber, Piccolo checks in looking for Saint, then leaves. • Gapjaw and Hammer watch Rowan and Leslin demonstrate the new security. • Saint tortured by Clef, Ingvald's brother, dressed as a Bluecoat in the wagon ride to Ironhook. • Piccolo cannot find Red or Saint, so he rejoins Gapjaw and Hammer and they kidnap Leslin, much to Safety's dismay when he extracts them on the steam launch.	2
18 Elisar	Silkshore. Barkul Market.	Inkletta and Niece try to mediate a clash between Bluecoats and a Skov riot led by Captain Rikard. Red Silver's bat Nails interrupts, the Bluecoats shoot the impostor Konrad surrendering as the captain but he escapes.	3

DAY ONE

Date	Place	Event	Chapter
19 Elisar	Silkshore. Mistshore Park.	Niece, Inkletta, and Nails find Red.	3
19 Elisar	Silkshore. Mauro Overview, Zephyr Street, Master Market.	• Niece drops Inkletta and Red off by the back door to the Overview. • Red tells Inkletta about the séance, confesses to ghost riding, and reveals the history of her curse and Razor Wind. • Inkletta meets Mistress of Tides, who explains Rowan has declared war, and Inkletta tells her about Red's curse.	3
19 Elisar	Silkshore. Boldway Canal Street Bridge Piling.	Niece survives a beggar assassin's attempt to kill her as she returns to the River Stallion base.	3
19 Elisar	Silkshore. High Six.	Soapstone captures Trellis, who escapes from the carriage when they leave, by Dannery Run. He takes Soapstone's spirit bane charm, so Soapstone will know it's him if he sends a message.	4
19 Elisar	Silkshore. Cramden's Public House, Attic.	Sanction is arrested while having his portrait painted, but Niece warns him and he escapes.	4
19 Elisar	Silkshore. Mauro Overview, Zephyr Street, Master Market.	Mistress of Tides resists arrests with her acolytes and kills a spirit warden and 3 initiates.	4
19 Elisar	Silkshore. Foggert's Sump.	Safety, Gapjaw, Piccolo, and the Hammer hide out after Piccolo stashes Leslin somewhere safe.	4
19 Elisar	Crow's Foot. Candle Street Butchers.	Niece goes to Rhya, it's a trap and she escapes, Rhya is captured.	4
19 Elisar	Dunslough. Ironhook. Interrogation Quarters.	Saint is interrogated by Soapstone but realizes Trellis is still free.	4

DAY TWO

Date	Place	Event	Chapter
20 Elisar	Silkshore. The Ease. Central Landing.	Trellis sees Soapstone, the Ministry, and Bluecoats go to the Canal Coordination Office then the Lending Commission gives them 3 days to pay all debts or 85% of the boats will be repossessed. He slips away.	5
20 Elisar	Silkshore. The Administrative Plaza.	Sanction in disguise meets with a clerk friend Jan to find out Barteus issued a report to the cabinet that High Six was toxic, if the committee accepts it they'll bulldoze it. Sir Dramach bringing a proposal to build a Spirit Warden compound there. Sanction tells her to collect reward money for spotting him, he leaves.	5
20 Elisar	Silkshore. Grotto Hill. The Mistyard.	The Mistress of Tides is confronted by the Fairpole Grotto Council Whisper, he rebukes her and sends her away from the safe house.	5
20 Elisar	Silkshore. South Stains near Grinder Hall.	Niece witnesses the Grinders getting firebombed.	5

DAY THREE

Date	Place	Event	Chapter
21 Elisar	Silkshore. Foggert's Sump.	Piccolo brings newspapers to Gapjaw, the Hammer, and Safety. • The navy firebombed the Grinders. • Gondolier repossession, pay by 23rd. News of fugitives, extension; get one dead, forgiven loan. Alive, six loans forgiven. Rowan Shipping will buy boats from the Ministry and hire on their former owners. Piccolo wants to kill Rowan's relatives, Gapjaw and Safety go along as the Hammer waits.	5

21 Elisar	Silkshore. Canter's Lowland. Ghost Market. Marker 36.	Piccolo put a modification in the paper for the evening edition to attract Sanction, who shows up but is followed. They head to the Ghost Market but an assassin attacks; Gapjaw is injured, Piccolo separated, but they kill the assassin under Lilora's Brew Pad.	5
21 Elisar	Silkshore. Canter's Lowland. Ghost Market. Marker 36.	They get to Marker 36 and Workshop uses alcahest to get rid of Sanction's tracker, and patches them up, for sapphires in payment.	6
21 Elisar	Six Towers. Breyan Street North.	The Hammer ambushes Captain Strank and cripples him, finding out Sanction was taken to Ironhook.	6

DAY FOUR

DATE	PLACE	EVENT	CHAPTER
22 Elisar	Silkshore. Canter's Lowland. Ghost Market. Marker 36. Workshop's lab.	Sanction, Gapjaw, and Safety are healing. Sanction talks to Workshop about not turning them in.	6
22 Elisar	Silkshore. Mauro Overview, Zephyr Street, Master Market.	Inkletta and Red Silver discuss the curse and decide to use a spirit well to address it.	6
22 Elisar	Silkshore. Fog Crest Rooftops.	Safety finds Piccolo, they rejoin Sanction and Gapjaw in a basement, plan the heist on the archive of the Ministry of Taxation in Silkshore, for tomorrow night.	7
22 Elisar	The Docks, Sorting Point.	The Hammer finds Niece as she pretends to be fresh off the boat, they decide to go find Trellis to get Rhya and Saint out of Ironhook.	7

DAY FIVE

Date	Place	Event	Chapter
23 Elisar	Crow's Foot. Runwater Corners.	Inkletta and Red Silver attack the Shrouded Queen's cult in a tower basement with the spirit well, Inkletta goes through the Mirror.	7
23 Elisar	Silkshore. Ministry of Taxation satellite office archive.	Sanction, Piccolo, Safety, and Gapjaw rob the archive and get Rowan's genealogical research.	7
23 Elisar	The Void Sea. Outside the Port of Doskvol.	Razor Wind sails into the harbor.	7
23 Elisar	Six Towers. Rowan House.	Saint recruited for the hunt by Rowan. After some luxury, he reveals the paper code, presses for more information so he can help better.	8
23 Elisar	Charterhall. Charterhall University. College of Immortal Studies.	Sanction, Piccolo, Safety, and Gapjaw interrogate Professor Stansby, find out about his blackmail operation, kill him, rob him.	8
23 Elisar	Crow's Foot. Tangletown. Empress of Gulls' Workshop Sloop Wreck.	Razor Wind talks to Empress of Gulls, who tells him about Rowan's party and the cursed woman he is pursuing. She says it won't end well for Razor Wind.	8
23 Elisar	Adrift in Dreams.	Mistress of Tides gets a dream from Inkletta.	8

DAY SIX

Date	Place	Event	Chapter
24 Elisar	Crow's Foot. Runwater Corners	Mistress of Tides finds Red Silver, Nails, and Inkletta as Bluecoats and Spirit Wardens take the site over to use a rift welder to repair the crack the spirit well caused. During the Blind Hour Mistress of Tides and Red Silver attack the basement, defeat the Wardens and Bluecoats, retrieve Inkletta, seal the spirit well, and escape, with the Wraiths in support.	9
24 Elisar	Silkshore. Fog Crest Overbuilt Basement.	Sanction tells Piccolo his whole plan, and begins the planning to inject Rowan's relatives.	9
24 Elisar	Brightstone. Unity Park, outside Sarool's House Cuisine.	Piccolo injects Lord Swint, Piccolo confronts him and escapes.	10
24 Elisar	Adrift in Dreams.	Razor Wind visits Lord Rowan, who tells him about Red Silver. RW asks for information to be left with the barkeep at the Gyroscope.	10
24 Elisar	Brightstone. Surban Estate.	Sanction gets Lord Danis Surban, half-brother to Cleith Rowan, into education and art.	10
24 Elisar	Six Towers. Rowan Mansion.	Saint tells Rowan about the 20th meeting with Sanction and a meeting on the 22nd aimed at Trellis. Workshop returned the corpse, the assassin group wants him protected in gratitude, then Workshop disappeared. Focus on Trellis, but Hive protects his family.	10

DAY SEVEN

Date	Place	Event	Chapter
25 Elisar	The Docks. Mather Outfitting Company.	Piccolo injects Lord Grainbalt.	10
25 Elisar	Nightmarket. Vancell Gardens.	Niece and the Hammer make contact with a cutout working for Trellis, go to an alley.	10
25 Elisar	Six Towers. Rowan Mansion.	Saint gives up the Brightstone asylum angle to reclaim the adept Leslin.	11
25 Elisar	Charterhall. Jayan Park. Lower Courts.	Piccolo injects a child age 10, #48 on the Lightning Eels team. Sanction owes Piccolo one for doing this.	11
25 Elisar	Brightstone. Inkwine Center for Refocusing.	Saint and Rowan get Leslin out of the asylum.	11
25 Elisar	Nightmarket. Ten Fringe Corridors.	Niece and the Hammer meet the Crolaange cult and escape to their hidden shrine pursued by an assassin.	11
25 Elisar	Brightstone. Arborside Conduit.	Piccolo injects Lord Rowan's mother in her convalescence home.	11
25 Elisar	Brightstone. Dorvale Estate.	Sanction takes Gapjaw, Piccolo, and Safety to rest and recover at the funeral barge.	12
25 Elisar	Silkshore. Crownwind Court.	Razor Wind goes to Red Silver's apartment, uses her rifle and landlord to cast a ritual to find her. He is joined by Elziraan, bone demon.	12
25 Elisar	Crow's Foot. Sails Alley.	Red Silver, Inkletta, and Mistress of Tides hiding out. Ritual chases them to seek refuge in the shrine to the Closed Eye. They are tricked into becoming drowning sacrifices, and when the Mistress of Tides cannot find a way out underwater, Inkletta ghost screams at the door.	12, 13

25 Elisar	Beneath the Gaze of the Fallen Star.	Niece and the Hammer are in the shrine and have a baptism ritual. It cleanses the tracer from Niece, kills the assassin following it, and inserts the Fallen Star to her timeline from birth to death; the demon is there when she dies. The Hammer is shocked to muteness.	12
25 Elisar	Nightmarket. Paper Street, Danse Park.	Niece and the Hammer come out with Nigel, who puts them on a coach that takes them to a boat, across the river to Strangford House on an island, where they meet Trellis and talk strategy. Six days until the next City Council meeting.	13
25 Elisar	Whitehall. Rowan Townhouse.	Saint meets Leslin, Rowan brings Mother Grine, Saint learns about the plasmic security system.	14
25 Elisar	Crow's Foot. Candle Street. Crow's Foot. Tangletown. Empress of Gulls' Workshop Sloop Wreck.	Mistress of Tides, Inkletta, and Red Silver decide to shelter with Empress of Gulls, who welcomes them. Ritual shielding hides Red Silver from Razor Wind.	14
25 Elisar	The Docks. North Hook Annex, Pier 18.	Saint goes with Leslin to the warehouse with the plasmic security system to see a demonstration.	14
25 Elisar	Overlooking Charhollow. Strangford House. Mastiff Library.	Trellis has essentials of the crew, and prepares a ritual with the Whisper Evergreen, Niece, and the Hammer to visit their dreams at midnight.	14

DAY EIGHT

DATE	PLACE	EVENT	CHAPTER
26 Elisar	Whitehall. Rowan Townhouse.	Saint wakes from a dream and tells Rowan etc. to tear off to Six Towers, Mistshore Park. He rides in a carriage with suspicious Mother Grine.	14
26 Elisar	Six Towers. Mistshore Park.	Rowan's agents catch two locals burying a box of Rowan's correspondence, and talk to an old woman who was at the dock so the steam launch could get everyone together. Mother Grine takes the box of correspondence, which Rowan insists is forgery.	15
26 Elisar	Dosk River to North Hook Channel.	Nine scoundrels (all but Trellis and Saint) are on the launch, which takes them to the Leviathan hunter the Constellation, at the docks, where they meet with Trellis in the map room and get some context for the way forward.	15
26 Elisar	The Docks. The Constellation.	Scoundrels plan a trip to the Sanctorium to talk to Elder Rowan and steal costumes. They plan to rob the Library Within of the Bellweather plans. They plan to rob the vampire Skannon Clelland, getting Dunvil blackmail.	17, 18, 19
26 Elisar	The Docks. The Constellation.	Razor Wind meets Elziraan, who points him to the Constellation. Razor Wind assaults the Constellation and kills the captain and many crew before a big tempest wave hits the ship and wipes him off the deck, covering the scoundrels' escape.	16
26 Elisar	Docks near the Constellation.	Inkletta confronts Elziraan and uses the power of the Shrouded Queen to pull the Selraetas tooth from the demon's bones.	16

26 Elisar	Brightstone. The Sanctorium.	Sanction chats with Elder Rowan about assuming the Rowan seat in the City Council while Trellis steals specialized costumes from the secret vault.	17
26 Elisar	Brightstone. Shining Mane Public House.	Gapjaw tells Soapstone to have church reps and Rowan at the test site.	
26 Elisar	The Void Sea.	Safety finds the Mistress of Tides, rescues her.	17
26 Elisar	Six Towers. Clelland Northshore Tower.	Piccolo poses as a sacrifice delivered by Zingh to the vampire Skannon Clelland, backed up by Gapjaw and Niece. They steal Dunvil blackmail and escape.	19
26 Elisar	The Docks. Pier 18, North Hook Annex.	Razor Wind stalks Red Silver into the test site. The security system disarms him, Red Silver kills him, and she is captured. Mother Grine tells Rowan he's off the City Council.	17, 18
26 Elisar	Whitecrown. Master Warden's Estate.	Trellis, Inkletta, the Hammer, and Sanction steal the original plans for the Bellweather Seminary bell towers from the Library Within.	18

DAY ELEVEN

DATE	PLACE	EVENT	CHAPTER
29 Elisar	Charter Hall. City Council Chambers, Doskvol Civic Palace.	Trellis attends the City Council meeting where North Port will be resettled, testing Rowan's security system, making peace between Council members and removing the pressure from the Silkworms and River Stallions.	20
29 Elisar	Whitehall. Rowan Townhouse.	Rowan unhappily releases Saint and Red Silver, and Saint makes demands for Soapstone's services, clothes, and final actions; Rowan agrees.	20
29 Elisar	Brightstone. Shining Mane Public House.	Saint and Red Silver get Soapstone, he writes letters and accompanies them on errands.	20

29 Elisar	The Docks. Arrivals and Departures Public House.	Saint and Soapstone recruit Clef as a Ministry liaison for Skov affairs.	20
29 Elisar	Dunslough. Dancing Gate, Ironhook Prison.	Soapstone, Saint, and Red Silver free Rhya and those imprisoned because of Rowan's hunt for the scoundrels.	20

DAY THIRTEEN

DATE	PLACE	EVENT	CHAPTER
31 Elisar	Silkshore. Flap-Flap Tavern, Barkul Market.	Trellis makes peace with Saint.	21
31 Elisar	Silkshore. Canal Coordination Office, Central Landing, The Ease.	Sanction makes peace with the gondoliers, offering them Ministry positions.	21
31 Elisar	Silkshore. High Six Radiant Garden.	The Hammer talks to Trellis about rebuilding.	21
31 Elisar	Silkshore. "Ribbons" Eel Shop.	Mother Grine makes peace with Safety (representing the scoundrels) on behalf of the Rowan family, the assassins, and the church.	21
31 Elisar	Silkshore. Training Chamber, Mauro Overview.	Mistress of Tides, Inkletta, and Red Silver figure out next moves.	21
31 Elisar	Nightmarket. Gaddoc Rail Station.	Sanction and Piccolo try to meet with Rutherford, who intercepts them to find out all is well.	21

PATREON SPONSORS

Thank you for your support while I was writing. You change what is possible.

Aslan Silva	Mark Robison
Benjamin Hamdorf	Matthew Gagan
Benjamin Seeley	Max Stevenson
Blaze Azelski	Michael Liebhart
Brett Casto	Miller Ramos
Chuck Dee	Nat Lanza
David Brock	Nicholas Serluco
edchuk	Noah Crisp
Eli Kurtz	Petri Wessman
Elizabeth Parmeter	Phyllis Hurshman
Ian Donald	RavenRavel
James Robertson	René Lößner
Jeremy Collins	Ryan Dunleavy
John Harper	Simon Forster
Jon	Tales From the Grim
Joshua Cender	Ted Soper
Kear	Thomas
Kevin	Todd Estabrook
Logan Waterman	Video Store Cowboy
MapForge	

Made in the USA
Las Vegas, NV
05 July 2021